FAKE DATING A
HUMAN
101

JENNIFER
KROPF

DEDICATION

I'd like to dedicate this book to Norah Clayton for those nights you promised your parents you were "going to bed" then clicked on your reading light when you thought they couldn't see so you could keep reading my books.

CHAPTER
BEFORE WE BEGIN...

0

Luc Zelsor and the Week After His Unbearable, Vile, Horrid, Pig-Faced Father Died

The study of people was, and always would be, far more terrifying than the study of any creature or beast one could come face-to-face with. One would learn *why* people do things when they study them. One might learn what they're thinking, and therefore one would likely conclude that people are far more dangerous than creatures. It's *people* who are almost always monsters on the inside, even if they show a pinch of goodness every now and then. Even if they set out to do the right thing in completely the wrong way.

Smoke engulfed the Shadow Palace even though there was no fire.

The bitter scent mixed with the sweetness of a perturbed and very focused nine tailed fox as he marched through the haze, bashing aside friend and foe and whoever else got in his way. When he reached the throne room eclipsed by a set of glistening black doors, he studied the gold-spun handles. He shook them a little, but the doors wouldn't budge.

"Oh dear," he bit out. "We'll do this the hard way then."

He took a measured step back, then he raised his leg and kicked the snot out of those doors.

They swung open in obedience, screeching on their hinges and slapping hard against the walls when they came around, announcing the fox's arrival with the lovely tune of clamour. He marched in just as the hall at his back filled with the noise of scurrying Shadows racing in to save their Queene. This would not be a good day for the royal family. He was sure the stories in his gaze said as much as he stopped before the great throne, upturned roots spiralling from the seat like a black sun with tangled limbs.

"Luc Zelsor." The Dark Queene's voice was calm, considering she must have sniffed him coming the moment he'd assaulted her fairy guards downstairs. Naturally, she didn't call him '*Grandson,*' or refer to him as family in any way.

Families were for losers. Luc would rather go without one anyway.

"Did you hear the news, Your Majesty?" Luc asked, slurring the words provocatively as his alluring fragrance filled the throne room. "The High Prince is dead." He didn't mean to—but he smiled a little. Whether it was because he was proud to be the victor, the next legend in the fox stories, or because he was absolutely diabolical, he wasn't sure. It was probably the second one.

The Dark Queene's eyes remained steady upon him. Her rhythms didn't change, however her fingers—they tightened just a teensy tiny bit on the armrests of her gaudy throne. That was all the reaction she gave though. She must have known the ways of the fox since her late husband was one. Perhaps she expected this. Perhaps she wouldn't even be mad—

"Apprehend him." Her voice sailed through the chamber, so cold and detached that Luc almost shivered.

Loyal Shadows crept into the throne room at Luc's back, and he sighed in disappointment. "That interferes with my plans, unfortunately. I have a *very* pressing 'to do' list this week."

Both his fairsabers were out in a flash, and right before the watching eyes of the aging bat who was repulsed at the mere sight of him for still being alive instead of his father—or, as some might call her, the *Queene*—Luc slayed the remainder of her fairy guards.

When he was finished, he took a look around at the purple blood on the floor, on the walls. Truly, the hideous throne room should have thanked him for redecorating a little.

The Queene inhaled to speak, but Luc's left saber swished to her throat, halting her words and making her freeze. Luc settled his silvery gaze upon the ruler of the Dark Corner who had a habit of being too greedy and killing everyone in her path to get what she wanted. The one responsible for most of the bad and annoying things that happened in the Dark Corner of Ever. Though, after today, he'd done the whole "killing everyone in his path to get what he wanted" thing, too.

It was different.

"I hope the entire Palace remembers this day. The day a lonely fox got revenge for the mother who was never allowed to sit at the Queene's table, was never allowed to stand in the Queene's presence, was never allowed to *stay*." He let that sink in a moment after he said it. "Tell me where she is, and I won't kill you upon your ugly throne that looks like a childling's tree fort gone wrong."

The Dark Queene's lip curled, her fingers tightened on her armrests again. Her hollow eyes narrowed, proving she was every bit the vault of silence Reval Zelsor had been. By the look on her face, Luc knew the Queene had been in on Reval's plan to hide Luc's mother away. He imagined her giddy at the thought of letting a fairy she despised starve to death slowly.

And for that, Luc decided there were probably other fairies nearby who could give him the information he wanted. Including the half-dozen

Shadow Army Commanders Luc knew by name who were flooding into the throne room, filling the space with the metallic commotion of their weapons being drawn.

The Queene found a peculiarly irritating sneer. "You'll never leave this place alive, Luc. Perhaps you're not that clever."

Luc stared so hard, his eyes went dry.

How.

Insulting.

Darkness swept over the room as the cloud of torment swallowed the last speckles of light from outside, and the layer of fog on the windows evaporated as smoky shadows brushed up the walls. Even the stones holding the walls together rattled just a bit as the Dark Queene's power rolled from the stick throne in waves.

From there, many interesting, tasty, and dreadful things happened.

Things to be discovered later.

A Simple Guide of Necessary Steps
to Fake Date a Human
*(And to Make Her Fall in Love
with You While You're at It)*

1.   Show up unannounced all the time so you're constantly in her face and in her space. (Human females love that.)

2.   Be a fae.

3.   Give her a heads-up along with fashion pointers when the outfit she's wearing makes her look fatter than normal.

4.   Borrow her stuff and don't put it back where you got it from. (Even better if you leave it somewhere she'll step on it later.)

5.   When she's walking past carrying something that looks exceptionally heavy, laugh and watch.

6.   Be gorgeous. Every day, without even trying.

7.   Show up at her workplace with two coffees. Drink them both in front of her.

8.　　If she ever disagrees with anything you say, ask her why she's in a mood and if it's her "time of the month."

9.　　Make all her coworkers obsessed with you so they talk to her about you all the time even when you're not there.

10.　　When she's mad because you didn't do the thing she wanted because you can't read her mind and you don't know every single one of her female thoughts, offer her words of comfort, such as, "If you can't tell me what's on your mind, I'll assume it's because you don't have one." And "Maybe you should try decaf from now on so you're less snippy." And, if necessary, "Let's break up." But then, of course, when she agrees, chase after her and drag her back because she's not getting away from you that easily.

CHAPTER

1

Lily Baker and the Thing that Happened Before Shayne Left
One Month Ago

On a glassy moonlit night, a young police officer moved from shadow to shadow. The cool wind kissed her cheeks and fluttered her blonde hair while starlight glimmered down the ink on her arms that told her life story in carefully woven pictures. She glanced over her shoulder every time a car passed on the road or a small animal scurried by. When she got to the back door of Desmount Tech Industries, she pulled her key card from her pocket and made her way inside.

Most of the halls were unlit, only flashing on via sensors when she entered them. She passed two people on her way to the stairs—overachievers who never went home, likely. Desmount Tech's hardest workers. She probably owed them half the credit for bringing her inventions to life. She trotted up the stairs, the patters of her shoes echoing through the empty, wide-open space in the lobby. When she came around the bend to her lab, she saw someone waiting for her in the hall.

Gabe Desmount looked up from the file in his hands. He slapped it shut and cast her a charming, boyish smile. The kid was fresh out of high school, but he was probably the most powerful person—well, human anyway—that Lily knew. Definitely the richest. It showed in his tailored suit and how his hair was perfectly styled even in the middle of the night.

"Did it work?" Lily asked as Gabe handed her the file.

"We've only tested it against the fae blood samples we had. Obviously it's difficult to shoot at *real* fae for our tests. But the bullets pulled left or right toward the targets and released our paralyzing toxin upon impact. One hit with our bullets, and any fae will tumble to the ground unable to move." Gabe opened the lab door and led the way inside. He lifted a gun from a pedestal on the centre table, and he handed it to Lily. "This one is different though—our newest one. This one targets to kill. It releases a fast-working poison capsule once the bullet hits a body."

Lily studied the gun, rolling it over in her hands. She lifted it as if she meant to fire. Then she lowered it to look it over again. "It feels nice. It's not as heavy as my normal gun," she said.

Gabe nodded. "We could make smaller versions of these and arm people across the country. Women could keep them in their purses. The goal is to make them so they'll do minimal-to-no damage to us humans, even if fired by accident, so it wouldn't be a safety concern. But people will be able to defend themselves if fairies try to kidnap them like with what happened to your friend last Christmas."

Lily handed the gun back, but Gabe shook his head. "You keep it. You're the one in the company of fae, Baker."

Lily chuckled. "My fairies aren't the ones we need to worry about."

The edge of Gabe's mouth tugged like he wanted to disagree. He turned for the table though and picked up a stack of papers. "You can look over the design if you'd like. I don't need these back." He offered them to her, and Lily tucked them under her arm along with the new weapon.

"I'll see you tomorrow then," she said. She turned to leave when Gabe spoke again.

"Isn't it getting hard?" he asked, stopping her at the door.

There was something in his voice that made Lily not want to ask what he meant, but she did anyway. "Is what getting hard?" she said over her shoulder.

"All the sneaking around? Working a full day at the station, and then coming here to work more in the evenings? Hiding the truth from the fae in your midst?" he clarified. Gabe slid his hands into his pockets. "You could quit being a cop and come work for me full time. You know I could use your expertise on all this specialty tech. And you could help me test the gear for the Canadian police forces, too."

Lily glanced at the museum of weaponry on the walls. Things she'd help build. Designs she'd thought of all on her own. Desmount Tech would probably pay better than the force. But...

"I have siblings to protect," she said. "I need to be a cop."

Gabe nodded and folded his arms. "Well, my offer stands now or later if you change your mind. Get home safe, Baker."

Lily waved as she left, closing the door quietly behind her.

She moved through the halls and tapped her way back down the lobby staircase. No one was around anymore when she made her way through the back halls. The gun and papers slipped when she reached for the back door, so she pulled them from beneath her arm as she pushed her way outside.

She came to a halt. The door slammed shut behind her. Wind prickled her ears as a strange, warm sensation dragged over her back like a finger running along her skin. *Or*, like someone's heated, magical gaze was sizing her up.

She spun and raised the gun, dropping her papers. The sheets of information and diagrams flew into the wind and dispersed as she took in a tall, annoying, admittedly handsome fairy watching her, his white hair ruffling in the breeze, his t-shirt flapping against his body. Shayne was barefoot on the cold sidewalk on top of being completely unwelcome.

Lily's papers glided down around him, then rolled away in too many directions for her to chase.

She moved to lower her gun, but Shayne grabbed it. He held it there. Aimed at him.

"What are you planning to do with this fairy killer, ugly Human?" he asked. His smile was taunting, but there was a thinness to his lips that made Lily think he was mad. She looked right then left as she tried to come up with an answer he'd buy. "Fine," he said first. "I'll go destroy everything I just saw up in that room, then." He nodded toward the building behind her.

"What room?" Lily asked, her mouth going dry. His dramatic, slow blinking told her exactly what room he spoke of. That he knew. He'd seen. "Don't touch anything," she warned, thinking of the months of work she had hiding away in *that room.*

Shayne yanked her gun, pulling her hand with it. He pressed the barrel against his beating heart—right where one single shot would end him. "Are you going to shoot me, Human?" he asked.

"Are you crazy, Shayne?" Lily rasped. She tried to jerk the gun back, but he didn't let go. In fact, he slid his other hand around hers, wrapping his thumb over her forefinger and placing a dangerous amount of pressure on the trigger. "Shayne!" she scolded. "This will kill you!" But when her eyes flashed up from the gun, she found he wasn't smiling anymore. She rarely saw Shayne serious; it made her words catch in the back of her throat.

"Never talk about killing a fairy to a fairy," he articulated. "And *especially...*" Shayne tugged the gun away, forcing Lily to lose her grip and stumble forward into his chest. In the same motion, he caught her waist and swung her around, pinning her against the wall of Desmount Tech. An eruption of butterflies spilled into her stomach when their faces came inches apart and his lips *almost* bumped into hers. "...never aim a weapon at one unless you're prepared to shoot it," he finished. Lily pulled her mouth closed and forced her gaze up to his eyes where it belonged.

4

"Now, tell me—who was that dashing human you just met inside?" Shayne asked, seeming in no hurry to stop sandwiching her between himself and the building. "I don't feel threatened, which means you must not be growing a crush for him. But there is something toiling in my fairy feels…" He glanced off, tapping the barrel of Lily's gun against his lip in thought.

"Jealousy?" Lily guessed.

Shayne squeezed an eye shut like he was thinking harder. "That can't be it."

She huffed. "Seriously, Shayne? Is this why you've been looking so tired lately? Because you've been following me around at night?" She tried to squirm out of his hold, but he flashed a smile, watching as she failed to escape.

"Why don't we say it is?" he said, and she stopped her fleeing attempt.

"For real?"

Shayne snorted a laugh, dragging the handle of the gun across his eyebrow to scratch it. Lily's skin tightened as the gun's barrel aimed toward his head, his heart, his everywhere else.

"If I look tired, *Lily*, it's because you're exhausting to fake date."

She grunted. "It's not my fault we're doing this. I keep telling everyone at the station we broke up, but then you show up the next day with coffee and assure everyone we're still together. Why is that, Shayne?"

"You're happy when I do," he stated.

She raised an eyebrow when he didn't elaborate. Then he laughed at himself.

"Your pupils dilate whenever I walk into your workplace. Your cheeks turn a smidgen pink. Your breathing even changes. You might hate my guts most days, Human, but I think I accidentally became your *happily ever after*. You miss me when I don't show up at the station— admit it." He grinned too much, and Lily made a face.

"I'm not admitting that," she said.

"Admit it. Do it."

"No!"

"Why, Human, why?"

"Because I'm not a liar, Shayne."

He tilted his head in thought. "See, that sounded like a lie to me."

Lily sighed and rubbed her temple. "I don't need a happily ever after, you weirdo. Those are just in fairytales."

"Did you forget what I am? And everyone wants a happily ever after," he objected. "Sure, we all think Cress is obnoxious every time he opens his mouth about his wedding, but he's right about one thing—and that's being happy. It's why my brothers and I chose to stay here. This is where happiness is."

"Yeah, well…" Lily shook her head in disbelief "…I always said I'd never get married. So stop telling me what I want, and grabbing me like this, and following me at night," she said.

"Hmm." Shayne eyed her. "I suppose only time will tell whether you're a liar or not. And you like it when I grab you. Let me walk you home."

"No way. I have two legs and I'm perfectly capable of walking myself home."

Shayne rolled his eyes. "Yes, yes. We all know you're a hero on legs. Now stop saying such sassy things with that curvy mouth of yours. It gets my insides all feely."

The last of Lily's papers took flight off the sidewalk in a gust of wind, creating a ruckus and disappearing into the city of Toronto where she'd never find them. She watched them soar away. "I'm pretty sure you've really lost your mind," she muttered. "Which one of your clueless brothers let you become *King* of the High Court of the Coffee Bean?"

Shayne sucked in a deep breath, and she caught him staring at her lips when she looked back. His mouth was pinched as he chewed on the inside of his cheek. Lily couldn't imagine what he had to ponder so hard about, but she failed to find her voice to ask when his grip on her tightened. His hand suddenly felt warmer against her back.

Out of nowhere, he shook his head like he was clearing it. "Go home then," he said. "Go to bed and stop making fairy guns and instigating other midnight mischiefs. You should remember that if you keep throwing rocks at fairies, eventually you'll hit one." He leaned in and whispered, "Then *all* the wicked fairies will come for you. Not just me."

He released his hold on her waist and pulled back, setting her free. The cool night spilled over Lily's body, making her wonder how he could be so warm in this weather in just a t-shirt.

"You want me to leave while you still have my gun?" she asked in disbelief.

"Yes." His eyes dropped back to her mouth, briefly. "Before this *brainless King* does something he'll regret and leaves you enchanted for the next two days." A wide smile returned to his face. "I'm sure I don't even have to use magic to do that."

Heat struck Lily's cheeks. She folded her arms. "Unreal," she muttered. "You can't just *keep* that gun. You're going to give it back, right?" The chilly evening didn't feel cold anymore, and she had the impulse to shake her shirt to cool herself. But of course, she wouldn't be caught dead doing that in front of Shayne.

Shayne laughed without answering. He continued to laugh as he headed down the sidewalk, not even saying goodbye. He twirled the gun around his finger. Lily watched—going rigid every time the barrel swung toward him—until he turned at the end of the block and disappeared into the cool Toronto night.

It took Lily several moments of coaching herself before she was able to step into Fae Café the next morning. The bell at the door had always brought her a sense of comfort, but today it sounded like a warning siren. She clasped her hands and took in a deep breath when she was inside, inhaling the fragrance of freshly ground coffee beans and hot-out-of-the-oven strawberry turnovers. Mor glanced up from the counter and shot her a partial smile before returning his attention to the coffee pot he was half emptying into a to-go cup.

Mor had smiled. Like nothing was wrong today.

Like Shayne *hadn't* told his Brotherhood besties what he'd discovered about her last night.

Lily's shoulders relaxed. She unclasped her hands and headed into the café. But she slowed her walk, her feet coming together when she felt the warm, phantom sensation of knuckles stroking along her arm. She cut a sharp glare over to the seat in the corner.

Shayne winked.

He was wearing a zip-up hoodie today with the sleeves pushed up to his elbows. He raised a coffee to his lips with theatrical slowness, keeping his gaze pinned on her as he did it. He didn't blink *once* as he sipped. As he lowered his burgundy mug back to the table beside him.

Lily took in a deep breath and put her attention back on the things ahead—on Mor who was having a nice day, on the kitchen where the smell of turnovers wafted from, on the quiet TV sharing upcoming show previews, on Dranian coming from the back room carrying a box of paper cups. Business as usual. That was all she cared to focus on.

Not the fairy assassin in the corner wearing the exact sort of cozy sweater she loved, with the sleeves pushed up to his elbows to show the strength in his forearms, watching her keenly with his *I'm-trying-to-get-your-attention* eyes.

She cursed the day she'd admitted out loud to Kate that she liked it when guys wore sweaters. That cozy sweaters made her want to snuggle right into their chest. She still blushed whenever she thought about how she'd realized too late that all the fairies in the next room were listening, and she'd even gone as far as to admit she always noticed when guys *'pushed their sleeves up to their elbows.'*

She wanted to die.

Lily bit her lips together, avoiding looking left. No, Shayne hadn't told his brothers about what she was doing at Desmount Tech, but he was sure making her pay for her crimes in his own way.

"Are you working here today?" Lily asked Mor, putting extra effort into making this day normal. She slid a to-go cup off the stack when she reached the counter, and Mor nudged the coffee pot over.

"Just for the morning. Are you heading into work?" He sipped his coffee, but his gaze slid over to *someone* sitting in the corner. Then back to Lily.

"Yeah." Lily only realized how unsteady her hands were when she tried to pour her coffee. She almost missed the cup. Mor's eyes flickered to her pouring, but he didn't say anything. She tried to lift a paper lid off the stack but ended up with three stuck together. She shook them. They were fastened like glue.

She shook it again.

Finally, Mor snatched the lids and flicked one off the top. He fastened it to her coffee cup then settled his brown-silver gaze on her.

"Queensbane, what's going on between you two?" He nodded toward the corner of the room.

"I stole her gun," Shayne admitted without missing a beat, causing Lily to spin and cast him a look of warning that was probably also filled with some worry and begging. She hated that fairies could hear human pulses, because right now hers rivalled the rhythm of a wild nightclub.

Mor scowled. "You're going to get a good beating one day if you keep stealing things, Shayne. And when did you graduate from stealing trinkets to human weapons?" He reached for the cloth behind the cash register and began washing everything like he was hardly listening to himself or waiting for an answer. He got particularly focused on a stain at the end of the counter.

Lily took the opportunity to cross the café and stand in front of the sweater-wearing gun thief. He flashed her a smile that made her toes curl in her shoes. The worst part was that she couldn't scold him. At least, not in front of the others. She heard Cress and Kate come out of the kitchen behind her, discussing something too quiet to hear. A chair squeaked where Dranian must have sat down to sort the cups.

"Where did you put my gun?" Lily asked Shayne straight-up. Instead of answering, he made a show of pushing his sleeves up a little more. "I need it. Where is it?" she tried again.

Shayne stood, making her step back. "Some place you'll never find it," he said. "But feel free to do a search." He opened his arms, stretching them wide and presenting himself along with his smile. "I should warn you though, I'm pretty ticklish."

"Wait a minute…" Kate's words filled the café. "Is that you, Dranian? Why are you on TV?"

Shayne's face changed. Lily was one turn away from seeing what Kate was talking about when Shayne's arms flew around her and dragged her into a hug.

"Shayne! What are you doing?!" Lily's words were muffled as he cradled the back of her head and smooshed her face into his shoulder.

"I'm here to make all your dreams come true, ugly Human. Feel free to snuggle happily ever after into the broad chest of a handsome male wearing a cozy sweater," he invited. His arms were a straight jacket around her, but Lily managed to lift her head enough to see Cress yank Kate toward him the same way.

"I have something important to discuss with you, Katherine," Cress said as he threw his weight into the kitchen doors and pulled her through with him. Kate was barely able to make a peep of protest before the doors swung closed after them.

Lily caught Shayne flicking his chin toward the TV. His eyes were tethered to someone across the room, and when Lily twisted to see, she caught Dranian on the other end.

Dranian nodded. He stood. Then he walked over to the TV and punched the life out of it.

Lily's jaw dropped. "Are you for real?!" she screeched.

When she whipped her head back to Shayne, she found him biting down on his lips and casting daggers into Dranian's back with his eyes as the whole TV came crashing to the floor, creating a ringing *smash* that must have echoed all the way down the street.

At the counter, Mor sighed and shook his head.

"What did you just do to our TV, Dranian?!" Lily shrieked. She tried tugging from Shayne again, and this time, he let her go. But he didn't take his thin-lipped smile or his wide, pointed gaze off Dranian.

"I'm curious about that also," Mor mumbled through his teeth.

Dranian looked from Mor to Shayne. To Lily. Then he said, "Oops."

"Oops?" Lily folded her arms. "*Seriously?*"

"It was an accident," Dranian said dully. But his face contorted a little. He bit his tongue like it hurt or was numb. Or like he was *lying*.

"Oh well," Shayne piped up. "I guess there's no more TV for a while." He strutted on past, whistling to himself like Dranian hadn't just bashed a hole through the café's expensive TV. Shayne began gathering mugs off bistro tables, suddenly prepared to resume business as usual.

Dranian, though, glanced back to the wall where the TV had been. His eyes settled on something resting on the shelf and he headed over to it. He grabbed the remote, held it up, and said to Shayne, "Ah. Is this what you were nodding to?"

Mor slapped a hand over his face. "So much for secret-y things, you fool," he muttered.

"Wait…" Lily let out a laugh of disbelief and turned toward Shayne. "Secret-y things?" Shayne didn't seem so eager to make eye contact anymore. "What secret-y things? What have you four been up to?" Lily put her hands on her hips, but she swallowed her words when Shayne spun back around with a look that said, *"If you ask, I'll tell them your secret-y thing."*

Lily dropped her hands from her hips as her gusto fled. She swallowed and made a show of looking at her watch. "You're lucky I have to get to work," she said. She pursed her lips and stared at the floor, pretending to see something interesting down there. Then she turned for the café door.

"Goodbye, Human. Your hair is quite ugly today," Shayne called after her in his most affectionate voice.

Lily's jaw tightened. "Your face is ugly," she snapped as she shot him a look over her shoulder. But he just smiled in an obnoxious way that made it clear he knew she was wrong.

She cringed at her own lame response as she pushed her way outside and pulled on her police cap. "Unreal," she muttered. Even a middle schooler could have come up with a better comeback than that.

The morning air tickled Lily's nose as she walked. She realized she'd left her coffee behind after all that. She sighed at the thought of having to drink the weak blend with the metallic aftertaste they had at the station. Officer Westbow had once cleaned out the coffee machine with vinegar, and the coffee had the sharp flavour mixed into it ever since. Lily considered going back to Fae Café to get her coffee, but…

Somehow, she became more helpless under Shayne's gaze than when she was looking into the eyes of a charged criminal. He shouldn't have been able to rattle her so much; she hadn't suffered through a lifetime of challenges and beaten the odds stacked against her just to be thrown off by a fairy who most people in her world only thought existed in children's books.

Lily adjusted her hat with a vengeance and marched all the way to work without looking back.

2

Shayne Lyro and the Present

The amount of glitter on the Lyro table was a form of eye torture all on its own. Shayne squinted when the late evening sun dipped low enough to pierce through the arched dining room windows and reflect off the thousands of silver flakes adorning the tablecloth around everyone's plates. It brought a whole new meaning to the term 'blinding sunset'. He covered his eyes and peeked through a slit in his fingers, his gaze falling on an empty seat at the far end of the table. A seat that had been empty for more years than he could remember now. Truly, he almost forgot he once had a sister.

Shayne sighed and dropped his hand, deciding to close his eyes for the rest of the dinner instead. He wasn't even hungry. He wouldn't have come to this feast at all if Hans-Der—Shayne's ever-smiling blood father—hadn't required everyone's attendance for whatever unimportant announcement he claimed to have to make. It made Shayne wonder what he was even still doing in this House.

He'd come to kill a dreamslipper. To rid himself of his nightmares. To sever the new, creative hold the House of Lyro had on him and be done with them *forever.*

Unfortunately, he didn't realize until he got here that he couldn't kill the pretty, trapped fairy. That he perhaps didn't want to—ever since the moment he saw her in that miserable gilded cage and read the story in her eyes that told him she despised the Lyro name just as much as he did. Truly, he'd expected to meet some powerful siren queene working alongside his brothers and laughing in the rewards of their mutual wicked deeds. But Mycra Sentorious wasn't that.

No, she was a night blossom with her petals torn off. A butterfly with ripped wings. A lovely beast with its ankle caught in a snare. She was, in every way, a prisoner.

And Shayne didn't kill prisoners.

He adjusted in his seat, his heavy boots getting caught on the floor because he once again forgot he was wearing them. Down the table, a few of his blood brothers and his father's esteemed guests lifted their heads at the boot-stomping ruckus. But they soon forgot about Shayne's tap-dance show when the wide doors were opened and the Lyro's favourite family prize was guided through their midst: their lovely, imprisoned dreamslipper with her wildly piercing green eyes and silk black hair.

The most powerful allies of Lyro grinned around the table, nodding their approval and clapping—including Lord Isbeth; former war fae with wind power that could rip up a forest. Many allies of the Lyro House were terrifying in their own way, wielding North powers so great they could freeze enemies or bury a fairy in the cold earth with a sweep of their hand. Shayne was no match for them, but that had never stopped him from chasing their daughters for kisses and challenging their sons to reckless duels in his youth.

In the grand doorway, a tetrad of Lyro guards held tight to gold chains clasped to the gilded collar at the dreamslipper's throat. Mycra Sentorious scanned the faces down the table from beneath her ink-black lashes. Even though she was being led into the feast like a dog, she looked as if she hadn't a care in the faeborn world, and for that Shayne mustered up a special smile just for her. When her gaze swept across the feast, it caught on Shayne's magnificent smile.

She didn't smile back.

Mycra did, however, swallow. The second her eyes met his, a fearful expression appeared.

But by the time the guards brought her to her seat at the foot of the table, the look was gone. Mycra lowered herself gracefully into her seat, and a heaping plate of spellbuns and hot squash was placed before her. She didn't touch her chopsticks. She didn't eat. Shayne wondered if her next ploy to escape this household was to starve herself to death.

Frankly, he'd observed her forced to attend numerous events since he'd arrived. She'd been decorated in the finest jewels, blossom wreathes, and gold-braided crowns, and paraded before the Lyro House's powerful friends like an expensive painting they wanted to brag about. Yes, Shayne guessed she would probably rather be dead than to continue living this way. His guesses were put on hold though when Hans-Der Lyro uttered across the space, "I've brought you all here to announce that I'll be leaving the House for ten days," he said. Then he nodded to his allies around the table. "As you can see, I've brought witnesses to this announcement. Which means, I expect you all to behave until I get back. Or you'll suffer my wrath and the wrath of my allies who will be checking in on you while I'm gone." Hans-Der seemed particularly intent on eyeing Kahn-Der—the oldest brother of the Lyro family—and Jethwire—Shayne's first younger brother—and Massie—Shayne's second younger brother—and, of course, Shayne.

That was it. Mycra's bright gaze darted to Shayne's. It was swift, and pointed, and full of warning. Her eyes dropped to her plate again, and the nonchalance returned like a beautiful mask.

Shayne leaned back in his chair, tapping a finger against the tabletop as he thought about that. For weeks now, Mycra had been warning him that his brothers planned to kill him, which he'd expected since the moment he'd set foot in his childling home. But today the pretty fairy looked different. Today, there was a tone of discovery in her eyes. Maybe she'd overheard something or stole information from his brothers' dreams.

Shayne dragged his attention over to Kahn-Der down the table. Kahn-Der ate his hot squash in modest bites, his shiny white hair falling out of place when he leaned forward. Even while eating, the fairy possessed a crooked smile. He hadn't reacted to the news of Hans-Der's ten-day-long departure, which meant he already knew about it. Which meant he might have even crafted a plan to make the most of it.

Shayne's gaze hopped to Jethwire next, where the flute he'd stolen from a sea siren rested quietly beside his dinner plate. Then to Massie. They were the only two Shayne thought weren't a threat, since they'd both made it clear they didn't desire the chair belonging to the heir of the household. But Massie lifted his head from his soup just a little. He stole a look at Jethwire, and Jethwire looked back.

A wide smile spread across Shayne's face. He set down his chopsticks, finding no use for them now. How could he eat when it was so painfully obvious his brothers had a plot to kill him? Even the smell in the room had changed to one of hushed hatred and stabby intentions.

Truly, he wondered what had taken them so long. Every day he'd waited for the cold iron stab of Kahn-Der's long-bladed fairsaber. He'd hardly slept in giddy anticipation of it. Shayne lifted his goblet of spiked citrus. He drank slowly, savouring the sweet and sour taste. It wasn't like Kahn-Der to show mercy, and Jethwire and Massie were possibly worse. Shayne guessed they planned to either torture him until he was an eternally broken fairy—unfit to be seen in public or to take his birthright chair—or they'd kill him outright. Probably the latter.

It was hilarious that his brothers thought they could beat him. Sure, the Lyros had always been masters of unfathomable torture. But Shayne had spent many years as an assassin, and he possessed no shortage of ways to end them in style. Now that he'd decided not to kill the poor dreamslipper, Shayne's plan had been to play along as the returned prodigal son for a while and sneak back out of the House when a good distraction presented itself. But maybe destroying everyone was the best way.

Since the announcement was complete, Hans-Der lifted from his seat while dabbing his lips with a cloth. "Shall we retire to the meeting room?" he asked his ally Lords.

Seven powerful fairy heads nodded. Seven fairies stood. Seven fairies left, until it was just Shayne along with his brothers in the dining room, a quiet dreamslipper, and a handful of lesser fairies in burlap carrying in sugar plums on bronze platters for dessert.

No one touched the dessert.

Shayne set down his goblet of spiked citrus and turned to glance at Kahn-Der down the table. He pulled his mouth into a smile. "Let's die together then. Tonight," he said.

And just like that, everyone in the room froze like an icy wind had blown in from the mountains. Like the words had been spoken by a ghost.

No, it wasn't the *suggestion* that shook the pebbles in the floor and made the curtains shudder an exhale. It was the words that every Lyro brother had heard once before. Words meant to remind them of the fairy who used to sit in that empty chair at the far end of the table.

Kahn-Der, of course, reached for a sugar plum after all and bit into it with all the fake nonchalance of a stage actor in the North High Court's seasonal Yule ceremonies. "What would make you say such a thing, Brother?" he asked. He licked the purple juices from his shapely lips, and his ice-blue gaze fired up to Shayne, sharp and laugh-worthy.

Shayne held his gaze like that, smiling just a little wider. "We're evenly matched, I think," he bluffed. Obviously, Shayne was *far* above Kahn-Der's level. "Therefore, chances are we'll both die in the end, right?" He took his goblet and downed the rest of his spiked citrus all at once to meet the absurd level of Kahn-Der's drama. Then he slammed the goblet on the tabletop, making glitter puff into the air and swirl in the breezy current fluttering through the room. "I've been waiting for this for weeks. Meet me on the roof—just like in the dreams you sent me. Unless you're a coward, of course? I can't imagine the embarrassment

17

you'd bring to this family if you didn't show up."

Jethwire choked on his plum across the table. He bit his lips over a diabolical grin, proving that even though he wished to see Shayne as a lifeless fairy corpse by the end of the week, he could appreciate a good verbal arse-whacking.

Kahn-Der was not so generous with his smiles. Instead, a death song chanted from his deep blue gaze. His fingers tightened around his plum, and streams of purple juice leaked through his fingers, running down his hand and dripping onto his silver plate like fairy blood. But the oldest Lyro brother kept a relaxed posture as he dropped the plum's pit and reached casually for a cloth. He dabbed his hand dry, *seeming* lost in his own dark world.

"I applaud you, Brother, for being willing to face me," he finally said to Shayne, "and for not running off."

Shayne sighed, smiled, and pushed his full plate away as he stood, letting his sliding chair send a sharp sound through the dining room. "Yes, well, not all of us are cowards."

Shayne whistled as he rounded the table and headed from the feast toward the maze of hallways he'd gotten lost in so many times as a child-ling. Just another trap Hans-Der had devised to keep his family close. To ensure they never found their way out.

Something tickled the back of Shayne's throat as he pushed open the dining room doors. He coughed, and then he paused, glancing back into the dining room where his plate rested, heaped with delicious looking, untouched food. He wasn't foolish enough to eat it and ingest whatever poison might have been hiding inside. He rubbed a hand down his neck, remembering how his throat often acted up when the dry snowy season approached. His shoulders relaxed, and when he saw Kahn-Der sizing him up, Shayne winked. Just a little bat of his eye—yet a full promise.

The frostiness of Kahn-Der's gaze followed Shayne until he kicked the dining room doors shut behind him.

It was less than three hours before Shayne realized his mistake. He stared at himself in the dull mirror of his bedroom, his reflection going in and out of focus. He'd tried to upheave the spiked citrus the moment his stomach grew warm, but it was much too late for that.

It started with his abdomen feeling pricky, and then it moved to his limbs, and it hit his eyes last. His breathing grew strained, and he leaned forward against his dresser as he fumbled around for his fairsaber, knowing he had to get out of this room. Knowing they would come for him any minute if he didn't.

Knowing he had a prisoner to free before it was too late.

The basement was far too dark for someone to live in, but it was where the Lyro family kept their prisoner, nonetheless. Not even a torch or a fireplace was lit. Shayne was sure he'd walk into something face-first and break his beautiful nose if he wasn't careful. He kept a hand along the wall, brushing over cool stones as he stumbled deeper into the space. He remembered running through these chilly tunnels in bare feet in his childling years; stealing tiny, rare items from the shelves, running his fingers along the weapons on the walls, pretending to fight shadows with a blade like they were real fairies.

Little did he know he'd turn out to be an assassin. That he would get quite good at fighting his enemies for real. That at full strength, he'd become nearly unstoppable.

He should have known his brothers would target his strength first.

Shayne hadn't exactly been given a warm welcome when he'd waltzed in the front entrance and announced himself months ago. Only his father had accepted him back in with open arms, which was odd considering Hans-Der was the one who'd sent Shayne away in the first place. It was his brothers and all the old House allies that had treated Shayne like he'd walked over from the House of Riothin or some other hated rival. Since that day, the threat of Shayne's existence had hung in every room he'd walked into like a loud, shiny, eye-catching chandelier. He'd become the focal point of several noble households' gossip. He was pretty sure the House of Calamity was already trying to marry him off to one of their blue-haired females.

A tiny light flickered on, illuminating an orb of space in the basement. Shayne glanced over to find a dreamslipper, with a particularly pointed look, holding a lantern. He smiled and went to meet Mycra at the bars of her cage.

"You almost walked right past me," she said. The lantern light made her bright eyes dance as she looked him over, taking in his state. "Tell me what you're doing down here," she demanded like she ruled the whole wide world, and Shayne sighed. "You're not well," she added with realization. "Don't tell me they poisoned you with a numbing weed or something."

"Fine," Shayne slurred. "I won't tell you."

Mycra's fingers tightened around her light. "Make a bargain for your life before they take it."

Shayne shook a finger at her. "Never make a bargain with a fairy," he said, using the same finger to flick a gold bar between them. "That's my motto."

Mycra blinked like she didn't know what a 'motto' was, and Shayne waved a hand through the air. "Never mind. It's a human thing," he said. "But forget bargains. I'm here to set you free."

Her face changed. "Why?"

Shayne shrugged. "Well, if they kill me tonight, they'll probably kill you next. I think it's obvious my blood brothers have caught on to our alliance." Her features went blurry, and he squinted, sure she was disappearing. That his surroundings were all melting. He tried to shake the dizziness from his head.

Mycra grunted in her high voice. "I'd love to see them try. I'll tear them to shreds from the inside out—mind first."

Shayne snorted a laugh. It was his favourite when she used her deadly words. "Tsk, tsk. Naughty siren. It's not even my birthday and you're offering up presents." He drew a short dagger from his pocket. "And you know full well you can only destroy one fairy at a time. If you target someone from my household, the rest of the House will come after you in the morning."

Mycra's face fell. She put a hand over the bloodlock on the door and said, "Wait."

Shayne paused with the dagger against his palm.

"You're not going to run away with me?" Her throat bobbed. "I thought we'd go find your friend together."

Shayne's smile widened. "Are you talking about *my* Dranian?" He laughed, and the sound echoed through the basement. "You and I might be allies today, but we have a long way to go before I'll trust a powerful dreamslipper to be near my forever friend."

Mycra's mouth pinched. It was hilarious, and Shayne almost barked another laugh.

"I could just wait until you sleep and steal the information of his whereabouts from you," she pointed out with extra-thin words. "The only reason I haven't already is because I thought we were on the same team."

Shayne dropped the dagger back to his side. Naturally, Mycra's eyes followed it, and a teensy flicker of regret crossed her face.

"You might as well join my blood brothers in trying to kill me if you want that information," Shayne stated. "Now, quit begging for things you can't have and get ready to run. The alarm will sing through the House when I break this lock."

Mycra's bright eyes widened. "Wait—"

Shayne slashed his palm and grabbed the bloodlock, but he ripped his hand back when low, dark laughter flitted through the basement. It was too late though—the wailing alarm vibrated through every staircase, room, and hall. Shayne whirled. His oldest brother was hidden by the darkness, but the scent of ripe plums and expensive linens floated through the space. He sniffed.

Many expensive linens.

Kahn-Der was the first to step into the lantern light. The glow illuminated the metallic-scaled lamellar armour and the long, thin fairsaber strapped to his hip. Shayne swallowed as more fairies emerged from the darkness. Jethwire and Massie wore cruel grins and the rich, red hanboks of Lyro. Behind them, others drew forward just enough for Shayne to know they were there—fairy faces of males Shayne once knew, fairies he once ran through the cherry blossom orchards alongside.

They all teetered along with the room. Shayne's vision, limbs, and senses betrayed him as he forgot every trick of his assassin training.

Kahn-Der smiled. Shayne wanted to tell him his smile was ugly, but his throat felt full of pins and needles. So, he balled his hand into a fist around his dagger instead. Not that he could swing it properly. He relaxed and folded his arms, huffing a laugh and looking at the floor. He cleared his throat, but his words still came out gravelly. "You must be a coward after all, Kahn-Der, if you brought all these fairies to kill me," he said. "How embarrassing for you."

"We didn't bring weapons," Jethwire promised, and Shayne glanced down at Kahn-Der's long sword with a doubtful face. "We just want to talk." Jethwire's twisted smile was a different sort of unsettling; a little too wide to be natural.

"Take him," Kahn-Der directed in a dark voice barely decipherable against the loud ringing alarm.

Shayne rolled the dagger over his fingers, waiting for the first of his brothers and former friends to make their move. A horrid, bitter laugh filled his stinging throat as he realized his one foolish mistake would make this the day he died after all, perhaps even the hour. But a sound lifted through the space; a low creaking of hinges being turned, and the dagger stilled on Shayne's fingers. A footstep sounded behind him. Then another.

Shayne dragged his wildly round eyes over to see the dreamslipper there. Standing beside him. Out of her cage. She looked unexpectedly frightening when she wasn't behind bars or herded on chains. When there was nothing standing between her and the person she was glaring at—which in this case, was Kahn-Der.

The heel of Kahn-Der's boot slid back an inch. His ever-present crooked smile remained, but the corners of his mouth wavered. The fairies at his back all reached for the hidden weapons Jethwire had lied about. It was a wonder what everyone was so afraid of while being wide awake, but maybe it was the slightly startling brightness of Mycra Sentorious's eyes. And that was amusing, so, even though it could cost him his life, Shayne decided to conduct an experiment.

He tossed her the dagger.

Kahn-Der tried to grab the weapon as it sailed, but he missed, and the handle fell right into Mycra's grip.

"Get that!" Kahn-Der commanded his allies. Massie reached for the dagger only to find his arm being sliced three times over, faster than anyone could blink.

Shayne's jaw dropped. He slapped a hand over his mouth when four fairies surrounded Mycra and she fell to a knee in a spin, stabbing exactly eight kneecaps. Four fae fell to the ground, and Shayne wondered if he was dreaming. If this dreamslipper was messing with his slumber and he might snap awake at any moment. But he knew it was real when Jethwire and Massie sprang forward and grabbed his arms. Still, he laughed. Because even if he died today, tossing Mycra that dagger was...

Absolutely. *Worth*. It.

A fairy pinned Mycra to the ground while two others wrestled the dagger from her grip. Shayne punched Jethwire and kicked Massie in his ribs to free himself, then he wobbled across the space and took hold of the fairy's head who pinned Mycra to the floor. With a quick twist and snap, the fairy seemed to have trouble still being alive. Shayne tossed the body to the floor and kicked the next fairy right in the teeth, sending him sprawling backward and giving Mycra a chance to jump to her feet. Shayne shoved her toward the basement door.

"Don't waste my death, pretty Fairy," he said as all the injured fae climbed to their feet, and those who hadn't struck yet began surrounding Shayne and giving each other hand signals they thought Shayne couldn't see. Mycra looked like she might protest, but she met Shayne's eyes. With his gaze, he told her how dissatisfied he would be if she died beside him today. And she seemed to understand that his death would mean nothing if she became a corpse after this.

Something heavy struck Shayne's head. His arms were grabbed, the backs of his knees were kicked. Vertigo spilled in, but even so, he growled at the fae and raged like a mad crossbeast, ripping himself from their grip only to have more hands latch on again. Mycra sprang back during his show, shooting him one last look of panic. Then she raced for the door, grabbing a spear handle from the wall display on her way out.

Shayne found a small, weak smile watching her escape. It wasn't even that he cared that much—she was still a stranger—but she must have had something to live for, or she wouldn't have run. He inhaled a mouthful of stale dungeon air as he was lifted to his feet, thinking all the while of how the beautiful, caged beast was free at last. The flower had a chance to grow new petals. The butterfly might fly again—

A rock collided with Shayne's temple, and he toppled over. From there, he was kicked until purple blood ran from his mouth, from his ears, from his nose. His cheek scraped the cold stone floor as his body became the stomping ground for a dozen sets of boots. Most fairies would have cried or begged for mercy in his position, but Shayne laughed. He laughed and laughed as his bones were broken and his flesh was torn. He laughed because he came to this House to end his nightmares, and as it turned out, he'd found a way to end them after all.

Truly, dying would solve a lot of problems.

At least, that was his thought until Kahn-Der grabbed his shoulders and ripped him to his feet. The fairy had a gloating sneer as he tossed Shayne back into the hoard. "Walk him upstairs," Kahn-Der instructed, and Shayne blinked through swelling eyelids.

"What happened to the whole 'killing me' thing?" he asked with a voice too dry for much sound.

Kahn-Der chuckled, his icy eyes grazing over Shayne's cuts and blood. He lifted a hand to smooth his white hair back into place, and he licked his lips. "We have you for ten whole days, Brother," he said. Past him, Jethwire's and Massie's blue eyes grew wild, their grins twisting, and Shayne swallowed against his tender throat.

Torment, then. His household's specialty.

Jethwire nodded toward the basement door and the hands on Shayne's body roughly escorted him to the stairs. They made him walk on his own two wobbling legs back to the main floor of the House, through the maze of halls, and into the dining room where he'd issued his first threat to Kahn-Der. Shayne fought a wave of nausea. He hoped he would at least barf on someone tonight.

His dining seat was lifted, carried onto the tabletop, and placed in the exact centre of the table. Shayne was hoisted up and shoved into it. Fairies grabbed his hands, and his forearms were tied to the armrests with vines. He watched it all past puffy eyelids. He didn't fight them. He didn't resist. There was no point.

He did, however, crack a small smile in the midst of it all when Kahn-Der said, "You will beg me for death in the end. And I shall grant your wish by flicking you off the roof of the pagoda and watching you fall a very long way to your death, just like in your nightmares."

The small smile wasn't enough. Shayne loudly chuckled. "Coward," he said.

He couldn't deny it—he was flattered. Flattered that Kahn-Der was too afraid of his Brotherhood of Assassins experience to want to take him on alone. That Kahn-Der would only face Shayne once he was in a weak state of battered body and mind. That Shayne was flat out amazing, and Kahn-Der was basic.

As the cold iron clubs swung, Shayne's last thoughts weren't of the dreamslipper who'd gotten a second chance, or of revenge on his family, or even of his failed escape.

They were of a simple café he loved, owned by a blonde human who could deliciously lie through her teeth, and a moody, one-armed fairy he hadn't even said goodbye to.

25

3

Dranian Evelry and the Homecoming

Everything in the Ever Corners was bad. Not fit for humans. The forests were dark, the paths were hard on the feet, the pines were prickly, the food was sour, the stories in the wind were grumbling about the latest rise in North Corner taxes—

Dranian looked up when Lily sighed. He found the human standing with her hands on her hips, waiting for him on the path ahead. The golden sun was just beginning to dip toward the hoarfrost-covered mountains in the distance, and soon ice would prism the light into all sorts of wretched corners, threatening to expose anyone hiding in the shadows or walking out on a wide-open path like Lily had insisted they do—

"I've cross examined guilty criminals less nervous than you," she said.

Dranian frowned. "I've escorted frivolous royals less daft in the face of danger than you."

Lily opened her mouth but paused as if she were trying to sort through his complex usage of words. "Did you just call me stupid?" she asked plainly.

Dranian stared. Blinked. He shook his head.

Lily made a doubtful face. "Liar." She turned to continue down the path, tightening the straps of her satchel of belongings that would be utterly useless in just about every situation in the North Corner of Ever. Dranian exhaled. He continued to follow as she looked in amazement at every detail in sight; the velvety starbud bushes that stared right back at the strange human strutting by, the streams of colour on the horizon, and the golden honey bulbs dangling from the most generous trees along the path, tempting every passerby with the promise of their sweet taste and a raging army of silver hornets that would stab any fool dumb enough to try and actually taste it.

This was going to be a long day.

Yesterday had been a long day.

The day before that had been a long day, too, and the one before that.

Dranian had no trouble remembering the way to the House of Lyro, but the House was on the furthest cusp of the North Corner, practically on the border of the East, and in the exact furthest possible spot from the gate to the human realm. He exhaled again. With every step deeper into Ever that Lily took, he regretted bringing her more. He could already feel the wrath Cress would exercise upon him for doing such a foolish thing. He could practically taste the rocks. Mor wouldn't even defend him this time, and neither would Kate.

He ran his tongue along his teeth like he expected to find grains of rock salt there already as he studied Lily's back. Her useless satchel. Her parted mouth and tiny gasps at each new fairy thing she observed. He made a grunty sound. Lily missed all the most important things; the creeping vines following a short distance behind them, the threat of Jackson Frost's fingers reaching through the air, the distant fae parties her weensy little human ears couldn't observe the horrors of. And for that, he found he was in a mood.

"This place is unreal," Lily breathed.

"It's totally real. Real enough to drag you into a pit to be chewed up by cossbeasts and spit back out again," Dranian muttered.

Lily turned and shot him a look. "If I didn't know any better, I'd think you were trying to scare me into going back home." She folded her arms.

Dranian blinked. That was exactly what he was doing. He was beyond astounded it took her this long to figure that out.

"Stop being so grumpy. What were you going to do if I stayed home? Come here by *yourself?*" Her gaze flicked to his one bad arm, and he bristled.

"Luc said he was coming after he does his other thing," Dranian returned.

Lily huffed and tilted her head. "You really still think he's coming? Are you crazy, Dranian? He ditched us for good—that's why we've been walking for days instead of airslipping to Shayne's house in a matter of minutes." She pointed to the forest. "That jerk is probably spying on us from a tree, happily waiting to watch us get eaten by something."

Dranian opened his mouth to protest but found he hadn't a thing to say. He closed it again when Lily turned and continued walking. He stole a wary glance up at the trees as he hopped after her.

"I had no idea you even talked this much. Do the others know you can run your mouth?" Lily raised a brow when he caught up. "Or is that a trait you saved especially for me?" She flashed a cute, yet painfully sarcastic, scrunched-nose smile at him this time.

Dranian grumbled a few indecipherable fairy curses and flicked an emerald leaf on his way past. He bumped Lily with his shoulder when she stopped walking. He thought to ask her why she halted, but he'd already been accused of talking too much and he figured she'd tell him without being prompted if he waited long enough.

As expected, she asked, "Do you hear that?"

Dranian followed her gaze to the forest. Cracks of darkness wedged around the trees beneath a roof of tangled branches blocking the light. Modest whispers leaked from the wood trunks, slipping around the grasses, crawling out of the flowers. Dranian felt a nudge to take a step toward it all, but he broke his stare and looked at the sun meeting the frosted mountain tops instead. He knew the things hiding in those woods. He knew better than to stare.

He also knew Lily couldn't hear any of that whispery mumbo jumbo. She was probably obsessing over a singing cricket.

"We should get to a safe forest before sundown," he mumbled. He decided to lead the way this time, rolling his shoulder and wincing at the shooting pain as he headed down the path. He heard Lily's footsteps following him, but their rhythm was random like she kept turning to look over her shoulder as she walked.

They said nothing else for a while.

It took Dranian thirty-seven minutes to find a forest safe enough for sleep. He waited for Lily to fall asleep first. And he meant to stay up and keep watch, but after days of walking, it only took him sixteen more minutes to achieve slumber.

Dranian found himself on a vast ship. Restlessness bewitched a dark sky, and waves crashed up the boat's sides onto the deck. The ship was sinking. How had he gotten here?

"Dranian!"

His faeborn heart tumbled off course, chasing hope without navigation.

"Are you here?" he shouted into the gloom. He did a full spin, but he did not see the girl with no name anywhere. "Where are you?!"

It had been well over a week since he'd met the girl in his dreams. She hadn't sent word about Shayne. She hadn't told him she was okay. She'd disappeared from him entirely.

"I'm here!"

He turned, and there she was; haunting green irises, shiny black hair, smooth red lips… Only, her eyelids drooped, dark crescents cradled her eyes, her fair lips were parched, and her black hair was tossed. Her chest pumped like she might faint. Dranian barely reached for her before she lurched to the side like she'd been thrown. She tumbled into the ship's rail, cracking the wood with her back. Dranian sprang after her, grabbed her hand, and pulled her to her feet in one strong tug.

Thunder crackled overhead, followed by streaks of electric light burning through the clouds. Dranian's brows pulled together. "Are you doing this?" he asked. Frosty air blew over his shoulders and down his spine. He got the strangest sense he was in trouble.

"I didn't mean to—I'm sorry." She fought to catch her breath.

"Did you give me a nightmare?" Dranian looked warily at the sky, at the sinking boat.

But she shook her head. *"I gave you mine."*

Dranian's grip tightened on her hands. *Her* nightmare. This was…

He looked around again, something dropping into the pit of his stomach. "Queensbane," he muttered. If he was a bolder fairy, he might have pulled her in and held her tight as she lived through it. But he didn't know if that was the sort of thing she would have liked.

The fresh scent of grapes brushed by, mixing with the eerie musk of angry clouds and hungry waters. Dranian's nose wrinkled as it all bled together strangely. "Were there grapes on your ship?" he asked.

The girl looked at him oddly. "No. That scent is coming from outside your dream." But her eyes narrowed, and her lips peeled apart. "Wait… are you in the North Corner?" And then, "Are you by a vineyard?"

There was no time to answer as a mouth of darkness opened above them and inhaled debris from the ship, water, and cloud. The girl with no name was sucked backward, her hands sliding out of Dranian's, her body blowing up toward the abyss.

Dranian leapt forward to try and grab her back, his hand raised and empty. But she was swallowed by darkness, vanishing right before his eyes, leaving his dream, leaving him trapped in her nightmare.

He shouted.

Dranian was slapped, and he startled awake.

He gasped, flinging up to a sitting position. Lily knelt there, surrounded by a quiet forest and the blue threat of early morning. She was staring at him like he was a lunatic. "Are you alright?" she asked in a voice higher than normal. "You were shouting in your sleep!"

So she'd slapped him.

Dranian swallowed, finding his mouth parched. His whole body shook. He was dizzy, too, his mind going blank—*no*. He could not panic at a time like this. Not alone out here with Lily who needed him.

He inhaled deeply. Exhaled. Repeated it three times over.

When clear thoughts returned, he looked down at his hands, imagining someone else's holding them. Imagining someone's fingers sliding out of his grip. Imagining her being torn away.

Seconds. He'd barely seen the girl for *seconds*, and she'd been in distress. Dranian dropped his head into his palms and gripped the hair above his pointed ears.

"What's gotten into you?" Lily put a hand on his shoulder. "You never yell."

There weren't exactly proper words to explain his situation to a human. He hadn't told Lily about his nightmares, even when they were trading secrets about Luc, and her secret fairy destroying police division, and all the other things. So, all he said was, "I had a bad dream."

Lily nodded. She slumped to sit beside him in the cool grass. After a moment, she said, "I get that. I could never sleep well when I was younger because there was no one looking out for me while I slept. So I always had these crazy dreams where I was alone and someone was hurting me, or chasing me, or whatever else." She plucked a stalk of grass and rubbed it between her fingers. "The worst part of having no family was being too afraid to fall asleep in strange places."

Dranian glanced over at Lily, thinking of when he first became haunted by a dreamslipper and how hard he'd fought to stay awake. He tried to picture a small human girl doing the same thing.

He wasn't sure he had any sort of comfort to provide, so he cleared his throat instead and offered, "Sometimes 'family' is something you find when you're a little older."

Lily's face broke into a smile. "That's super deep, Dranian." She patted him on the shoulder. "Nice job."

He couldn't tell if she was being sarcastic or if she meant it, but she did look grateful as she rose to stand and extended a hand to help him up. Dranian climbed to his feet on his own though, using both his good legs to do it.

"Do you feel like jogging?" Lily asked.

Dranian scowled. "Jogging?"

"Yeah. We'll get there faster if we run." She pulled her satchel onto her shoulders and headed back toward the path. She broke into an easy jog without warning or waiting for him to agree to it.

Dranian scrambled after her, making sure to keep up—no, making sure to *pass her* once he reached the road. Fairies were far superior to humans in strength and speed. He imagined this exercise might be rather humiliating for Lily, though when she sped up to match his pace—no, to pass *him*...

Dranian's eyes widened at Lily's back. Her face was relaxed, her strides appeared easy; she looked as though she could run for the next several hours.

Of all his traits, competitiveness was the one Dranian cared about the least. Being good at things often brought unwanted attention, often demanded speeches to be made, questions to be asked, all of which were best avoided. So, that wasn't what this was. This wasn't a competition. This was by no means an actual race.

But he couldn't exactly be outgalloped by a human.

Dranian lifted his nose into the air, tilting his head back as he put his greatest effort forth to sprint past Lily, leaving no room for her victory whatsoever. He raced and raced and raced, breaking out of the forest into the morning sunlight, past the glistening gold vineyards, until he came to the end of the path where an abandoned stick hut rested in the shadow of a stalky pine. Beyond the hut's broken door, Dranian spotted a chair. He huffed with an almost-smile and headed toward the hut, wondering if it would be considered gloating if he were to pull out a chair and sit to wait for Lily until she caught up.

CHAPTER

4

Lily Baker and the Rules

The music didn't start right away. Lily only heard it after three days in the Ever Corners, and even then, she wasn't convinced of what she was hearing. The tune mixed into the wind, hardly a sound at all, just a high note of a woodwind instrument. But the crazy part was that Dranian swore he couldn't hear a thing.

Lily shook off the thought as she followed him into the village, accidentally kicking up dirt as her feet dragged. She was sticky with sweat from running for so long. She could have smacked the grouchy fairy for making her sprint like that, but when she'd finally reached him, he had a look on his face that somewhat resembled a smile, and Lily figured she shouldn't ruin such a rare and precious thing. If she'd had her phone, she would have snapped a picture of his expression before it went away, just to prove to the others it had really happened.

Dranian strutted a little taller now, and Lily smirked and shook her head. If all she had to do to get him to change his attitude about this trip was to let him run ahead of her for a while, she would have done it ages ago.

"The girl who can survive anything... can she survive us?"

Lily's feet came together. The music tickled her ears like it was a physical substance.

She wasn't crazy. It was really there, and now the song had... words?

She turned to look behind her, scanning the strange village streets with their crooked trees, their braided stick arches, and their glowing flower curtains. Something told her to go find the source of the music. It was the same feeling she got when she had a case to be solved that cost her sleep and days of mildly unhealthy obsessive attention. That addictive behavior was the reason Chief Adams wanted to promote her to detective.

The girl who can survive anything.

This freaky fairy park couldn't have possibly known to use that word—*survive*. The song couldn't have been talking about her.

"Lily." Dranian only used her name when he wanted something, was strangely trying to apologize for something, or was feeling impatient with her and didn't want to outright say it.

"Do you seriously not hear that?" she asked him. It sounded like the tune was coming from the faraway hills, which was totally impossible. It also seemed louder now, like they were getting closer to it.

But, once again, Dranian said, "No."

Lily sighed and turned to face him just as he reached for the hood of her police hoodie and yanked it up over her head. He positioned it around her face, roughly stuffing her hair inside.

"If you can," Dranian murmured, "conceal your scent as much as possible. And *especially* keep your eyes down. Don't make eye contact with any fairies we pass in this village."

"For real? How do I conceal my scent?" Lily folded her arms as she waited for him to finish his fussing.

Dranian leaned forward and sniffed. He made a face. "Unfortunately, it will be difficult," he admitted.

Lily burst out laughing. "Well, I wouldn't smell so bad if *someone* hadn't made me run a marathon today," she pointed out.

Dranian opened his mouth. He closed it again. Another shadow of a smile almost showed itself. "Stay close. If anyone grabs you, scream so I know. If anyone offers you gems, refuse even if you see visions of a wealthy life. If anyone offers you a drink that's bubbly and silver, refuse even if you—"

"How about I just refuse everything?" Lily offered.

Dranian nodded. "That will work." He turned and led the way onto a busy street where garland wrapped fences and white cottony dust covered the roads as if it was placed there to mimic snow. Tiny, glowing fairies buzzed above them like fireflies, and pretty, pointy-eared creatures moved into their path, eyeing Lily and Dranian while sipping on steaming drinks from crystal mugs. They wore long, deep blue gowns, vests with glittering green threads, chunky scarves, and large coats with fur-lined hoods. Some wore wreaths with flowers that sprouted as they passed. Dranian ignored them all, walking like a military man on a mission.

"They're preparing for the two months of Yule ceremonies," he muttered over his shoulder. "That's why everything is extra flashy."

"Ah." Lily wondered if the House of Lyro would be decorated like this; frost-kissed and smelling of pine. "What can we expect the House of Lyro to be like?" she asked. "You've hardly briefed me on it."

"You won't be going in there," Dranian stated.

Lily stopped walking again. "What do you mean I won't be going in?" A nearby fairy took her hesitation as an opportunity to show her a dazzling velvet gown that somehow looked to be exactly her size.

"I made this gown for you, can't you tell?" the fairy asked.

Lily glanced over at the dress, but only until Dranian swept back, grabbed her shoulder, turned her toward the road ahead, and continued walking.

"If you go into the House, you'll never come out. I'll go in. I know this family. I can withstand their torture." Dranian's voice wavered—a clear tell that he was lying. Lily looked over in time to see him bite his tongue.

It was strange to be the least educated person on an assignment. Connor always let Lily do the research ahead of their tasks, making her the natural leader. She didn't know whether to try and convince Dranian to let her help, or if she should heed his advice since he understood this magic stuff. It was difficult to tell if he was being reasonable or overly cautious.

She decided to change the subject. "I'm starving."

"Swallow some air then, Human, because that's all we have to eat," Dranian grumbled.

Lily grunted and stuck her tongue out at him. She did it half to lighten the mood, and half from legitimate dissatisfaction of the growling hole in her belly. What she didn't do it for though, was for someone to place something on it.

She wasn't prepared to come face-to-face with a black-haired fairy, or to have him drop a coin on her tongue at lightning speed. Or for the vicious smile that followed.

She was too shocked to move for a split second as it settled in.

Lily tried to spit it back out. Her spitty sounds filled the street, turning heads. But the coin stuck to her tongue like glue, weighing it down so she couldn't even speak.

"Now you won't be hungry forever," the fairy said like he'd heard her comment and was kindly solving her problem.

Dranian punched him.

Lily shrieked, trying to pull the metal out of her mouth as the black-haired fairy fell into the dirt. The fairy howled a laugh, then he pointed at Lily.

"Is that female what I think she is?" he asked Dranian.

Dranian's eyes widened. He brushed a hand over his injured arm.

Lily had never felt more out of her element as her legs turned numb and began wobbling. Heat soared through her body as if a paralytic drug was leaking from the coin. She reached for the gun tucked into the back of her belt, but found she couldn't move her fingers to grab it.

"I'm from the Brotherhood of Assassins!" Dranian barked over the street. "The death-bringers of Queene Levress herself! Cross me at great cost!" Before he'd even finished his announcement, he lifted Lily, his face contorting as he tossed her over his shoulder and hauled her through the village.

His sprint into the woods was filled with grunting and quiet, anguished sounds. Lily's mouth had no feeling as he laid her flat on her back behind the cover of the trees. "Don't touch anything!" he growled. "Don't eat anything! Why is that so difficult?!" He jammed his fingers into the dirt and rummaged around until he found a stone. Then he squeezed Lily's jaw to open her mouth, and he dropped it inside.

The second the stone touched the coin, it loosened from her tongue and the feeling came back into her body. She flung herself up and coughed, spitting out the coin and the dirty rock at once.

"That was totally not my fault!" she said in a shriek. She coughed again. "Ugh, that rock tasted like mud." She put a hand on her stomach as a terrible, overwhelming wave of starvation rushed in, so much greater than the hunger she'd felt before the whole coin thing. Thoughts of food screamed through her mind; pizza, pasta, Thai food, cake— "How much further is it to the House of Lyro?" she asked. *"And is there going to be food there?"* was what she wanted to ask.

"House of…" Dranian looked like he might explode behind his dull mask of expression. "Forget the House of Lyro! Now I'm going to be fighting off a whole village! They all saw you!" Then, "Do you know how valuable you are? Hunters will fill these woods within the hour!"

Lily nodded. She closed her eyes and shook the manic thoughts of pizza away. "Did that coin trick make me crave food like a crazy person?"

"It might have," Dranian snapped.

She thought of that fairy's vicious smile, how fast he'd put her in a state of paralysis, and suddenly she wanted nothing more than to get far away from this village. In fact… it was the first moment she wondered if maybe Dranian had been right in his warnings of this place, and that she was crazy for wanting to come here. The first moment she realized she had no idea what she was doing against fairies.

"Let's go," she said. Everything in the trees was darker, the air thicker, her knees weaker. "Dranian, I want to go," she said again, pulling her legs beneath her.

"Your body isn't used to fairy meddling. Are you sure you can walk?" Dranian asked. He stole a look into the woods. Glanced over his shoulder.

"I'm fine!" Lily promised. She stood and inhaled deeply.

She passed out.

Her limbs crumpled, she hit the dirt, she was gone.

There was no dream. There was just spinning blackness that swallowed time and thoughts and reality.

It felt like only a few seconds had passed when she heard Dranian mutter, "I haven't fought that hard in ages, *Human*." And some time after that he said, "We'll have to hide here until I regain strength in my one good arm."

There were only two kinds of people in the world. Those who solved problems and those who made them. Despite her upbringing and unlucky childhood, Lily had refused at an early age to be the latter. And that one resolve had made her a different sort of girl. It had made her a survivor.

That was why, when the sound of shattering glass made her eyelids peel open to see a ceiling over her head and walls around her, her first move was to roll out of bed, grab her gun, and move into the next room before she'd blinked the sleep from her eyes. It was why she punched as soon as she saw the young woman raise a weapon against Dranian, their colliding spears sending a metallic echo through the cabin.

The woman took Lily's punch, the spear in her hand swinging around so fast, Lily would have been impaled through the neck if she hadn't leaned back. Lily kicked as she came up. The woman dodged it in a graceful dance, appearing before her again with the tip of her spear at Lily's throat. Lily's gun was against the woman's head, right between a pair of wild green eyes.

The woman's gaze flickered over to Dranian—whom Lily only now realized had stopped fighting. He'd become pale and rigid, and he looked like he'd seen a ghost.

"Drop your spear, or I'll shoot," Lily warned the woman anyway.

Dranian dropped his spear, and Lily cut him a look of disbelief. "I wasn't talking to you!" she said. But his expression didn't waver, and Lily looked from Dranian, to the woman, then back to Dranian again, who seemed like he couldn't spit out whatever he wanted to say.

Then, as if all the weirdness in the room wasn't enough, Dranian miraculously found his voice to ask her, "Where's Shayne?"

Lily almost demanded to know why Dranian would ask that question to a stranger, but the young woman's face fell, and the next thing Lily knew, the 'stranger' spoke words that made Lily drop her gun. Made the beats of Lily's heart slow, and made none of this seem real.

"You came too late," the woman said.

Too late.

Too *late*?

Was this woman a psycho? She clearly had a few screws loose, but numbness filled Lily's chest when she studied the woman's face and saw actual regret there. It was as if this stranger might have really known something about Shayne in her glowing-eyed, tangly-haired head. And that... Lily couldn't handle that. Not even a peanut's worth.

"What does that mean?" Lily asked in a low, articulate voice. She nearly raised her gun again. Heat burned around her eyes out of nowhere, even though crying wouldn't solve anything. Even though crying was for people who didn't know how to survive like she did. "Tell me what that means!" she repeated. She cut her glare over to Dranian who stood there with parted lips, hugging his injured arm to himself, still staring at the intruder. "Who is this?" Lily asked him instead, pointing to the psycho-woman with her gun.

Dranian didn't answer. Didn't move a muscle. Didn't help *at all.*

The woman spoke instead, "It means Shayne Lyro is probably already dead. And if he's not... he likely wishes he was," she stated. Her voice was high and sweet like a melody, but it didn't make the things she said any better. "And running at full speed to that horrible House won't get us there in time even if the sky deities have kept him alive until now."

Lily bit down on her lips and drifted a step toward Dranian, forcing him to peel his eyes off the psycho-woman and meet her gaze. "What is she saying, Dranian?" she demanded. "What is this psycho saying?"

Dranian's mouth moved, but he didn't answer.

"What in the world happened, Dranian?" Lily roared this time. She tightened her grip on her gun while losing her grip on herself. "I know all you *brothers* were in on something back in the summer. Did that have to do with why Shayne lied to us and came here and ended up like this?!"

Dranian slid back a step. A crease formed between his brows as he shook his head. "Our secret-y thing had nothing to do with this," he swore. "And I promised my brothers I would never tell of that incident, so don't ask me about it—I beg you, Lily."

Lily stared at him with a look that spent the last dime of energy she had left after hearing the woman's news. "We'll be too late even if we run; didn't you hear?" Lily enunciated every syllable. "We're too late, Dranian! We're too late for Shayne!" She hiccuped an inhale as that settled in. "So yeah—I'm going to ask about it. And you're going to tell me every 'secret-y' thing you fairies were involved in before Shayne left."

5

Shayne Lyro and the Secret-y Thing
that Happened Before He Left

Two Months Ago

The floor of Kate's apartment was filthy. Shayne hadn't noticed it until he laid upside down on the couch in the living space with his legs up the backrest and his white hair sweeping the floor.

Mor sighed loudly when he came in. He didn't bother asking what Shayne was doing or why he was upside down. Dranian didn't ask questions either; he came into the apartment as straight-faced as ever, glanced at Shayne's toes dancing in the air, and kept walking until he reached the kitchen island with Mor. He pulled out a stool and sat down.

Cress, however, was entirely incapable of passing by without a word.

"Your feet are ghastly, Shayne!" he scolded. "Look!" His finger did an up-and-down sweep of pointing out all the dirt Shayne had collected on his foot-bottoms over the last day. "I shall cut off your feet altogether if you *ever—*"

Shayne slid his leg over and tried to poke Cress in the eye with his toe. The fearsome, severely over-glorified Prince of the North Corner swatted toward Shayne's quick feet, missing over and over until he gritted his teeth and pointed at Shayne like he was about to announce something very important. Shayne grinned. It seemed to only make matters worse though, and Cress's lips thinned as he grappled Shayne's legs together. Shayne laughed as he was dragged sideways off the couch and tossed into a heap on the floor.

"Agh!" Cress looked himself over in disgust as if assessing his body for damage. He wiped his hands down his shirt to rid himself of Shayne's nonexistent filth.

Shayne brought his arms up and clasped his fingers behind his head as he watched from the floor. The second Cress moved to take a step toward the counter where Mor and Dranian waited, Shayne stuck out his leg and tripped him.

The squealing of a gracefully falling fae prince filled the apartment. Even Mor pressed a fist against his mouth to hide his laughter this time. Then, through his fingers, he said to Cress, "You know he only does things like that because you react so strongly."

Cress ripped a cushion off the couch and hurled it at where he must have thought Shayne was. Shayne watched the cushion sail by, fling off the nearest chair, soar into the kitchen, and smash against Kate's mug collection. Ringing sounds of shattering goblets overtook the apartment, the catastrophe hidden from Shayne's sight behind the island. Only Mor sprang for the mugs, but he didn't catch a single one before the whole collection met its end. Mor's hands remained out and empty as all four fairies went rigid and exchanged looks.

A light croaking sound came from Cress. He slapped a hand over his eyes. "We're done for!" he shouted. Then he pointed at Shayne with his other hand. "This is why we were told not to engage in shenanigans in Katherine's apartment anymore!"

Shayne propped himself onto his elbows. "How bad is it?" he asked

43

Mor, cringing.

Mor glanced down toward the floor. "It's not great," he admitted. "I'll get the broom—Cress! What are you doing?"

Shayne scrambled backward when he noticed Cress marching toward him on his knees with a new cushion, his turquoise eyes narrowed and lethal.

"I'm suffocating the problem once and for all!" Cress declared. He lunged for Shayne, holding the cushion toward his face. Mor suddenly appeared, grabbing Cress around his middle and holding him still as Shayne scrambled to his feet. Shayne wasn't sure why Mor bothered since he was perfectly capable of fending off Cress on his own, until Lily's voice came from behind him.

"Are you crazy, Cress?!" she asked.

Shayne's smile widened. He looked Cress dead in the eyes, and he shot him a perfectly timed look of gloating. Cress wouldn't dare try anything deadly with Lily present.

Lily even appeared in front of him, her back all tense like she was going to *protect him from Cress*, and thus, fulfilling all Shayne's hopes and dreams in one single second. It was adorable. As if she could do anything against Cress. She'd be lucky to give him a papercut, and she'd spend all her energy doing it.

Honestly, Shayne just wanted to hug her from behind and squeeze her like a human teddy bear sometimes.

He tore his gaze off Lily's back when she whirled around.

Far across the apartment, a bug crawled up the wall. Shayne focused all his attention on it. That, and doing everything in his power not to smile right in her face. Because she'd tried to *save* him.

Oops—a smile slipped out. And a little sniffle-laugh.

"Shayne!" Lily shouted. "What happened? What was that huge crash?"

Shayne settled his gaze on the human he accidentally thought about all the time for no particular reason. How irritating she was to be the one who popped into his mind whenever he awoke from his night terrors. To be the sole provider of the happy thoughts that reminded him what was real and what was a nightmare. Lily Baker was greedy for stealing so much of his brain's time.

A strand of her maize hair had escaped her ponytail, likely from her race up the stairs. "You have nothing to worry about, ugly Human," Shayne assured her, patting her on the head. "Now, go do something with that horrid lion's mane of fur you call hair."

Lily was pretty when she scowled. Truly picturesque. Her stink-face would go nicely on a calendar, and Shayne wondered if he should take the idea from Mor and create a calendar for the café with all of Lily's most horrid faces. She'd love it.

"Anyway—" Shayne wrapped an arm around her shoulders and guided her back toward the stairs before she might take a step deeper into the kitchen and spot the sea of mug crumbs on the floor, "—say hi to Officer Greene for me today. Tell him I'll bring him those tartlets he asked for next time I come in..."

Lily made a sound and moved toward the stairs, but Shayne found himself tightening his grip on her shoulders. She looked up at him with a strange blend of accusation and question as he held her there, tilting his head and scrunching his nose as he inhaled.

"Human, I don't suppose you've come into contact with any fairies you haven't told us about, hmm?" he asked. His fingers dug in a little as her eyes widened and her lips peeled apart.

"What? No way!" she said with a tone that was wobbly and all over the place.

Shayne whirled her to face him, dragged her forward, and brought his face right into her messy hair. He breathed in, eyeing a loose hair and winding it around his finger.

Two hands came against his chest and shoved him back. He let Lily push him, falling away a step or two.

Shayne chewed on his lip, then he smiled. "Have a good day at work." It was as sarcastic as sarcastic could be. Lily seemed to know it, too. She looked back and forth between his eyes for a moment and finally grunted, heading for the stairs with folded arms.

Shayne waited for her to leave. Waited until the door swung shut behind her, until her footsteps promised she was downstairs. Then he turned to his brothers.

"Now I'm sure of it. She's hiding something, and I can't stop thinking about it," he stated. "It's driving me faeborn mad!" He released a long, melodic huff.

Cress scowled. "You always think everyone's hiding something." He tossed his cushion weapon back to the couch.

"Just ignore him," Mor murmured to Cress. "He's only saying this to get you riled up again. Why do you always fall for it?"

"I'm not just saying it!" Shayne stated. He crossed his arms. "Her hair smells like fairy blood. Why in the name of the sky deities would one of our humans smell of fairy blood?"

Mor sighed and went to get the broom from the closet. When he pulled it out, he started sweeping the kitchen. Large mug chunks went straight into the garbage.

"Perhaps your senses are off," Dranian mumbled.

Cress nodded. "He's right. You've been living in the human realm so long you don't know what you're smelling or sensing or whatever." He waved a hand through the air as he went to fetch the other cushion.

"Smell this." Shayne held up the hair he'd stolen from Lily's ponytail. "Then you decide if I'm going mad for nothing."

Mor released an exasperated sound and marched across the apartment. He took the hair as if he had a thousand other things he'd rather be doing, and he sniffed it. "It's normal," he stated, but his brows pulled together. He blinked down at the hair. Slowly, he lifted it to his nose again, and this time when he smelled it, he inhaled deeply, rolling it between his fingers.

He dropped his hand to his side and glanced off. He didn't say anything for a moment.

"What is it, Mor?" Cress leaned forward, eyeing Mor's hand. "Is it plain and normal and all that?"

Mor's brown-silver gaze became level with Shayne's. "If you're wrong about this, and Lily finds out we're snooping into her human life, *you're* going to be the one to pay for it."

Shayne smiled and thrust a victory fist into the air.

"I suggest lashings as punishment if he's wrong," Cress said.

"I'm not wrong," Shayne promised. "Did you know Lily frequents a secret building across the city? It's called *Desmount Tech*—the same company that equips the police force with some *very* astounding gear—"

"What exactly are you suggesting?" Mor asked.

Shayne grinned again. "I'm suggesting we handle it like we would have in the Brotherhood. We go at night, we infiltrate, we interrogate, and we get the answers we need."

"And if you're wrong?" Mor challenged.

Shayne tapped a finger against his chin. "If I'm wrong, Cress can give me six lashings—"

"Ten," Cress decided.

"Fine, ten. But if I'm *right*—"

"If you're right, you'll just be faeborn right. That's all there is to it," Mor cut in.

"No. If I'm right about this, I want you to erase my memories of the Four Corners so that I only know of this place." Shayne twirled a finger around the apartment.

Dranian nearly fell off his stool at the island, and Cress gasped.

Mor stared though. The Shadow Fairy didn't say anything—didn't mention to the others that this was not the first time Shayne had asked him to do this.

"That is preposterous, Shayne!" Cress announced. "Why would you want to forget the things of your youth and childling years? The lessons we learned to evade fairy tricks? Your assassin training? And... all the other important things?"

Shayne held Mor's gaze. Mor was the one who knew the extent of

Shayne's nightmares. He was also the one who'd endured Shayne's incessant, obnoxious begging over the last few days to have everything erased in hopes it might cure him of his sleeping torment. Even so...

"I'm not doing that," Mor stated.

Shayne sighed and stuffed his hands into his pockets. He found a button in there. One he'd stolen right off a snobbish human's coat. "Fine. I'll take the *just being faeborn right* thing. Being right about this is satisfaction enough." He pointed to Cress. "Unless I can give Cress lashes?"

"Absolutely not!" Cress snapped back as he marched over. "I was once a *prince* of the North Corner of—"

Shayne threw the button into Cress's open mouth.

Cress gagged and Mor bit his lips over a smile. He turned his head away so Cress wouldn't see it.

"Dranian and I will plan our heist for this evening and give you details within the hour," Shayne said to Mor as Cress spat the button out. Shayne leaned to see past them and called to Dranian, "You coming?"

Dranian slid off his seat without a word and hastened to the stairs.

"I could use a coffee," Shayne added as he pushed out the apartment door and led the way down. "I call the good chair by the fireplace—"

Dranian rushed forward, and Shayne sprang after him. They shoved each other, fighting for position at the bottom of the stairs. Dranian nudged Shayne aside with his hip and managed to exit the stairwell first, but in the end Shayne latched onto the back of Dranian's shirt, yanked it so hard it ripped off, and took the opportunity of Dranian going dead-still in the middle of the café with his rippling abs exposed to spring past him and land in the café's best chair.

The moon was a heavy bulb lighting the sky, marking the path for four fae assassins in black to infiltrate a highly secure building. The whole escapade made Shayne realize that humans were a rather dumb species. Sneaking inside Desmount Tech was nearly as easy as the walk through the city to reach it. The doors weren't even locked, and several lights were left on inside as if the fools of Lily's big secret were *inviting* the fairies to come spy on them.

An itch arose on Shayne's back as he headed down a curvy hallway. He twisted his arms this way and that to reach beneath where his crossbow was strapped, never quite finding it, until someone else's fingers scratched the spot. Shayne released a sigh of relief.

"All that twisting was horrendous to watch. You looked like a writhing hogbeast suffering from worms," Cress explained as he passed Shayne to peer around the hall's edge. He mirrored the dangerous killer he once was as he inched his way forward to scout for enemies. Once satisfied, he signalled to the brothers behind him that it was safe to progress, and he slowly drew his glimmering fairsaber. A brief beat of pride moved through Shayne at seeing Cress back in murder-mode after all his time in the human realm. Shayne would rather die by a thousand hot flames than admit it, but Cress had always been the best killer among them. There was nothing quite as terrifying as seeing the coldness in Cress's eyes when he was entering enemy territory.

A strange sound lifted in the hall as they rounded the corner. Shayne looked back and forth in confusion until Mor said, "Cress, are you *humming*?"

The sound stopped.

"No," Cress said.

Shayne felt a grin form. "Was that the theme song of that spy movie we watched last night? What was that movie called again?" He tapped the side of his head, then he snapped. "A Mission Probable!"

"That was *not* it," Mor muttered.

"A Mission... Pretend-able?" Shayne guessed again.

"Mission Possible," Dranian murmured, almost too quiet to hear.

"Ah! Yes, that was it. *Mission Possible*. Cress, that's what you were humming, right?" Shayne nudged Cress's back as they came into a room cloaked in black curtains. "Were you pretending to be that astounding human male who—"

49

"I don't need to pretend to be a human, Shayne. I am far more fierce than any human spy…" Cress's voice trailed off as he flung a black curtain aside and stepped through. Shayne followed and almost walked into Cress, but he spun off to the side, making way for Dranian to bump into Cress's back instead.

Shayne blinked as blinding lights burned across an enormous space. A few dozen people were quietly moving about, including a small herd of dolled up human females at the far end. Every being was unarmed and seemingly unthreatened by the spies who'd infiltrated their building like the handsome human in *Mission Possible*. Only, unlike in the movie, this place felt safe and cozy and suspiciously cute.

A large banner hung across the wall that read: LAST DATE. LAST HOPE. LAST CHANCE FOR LOVE.

The quietness was interrupted when a female saw the assassins standing there. Her round face lit up and she rushed for them. The speedwalk triggered Cress's fairsaber to twitch forward, so Shayne grabbed the sword and yanked it from Cress's hand. He held it behind his back, and Mor silently took the weapon without a word. Shayne pulled off his crossbow and handed that back to Mor, too. A shuffling sound lifted by one of the curtains where Shayne imagined Mor was hiding all the weapons.

"You must be the bachelors for *Last Date!*" the human female exclaimed. She did a shameless gaze up and down their bodies. Dranian crossed his arms like he was trying to cover himself. "Wow, the recruiting team deserves a raise!" The female giggled and waved them forward. "Come fill out the forms so we can get started filming! Are you excited to learn which resort we'll be sending you to? Are you excited to meet the ladies?"

Not a single fairy foot moved. Rather, Cress's cold turquoise gaze— the one Shayne had been proud to see only seconds ago—landed on him with various tones and threats.

"What did she just say?" Cress asked slowly.

Shayne looked around at the décor, at the cameras, at the new people filtering into the large space. He scratched his head. "There's a *chance*," he said as he clasped his hands tightly together in front of him, "that we might be in the wrong building."

A shadowy chill crawled over Shayne's flesh, making his bones shiver and his limbs prickle with frostbite. He was sure he'd be frozen to the floor by Cress's ice powers and terrible mood if he wasn't careful with the next words that came out of his mouth.

"I take back my agreement about the lashings," Shayne settled on.

"Do you mean to tell me…" Mor said in a way that made Shayne picture him speaking through his teeth "…that we've walked onto a *dating* show? That these humans think we're *available* bachelors?"

Cress pinched the bridge of his nose. "Of *course* they think we're the bachelors, Mor. We're unfathomably gorgeous!"

Shayne accidentally grinned. Dranian nudged him, making him snap out of it and force the smile off his face before Cress or Mor might notice.

Cress turned slowly to face the fairies. He raised a finger and held it mostly in Shayne's face. "We can *not* be caught trying to spy on Lily," he stated in sharp, threatening words. "We shall do whatever these humans ask so we blend in. We will not blow our cover—*no matter what!*"

"Are you coming?" The same round-faced female returned on her tip toes. She fiddled with her curly hair as she waited. Four sheets of parchment and four ink pens were in her hands. "We can start with the questionnaires."

"We aren't prepared for an interrogation," Dranian murmured quietly. "What shall we do, Cress?"

Cress seemed frozen in place at the sight of the questionnaires. "Don't tell them any secrets," he instructed. "And no matter what, don't reveal that you're a powerful fairy that could crush their bones and mop this floor with their spilled blood."

Shayne chuckled and waved a hand through the air. "This is easy. Just be flirty and fun. Say you enjoy things like 'long walks on the beach.' That's fake dating a human 101. I should know since I've been fake dating a human for ages now," he bragged.

Cress glanced over at him. "What does *won-oh-won* mean?"

"It's when you're teaching someone a lesson. You say the topic, and then you say, *101*," Shayne explained.

Mor released a growly sigh. "Stop being so suspicious. You two are whispering right in front of that human," he scolded. He shoved Shayne out of the way and went first. They all watched as Mor approached the human female and took the piece of interrogation parchment she extended toward him.

Dranian turned back for the hall.

"Where do you think you're going?!" Cress whispered after him.

"I'm going to find the real human bachelors and lock them in a closet so they don't expose our ploy," he said back.

Four long hours later, the quartet of fairies stood before a large TV, staring at a collection of interviews all filling the screen at once. 'Editors' worked on the 'clips' to prepare the 'intro episode'.

Mor's interview took up the whole screen for a moment, and the name "*Jeff [No Last Name]*" appeared below, along with: *Occupation: Long Walks on The Beach.* Shayne nearly lost control of his bachelor façade when he read it.

"Don't you dare laugh," Mor threatened. "This is all your fault."

Mor's interview disappeared, replaced by clips of Cress's. Cress had chosen the name: *Cresstopher Alabrungerton.* And: *Occupation: Being a High Prince.* Shayne slapped a hand over his face.

"What?" Cress scolded. "It's not like anyone is going to believe it. Make your lie as close to the truth as possible without actually telling the truth. That's deception *won-oh-won.*"

Far down the line of editors, a human snickered. He leaned to the male beside him and whispered, "Did this guy's parents really make him believe he's a prince his whole life?"

Mor grabbed Cress's elbow to hold him still as Cress's gaze drilled the editor's back. "Do they think we can't hear them?!" Cress asked through tight lips.

"Probably," Mor pointed out. "Most humans couldn't."

"Of course I was told I was a prince my whole life! That's a *won-oh-won* lesson of prince-ing!" Cress argued, even though no one was disagreeing with him.

Shayne leaned forward to watch as his interview came next. He was the only fairy who'd flashed dreamy smiles and answered the questions naturally.

"You chose the name *Thomas Cruise?*" Cress folded his arms. "I wish I'd thought of that."

"Yes," Shayne said proudly. "And my occupation is *Possible Missions*, in case you didn't notice." He pointed to the TV screen.

"Hmm." Cress nodded. Then he said, "Trade names with me."

"Absolutely not," Shayne returned, but then he thought better of it. "Unless you lift my lashings punishment. Then I'll trade with you."

Cress tapped a finger against his chin as if considering.

When Dranian's interview appeared, the chatter died off. Shayne, Cress, and Mor all glared at Dranian at once.

"Why did you use your real name?" Mor murmured.

Dranian opened his mouth, then closed it. After a moment, he whispered, "I couldn't think of anything else."

"Queensbane, Dranian, please tell me you didn't put…" Cress gave up when the words *'Occupation: Assassin'* filled the screen. The three of them moaned.

Dranian pouted a little. "I'm not as creative as the rest of you," he muttered.

"Well, we've been exposed. Let's sneak out the back," Cress decided.

Shayne shook his head. "They're going to put this on TV. We should destroy everything first."

One of the editors looked up from where he sat with a horrified face, so Shayne flashed him a smile to promise he was joking, even though he wasn't.

"No time," Cress said. "We need to get back to the café before Kate and Lily notice we're missing and begin to devise suspicions and conclusions. It's clear one of us performs poorly under interrogation—" he cut a look toward Dranian "—so we'd better hope they don't ask any questions of our whereabouts this evening."

"What about the thing Lily is hiding?" Shayne asked as he followed Cress toward the curtain where Mor had stashed their weapons.

"What about it, Shayne?" Cress snapped. "Lily isn't the sneaky sort. And if I'm being faeborn honest, *you're* the sort to take everything too far. So, we're leaving this alone before my human fiancé finds out and throws an outrageous fit over it."

"But—"

"I'll not have you utter another word about it," Cress stated.

"I second that," Mor said as he dragged the fairsabers, spear, and crossbow out from beneath the curtain. A few humans murmured questions; one even gasped when they noticed all the pointy arrows and sharp edges.

Shayne sighed. "Fine. I'll figure it out on my own then. But you're all going to feel like fools when I prove I'm right." Shayne yanked his crossbow from Mor and pulled the strap on over his shoulders. He led the way to the halls. "You watch. Finding out everything about Lily Baker is going to be easy-peasy."

Nothing was easy-peasy after that—*except* figuring out that Lily was building secret fairy-slaughtering weapons behind the assassins' backs. That had, as Shayne had claimed, been easy.

Everything else came with difficulty over the next days. Sleeping. Waking up from terrible fits of fighting his blood brothers in his dreams. Experiencing the feeling of being thrown from high cliffs or drowned in the fountain in front of his childling House.

Nightmares. Dozens every night. Over and over. Nightmares that finally drove him to craft a lie about going on a trip; a lie so well planned that not even Mor could see through it. He loudly asked his brothers about the kingdom of Florida, about sunscreen and sunburns and fishing. He purchased new sandals and a 'beach bag'. He asked about catching fish, even.

"Why do I need to use a fishing pole? I can catch a fish with my bare hands," he said.

"Because humans don't catch fish with their bare hands, Shayne. You'll look preposterous," Cress claimed.

Shayne smirked because he already knew that. He watched his brothers flutter around the café. He watched Kate and Lily as they whispered things they forgot the fairies could hear. He watched all the people he wished to live alongside forever in their merry little ways.

But he couldn't do that. He couldn't live merrily or peacefully as it was while every night he grew more and more mad.

So, days later, he strapped on his navy Brotherhood uniform, hefted his crossbow onto his back, and headed for the gate to assassinate a dream-meddling wench so he could live out the rest of his faeborn life with his humans. It wouldn't take him long—just a week or two to infiltrate, eliminate the problem, and flee. Then he'd return, move into a box of space with Dranian, and the two of them would live happily ever after.

6

Shayne Lyro and the Present

A dull pulse was trapped inside Shayne's head. He peeled his eyes open, finding the dining room empty for once. Most of his fingers were broken, creating an obnoxiously painful sensation he couldn't fix while his arms were tied down. The first thing he'd do once he got out of this chair was snap all his fingers back in place so the bones could meld and then he'd use his fresh hand to punch Kahn-Der in the face.

A coarse, quiet laugh escaped his lips.

If he ever got out of this chair.

Old food littered the table by his feet. Not only had his brothers turned him into a centrepiece, they'd eaten their meals around him: morning, midday, and evening. They must have thought he'd be jealous at the sight of their crispy hogbeast meat and berry pudding. But as it was, he felt no hunger, even though having meat and vegetables thrown at him was the closest he'd come to eating anything in days.

His throat was too raw to shout anymore—he'd done enough shouting, insulting, egging the three other Lyro descendants on over the long days, but there was one thing he had not tried to nuisance them with yet, and that was his horrible singing voice. He wasn't sure he had the strength to use it, but he cleared his throat, wincing when he was reminded how tender it was. And he began to gift the House of Lyro with a ballad in a raspy, high melody that could hardly be called a melody at all. "Kahn-Der is a coward," he sang, "and Jethwire is bad at playing the flute. And Massie is seriously messed up. None of the Lyro brothers are handsome, except for *one*—"

The doors to the dining room opened. Kahn-Der wore his lamellar armour again and carried his long sword. Shayne slumped back in the chair, finding his energy spent after just a few lines of his song. His eyes slid closed too, and his heart grew weak at the mere sight of his brothers returning. He stifled a moan as he considered what torment they had in store for him today.

He missed hot coffee and butter tarts. He missed sleeping in on weekends and taking pointers from cheesy romance novels read by the fire. He missed arguing with human store owners about why he couldn't enter their store in bare feet.

Today, and yesterday, and the day before that, there were moments when he'd wished for death, followed by moments he'd wanted to destroy Kahn-Der so badly he dreamt about it during the restless minutes of sleep he'd managed to find. He wondered if the sky deities would grant him one wish after he took his last breath. He wasn't sure exactly what he'd wish for, but he knew there was something in his faeborn heart he wanted. Unfortunately, he couldn't quite pinpoint what it was. Maybe he was just too tired to think right.

"Cut his vines," Kahn-Der instructed, and Shayne's eyes slid open. His gaze settled on his eldest brother whose crooked smile gloated like he'd beaten Shayne in this game. Like he'd enjoyed every moment of pain and discomfort he'd brought the former heir. Shayne had watched the oldest Lyro descendant do his fair share of terrible things in his years—stealing, murder, conspiring. Deep down, Shayne supposed he'd always hoped he'd be able to face off with him some day and annihilate the brute. The Ever Corners would be better off without Kahn-Der in them.

Massie hopped onto the table with a dagger and cut the vines in rigid strokes. Shayne's arms fell onto his lap. He raised his hands to study his strangely bent fingers. Then he started snapping them all back into place. "Faeborn-cursed monsters," he muttered beneath his breath as he fixed himself up.

"Come with me to the roof, Brother," Kahn-Der invited, and a weak smile spread across Shayne's face.

"Finally," he rasped. Shayne tried to stand but discovered his legs were drained of usefulness, and he fell right back into the chair. He gripped the armrests so he wouldn't slide out of the seat as Massie chuckled. Shayne took in a deep breath. He forced himself back to his feet, keeping his eyes wide open and...

"Queensbane," Shayne muttered to himself when he looked around at the table. He had no idea how he was going to get down without simply falling. He wasn't sure how he was going to take his first step forward either.

Massie solved his problem though when he shoved him.

Shayne fell sideways, off the table, over a chair, and toppled onto the floor. The dining room spun for a moment; the chairs were caught into a whirlwind, the smell of day-old pudding flying around with it, and the large painting on the wall of five white-haired Lyro children with two of the faces scratched out whisked by like a magic carpet. Despite his delirium, Shayne smiled. One of those pretty, scratched-off faces was his.

For a split second, Shayne wondered what his Brotherhood brothers would think if they saw him like this, and his smile fell off. He could not think of Dranian, Cress, and Mor right now. He could not think of them in his last moments, or he might decide he wanted to live. And he was long past that option.

Kahn-Der grabbed Shayne's shoulders and hoisted him to his feet.

The handle of a long fairsaber was shoved into Shayne's hand. Shayne was turned around, and Jethwire and Massie waved goodbye as Kahn-Der led Shayne to the stairs and shoved him, step by step, up to the roof of the pagoda—a journey that felt like hours by the time they reached it.

Shayne took in the red and gold dragon statues at the roof's four corners. He leaned a little to peer over the roof's edge, seeing thick pillars the width of a bathing pool below with flat tops. If he'd had any energy, he might have tried to leap onto the nearest one and spring from pillar to pillar to escape.

But if he tried to jump in his state, he'd fall. Fall and fall and fall. He'd do Kahn-Der's work for him.

"A death trial for the highest chair. I've wanted this since the day our father chose you as the heir instead of me," Kahn-Der said—Shayne only half listened. He already knew all this boring stuff. His return had likely made Kahn-Der worried that Hans-Der would hand the title of heir back to Shayne.

"He changed his mind about me after he chose me," Shayne mumbled anyway. "He sent me away and gave you everything you wanted."

Kahn-Der snarled. "Not everything. He let you live."

Rain spat upon the roof, turning the flat area slick. Shayne released a light chuckle from his sore throat as he lifted the shiny sword in his hand to gaze at it; the sword of his childling years. A special sword everyone in the House of Lyro knew how to use. Long and thin; meant for quick slicing.

"He let me live because he knew you were the real culprit behind our sister's death. He really only sent me away for being wild and hilarious and fun—something the rest of you haven't a clue how to be. *Maybe* he even hoped I'd return some day and slay you." Shayne rolled the fairsaber in his grip. He teetered as he tried to find his stance. Then he smiled—one last smile for the insufferable brother who'd destroyed so many fairy lives. "Enough chit chat. Let's play." He raised his sword.

Kahn-Der's crooked smirk returned, his ice-blue eyes narrowing, his white hair turning to glassy strands in the rain. "This will be a good day for me," he said as he raised his fairsaber.

Shayne didn't dare try to run at him. Running would make him tip over. So he waited, and sure enough, Kahn-Der struck first.

The blade came down so heavily that Shayne fell backward when he blocked. He rolled out of the way as Kahn-Der stabbed the roof, over and over, only ever missing by a thread. Shayne threw his leg up into Kahn-Der's stomach, revelling in the sweet sound of bone snapping.

Kahn-Der growled, finally hesitating long enough for Shayne to climb to his feet.

Shayne reached over and patted himself on the back. "I'm not doing so bad considering how unfair this fight is, don't you think?" he asked. Kahn-Der didn't give him time for more thoughts; his fairsaber swung at Shayne with the speed of the wind, and Shayne took it.

He took it...

He was too fatigued to see it coming, too weak to dodge it.

The blade tore through his flesh, right across his front, and Shayne released a guttural cry. He dropped to a knee, using his sword for support as purple blood raced down his body, mixing in with the rain puddles. He checked to make sure he was still breathing, that his faeborn lungs hadn't stopped working. Then he clenched his jaw.

This fool. Did he even know he'd stolen Shayne's happy life without a care?

Kahn-Der swept in to finish him off as Shayne's eyes threatened to fall closed. He took in one last breath and slashed through the air, catching Kahn-Der's midsection so their cuts matched. Kahn-Der gasped and grabbed his stomach. He looked up at Shayne in surprise.

Shayne flashed him a smile. "Twinsies," he said.

Kahn-Der growled and kicked Shayne backward. The second he was down, Kahn-Der kicked him again, forcing Shayne to roll dangerously close to the roof's edge. And with Kahn-Der's last kick, Shayne tumbled off, his hands weakly grabbing for something to catch and finding nothing.

Wind and rain slapped his cheeks on the way down.

Shayne collided against a flat surface, his ribs bending inside of him, his body skidding to a stop. He realized he'd landed atop a pillar when his fairsaber tipped over the edge and soared far below to the ground where he'd never get it back.

Kahn-Der landed beside him and used his boot to flip Shayne over.

Rain fell into Shayne's eyes, blurring his brother's crooked smile. A brief break in the dark clouds sent light burning over them, turning Kahn-Der into a silhouette as he raised his fairsaber high above Shayne's chest, blade point aimed for Shayne's heart.

So, this was it.

Shayne braced for it. He almost closed his eyes, but...

A new silhouette appeared with a flash of ruby-red, eclipsing the light beside Kahn-Der. It was followed by a confusing, bone-snapping shuffle that ended with Kahn-Der *flying* off the pillar. Shayne blinked as Kahn-Der's limbs flailed, as he didn't catch himself, as he disappeared over the edge.

Shayne tilted his ear to listen, sure he heard the echo of Kahn-Der's wail like the fool was falling... still falling... and...

"Oh dear. I hope you weren't planning to keep him alive? I think he's very much splattered."

Shayne's blurred gaze drifted back to the new silhouette. Was this fairy speaking to *him*?

A sweet, furry smell wafted through the air as Shayne lifted a hand to block the sun, to see who this glowing savior was. But the sun slipped behind the clouds again, everything turning back to shadows, and Shayne found himself staring into the face of an enemy fox he was sure was a hallucination.

Luc Zelsor stared back at Shayne. "North Fairies," he muttered in a bored tone.

Through the teetering in his mind, Shayne recalled a dagger hidden in his boot. Boots weren't good for anything really, except hiding daggers. He dropped his arm; it slapped against the stone beneath him and stayed there for a moment until he could muster the energy to move it again. Then he inched his hand toward his boot. Bit by bit.

Luc Zelsor blinked. Watching it all.

Shayne tugged the dagger free anyway. He tried to throw it quickly, but the toss ended up being so weak that the fox simply swatted it from its slow, pathetic float through the air. The blade bounced off the pillar and fell, down, down—just like Kahn-Der had.

Suddenly Shayne laughed. Was Kahn-Der really the one who'd met that fate? Agony ripped through his body with the chuckles, and he winced, deciding laughing was off limits.

The fox still stood there. Arms folded. Watching. After a moment, he scowled and said, "You really are mad, North Fairy. I thought Lily Baker was fibbing about you being crazy, but I can see now that you're a pure-bred lunatic."

Shayne's smile fell. He felt less dizzy as he lifted his gaze to the fox. Something predatory came over him, and he gritted his teeth, pulling himself up to a sitting position as his swollen flesh and aching muscles screamed in protest.

"Whose name did you just utter from that vile mouth of yours?" Shayne asked from a dry throat. "When did you speak to *my* Lily? I swear, if you so much as *touched* her—"

Luc kicked him back down. Shayne's spine smacked the stone, and he choked to catch his breath.

"There's only room on this pillar for one fairy who talks a lot, I'm afraid. And I call dibs on being that fairy." Luc tilted his head. "Honestly, I'm not convinced you were worth saving. There's a perfectly good dog back in my apartment that possesses everything necessary to replace you." At that, Luc sighed, dropped to a knee, and grabbed Shayne by the arms.

Shayne gasped as he was sucked from the pillar. The realm turned to wind around him and he was overcome with the sensation of floating, speeding, slipping through spaces. After a second of it, he realized he was being cutely *held* by Luc-the-enemy-fox-*Zelsor*. Shayne tried to push the fox off him, tried to peel himself out of the fox's grip, but the

62

attempt brought a fresh dizzy spell over him, and he slumped—accidentally letting his head fall onto Luc's shoulder. A grunt of revulsion filled his ear.

It may have gone on for seconds, or minutes, or longer; the fox's kidnapping attempt. Time patterns were confusing as Shayne fell in and out of consciousness. As he became aware of his surroundings slowing down.

The next thing Shayne knew, he was dropped onto a cold, hard floor. He rolled onto his side and curled into a ball to sleep there, caring nothing of the place, the time, the circumstance. But then he heard a voice that made him feel all warm and good inside. A grumpy fae voice. It said, "I thought you were going to meet us there later?"

A treacherous fox voice returned, "The thing I had to deal with first ended sooner than I anticipated." And then, "You're lucky I made it to that tacky red House early, North Fairy. Your lunatic barefoot friend owes me his life, you know."

When Shayne managed to open his eyes, everything was blurry again. But as his vision sharpened, he thought he could see Dranian standing there, the fool's scowl as perfect as ever, his eyes filled with worry. Shayne released a dry chuckle as he wondered if he really had died in that moment on the pillar. If Kahn-Der had ended him, and the rest had been an afterlife illusion. Because he was sure this was fairy heaven—or even better, human heaven. Luc Zelsor must have been a grim reaper sent to try and steal him from his true destiny among the clouds.

Shayne's theory was confirmed when a pretty, blonde-haired human came racing into the room. She dropped down beside him and shouted, "Are you crazy, Shayne?!"

"Only crazy for you," he tried to say back to human-heaven's-Lily

as he reached a weak arm toward her to see what she might feel like in heaven. If her body was solid or made of light where his hand would move through. But Shayne found his mouth didn't work anymore to say his brilliant comment, and his arm was too heavy. His hand dropped back down, his eyes rolled closed, and his head fell to the side as the visions of human heaven drifted away.

CHAPTER

7

Lily Baker and the Switcheroo

The early morning hours in the Ever Corners had a different feel than the ones in Toronto. On her bed, Lily hugged her knees to herself as she stared out the window of the worn-down cottage and watched silvery 'fluffs' lift from the woods. They did a shiny dance of nature, dusting against a backdrop of the richest green leaves she'd ever seen. The scene was accented by gold sunlight spearing through the branches overhead.

When she was young, mornings had been something like this. She'd often woken up in a room alone and hugged her knees as she stared out the window at the long laneway of the children's 'in-between' safehouse building, wondering if a family might come driving down that lane and decide to take her home. Before she'd died, Tanya Baker had been so certain one of her friends would take Lily in once she was gone. She'd assured Lily it would all be okay as she'd laid on a crisp white hospital bed. But when the day came, the friends she'd mentioned never reached out—in fact, it was the opposite. Lily overheard the repeated disappointment in the child service worker's voice after several phone calls were made, and the people who'd made Lily's mother a promise suddenly didn't want to be contacted.

In the summers growing up, Lily would spot milkweed fluff in the air and think of her mom. Her mom had once told her that milkweed fluffs were really fairies in disguise, and if you could catch one, you could make a wish. She'd said the same thing about snowflakes in the winter.

But Lily had caught dozens of milkweed fluffs. She'd captured hundreds of snowflakes from the air with her mittens. They never granted her wishes. They never brought her mother back or brought her a family who wanted to keep her past a couple of months.

That was, until she met the Lewis family. But by that time, Lily no longer believed in fairies or wishes. She believed in working hard to be a good person as a way of being grateful to the only people who'd chosen to love her. She believed in returning kindness by protecting the Lewis family.

It was why she didn't care about anything as much as protecting Kate and Greyson from the cruel world she'd known.

As an adult, mornings in the city came with droplets of dew, a crisp chill, and the warm scent of brewing coffee. It came with eating a quick breakfast, putting on makeup, finding her badge, checking in with her siblings, and heading out to save the city from criminals. Or, more likely, saving cats stuck in trees, following up on neighbour disputes, and writing up reports.

Still. Mornings in the city were perfect. There was nothing that should have messed with them. Nothing that should have drawn her away from those moments where the troubles of the past seemed like a distant memory.

Except that something did. *Someone* did.

Up until the second Luc had shown up with Shayne in his arms, Lily was sure she'd made the biggest mistake of her life in coming here.

Lily slid off the bed and reached her arm through a gaping hole in the window. She splayed her fingers as the silent silver dust balls swept by. One grazed her finger, and she slowly clasped her hand around it, pulling it into the room to study it. It looked like a tiny milkweed fluff, but it shimmered in the light and left a buzzing feeling on her palm.

Still. She thought about making a wish.

"The girl who can survive anything... can she survive us?"

Lily's gaze darted back to the window. She peered into the woods, taking in the darkest parts of the trees. The music drifted in and out, like someone was turning their phone volume up and down, but one thing was certain; the gentle woodwind instrument was louder and clearer than it had been last time. Whatever this music was, it was getting closer.

"*Your* friend? Ha!" Shayne's voice lifted from the cottage's living space. Lily's stomach tightened at the sound of that voice, the one she hadn't heard in months. The one belonging to the person she came into this horrid, magical world to find. And now, by some miracle, he was here.

He'd been sleeping for a full day and night, barely even moving.

But now he was awake. And yelling.

Lily shoved the fluff out the window and headed for the bedroom door.

"Believe whatever you like, North Fairy. Dranian and I even have a dog together." Luc sounded like he'd rather be doing anything in the world than having this conversation.

"Don't speak for Dranian, you flappy-lipped fox. Dranian Evelry is a mighty fae warrior who singlehandedly assassinated the Low King of the Third Region's Shade Forest with nothing but a handful of mud! He can speak for himself."

"It was poisoned mud." Dranian's murmur reached Lily as she came into the living area. The bedroom door squeaked closed behind her. "So it wasn't that difficult—"

"Quiet Dranian, I'm telling off this fox for you..." Shayne's words fell away when he glanced toward the squeaking sound and his blue gaze landed on Lily standing there.

A flutter moved through Lily's stomach when he didn't say anything. When he just stared.

Two large bruises covered the side of Shayne's pale face, and one of his eyes was set in a purple ring, but even so, Lily wanted to smile. To grab him into a hug that would be completely out of character for her. She even had one fleeting, bizarre thought to kiss him right on his busted mouth to thank him for being alive. But she cleared her throat, keeping her whole face in check.

Shayne wore a fastened, red, imperial coat-like garment she didn't recognize. The midsection had a tear and the collar was stretched. She hadn't been able to stand looking at him before while he was in such terrible shape, but now that he was awake, and alert, and hollering at everyone, she took in every bloody notch in his skin, every bump on his face, and especially his frown.

His frown.

Shayne never frowned…

There was a moment where everything in the room was so quiet, Lily thought she'd gone deaf.

"That…" The word was coarse when Shayne finally spoke. He blinked. He squinted. He blinked again. "…better not be what I think it is."

The front door of the cottage opened, and Mycra—the psycho woman—walked in with a basket of gold-coloured grapes.

"Don't you mean *whom* you think it is?" Luc sighed. "If you're going to talk so much, you should at least learn how to speak."

Shayne reached up and pinched his own arm. He made a face, and as if realizing this wasn't a dream, his expression turned wild. All of a sudden, louder than a thousand police sirens shrieking in the dead of night, he *shouted*, "You're not angel-Lily from human heaven?!!"

"What?" Mycra murmured by the door. She looked around like she was trying to figure out what she'd walked into.

Lily went over Shayne's words twice in her head before she decided she had no idea what he was talking about. "Did you fall face first into an alternate reality, Shayne?" she asked. Shayne hadn't blinked in way too long, and—why hadn't he smiled yet?

But then...

"I'm going to kill you," Shayne whispered.

Lily's mouth parted. She slid back a step until Shayne's stare fired over to Dranian instead and she realized he wasn't talking to her. "You're dead."

A second ago, Dranian's lips had been quirking upward like he was enjoying watching Shayne and Luc fight over him. But now, his eyes grew big. He sprang back when Shayne reached for him.

Mycra appeared out of nowhere, grabbing Shayne's hand and twisting it at an awkward angle, halting Shayne's assault attempt. She edged her way in between the two, her bright eyes pinning Shayne more securely than whatever pain she caused his body from her limb wrangling.

Shayne's lashes fluttered for a moment. He teetered slightly.

Luc stared at it all with a completely uninterested expression. Yet, still, he said to Dranian, "Hit him back, you fool."

Dranian looked from Shayne to Luc. To Mycra. Back to Shayne.

His mouth quirked up at the corners again.

"Unreal," Lily said. "Put an end to this like a normal person, Dranian. They're not all fighting over *you*." Though she actually wasn't sure.

"Nope." Shayne's arm flew up; he held a finger before Lily's face, but he didn't look at her. "No, you can't talk, ugly Human. You aren't here, and therefore, you can't speak."

Lily shoved his finger out of her face. "I'm here, Shayne. Deal with it."

Shayne dragged his thin-lipped face around to look at her once and for all. "Do you know the kinds of horrible things fairies like to do to humans, *Human*?" he asked. He took a fast step toward her, tugging himself from Mycra's grip. "Do you have any idea what will happen to you if you're caught here?" The purpling ring around his eye looked worse close up.

"I can take care of myself," Lily promised.

Shayne threw his head back and laughed. He laughed until he nearly lost his balance. Then he winced and inhaled sharply, grabbing the wall for support and clutching his midsection.

"There's a pool of healing water a few feet into the woods," Mycra said. "Go toss him in there for a while," she said to no one in particular. But then she glanced over her shoulder at Luc.

Luc raised a scarlet brow. "*I'm* not doing it." He looked at Dranian after he said it, his glance falling to Dranian's arm. His gaze fired over to Lily next, and his nose wrinkled. Finally, he looked Mycra up and down, eyeing her slender frame. He released a heavy, annoyed sigh and marched across the space.

Shayne still stared at Lily, even when Luc reached for his arm.

"No." Shayne swatted Luc's fingers off the second they touched him. "I need to punish this human first for doing something as foolish as coming here."

Shayne looked ridiculous with his bruised face, wild white hair, teetering body, and eyes full of accusation. Lily fought an unexpected smirk. The second it appeared, Shayne's eyes widened and his hand smooshed over her mouth.

"There's no smiling allowed either," he said. "You're not really here, and therefore, you can't smile."

Luc huffed. "Whatever," he said, reaching for Shayne. Lily didn't realize he was reaching for her too until the fox had her wrist. She was sucked into a tunnel of whipping wind and smeared colours. A second later...

Her body splashed into a pool of water. She gasped as she caught her balance and glanced down at her drenched police hoodie. The water came up to her belly, but she could hardly see it past Shayne's hand still over her mouth. He remained staring at her through the droplets running down his face, and she realized his other arm was wound around her waist, holding her.

"Let me go, Shayne," she said through his fingers.

"Absolutely not. I'll never let you go, Lily Baker. You can't leave my side now—and don't blame me for it; you signed up for this the moment you decided to pitch your human brain into oblivion and set foot in the Ever Corners." Shayne released her mouth and reached around to clasp both hands behind her back instead. He hoisted her against him tightly. "Foolish human."

Lily didn't realize Luc was there, hunched forward on the grassy area around the pool with his hands on his knees, until his panting filled her ears. He stood tall and gazed down his nose at the two of them. "You're all insufferable to watch. What a gong show," he said. "And don't you know how difficult it is to carry *two* people through the air at the same time?" With that, he turned and headed back through the trees toward the cottage, patting off his sleeves as he went.

"Let me go," Lily tried again, pushing against Shayne's chest this time, but he tightened his arms and shook his head.

"Nope."

"How are you even—" She gritted her teeth and attempted to use her weight against him. She even smacked his shoulder, but he wouldn't budge. "—doing this?" she finished in one exasperated breath. A minute ago, he'd seemed too injured to stand on his own two feet. Now it was like his arms had turned to tungsten.

"These waters work quickly—that's something I know because I'm from the Ever Corners and *you're not*—and I'm suddenly feeling as if I possess the strength of a thousand elven bulls. Which is rather convenient since I plan to hold onto you like this until I get you back to the human realm where you belong."

"Get *me* back? The reason we came here was to bring *you* back with us," Lily objected.

Shayne released a raspy sound. "Though I do love to whack a wasp's nest and then leave, I'm not going back…" He paused, then said, "unless you beg."

There it was. He smiled.

Lily caught herself staring at it; the easy curl of his closed-mouth grin. That infectious smile that sent a tiny ripple through her abdomen. It had been easy to ignore his smiles back in the city, back when she was around him more and saw his grins every day. It felt different seeing one now; like she'd become addicted to them at some point and didn't know how much she'd craved the sight of one until it was happening right in front of her.

She realized she was standing way too close to Shayne's face to be staring at his mouth, of all things.

It was too late though. He noticed. And when his grin grew, she blushed.

"It's alright, ugly Human. I have that effect on females," he bragged. "Sometimes it's a burden to be gorgeous all the time without even trying."

Lily made a noise in the back of her throat. "You should shove your face into these healing waters a little longer before you say things like that," she advised, eyeing his busted chin.

"Hmm."

He let her go—no, he *pushed* her.

Lily fell back into the pool, and warm liquid rushed in. She splashed until she regained her footing and stood with the new weight of water saturating her hair and whatever parts of her sweater that had stayed dry up until now.

Shayne laid back on the slanted poolside, the hem of his red coat floating around him. He closed his eyes.

"Seriously?!" Lily folded her arms.

"Shhhh. I'm healing."

Lily shook her head as she waded toward a stone ledge beside him. She grabbed the grass above to keep balance as she lifted herself onto it. She almost took a step out of the pool, almost escaped to the forest, when a hand wrapped around her ankle. She shrieked as she was yanked.

"Nope." Shayne dragged her back into the pool, then grabbed a handful of her sweater and tugged her over. "Nice try." He tucked her in nicely beside him, then he laid his head back and closed his eyes again.

Lily took in a deep breath and let it out slowly. She stared up at the sky beginning to glow and interlace with prismed colours. Even if she wasn't too tired to fight back against Shayne's rapidly rejuvenating strength, she had to admit the serene woods were relaxing. The water was warm, and the view was remarkable, too. She glanced over at Shayne when she heard the slow, steady rhythm of his breathing. His lips peeled apart and his head rolled gently to the side, shifting his white hair. She wondered how long it had been since he'd gotten any real sleep. How many nights he'd been forcefully kept awake to end up in this kind of condition. But most of all, she wondered how she'd been lucky enough to get him back. To have him right beside her, alive and breathing, and sleeping peacefully.

"You lunatic," she whispered.

What if he'd never woken up after Luc arrived with him? What if she'd really lost him? For over a day they'd been waiting for Shayne to wake up so they could go home. Dranian had practically turned into a nurse.

Lily raised a hand to cover her mouth when her eyes grew hot with tears. A sob threatened to slip out, but she stifled it, taking another deep breath and blowing it out quietly. She'd die before she let someone see her crying over Shayne, of all people.

She'd come to this terrifying place on a search and rescue mission. Shayne had been rescued. Now all she had to do was get him out of here, and everything could go back to normal.

Lily found Dranian sitting on an open hillside before a view of rolling hills, golden vineyards, and distant blue mountains. Luc laid flat on his back with his eyes closed beside him like he was napping. Dranian said nothing, but he stared particularly hard at the hills as if waiting for something to pop out of them.

Lily still wasn't comfortable leaving Dranian alone with Luc, regardless of whatever heroic act Luc had found within his warped, serial-kidnapping personality to do. But Dranian didn't seem afraid. In fact, his body language had only improved since Luc had shown up. It had gotten better when Mycra had first shown up too, though neither the bright-eyed, goddess-faced girl or the savage, secret-stealing sociopath had provided Lily with enough details about themselves or their motives to leave her completely relaxed in their presence. She was also still pretty stumped about how Dranian and Mycra knew each other, and why they understood each other without saying anything at all.

When Lily reached the duo on the hill, she wedged her way in between them, nudging Luc over so she could fit. Luc snorted and peeked one eye open. When he saw Lily, he rolled his one eye and closed it again.

Lily studied the nine tailed fox for suspicious tells. Not everything she'd read about creatures like him fit Luc's description. Some people considered nine tailed foxes to be gods. But apart from having a god-complex, Luc was far from that. Only now did Lily notice he wore a long black coat that looked like a combination of something an English prince might wear and Count Dracula's go-to hunting outfit.

"What happened to your hands?" she asked Luc when she spotted lacerations over his knuckles and wrists. The cuts were thin like whatever had caused them was sharp, although bruising above his left thumb told her he'd also had a collision with a blunt object.

Luc's mouth pinched a little. He stuffed his hands into the pockets of his Dracula coat and didn't answer.

"Has Shayne awakened?" Dranian asked.

Lily shook her head. She'd watched for nearly an hour as the bruises on Shayne's face disappeared and his cuts closed up before she'd crawled out of the water. During that time, she'd made a short study of the crystal-clear turquoise pool. A pool of water that *healed people* could have changed the whole human realm.

The human realm.

Kate.

Lily suddenly sat straight. "What day is it back home?" she asked Dranian. She patted her sweater down for her phone before remembering she didn't have it. Then she lifted her hands and began counting back the days.

"November must be almost over by now," Dranian murmured in reply. "I don't know the day, exactly."

"It's December first," Lily realized, dropping her hands to her knees. "I should be home. There's only fourteen days left." She pulled out her elastic and refastened her ponytail.

"Why? What happens in fourteen days?" Dranian asked.

Lily smoothed her hair down and flicked dirt off her sweater as she sorted through how she was going to explain herself to Kate and Greyson once they got back.

"It's the anniversary of Grandma Lewis's death," Luc piped up from the grass.

Lily and Dranian both turned toward him, Dranian leaning to look over Lily's shoulder. Luc's eyes were still closed. He yawned.

A flit of guilt moved through Lily's chest at the thought of her grandmother. She'd been so busy with work and the café this year that she'd hardly had time to think about the old woman. How had a whole year passed already?

Lily cleared her throat. "How do you know who Grandma Lewis is?" she asked Luc.

"Her name and death anniversary were written on the calendar in Fae Café," he said back as if it was obvious.

"Ah." Dranian nodded like that made sense, but he stopped. He looked back at Luc again. "When were you in Fae Café while I wasn't there?"

Luc opened his eyes and lifted his head to steal a look at Dranian. "That's an excellent question." A broad, admittedly attractive but notoriously creepy smile took over his mouth. He laid his head back and resumed his nap without explaining anything.

A shout came through the forest. The first words were muffled, but something along the lines of, "ugly Human" was among them. Then came, "Where are you?!" It was called like a warning, and Lily shifted uncomfortably on the hill. "Dranian??" came next.

"I guess he's 'awakened'," Lily said.

Luc stretched, his scarlet hair glittering in the sun with the movement. "You two go deal with him." He flicked a hand at Lily and Dranian. "I've already dealt with him enough."

Shayne came bursting from the trees, swatting a branch out of the way and sending four leaves spiraling through the air. Lily thought he'd be normal and sit down beside Dranian where there was space, but she should have known Shayne did nothing normally. His hands appeared beneath her arms and she was lifted from the grass, plunked onto her feet, and turned around. He was smiling, but it was too wide and a little wild.

"I made you a bracelet," he said, and Lily raised a brow. "You're going to love it." He reached behind him and pulled out a short stem of green vine. "Allow me to put this on you." As soon as Shayne took Lily's hand, Luc grabbed her wrist and shoved Shayne back a step. Lily hadn't even seen Luc climb to his feet. She glared at the fox and yanked her wrist away from him.

"Don't put that on, dear Lily," Luc warned. "Not unless you want to be tethered to this lunatic by an enchanted vine." He bristled. "Trust me, it's astoundingly frustrating."

Lily's gaze fired back to Shayne. "You tried to cuff me? With a weird fairy plant? Seriously?"

Shayne was too busy glaring at Luc to hear. He took a step toward the fox, bringing out Luc's broad, intimidating smile. "Don't touch my things, Foxy," Shayne warned. "These two things," he pointed between Lily and Dranian, "are mine."

"How about you pick one to keep, and I'll have the other? You decide which one you want most." Luc's voice turned sweet and alluring, like the promise of sugar and dreams coming true. Lily found herself leaning in to hear him better. She'd never noticed his lips were heart-shaped or that his skin was so smooth. She shook the strange thought from her mind, sure she was sleep deprived until Luc said, "I'm sure I can win Lily Baker over since she's already being lured in by my fox charm. Can't you feel it?"

Shayne tilted his head, his smile turning thin. "Remember how I killed you once?" he asked.

"Remember how I haven't gotten revenge for that yet?" Luc's silver-brown eyes narrowed, and Lily snapped out of her daze.

She stepped in and pushed Shayne and Luc away from each other, holding tight to a handful of each of their coats to keep them apart and cutting Dranian a look as if to say, *"Stop enjoying this and help a little, would you?"* Dranian only shrugged in response, but his almost-smile was back.

"Oh dear. I think she likes touching me, too," Luc said. He placed his pale hand over where Lily held his coat at his chest. It wasn't warm like it should be—Luc's skin was ice cold.

"Gross," Lily said, dropping his coat. But she kept a hold on Shayne's, and Shayne flashed Luc a gloating grin.

"Uh oh," Shayne said. "You'd better not ask them to choose between us, Zelsor. I think they'll both choose me."

Luc's smile turned to a scowl. He rolled his eyes and said, "Anyway, we should move from this defenseless cottage before the rest of your household shows up in their gaudy red coats." His gaze flickered down to Shayne's outfit as he said it.

"They'll never find us out here," Dranian stated. He raised his chin. "This cottage is riddled with North rash weeds that will mask our scent and keep unwanted guests away."

Luc's face blanched.

"They've found us!" A shrill voice lifted in the distance.

Lily spotted Mycra racing over the hills, her dark hair lapping behind her. Her strides were impressive, even with a short spear in her hand. "The House of Lyro is coming!"

"What?!" Dranian growled.

"Did you say *rash weeds*?" Luc shouted. He yanked the hem of his coat around as if checking it.

Lily's flesh pulled tight as she gazed over the hills. She couldn't see anyone coming yet, but she wanted to look into the faces of the people who'd put Shayne into such a battered state. Who'd cast him out of their home when he was younger. She wanted to see what his heartless family looked like, but even more than that...

She wanted him to escape from them.

"Let's airslip back to the café!" Lily turned to Luc. "Hurry!" she added.

Luc nearly choked. "Do you really think I can carry *all of you* through the wind, dear Lily?"

Her spare hand drifted to the pocket of her hoodie where she usually kept her phone. "Carry one of us at a time," she returned, and Luc's heart-shaped lips twisted.

"I don't think you know how things work among fairies," he said. "We can't just leave when they're this close or whatever Shadow Fairies they're working with will follow us through the gate—as my own past has proven. Either we fight until they're dead or we're dead, or we make a bargain for our lives, *or* we find a way to fool them into *thinking* we're dead. But we don't just 'slip away' without consequences." He nodded toward Shayne. "Did this fool never tell you that?"

"Why do they care so much? Why can't they just let us go?" Lily finally dropped Shayne's coat and folded her arms, squeezing them tight. "This doesn't make any sense."

Luc sighed. "It does, actually. I killed the heir to the House of Lyro the other day."

Shayne released a deep moan. "I was hoping I'd dreamt that part. Couldn't you have just messed Kahn-Der up a little? Broken his legs and smashed a few ribs? Did you really have to toss him off the top of a pillar like a bag of spoiled potatoes?" he asked Luc.

Luc examined his nails. "I enjoyed it."

Shayne thought about that. Then he admitted, "So did I."

"Didn't you hear what I said?" Mycra shouted when she reached them. She scooted to a stop, kicking up dirt. "The House of Lyro is coming. They'll be here in minutes. We should run before it's too late!"

"That won't solve anything," Luc said, more to himself.

"Sure it will. Let's get out of here and sneak back to the human realm while they're not looking," Shayne said. He extended a hand to Lily, but she cast him a look to remind him she could walk on her own.

"Jethwire is leading the army," Mycra added, and Shayne's mouth twisted.

"So my father isn't with them?" he asked.

"I doubt he's back yet," Mycra said. "But it doesn't matter; it's the hunting army. They'll have already been promised rewards. Anyone spotted in your company will be black marked, and they'll shoot to capture, not to kill."

Shayne dragged a hand through his white hair, making it stand on end.

"Isn't that better?" Lily asked.

"No," Mycra, Dranian, and Shayne all said at the same time.

Shayne nudged Lily toward Dranian. "We should split up then," he decided. "Lily, stay with Dranian. Why don't you two head home first?"

"That is a *terrible* idea," Luc said. He cast Shayne a sidelong glance. "You should be quiet if you only have bad ideas."

"We don't have time for this!" Mycra objected.

"Exactly," Luc said. "They'll catch us if we run, and they'll corner us if we split up, which means we must fight."

"What?! You want me to... *fight* fairies? Here in the Ever Corners?" Lily asked. Her chest tightened—she couldn't seem to take in a full breath anymore.

"Yes. And in order to do that, we need a little more power, don't you think?" Luc tapped a finger against his chin. "Oh dear. I think that means it's time for my backup plan."

Flickering shadows rippled over the hill, and Lily looked up. Her jaw dropped as *thousands* of flapping birds filled the sky. Only they didn't appear quite normal; they looked... flat and bright red.

"They've spotted us," Mycra warned. She gazed at the sky warily. "We should run, Shayne. I can't... I don't want to go back there." Dranian's attention snapped to her and stayed there, even as one of the birds fell from the sky and spiralled down, landing at Shayne's feet.

Shayne stooped to pick it up, showing the birds were made of paper when he unfolded it and studied the sheet. A muscle feathered in his jaw.

A second later, a bird fell at Luc's feet, too. Luc snarled at it a little, but he reluctantly snatched it and unfolded the paper. "For the offense of executing Lord Kahn-Der, son of Lord Hans-Der of the Silver Castle High Court, you have been established as an enemy of the House of Lyro and our allies. Surrender or die." Luc grunted, then to Shayne, he said, "What does yours say?"

Shayne crumpled his and stuffed it in his coat pocket. "Nothing important. I agree with the obnoxious fox. Let's fight."

Lily couldn't believe her ears. Only a second ago, Shayne had been determined to run. She watched his gaze flicker up to the crimson birds in the sky circling like a swarm overhead.

"I have a present for you, North Fairy," Luc said to Dranian now. "I've been keeping it with me for insurance." He reached into his pocket and pulled out something almost too small to see. He held up a nut—or half of one at least.

"What is it?" Dranian asked, brows furrowing.

"It's something that will save us," Luc returned.

Lily was a breath away from calling Luc crazy when Luc tossed the nut to Dranian. Dranian fumbled to catch it.

"Eat it fast," Luc instructed.

"Wait—" Mycra reached for Dranian's hand, but it was too late. Dranian popped the nut into his mouth and swallowed it like a pill.

"Do you really think that's a good idea right now?" Shayne asked Luc with articulated words.

"You would think so if you knew who ate the other half." Luc's broad smile returned, and a twinkle lit his eyes.

Shayne blinked. He grasped Luc's shoulder and shook it. "Who ate the other faeborn-cursed half, Foxy?"

Lily glanced at the darkening, bird-filled sky as she asked, "Am I seriously the only one who doesn't know what's going on?!" When she dropped her gaze back to Dranian, she found him shaking. Her eyes widened and she stepped toward him. "Dranian…?"

Luc seized her arm, holding her still. "Wait," he instructed. In the same second, Shayne reached across and smacked his hand off.

"Keep your fox paws to yourself. She hates being grabbed!" he snapped.

Lily watched as Dranian shuddered. She brought a hand over her mouth, her mind racing with all the training she had to aid someone experiencing a panic attack. She realized Luc was smiling—like this was *funny*—and her hands balled into fists. "If we get out of this, I'm arresting you the second you step back into the human realm…" Her words caught when she looked back at Dranian.

No. Not Dranian.

Lily blinked. "Cress?"

For a second, she thought she woke up from a strange dream and was back home in the café.

Cress stood there, looking down at his clothes. His arms. His hands. He wore an expensive looking navy suit complete with a collared shirt, a jacket, dress pants, and a strangely familiar grouchy expression.

Shayne's jaw dropped. He whirled on Luc. "Cress?! You fed the other half of the walnut to *Cress*?"

"Yes," Luc returned. "And without him knowing it, too. Poor Cressica. I wonder what he'll do when he realizes he's trapped inside the body of a three-legged guard dog at home." He shrugged.

Cress—or, Dranian-in-Cress's-body, if Lily was understanding—muttered, "He'll make me eat rocks."

Shayne suddenly laughed. He almost lost his balance as he tried to collect himself. "Queensbane, Cress is going to be furious," he said.

81

"I hope so. He did kill me, after all. And I always get my revenge."
Luc sliced Shayne a look as if that was a promise. Then, to Dranian-in-
Cress's-body, he said, "Welcome to the fight, Dranian. Now you have
the powers of flight, faestone, past peeping, icy weather, and whatever
other magnificent gifts the mighty Prince of the North possesses. Let's
fight." He pulled a ruby from his pocket and rolled it over his fingers. He
lifted something else out of his pocket too; it looked like a crumb of
bread. He stared at it for a moment, then he flicked it into the grass.

Red poured over the hills in the distance, and Lily's mouth parted as
she beheld the giant antlered beasts carrying fairies in red coats that
looked like Shayne's. They moved so fast; she realized Luc was right—
they wouldn't have made it far even if they'd tried to run.

8

Dranian Evelry Being Epic

There weren't words to explain what had happened the moment Dranian laid eyes upon the woman of his dreams. For a split second, he'd thought he wasn't actually awake when she'd appeared in front of him in the cabin. He thought he was stopping an intruder, that someone from the village had followed them in hopes of kidnapping the human under his charge. He'd locked spears with her—the female. He'd nearly fought with all he had left until he realized...

It was her.

The girl with no name stood before him.

His surroundings hadn't been teetering and stormy and nightmarish. Everything was bright and the air was crisp. He was awake. He was awake and she was there and she was looking at him.

Dranian would relive that moment every second of every day. He stole another glance at the girl with no name now where she stood on the hill beside him. Her throat constricted as she watched the enemies in crimson flooding the valley. As she prepared to face the very souls who had imprisoned her these last years. How his blood boiled with fresh rage when he thought about all she'd been through in her time. He'd hardly been able to sit still when she'd told him mere bits and pieces of what had happened in her life since they were separated in Ashi-Calla village.

Him. Enraged.

Feeling feely things.

Dranian's chest had gotten warm the last few days. He couldn't make it stop, even when he'd tried plunging into a cold healing pool. He feared his chest might heat to oven temperatures and bake his insides if he couldn't make it stop. That his body would turn to a tasty meat stick for the birds and he'd die like that.

A meat stick.

Dranian rubbed his chest when he thought about it. He decided to forget about his troubles though as he watched the girl with no name's fingers fidget around the short spear he'd once given her for slaying a hogbeast. A thing she'd kept all these years like a trophy.

She was visibly nervous. And for that, Dranian wanted to defeat the House of Lyro all the more.

He opened his mouth to say something consoling, but he realized two things. The first was that he didn't know what sort of nice consoling thing might work. The second was that he didn't know what to call her. The others called her *Mycra Sentorious*, but Dranian wouldn't. He knew what that name was. He knew the horrors she'd faced on that ship, and why she should not label herself with such a bad memory.

He would choose a new name for her someday. But today...

Dranian turned his attention to the crimson swarm. A hoard of fae he had once worked for. Friends of the House who had joined in beating him up and tormenting him for fun. Friends who had been able to get away with it at the time, until Shayne had done something about it.

But not today.

No, Dranian wasn't going to smile or anything outrageous like that.

But maybe he was looking forward to facing these fae again in a body like Cress's. Maybe he would give them all a taste of their own faeborn medicine. And he would look dazzling doing it, too, in this fashionable suit.

Dranian should have been worried about the retaliation for what he was about to do. Cress would lose his mind if Dranian brought any harmful scrapes to the Prince's well-kept body.

But he wasn't worried.

Today, Dranian wanted to be epic.

Today, he was Epic-Dranian.

Cress could shove it.

9

Shayne Lyro and Paper Cranes

Red fire rained from the sky as the paper birds burst into flame and plummeted toward Shayne every two seconds. He growled when a cinder burned across his back, but he kept his eyes open, half his attention on the human shooting her fairy-killing gun at fae hunters wearing the colours of his former family. She was supposed to stay on the hill. She was *supposed* to stay back and hide with Mycra. But somehow she'd been sucked into the cursed middle of the army along with him.

Dranian in Cress's stolen skin was a sight to behold. The fool raced through the hoard with his fist turned to stone and punched everything in sight—deer and fairy. He thrust his spear into a neck, then shot himself into the sky. Shayne wanted to laugh, wanted to tell Dranian he was better at being Cress than Cress was. But smiles were a luxury for whoever survived this chaos, and Shayne couldn't find his laugh amidst the fear of his own family destroying the things he cared about most.

A head of silken red hair flashed before him, appearing and then disappearing in the blink of an eye. Luc stabbed fast and ruthlessly; Lyro's allies didn't know what had hit them. The fox barely stood still long enough to impale a duo of fairies at Shayne's back before he was onto the next victim. But Shayne saw him stop before a silver-brown-eyed fairy. Luc's opponent had a fairsaber raised, but after he stared at Luc for a moment, he dropped his blade and surrendered. Luc's lips curled into a smile, and he disappeared again in a flash. It was suspicious—

Shayne almost yelped when Luc appeared before him with a crossbow in his hands. "For you, North Fairy," he said, extending the crossbow and a quiver of arrows. "I know it's your favourite." There was an edge to his words as he tapped a very specific spot on his chest where an arrow had once pierced.

Shayne grunted and took the bow. The second he did, Luc was gone again, leaving a path of destruction through the hunters until one of them managed to toss a net around him. Shayne watched, raising his crossbow to fire as Luc was bound, asking himself *why* he wanted to save Luc, when Dranian appeared and ripped the net clean in half with Cress's brute strength. So, Shayne slung the crossbow onto his back and drew up his fairsaber to slash a nearby hunter instead. The fairy fell off his deer, and Shayne stole it, mounting the creature in one leap and turning it to face his blood brothers watching from the hill.

Jethwire and Massie seemed comfortable atop their reindeers, uninterested in getting purple blood on their hands and hanboks. Even their hair was neat—Massie's long locks were in a tight topknot high on his head with not a strand out of place. Words that desperately needed to be said burned on Shayne's tongue. But his attention snapped to Lily when her shriek rang through the fight. She was flat on her back; she raised her gun as she scooted backward over the grass, firing and levelling a hunter. Then she rolled up to her feet and switched out her gun's cartridge. She was shooting again before she stopped to blink.

Shayne cut up a few more hunters before he could look back at her.

Astoundingly, Lily didn't look afraid, but Shayne could rarely catch a tone past her well-sealed fortress of emotions to know for sure. He realized this was the first time he'd seen her fight. It was the first time he wondered if maybe she really could take care of herself...

Lily went to fire, but no bullets came out. She tried again.

Click.

Her face paled as she lowered her gun. As she padded down her sweater pockets. As she watched a hunter in black armour racing toward her on a deer with his spear out.

Shayne abandoned his blood brothers and grabbed his reindeer's antlers, veering the creature toward the hunter eyeing Lily instead. In one smooth motion, he pulled his feet up and leapt from the deer's back. He lost his fairsaber when he collided with the hunter and ripped him off the saddle. They both plummeted to the ground and rolled twice before Shayne jammed his knuckles into the fairy's eyes and stole his sight.

"That's what you get for looking at one of *my* humans," he informed the fairy.

Ahead, Dranian appeared at Lily's side, holding up a stone forearm to deflect an arrow. Shayne climbed to his feet and marched over, but when he saw Lily's brows pull together, when he heard her rhythms change from pounding and fast to slow and strange, he halted.

She looked around like she was lost. Her pretty, messy hair fell across her face as she did a full turn, searching desperately for something.

"Lily," Shayne called sternly.

It worked—she snapped out of it. But only for a moment.

Dranian held off the Lyro forces best he could, but he looked over his shoulder at Lily in question as she stood there. As her gaze detached from Shayne again and drifted across the hoard of red, up the hill, and fell upon the two descendants of the House waiting there. Like they'd called her name.

Shayne looked to the hill.

Jethwire and Massie had dismounted their reindeers. Jethwire held a flute to his lips. The music was silent, but as he inhaled, then blew,

Shayne knew he was playing it. He also knew that no flute was completely silent. That it always played for an audience, even if it was for an audience of one.

Shayne's gaze snapped back to Lily. He broke into a run.

Across the grass, Luc was captured again. The fox fought ruthlessly to free himself from a tetrad of vine lassos. Just past him, Mycra was forced to her knees, a hunter grabbing a fistful of her hair to keep her still. She still kicked outward and snapped his knee, inviting three other hunters to leap on top of her and pin her down.

"Lily!" Shayne caught her shoulders and turned her around to face him.

Dranian tore into the skies the moment Shayne reached them, aiming for Mycra as Luc tore from his restrains and unleashed bone-snapping chaos upon the hunters who'd captured him.

Shayne put his hands over Lily's ears. "Look at me," he said to her. "The siren-song will only get louder if you listen to it." He knew she couldn't hear what he said through his hands, but he said it anyway. A fiery paper crane spiralled down, burning across his arm. He gritted his teeth, shaking it off and keeping his gaze on hers.

Lily looked back and forth between his eyes. Her hair had mostly torn from its ponytail, her cheek was flecked with fairy blood, and her flesh was slick with sweat. Still, she was quite possibly the prettiest thing Shayne had ever seen, and thus, he knew she was an appealing target for any fairy with a spec of greed.

"Why are you here, Lily Baker?" Shayne muttered.

He released her ears only long enough to slay an approaching trio of fairies in red and black. Then he swung around and put his hands back on her ears again. But this time, Lily said in a quiet voice, "I'm fine, Shayne. Let me go."

He bit down on his lips. "Never."

A growl lifted to their left. Shayne glanced over to find Luc flipping a fairy onto his back with a repulsed sound. Luc raised a brow at Shayne and Lily as if wondering what Shayne was doing holding Lily's face instead of fighting, but then he seemed to decide he didn't care. He picked up a spear off the ground and hurtled it across the hill. It slammed into a hunter who sailed at least ten feet before he fell.

"Foxy," Shayne said. He nodded up the hill to where Jethwire had stopped playing his flute to cast Shayne a devilish, crooked smile. "Get me up to them. And then come back and take our human far away from here. This fight is over."

"Oh dear." Luc sighed. "This fight is barely half over. Learn math." He waved a finger around at all the remaining hunters.

"Luc," Shayne said, using the fool's real name for the first time. He cast the fox a solemn, pleading look. He was too proud to ask an egotistical nine tailed monster for help in any situation, except for this one.

Luc released a loud huff. "You all seem to ask a great deal of me, you know. If you had any idea how powerful I've become, you'd think twice about bossing me around." He grumbled the last part as he walked over and grabbed Shayne's wrist.

Shayne pulled his crossbow around as he was torn into the wind. Luc dumped him so fast, he almost didn't catch himself on his feet. But when the hill formed around him, Shayne already had the crossbow pointed at Jethwire's back, right against the fairy's spine.

"Call the hunting party back to the House. Or I'll make sure you end up like Kahn-Der," Shayne said.

Massie looked over at Shayne with a startled face; Jethwire didn't move a muscle.

"Brother," Jethwire greeted. "Did you think this was over just because you left the House?"

"I'd hoped so, but no, I didn't really expect that." Shayne nudged the tip of the arrow a little harder against Jethwire's back. "Call off your hunting dogs," he said again.

Jethwire obediently raised a hand, and the hunters who noticed stopped their pursuit, mounted their deer, and headed away. Many hadn't seen though.

"Perhaps my best bet is to finish you both right here. Save me the trouble of having to do it later if you follow me again," Shayne thought aloud.

Massie's slow grin appeared. His sparkling eyes narrowed on Shayne's crossbow like he wanted to see if Shayne would really shoot Jethwire through the back. "I imagine you know how our father wouldn't sleep until he destroyed you if you did that. He's still sore about Panola. I wonder what he'll do when he finds out about Kahn-Der." Massie twirled a silver dagger over his fingers. Shayne hadn't seen him pull it out.

"Perhaps he'll throw a celebratory feast now that his oldest and most incapable son no longer craves his inheritance," Shayne guessed. "We all know Kahn-Der was a greedy hog. Which one of you is going to get his enormous, excessively decorated bedroom? Hmm?"

The hunters congregated at the foot of the hill. Dranian retreated at the other end of the valley, soaring into the air with Mycra in his arms. Dozens of dead hunters in red coats spotted the grass; the battle's ending almost looked laughable. Dranian and Luc had caused all this destruction, and now Jethwire and Massie had finally seen what Shayne and *his* allies were capable of.

He decided this unbearable subject of conversation was over. He had other words to use against his brothers, other things he needed to address now, but then Massie said, "She's pretty."

Shayne's fingers tightened on the trigger of the bow. His mouth opened, but he didn't ask who Massie spoke of.

"Your human," Massie said anyway, nodding down the hill to where Luc pulled Lily to himself. The fox took one last look up the hill before he vanished with her, and Shayne breathed a sigh of relief. Massie turned an inch toward Shayne—his strange smile was still there. Shayne was tempted to shoot it off. "Did you know you were in love with a human?" Massie asked.

Shayne's finger faltered on the crossbow trigger. He nearly fired the arrow through Jethwire right then and there.

Massie's warped smile only grew when Shayne forced a laugh. "Nonsense." He wondered if he ought to just leave—he could cast his important words at these fools another time.

"It's true, Brother. When our dreamslipper informed us you had a fairy crush, that you dreamt of a golden-haired female, we thought to send a few tunes of invitation into the wind to see if we could draw her to us and meet her in person. It took us a while to realize the reason she never came was because the two of you were in another world entirely and she couldn't hear it. Because she was a *human*." Massie tilted his head. "How foolish you must feel for letting her come here."

"Give me your flute, Jethwire," Shayne demanded.

"It's too late," Jethwire replied. "All the tunes are already floating through the wind, searching for her weaknesses and desires. They've been waiting for her since last year's snow. And you brought her here to face them."

Shayne flexed his jaw. "What do you want?" he asked.

"You know exactly what we want, Brother," Massie said, his smile disappearing. "And why you can't kill us." He reached over and pushed the nose of Shayne's crossbow down.

Jethwire finally turned around. "And you know why we will keep coming, regardless of the *supposedly dead* Prince of the North being in your company. We've been trying to decide for months if we should tell our High Queene he's alive and has been in hiding," he added. "You'd better consider our deal quickly. Our father returns in three days, and by then it'll be too late. If he learns you've fled, you know what he'll do."

Shayne took a few steps back. He scanned his brothers, calculating his best shot. "This conversation is over," he said. "I need time to think. Don't even dream about capturing Cressica Alabastian for a reward, or sending more hunters to drag me back, or luring in that human to use as bait."

Without waiting for a response, he fired an arrow into Jethwire's leg. It punched through and speared into Massie's leg, too, pinning them together and finally splattering purple blood on their precious hanboks.

Jethwire wailed a shriek and stared down at his leg in horror. Massie's blue eyes twinkled as he gazed at the blood.

"That's so you can't snatch me up as I leave," Shayne stated. He slung the crossbow onto his back and turned to race over the hill.

The colour shifted in the sky, darkening from aqua to a navy-gray and filling with rainclouds. It seemed Dranian didn't know how to control Cress's weather powers yet. Shayne inhaled the icy turn of the wind as he met the trees, and only when he was behind the cover of a trunk did he stop to catch his breath and peek back at the dozens of remaining fairies in his family's colours. His hand found its way into his pocket, his fingers curling around a paper crane. He drew it out to read it again, despising the words just as much as the first time:

Neither of us wish to be the Lyro heir. This is your birthright, Brother. Return to the House to take your place, and we won't have our scouts pay a deadly visit to your humans in the tavern across the gate called
Fae Café.
Did you think we didn't know about that?
We had your dreams hostage for months. We know everything. We know about Kate Kole, Violet Miller, Greyson Lewis, and especially
Lily Baker.
Come home and bring our dreamslipper with you before this gets unpleasant. We'd hate to do to your humans what we did to all those fairies who crossed us in our childling years.

Jethwire & Massie

Shayne wasn't quite ready to see Lily, but there she was, standing in her cute little *Regional Police* sweater, appearing as shaken as could be expected after what she'd just witnessed. His gaze got caught on her for a moment, until she turned around at the sound of him crunching over sticks and stones through the forest, and then he yanked his gaze in another direction and plunked it on the dreamslipper.

Mycra.

He marched for the female where she stood beside Dranian in Cress's body and Foxy Luc. The group of them hid in a small clearing in the woods surrounded by thick pines and spindly black branches. Mycra was looking intently at Dranian, studying Cress's body and face a little too closely. Eyeing his cold turquoise irises most of all.

Shayne meant to let Lily be, but her scent wafted over him when he brushed by her and his wretched feet came together, right in a squishy patch of mud. A strenuous amount of her tension tickled his faeborn chest, coming off her in waves. It could have been fear, though it was hard to know for sure since she was practically a she-wizard with the way she could ward off meddling fairies interested in her secrets.

The mud's moisture leaked up through Shayne's toes as he exhaled. He turned around.

Lily's lashes were all stuck together. One thick strand of hair covered part of her face, but neither of those things stopped her from staring into his eyes. Probably using her wizard powers to see right into his soul like she did with unruly humans on investigations.

Shayne slid off his crossbow and tossed it against a tree, then he reached for Lily and dragged her gently into a hug. He held her against his chest for just a moment. Then he asked, "Are you alright, ugly Human?"

She inhaled—the breath was shaky, he noticed. He almost smiled, not because of her distress, but because even though she hid herself better than most humans, Shayne had her mostly figured out.

"I'm fine," she lied.

He held her a little longer anyway.

"Of course you are." Shayne wasn't stupid; it was clear she was loving this hugging business by how she didn't try to pull away from him. "But it's okay if you're not fine," he said. "No one's invincible. If you

94

want to cry—"

Her hands came against his chest, and she shoved him back—he let her, as usual. She wasn't that strong, which was part of her charm. "I said I was fine," she repeated.

Shayne nodded. "Right, right. You did say that." He reached for his crossbow and lifted the strap back over his head, fastening it slowly as he held her gaze. "Feel free to use my robust, shapely shoulder to cry on when you change your mind."

He flashed her a smile. Not because he needed it, but because she did.

When he turned, he planted his attention on Mycra. "Pretty Fairy," he called. "I need a word."

Luc raised a brow. He looked between Lily and Mycra. "Well, that's rude," he said. "Calling one of them pretty and the other ugly."

"No one asked you, Foxy Luc," Shayne stated. "I have my reasons."

The sound of Lily's teensy feminine grunt lifted behind him.

"I've met the person who owns this body," Mycra finally said, still looking at Dranian in Cress's skin.

"You have?" Dranian asked.

"I crossed him many years ago." Mycra's expression turned wary. "He led a raid that killed someone I cared deeply about."

"Ah. What a relief. I was about to make you explain why you were ogling Cress," Shayne stated. "He's taken, you know."

Mycra's bright eyes expanded, and Dranian blushed, turning Cress's shapely jawline redder than anyone had probably ever seen it. Shayne smirked, wishing he could have taken a selfie with him and put it as the background image on Cress's phone.

His smile fell though when he thought of Cress's phone. Of Cress. Of Mor. Of Kate, and Greyson, and Violet. When he thought of what Cress and Mor might have to face soon because of him. He imagined them fighting off the Lyro scouts in the street outside Fae Café. They would be all right as long as Mor airslipped to the Sisterhood's yarn store and called in a favour. Cress would have to hold them off until the Sisterhood got there…

95

In Dranian's body.

Shayne ran a hand down his face. He turned to Luc. "You know the first thing Mor and Cress will do once they realize who's responsible for this little body-swap robbery is try to figure out where we are. If they get even an inkling we're in the Ever Corners…" He couldn't finish the sentence or fathom the thought.

A broad smile took over Luc's face. "Oh dear. You mean the High Court of the Coffee Bean may *finally* come to my rescue?" He batted his lashes. "It's about time."

Shayne's lips tightened. He'd spent three hundred and thirty-six dollars in the human mall on 'vacation wear' to support his lie of going on the exact sort of fun-filled beach holiday he'd read about in a magazine— all so that no one would actually *come here*. "You might not care, Foxy, but if anyone in the North Corner reports seeing this body and thinks this is Cress—" he nodded to Dranian "—we'll have far more than my family chasing after us. The whole Brotherhood of Assassins will take Dranian captive for Levress and we'll never get him out of the Silver Castle. It'll be goodbye forever."

Luc shrugged and began carefully rolling up the sleeves of his over-the-top imperial coat. The threading on it was so detailed, it made Shayne go cross-eyed to look at. "Then I suppose Prince Cressica had better hurry here if he wants to get his body back in one piece," Luc said.

Dranian's red face turned white instead, and Shayne stifled an eye roll. "Don't be so dramatic. I was careful to cover my tracks when I left the human realm, so unless someone *hands them* a map, they won't find out we're here," he promised. "And you're trying way too hard with that coat. Is this your attempt to dress up as a king for Halloween? Because Halloween is long over," Shayne said.

Luc only smiled. Then he pulled out a tiny piece of human-world bread from his pocket and flicked it at Shayne. It hit Shayne's stomach and fell to the ground.

Shayne grunted. "You'll have to try harder than that to poison me," he said. He turned to Mycra. "I'd like a word," he repeated without missing a beat. "*Now*, dreamslipper."

Mycra's expression changed when he called her that. He was the best at nicknames, and that last one held implications he was sure she'd pick up on.

Sure enough, Mycra swallowed and nodded. She headed into the trees and broke into a jog. Shayne followed, keeping a few paces behind. Once they were far enough away that Dranian's and Luc's fairy ears wouldn't pick up their whispers, Mycra slowed to a stop and turned to face him.

"What exactly did you tell my family?" Shayne asked immediately. "Actually, what did you tell my brothers, specifically? And does my father know about the humans, too?"

"I told them only what you dreamt about," she said. "Dreamslipping is a complex art and originally, I wasn't told to investigate. I was only told to send you nightmares that would drive you home. But you fought against me by pulling your happiest thoughts into your slumber. Most often you dreamt about..." She glanced back toward the way they came.

Shayne shook his head. "I know what I fought back with," he said, stepping toward her and grabbing his hair. "You told them about that?"

"I just told them about the humans and your feelings toward them. And I told them about the other fairies I saw—the North Prince, and the Shadow Fairy. But I never told them about Dranian. As soon as I realized he was still with you after all these years, I stopped telling them anything." Mycra bit her lower lip. "I'm sorry, Shayne. It was my job. I didn't know we'd become allies. Honestly, I thought if you ever returned to the House, you'd try to kill me."

Shayne paced in a circle. "You should have warned me the first day we met. I had no idea." He pointed back toward the clearing. "How much do they know about *her*?"

Mycra swallowed. "They know you need her," she admitted. "They know that if they can get her, they'll control you."

Shayne's exasperated groan echoed through the woods. "Don't you understand the position you've put me in?! Simply killing off Jethwire and Massie isn't an option anymore! If they're gone, my father will only be more desperate to get me to return for the chair as his last living inheritor. So I can't leave them alive or they'll go after my humans, but I can't kill them either!"

Mycra nodded and clasped her hands together. "I know. I'm sorry."

Shayne squatted and grabbed his head. "I'm going to have to go back to the House," he realized. His heart felt like it had turned to faestone, sinking deeper and deeper into the pit of him. "I'll never return to the café, will I? I'll become the next Lyro High Lord. I'll be trapped in that seat forever."

He'd saved Mycra Sentorious. He showed her mercy after she'd haunted him. And when he realized how Dranian felt about her, he was glad he did it. But she hadn't told him the greatest danger of all. Shayne had to find out this way; from a paper crane.

When Shayne found it within himself to look up at Mycra again, he saw a large tear sailing down her cheek and something broke within him. He closed his eyes, grappling every loose thought and reeling them all back in. "I'm sorry, too. This isn't your fault." He stood. "This is my family. You were their prisoner, like me."

"Don't apologize to me," she said. "I sold you out to them. I'll help you fight them if I must. I'll do whatever it takes to free you from their grasp."

Shayne cast her a weak smile. "You're afraid of them. Admit it."

Mycra closed her mouth. It was answer enough.

He looked down at the mossy rocks beneath his feet. "You'll go back to the human realm with Dranian and Lily. You'll keep *my* Dranian safe. You'll be there for him when I can't," he said. His throat grew thick. "And if I ever hear of you hurting him, with your dream powers or in any other way, I'll..." He shook his head, feeling too uncreative to be clever.

Mycra's face changed, her eyes turning sharp. "You'll what?" She waited. "You'll haunt me?" she guessed. "Will you torment me, Shayne Lyro? Will you make me go mad?" She took a threatening step toward him. "Because those are all things I could do to you. You might know Dranian now, but I've known him longer. I'm his fairy guard."

Shayne folded his arms as he listened. He didn't spot any lies in her tone, but she was an actress; he'd seen it. "I still know very little about you," he pointed out. "And what sort of fairy guard abandons such a vulnerable fairy? Where were you when he suffered in my House? Where were you when he shook and trembled beneath the weight of his fears all these years? Where were you when his arm was taken?"

Mycra fell back a step like she'd been slapped. Her mouth hung open.

A cluster of blossom bugs floated by, spiralling in the breeze. Shayne watched one land on her cheek, but she didn't seem to feel it.

After a moment, Mycra cleared her throat. Then she said, "I'll be his lost arm. I'll be his strength and his weapon. He doesn't need his arm when he has me."

Shayne squinted as he thought that over. He knew he'd taken it too far with his comments, but he needed to know for sure she was going to stand by his friend. Finally, he nodded.

"And I'll find the fairy who took his arm," she went on, "and I'll destroy the culprit from the inside out." She vowed it with all the ferocity of a scorned beast.

A slow smile spread across Shayne's face. He couldn't have orchestrated that better if he'd tried.

"Perfect. You pass," he said. He held up a hand in the direction of the others as if to allow her to go first. "Let me know if you need any help finding the culprit. I'm happy to point you in the right direction."

As he followed Mycra back to the others, Shayne went over the words of the note sitting heavy in his pocket. The terrible decision he had to make hung before him like a black cloud.

And he only had three days left to make it.

CHAPTER

10

Lily Baker and the Lady of the Lake

There was only one time in Lily's life she remembered walking for an entire day without stopping. It had been pouring rain, and she'd gotten a terrible cold trying to escape her sixth foster home with nothing more than a backpack of soggy homework and half a bottle of juice. When she'd finally stopped to rest on a park bench, she discovered her heels had bled right through her shoes. She was so hungry that the blinding red and blue lights didn't make her spring off the bench and keep running when they showed up against the playset in her view. She waited. Because she knew that if the cops picked her up, at least they'd feed her.

Now, as Lily walked for hours on end until dusk rolled over the skies, she was far more determined than she'd been back in her youth. Her stomach growled, but she didn't peep one word of complaint, even though all she wanted to do was fall flat on her face in the grass and sleep.

Luc, on the other hand, complained the whole way since, "Walking

FAKE DATING A HUMAN 101

was for less gifted fairies than him," and "It's criminal to make a Shadow Fairy walk so much," and "You're all fools for not realizing who you're messing with."

If Lily was reminded *one more time* that Luc was a great, powerful fox of legend, she would lose it.

She craved a bath, a hot tea, and a soft bed. She tilted her head from side to side to stretch, moaning at the ache in her shoulders. She'd never fought for her life like she did back on the hill. She could still see the bullets whizzing, landing, the fairies falling...

A shiver moved down her spine, and she swallowed. When her breathing became thin, she stuffed her hands in her pockets in case they were shaking. No one else seemed affected by how they'd had to face off with such vicious creatures in a valley-wide death match earlier in the day.

Luc fell into a stride beside her. He had a strange, terrifying smile.

"What?" Lily asked. She took a step away from him as she walked.

"How are you feeling, dear Lily?" he asked anyway, closing the gap just as quickly as she'd made it.

She looked at him like he was crazy. "Seriously? Why do you even care?"

"Oh, I don't know, really." He was still smiling. "I suppose it's the natural therapist within me." He sighed. "I can't help but notice when a human's *psychological trauma* is flirting with the surface of their brain."

Lily burst out laughing.

It made Shayne and Dranian slow down up ahead. Shayne's gaze darted between Lily and Luc. "Stop making her laugh," he warned Luc. "You're not that funny."

Lily bit her lower lip to holster her chuckles. "Actually, what he just said was *very* funny," she corrected, shaking her head.

As if Luc had even a bead of empathy inside him.

Luc twisted his lips. "Fine. I won't therapist you, dear Lily. Your loss." He walked a little faster. A second later, he glanced over his shoulder as if checking to see if she was chasing after him—as if he actually thought she might come and beg him to change his mind.

Lily had never rolled her eyes so hard.

"Are you sure this is the way back to the human realm?" she called ahead. "We've been walking all day. This is totally not the way Dranian and I came."

Shayne's shoulders tightened a little. "Have some patience, ugly Human. I have a plan."

"What plan?" Dranian asked. "You never said anything about a plan."

"Well, no one asked where we were going until this moment," Shayne said.

"I did," Luc pointed out. He pulled a breadcrumb out of his pocket and tossed it on the ground like he was bored. "I asked several times—"

"Anyway, I have one last trick up my sleeve. A chance to make this right," Shayne stated. Lily caught Mycra staring at Shayne's back with a wary expression. It was all strange, and Lily slowed her walk. "And if this doesn't work..." Shayne's throat bobbed even though he was smiling. "I have a plan for that, too."

"You're all going to die," Luc stated. He waved a hand through the air when Shayne's gaze rolled up to the sky and thumped down upon him. "Not me though. I'll be long gone before I let myself get ruined by your issues, North Fairy. I'm not selfless like that. Ask anyone."

"No need. The evidence on that is pretty clear," Lily assured.

"If you all practiced studying people a little harder, you might realize that Shayne Lyro has been lying to us since back at that hill," Luc added. Then he said, "Fools. If you wish to walk to your death, you all go ahead. I'll happily disappear and leave you to it."

"*Please*," Shayne said, extending a hand to the air, "be my guest."

Luc turned his attention to Dranian. "Ask him," he advised. "Ask him what his plan is. See if I'm wrong."

Dranian's solemn face tilted from Luc to Shayne. Then he looked at the ground. "I don't want to," he murmured.

Lily huffed. "*I'll* ask him. What's your mysterious plan, Shayne?"

she demanded with ample sarcasm. "It can't possibly be worse than charging into a hoard of death-bringing fairies like we just did."

Luc raised a finger. "Actually, that plan was excellent. We survived. You're welcome."

Wind tossed Lily's hair and she dragged a hand up to smooth it down. "Shayne?" she asked when he didn't say anything. Shayne didn't even meet her eyes—he looked past the treeline at something in the distance.

"Let's stop for the night," Mycra cut in. She swooped around the others to Dranian's side. "We all need sleep. I'll guard everyone's dreams so we have strength for tomorrow."

"If you think I'm letting you into my dreams, you're mad," Luc stated. "I'll guard my own dreams tonight, thank you very much."

"There's a House at odds with the House of Lyro," Shayne stated, making everyone quiet down. "That's my plan. I mean to pay a rival House a visit," he finished.

Mycra's brows tilted in. Her hand rested idly on Dranian's arm. "Which House? Who are you speaking of?" She asked it like she didn't actually want to know.

Shayne flashed her a smile. "Oh, no one too fancy. The House of Riothin is *technically* the enemy of Lyro, but—"

"The House of Riothin?!" Dranian shouted, startling Lily more than it should have.

"Yes," Shayne said back. "I've always wanted to see the great House of my enemies. Weren't you ever a teensy bit curious about it, Dranian? You must have wondered about it at least once."

Mycra shook her head. "Shayne, we can't go there. You'll be sacrificed on the spot because of your last name."

"Not necessarily. Not if I can convince them to join hands with me against my brothers and father. I am rather charming, you know. They might go for it." Shayne flashed a smile that turned something in Lily's chest. "Maybe one of their daughters will wish to wed me and we can form an alliance through marriage."

Luc laughed and batted his lashes. "Oh dear. I think I might actually like this idea."

A pulse beat against Lily's neck. She realized her hands were balled into fists, and she unclasped them slowly. She wasn't sure why she felt like she couldn't speak all of a sudden, like the conversation had gotten away from her too fast and she no longer had any control.

"Let's just sleep on it for now," Mycra said. "We'll discuss this in the morning when we're not all exhausted." Then, to Dranian, she said, "Let's get a fire going. Can you summon flame?"

Luc snorted. "Prince Cressica can only influence weather patterns. He's not a sky deity." He turned for the trees. "I'll gather wood, you useless fairies of the North." He vanished.

"Do you know how to make a fire?" Mycra asked Shayne next.

"Absolutely not. You know I grew up rich." He folded his arms. "And in the human realm, we have these magical sticks with buttons called '*lighters*'. I had no need for learning this sort of thing."

Lily swallowed and finally pulled her stare off Shayne. Everyone had moved on so quickly.

"You guys are unreal," she said. It came out quieter than she meant it to. She grabbed a sharp-edged stone and headed to a flat patch of dirt. "Hand me your dagger," she said to Myrca. And then, "How can I possibly be the only one here who knows how to do this?" She brushed dry leaves into a pile, stacked a few sticks, and began slapping the spine of the dagger against the rock the way she'd read about in basic survival guides.

All the fairies leaned in to watch her.

It took a few tries, but eventually a spark shot out and hit the leaves. Lily lowered herself to blow on the flame until it caught. Luc returned with an armful of dry sticks, so Lily added them to the fire. Minutes later, one human and four fairies sat around the lapping flames.

Everyone chatted about this and that. Mostly, Shayne, Luc, and Dranian took turns asking Mycra specific questions about her past. Lily couldn't follow the conversations. Every time she tried, her gaze wandered back to the blue-eyed, white-haired fairy in the long red coat.

Though she hated the thought of agreeing with Luc, she had to admit Luc was right. On the hill, Shayne had changed. It was right when he'd read the note on the paper bird. One second, he'd wanted to run. The next, he'd wanted to fight.

And now... now he wanted to stay in the Ever Corners and visit a rival House instead of going home? Was he out of his mind? Lily hugged her knees to herself as she thought about it.

Dranian fell asleep first, his snoring echoing through the forest. Then Luc drifted off, sitting with his back against a log. Mycra yawned and lowered onto a patch of grass, so Lily unzipped her hoodie and shrugged it off. She arranged it flat on the dirt and laid back, but her gun dug in, so she unclipped her holster and set it beside her.

Stars twinkled through the leaves overhead. She wondered if Kate was looking at the stars too, wondering why Lily had never returned from that 'work trip out of town'. Connor was going to start flipping out with her not responding to calls and emails. She released a quiet sound when she thought about how embarrassing it would be if she ended up on the Missing Persons list.

"Ugh."

She had to get home. But how could she leave Shayne here after everything she'd seen of this place? After the horrible things his own brothers had done—were *still* doing—to him?

Lily tilted her head to spy on Shayne across the fire. The flames blocked most of her view. She lifted a little to try and see better, but she couldn't make out his silhouette anywhere on the other side. She jumped when his voice appeared beside her.

"You didn't destroy it."

Lily's gaze snapped over and there Shayne was, lying in the dirt. Her gun was in his hands. He turned it over, studying it.

She moved to retrieve it, but he yanked it away to where she couldn't reach. "I should toss this into a river," he said. "Before you use it, ugly Human. Before you get bold and make enemies with the wrong High Lord or kill the wrong fairy and land yourself before the wrong court, or worse."

Lily sighed and gave up trying to steal it back. "I've already used my gun. And it was a good thing I had it on me. In case you didn't notice, that fairy-killing weapon saved my life today."

"Hmm. It looked to me like you ran out of ammo and almost died," he said.

"I didn't run out of ammo. I just didn't have time to dig into my stash." She lifted her leg and tapped her ankle where she'd stuffed her spare cartridges in her sock. It looked ridiculous but it kept them close. "I only keep a few in my sweater pockets because it's easier to move around. Would you rather I have walked into that fight with nothing and been pummelled by antlered monsters?"

Shayne stared at her for a moment. Then he bit his lip over his smile. "Sometimes when you talk, I want to tell you to stop talking. Especially when you get sassy like that."

She tsked and raised a brow. "Why?"

He tapped the end of the gun against his chin, and Lily's stomach tightened. She fought the impulse to bat the weapon away from his head before he shot his own face off.

"Because your mouth keeps moving. And when your mouth moves and says things I like... I'm not sure. I suppose I want to kiss it." He shrugged. "You should be careful what you say to me, ugly Human."

Heat blossomed in Lily's neck and cheeks. She dragged her wide eyes back to the sky above. She would never understand why he said things like that—why he thought aloud. Why he would blab a bunch of nonsense about liking her mouth minutes after having a great idea to marry some fairy woman from the House of his enemies to solidify a peace deal.

"You just called me ugly twice in under thirty seconds," she pointed out. "I don't care if you hate my look, but even the fox knows it's rude to keep saying it." She rolled onto her side to sleep, facing away from him. Knowing she probably wouldn't actually sleep at all after everything she'd seen today.

Shayne's chuckles lifted through the dark. "I told you I have my reasons," he said. "What would you like me to call you then? Messy-Haired Scarecrow? Dagger-Eyed Demoness? Human-with-lips-that-like-to-lie?"

She flipped onto her back to glare at him. "What did I lie about, Shayne?" She wasn't sure at what point in this conversation she'd gotten angry or why every one of her emotions stood on end. Even for the walk, her eyes had been darting between the trees, and her heart had leapt from her chest every time someone stepped on a branch and made a sound.

"Oh, I don't know, Messy-Haired Scarecrow. You lied about this, for starters." He held up the gun. "We both know your fun little activities this year had nothing to do with working overtime."

Lily released an exasperated sound. "This again? You're really not going to let that go?"

"Probably not," he admitted. "I suppose I'm still curious why you thought you had to defend yourself against us."

"Not against *you*, Shayne." She saw an opportunity and grabbed the gun back. Then she tucked it into her sweater on the opposite side. "It's all the other fairies I'm worried about. I told you that."

"Why, Scarecrow, why? Why were you so worried all this time? You didn't think we'd protect you?" he asked. "Because as I recall, the one who stepped into this dungeon of fairy terror *by choice* was you." He waved a finger around at the forest. "You. Are. A. *Hazard*. To. Yourself."

Lily closed her eyes in disbelief. "Maybe, but I can also take care of myself, Shayne," she said for the hundredth time. "I've been doing it my whole life. I never had money, or a home, or real guardians before I met Kate, so I learned how to survive without a family." She pointed at him. "You're not my family! And I'm not a damsel in distress who needs saving. I'm perfectly capable of doing what I need to in order to survive on my own!"

Shayne dragged his round eyes to hers. He looked at her so intensely, she swallowed and tried to think of something else to say. She wasn't sure apologizing for raising her voice was the right thing...

He suddenly rolled on top of her, and she gasped. "When did I ever say I would take care of you, Lily Baker? Hmm?" he asked while his body pinned her down. She tried poking at his eyes to make him get off, but he grappled both her hands and restrained them above her head with one of his. "Do you really think I'm obsessive about guarding you—for *you*?" He used his free hand to shake a finger in her face. "No, no, no. I'm loyal to my master, *Kate*. Imagine the devastation she'd feel if something happened to you here."

Lily's body relaxed against the ground, her hands going slack in his grip. Anything sensible she might have replied with lost their value as Shayne leaned a little closer, leaving his mouth hanging an inch above hers. His lips parted, and Lily's gaze flickered down to them.

"You seem ever so determined to remind everyone that you can take care of yourself. But no one is invincible. *Especially* humans, and *especially* here. You know that full well after fighting those fairies on the hill. Your hands are still shaking. So what exactly did you go through in your human life that made you need to put on this façade—even when you feel this way?" he asked.

The quiet squeaks of nighttime bugs lifted through the woods. A gust of wind sailed in, making the flames dance and the gold light flicker on Shayne's cheeks.

He didn't move. Neither did she.

"Let me go, Shayne." She whispered it this time. Her eyes grew warm, and only the chilly wind brought them relief.

Shayne studied her, his deep blue gaze roaming over her face, his white hair fluttering in the breeze. Then he rolled off.

The coolness of the night rushed in like a wave the moment his body left.

The same bugs whistled from their hiding places among the trees. A mocking audience.

After a moment, Shayne spoke again. "To grow up without parents is a difficult feat. But there are several fairies around this fire who will tell you that sometimes growing up *with* parents can be worse."

Lily's throat felt thick when she swallowed. The stars blurred above. She blinked until they became sharp again. She hadn't meant to complain, but she was sure that was how it must have sounded to someone like Shayne who was currently running from a family that had done so many vile things to him. He'd been unable to walk by the time Luc found him. Lily had never experienced a physical altercation that had left her anywhere near that condition.

"I can only imagine what your parents are like if your brothers want you dead," she rasped.

Shayne released a quiet laugh. "I have no mother, and my brothers don't want me dead." He fiddled with a loose thread on his coat.

The way he said it stirred something in Lily's chest. It was the sort of gut feeling that came over her when a crook had something to hide during questioning.

She asked, "You're coming home with me, right?"

Shayne's fingers stilled on the thread.

Dranian murmured in his sleep on the other side of the fire. It was the only response Lily got in the first three seconds.

"I know you made comments about staying here, but you were only joking like always, right, Shayne? You were just trying to get me to beg or whatever?" she tried again. "You wouldn't actually let me and Dranian go home without you?"

Shayne rolled onto his side and propped his head up with his hand. His smile was dazzling, the sort of heart-melting expression he always walked into the station with when he was trying to convince the whole police force that he was the world's best boyfriend.

He looked her dead in the eyes, and he said, "I'm coming with you, of course." His grin turned tantalizing. "You can't get away from me, Lily Baker. Soon we'll go home, we'll make coffee, I'll force you to give me hugs in front of your coworkers, and we'll never think of this place again."

He didn't break eye contact or let his smile slip for a second.

Lily's shoulders relaxed. She nodded. A second later, she stretched, feeling for the first time like she might be able to sleep. She closed her eyes and shivered as the night grew cool.

Dranian's murmuring only got worse for the next hour until Luc stirred awake and kicked him.

"The girl who can survive anything... can she survive us?"

When Lily opened her eyes, she saw an ocean. She sat up quickly, blinking against the salty air, her mouth parting as she took in the emerald waters all around, splashing against the small island of black rock she was stranded upon. Clouds formed in the distance, and a great, blue sea storm rushed in.

She blinked.

And it was gone.

Lily looked around the forest. Early sunlight glowed against the bright leaves overhead, and a tiny horned creature skittered up a tree trunk.

Luc was gone.

Everyone else slept soundly around the dwindled fire.

Lily climbed to her feet and brushed the dirt off her jeans. She'd just picked up her sweater when it returned:

"The girl who can survive anything... can she survive us?"

She whirled.

The song trickled into the forest in waves: a high flute, soft like a whisper. A laugh followed, sweet and feminine. Then low, like a man's.

"You may wish to save him, but we will never let him go."

Her gaze darted down to Shayne. His red coat was unbuttoned and splayed, his head was tilted to the side, his eyes were closed, and his chest rose and fell peacefully. He looked young this way, without his worries on his face or his shoulders tense. It was sad Shayne only looked free when he slept.

"Who won't let you go, Shayne?" she whispered.

The song rose again, seeping in along the wind and coiling around her ears.

A shadow moved through the trees, and Lily squinted her eyes. It looked like a person was hiding there, and when the laugh returned, she knew.

She grabbed her gun and marched for the woods, kicking dirt and stones out of her way as she slid past trunks, trying to catch the stalker before he might escape. She scurried over a large rock and tiptoed over a short patch of yellowing moss. She couldn't see the person, but she could see their shadow rippling over a pile of dry leaves. They hid behind a tree thirty feet ahead.

Two hands grabbed her before she could raise her gun. She moved to strike as she was whirled around, until she saw Shayne's messy white hair. His hands were over her ears. She didn't even notice until he tried to say something and she couldn't hear it.

She watched his lips move, but she still had no idea what he was telling her. His coat was wrinkled, his hair fell in his eyes, and his eyelids hung half open like he'd been startled awake.

"Seriously. If you want me to listen, you're going to have to take your hands off my ears," she said. "Otherwise, I'm just going to assume you don't know how human ears work."

His lips slowly spread into a smile. This time she could read his word when he said, "Stop." And then something along the lines of, "You're killing me, ugly Human." His gaze darted down to her mouth.

"Are you going to take your hands off my ears now?" she asked.

He chewed on the inside of his cheek as if pretending to think. And he mouthed, "No."

She sighed. "Someone's watching us. I was about to find out who." His smile vanished. "If you let me, I might still be able to catch them before they get away..."

Shayne dropped her ears. His brows furrowed. "How long have you been hearing music?" he asked.

She blinked. Then she folded her arms. "How do you know I'm hearing anything?"

"Since you got here?" he guessed. "And is it music the rest of us can't hear? A tune that makes you think of a deep jade ocean?"

Lily blinked. Her expression must have told him enough.

Shayne nodded. "It's a Lady of the Lake. A siren's voice that's been trapped in a flute. Tell me whenever you hear it so I can keep an eye on you, and *never* follow the music." He took her hand and began leading her back to the campfire. "I need to get you home," he muttered under his breath like he was talking more to himself now.

"But..." Lily pointed back toward the woods with her gun. "The stalker..."

"There is no stalker, Lily." He used her real name for once. "There are just my brothers waiting for you at the other end of that song. Don't listen to it."

Lily looked back at the forest. She didn't see the shadow anymore. She didn't hear the music, either. "Would that be so bad? Seeing your brothers?" She thought about how she wanted to look them in the eyes after all they'd done. Obviously, she wasn't stupid enough to go pick a fight, but it might have been nice to see them, just once.

She realized Shayne had stopped walking. And he was glaring.

"What?" She folded her arms. "I was just joking."

"I'm not sure you were." He took a loose hold of her chin and lifted her face so their eyes met. "Let me make one thing clear, *Human*. If you ever go see my brothers by choice, I won't go after you. I won't help you. I'll leave, and you'll never see me again," he stated.

She raised an eyebrow. She actually couldn't tell if he was bluffing. "Why?" She nudged his hand off her chin—he let go.

A shadow came over his face. "Because that would mean you did something so unthinkably stupid. And I don't have it in me to reverse someone's stupidity at that level."

Lily made a sound of disbelief. She couldn't believe this was the same person who'd been making flirtatious advances on her for the last six months. Who tricked customers into eating fresh butter tarts at the café on a regular basis so they'd keep coming back. "You know, you used to talk a lot nicer to me. Even if you were being a turd, you were at least joking around. Right now, you're ice cold."

Shayne smiled a little, but it wasn't sweet or caring. It was the closest thing to a snarl Lily had ever seen on him. "I'm not joking around about this."

"Wow. Fine. I get your message loud and clear, Shayne. If I get snatched, I'm on my own." She brushed past him.

"Just don't get snatched in the first place," he called after her. "That's my point."

She ignored him and kept walking.

As if she'd *willingly* get taken. Did he think she was stupid?

She stuffed her gun away when she reached the campfire, and she shook out her hoodie. There was no getting the worst dirt stains out, but it was wearable at least. She slid it on and tried to do something about her hair.

Dranian and Mycra were awake now. Mycra restarted the fire as snowflakes spiralled around them, bringing in a gust of bitter cold that bit at Lily's nose. She shivered and sniffed.

Luc appeared beside her out of thin air, and she jumped back in surprise, balling her hands into fists and raising one. "Seriously?!" she scolded when she realized. "I almost clocked you!" His scarlet hair looked windblown and his cheeks were slightly flushed. She lowered her fists. "We should get you a horn to announce your arrival or something. You're going to give someone a heart attack."

Luc looked her up and down. He sighed and shucked off his Dracula coat. He extended it toward her.

She glared at him like he was crazy.

When she didn't take it, Luc shook it a little. A sweet fragrance wafted off the material, tickling Lily's nose. "It's in pristine condition," Luc told her. "It's not dirty like your sweater. It won't do you any harm to wear it."

113

"I beg to differ. You're clearly keeping snacks in there." She thought of the breadcrumbs he kept finding in his pockets.

Luc smirked.

Shayne was the one who finally took the coat. He slapped it back against Luc's chest. "She doesn't need this. She hates being taken care of."

Luc's pale fingers curled around it as he made a study of Lily. "Could have fooled me."

Shayne looked back at Lily then. She stifled a shiver, and his mouth twisted.

"This isn't because I think you need it, ugly Human," Shayne clarified as he tugged his arms out of his own coat. "It's because I don't want it." He didn't try to hand it to her—he opened it and wrapped it around her without giving her a choice.

Shayne's leftover warmth seeped into Lily's shoulders. The material inside was silky and soft and she snuggled into it before realizing what she was doing. Shayne's mouth twitched up a fraction, but he otherwise seemed like he didn't notice.

The buttons down the coat looked like real gold; Lily tilted one up to see it better. Something turned in her stomach when she realized it actually *was* real gold. When it dawned on her how much this lavish red coat must be worth.

Luc snorted a scoff and turned to Dranian. "Do you want the good news or the bad news?" he called over the firepit, though it seemed like he was shouting it to everyone.

Dranian glanced around at the others. When no one offered their preference, he decided, "Bad news?"

A loud crack rang through the forest, sending small birds squawking and racing from the leaves. Everyone's attention shot to an entire tree snapping off its base. It soared down to the mossy floor, nearly swatting Dranian—he sprang back a step before it could smack him like a flyswatter.

"Ah. It looks like the bad news has just arrived," Luc said.

Two fairies stood where that tree had just been. Lily started at the sight of Mor in his familiar jean jacket and a perturbed frown. And Dranian was with him—no...

Cress.

In Dranian's body.

Lily's hand came over her mouth. "What are you two doing here?" she asked through her fingers.

"Ah." Luc snapped. Then he pointed at Cress and Mor. "Interestingly enough, this is also the good news. Funny, isn't it?"

Lily couldn't decide if she was more worried about their reaction or relieved they were here. She got the strangest urge to cry, which made her think she felt mostly relieved. But when she turned to the others, she realized Shayne was pale and frozen in place. He stared at Cress and Mor with his mouth open like he was sure he was imagining them. It wasn't exactly an *"I'm happy to see you after all this time"* sort of reaction. Lily dropped her hand.

A twinkle lit Luc's eyes. "You look terrible, Trisencor. Almost like you've been walking in circles all night," he said. Mor ignored him and took in the firepit along with the people he knew standing around it.

"You!" Cress in Dranian's body said to Dranian in Cress's body before any other questions could be asked. "Come here so I can cut out your tongue!" he shouted. Cress took three full strides toward Dranian. "And..." Cress's gasp was so sharp, Lily almost covered her ears. "IS THAT MY SUIT?!"

Dranian scrambled backward, releasing an unnatural shrieking sound. He turned and leapt over the firepit, keeping just out of Cress's reach. When Cress sprang after him, Dranian shot into the sky.

Cress growled. "Get back down here, you fool! This horrid treachery is outrageous! You are in for a royal beating!" he shouted. "And that's *not* how you use my talents! They're meant to be used with the elegance of a prince! You're ripping around like a wild, blind hogbeast!" He raced into the woods in the direction Dranian had disappeared.

Through all of Cress's shouting, Mor found it within himself to finally pay attention to Luc. He glared. He took a break only to glare at Shayne next. At Lily—he studied her rich red coat. Then he glared at...

"Who are you?" he asked Mycra.

She didn't answer. No one else did, either.

Mor sniffed as though he smelled something unusual, and his brows tugged together as he eyed her pale skin and bright features. "You're dangerous—"

"I'm Dranian's fairy guard," she said, cutting him off.

Mor's expression turned doubtful.

"There's no time for introductions anyway," Luc said. "I expected you to get here *way* sooner, Trisencor. What took you so long?"

Mycra stole the opportunity to leave. She jogged off in the direction Cress and Dranian had gone. Mor followed her with his gaze, his eyes narrowing when she pulled out a short spear. He still didn't look happy when he settled his brown-silver stare back on Luc. "The breadcrumb trail you left didn't exactly make a straight line," he said in a low voice.

"Breadcrumb trail...?" Lily glanced over at the Dracula coat in Luc's hands. She huffed a laugh as it dawned on her why Luc had been tossing bread around the last few days.

"What in the name of the sky deities is going on?" Mor asked. Lily, and everyone else, stole glances at Shayne.

Shayne closed his mouth, snapping out of his daze. His throat bobbed, and he shook his head. "You can't be here," he rasped. "Mor... you need to go back!" Shayne took a step toward Mor and grabbed his arm. "This... This is...."

Mor frowned. "This is what, Shayne? Unexpected? After you strutted around in flip flops to fool us?" he said. "You'd better explain to me what you're doing here, or Cress isn't the one who's going to throw a fit this time."

Shayne tugged both hands through his hair. He paced around in a circle, his eyes glazing over like he was in another place. His breathing shallowed, and his lashes fluttered like he was going to collapse. He almost stepped right in the fire without realizing it, until Lily cut him off and grabbed his shoulder.

"Shayne," she stopped him. "What in the world has gotten into you?"

Shayne looked at her like he wasn't really seeing her there. He didn't blink. After a moment, he rasped, "I can explain."

"No you can't. You haven't explained anything since the start," Luc stated. He reached his slender fingers into one of his inner pockets and pulled out a red paper crane.

Shayne's eyes widened at the sight of it. He spun back to Lily and padded his hands over his own coat pockets even though Lily still wore it. She squirmed away as his hands flattened against her hips.

Shayne pointed to the crane in Luc's hand. "That isn't…"

"Yours? Oh dear. It is yours, isn't it? How ever did I get my hands on it?" Luc answered.

"What does it say?" Lily asked.

Luc yanked the crane back when Shayne stepped toward him. The two were the same height, their silvery and blue gazes level as a beat of silence moved over the campsite. Only Cress's shouting could be heard through the trees.

Luc tilted his head, a broad smile creeping across his mouth. "Lucky for you, North Fairy, I rather enjoy secrets. When I find one, it only makes me hungry for more, did you know that?" Without warning, Luc tossed the paper crane into the fire. It withered to ash in seconds.

"Wait!" Lily tried to kick it out of the flames, sending the last remaining bits of red floating into the air. She sprang back when her shoe caught fire, and she dug her toes into the dirt until the flame went out.

"What's he talking about, Shayne?" Mor asked in his low voice.

Shayne and Luc seemed telepathic, having a conversation in complete silence. Finally, Mor stepped to them. He paused. Then he shoved them both away from each other. Luc staggered back into a heap of moss, and Shayne nearly tripped into the fire.

It was almost funny, except that Shayne's reaction to Cress's and

Mor's arrival had been so strange. Lily couldn't shake the feeling that had been curling her instincts for the last twenty-four hours: that the current problem wasn't that Shayne didn't *want* to come back home, it was that he *couldn't*.

All it had taken was Luc waving around that red paper bird for Lily to know for sure.

It didn't seem real. Lily looked back into the woods where she'd seen that shadow. Where something had been stalking them, and laughing at them, and singing.

Last night, Shayne had promised to her face that they would be home soon. That they would drink coffee together.

Suddenly it was so painfully obvious he was lying.

This wasn't a manhunt. This was a hostage situation.

Shayne didn't need to be found, he needed to be rescued.

Lily huffed at herself. She couldn't believe she hadn't figured it out until now. That the brothers Shayne had told her to avoid were holding him on a leash.

CHAPTER

11

*Luc Zelsor and the Thing He Did Right After His Visit
to the Dark Corner*

Five Days Ago

No matter how many times Luc scrubbed his fingers with soap, he couldn't get the purple out from beneath his fingernails. He tossed the scrubby brush away and grabbed the sides of the sink to rest, dragging his lovely gaze up to peer at his reflection in the bathroom mirror.

Considering how many fairies he'd just executed, he didn't look half bad. There was a light speckle of bruising along his neck, but his face was untouched, and that was possibly the most important part. His hands though…

He raised his hands and grimaced at the cuts. A blueing bruise wrapped his thumb, too. It had nearly been broken clean off, but it seemed to have melded okay now that everything was reattached.

The apartment was quiet with Dranian off on his adventure and Dog-Shayne staying with clingy Beth. Luc smoothed down his scarlet hair and brushed his teeth for the road as he revelled in the silence. It had been so loud in the Shadow Palace. His ears still rung. His eyes stung too from all the pesky smoke.

He only had one thing left to do before he returned to the Corners of Ever, and that was to get some protection. He wasn't sure how things were going to land for him in the near future, if all was well or all was lost. It would depend on the vote. And once that was decided, he might need a rather terrific bodyguard.

Luc airslipped from the apartment and headed down the street where snow lightly dusted the roads and shop owners were stringing up Yule Celebration lights. He scanned the shops' windowsills, trying to remember where he'd seen a basket of forest debris that morning as he was passing by. It took him a few minutes, but he spotted the basket inside a 'loose-leaf tea' shop.

Luc chuckled at the thought. Loose leaf tea. Wasn't all tea made of loose leaves?

He nudged his way in and coughed to fetch the attention of the shop owner. But the man was in the far back helping a customer, and Luc was short on time. So, he waited until no one was looking. Then he reached over to the basket of forest debris—shelled nuts and fruit—and he slipped a walnut into his sleeve.

He turned to go with his prize.

"Merry Christmas!" the store owner called after him as he left.

Luc flashed back a smile and waved. The door slid shut behind him and he stuck his hands into his pockets as he headed down the road toward a small café with a purple awning and the scent of a pretentious North Prince's ego wafting out of it. Luc lifted the nut and sang a sweet, magical tune into its ear. Then he slid it back into his pocket and crushed the shell in his palm, spilling its yummy fragments out.

Fae Café had its fireplace going when Luc walked in. He hesitated at the door when he sniffed the wave of Shadow Fairy inside. "Oh dear," he muttered. He hadn't expected Mor to be here. Everything got more complicated when Mor was around.

Nevertheless, Luc pushed his way in and offered his sweetest smile. He accidentally saw Mor first, and his smile faltered.

"Trisencor," he greeted anyway, "I see you have a new holiday menu."

Mor's judgemental gaze settled on Luc as he slid onto a stool at the counter. A cringeworthy green apron was draped over Mor's muscular frame now instead of the tacky burgundy ones his High Court usually wore.

"What are you doing here, Luc?" Mor asked. When he folded his arms, it sort of seemed like he was flexing.

"I came for a coffee, naturally. Don't you know I drink coffee now?" Luc eyed an enormous slice of blueberry pie at the end of the counter.

"Don't you know you can go somewhere else to get it?" Mor said right back.

Luc pointed to the pie. "Can I have that?"

"No." Mor slid the pie away a little further. "That's Cress's. So unless you want your last fox life crushed beneath a faestone elbow, don't touch it."

Luc smiled. "I wouldn't dare."

Mor looked like he was stifling an eye roll as he rotated and fetched the coffee pot. The second his back was turned, Luc slid a chunk of walnut from his pocket. He reached across the counter and stuffed it inside the pie, right between two gooey blueberries.

"I'll ask again," Mor said as he turned back around with a filled paper cup. He reached for a lid and fastened it to the top, then he slid it across the counter to Luc. "What are you doing here?"

"I was in the neighbourhood. Isn't that what humans say?" Luc said as he received the coffee and took a whiff of the delicious bean scent.

"That's not an answer." Mor picked up a newspaper, rested it on the counter, then leaned forward and began to read like he'd suddenly decided Luc was no longer there, or was more likely waiting for Luc to leave.

Luc sighed. "What do you want to know, Mor? Fine. I was rescuing puppies from trees and saving babies," he said.

This time, Mor didn't stifle any of his eye roll.

"Don't you know I volunteer in an old-people's-home now, too?" Luc went on, and Mor shoved the newspaper aside. He bit his lips together like he'd run out of ideas of how to ignore Luc.

"Luc," he said. Surprisingly, it wasn't said with distain or annoyance. "Are you really going to keep living with Dranian?"

"Yes." Luc lifted his coffee and took his first sip. He gagged. "This is black," he stated. "It's horrid."

Mor let out a long breath. He took the coffee back and mixed in some sugar and cream. When he returned with Luc's coffee, it was clear the quiet barista had something to say. So, Luc tried his drink while he waited. This time, it was delicious.

"I still don't think I can trust you," Mor admitted. "And I'm not sure what to do about it, since we've established I can't kill you. And I'm worried that grumpy fool has actually taken a liking to you, which is absurd."

"Ah." Luc nodded. "It's absurd to you because you abandon people, Trisencor. Dranian, on the other hand, is loyal." He took another sip of his coffee and stood from the stool. "And no, you can't trust me. Not with anything—*except*, you can trust me with Dranian. Someday I might even prove it to you." He dug into his pocket and pulled out a few pebbles for payment. "Here. Put these in the register and tell whoever asks that they're gold."

Mor blinked slowly. "I'm not doing that," he said.

Luc shrugged. "Your loss."

In one sweep, Mor flicked all the pebbles off the counter. They splattered onto the floor and bounced everywhere.

"Queensbane, what is this mess?" A low voice filled the café, and Luc beheld the great Cressica Alabastian emerging from the staircase in an exceptional, perfectly tailored navy suit. The Prince looked like one of the rich characters in a TV series as he fiddled with his cuffs, as he glided over the floor, as a sunbeam soared through the window like a spotlight, and Luc could have sworn a gust of wind breathed across the room and fluttered Cress's shiny hair in slow, wispy motions. Music came from somewhere too, and Luc was sure no moment could be this flawless without magic.

Luc's smile broadened. The North High Prince was perfect.

The idiot was in for a great surprise.

"Look at me in this suit. I think I'll wear this every day, Mor," Cress stated, too self-absorbed to notice Luc standing there.

"If you get one drop of pie on that suit, Cress, you'll lose your mind and we'll all be hearing about it until Spring. Take it off and don't you dare put it back on again until your wedding," Mor scolded. He yanked the pie plate away before Cress could get it, and Luc frowned. "Promise me," Mor demanded, holding the pie at bay.

Cress sighed loudly. "Fine. I won't."

Luc grunted a laugh. He knew a lying face when he saw one. He sipped his coffee as he turned to go, and he glanced over at the clock beside the calendar on the wall, calculating the long journey through the wind ahead of him.

He'd just pushed his way outside when he overheard Mor murmur to Cress, "I told Dranian to move out of his apartment. I told him he could live with me."

The door slid closed, but Luc's delicate ears tilted back to hear Cress reply, "Dranian can handle himself." Cress sounded distracted, like he was still ogling at his suit. "He'll tell us if he needs us, Mor. We all have an agreement now to not keep secrets, and Dranian is easy to interrogate. Also—he hates your cathedral."

Luc stepped to the side, keeping out of sight of the Fae Café windows. He waited. He wasn't sure why; he had a place to be.

"I suppose," Mor replied. "But I'm just nervous with Dranian after he went against those Shadow Fairies on his own. I wouldn't be able to handle it if something happened to any one of you and I wasn't there to do something about it."

Luc's fingers curled around a brick in the wall at his back. He accidentally broke a chunk off and it smashed to the sidewalk. A middle-aged human female started as she walked by until Luc flashed her a sweet smile filled with fox charm. She relaxed and dipped her head in greeting, blushing as she left.

Once she was gone, Luc closed his eyes, leaned his head back against the wall, and sucked in a slow lungful of air.

What a herd of losers.

Their barefoot friend was flirting with death, likely going to die. And now Luc was going to be the heartless fool who'd stared Mor in the eyes and hadn't said anything about it.

"Why do all these North Fairies keep ruining my life?" he asked the sky deities.

He had no interest in helping or saving the High Court of the Coffee Bean. But maybe there was a tedious, ever-whining part of him that sort of wanted to prove something.

When Luc peeled his eyes open, his gaze settled on the bakery across the street where fresh loaves were being wrestled into plastic bags and placed on shelves. He was getting a little tired of using enchantments on everything, but one last one wouldn't hurt.

12

Shayne Lyro and the Fox

Two days left.

Shayne could not believe Luc. He couldn't believe that self-centred fox stole his note, read his secret, and *still* brought Cress and Mor here. That he hadn't even seen the error of his ways or apologized now that Kate, Greyson, and Violet were alone and in danger of being approached. In fact, the moment everyone agreed to switch locations so the House of Lyro might not track them, Luc disappeared. He must have thought no one was watching—but Shayne saw it.

The fox returned thirty minutes later and slipped into the back of the group.

Dranian evaded Cress as they marched through the woods. Cress continuously tried to sneak up on him, tried to smack the back of Dranian's neck or poke Dranian's hand. Ever since Luc admitted that all they had to do was touch to get their bodies back to normal, Cress hadn't let Dranian out of his sight.

"Just give him his body back," Mycra murmured to Dranian after Cress's fourth failed attempt. "You don't need it anymore."

Shayne watched Dranian shake his head. And despite Shayne's troubles, he smirked.

The situation was everything Shayne could have ever dreamed of. But his laughter fizzled out when reality set it. He'd lost his smile somewhere between his decision not to kill a dreamslipper and having his human home threatened.

He released a heavy breath and fiddled with a button on his coat now that Lily had returned it to him. It was all he could do not to stare at the pretty human as she led the way up front with Mor like she owned the forest. Like she belonged here, which she didn't.

Lily, Lily, Lily. What was he going to do with her?

Shayne noticed Cress scheming another sneak-up attempt on Dranian. He almost made it too, but Shayne flicked a pebble ahead with his toe. It hit the back of Dranian's leg, and Dranian whirled just in time to duck Cress's swinging fist.

Alright, he couldn't help it. Shayne laughed.

But once again, his laugh fell off, hit the dirt, and was trampled beneath his bare feet as he walked.

He had to tell them. He had to tell Cress, and Mor, and Dranian. He couldn't let his true brothers stay here when Kate, Violet, and Greyson were in trouble. They had no idea how important it was that they return before the two days were up. Shayne pressed his fingers against his faeborn heart, an ache forming there. He wasn't sure he could solve his problem to begin with, but now that Cress and Mor were here, it only made sense for them to take everyone home with them. Except for Shayne.

Shayne would tell them their humans were in trouble as soon as he dealt with the fox. And then he would head to the House of Riothin to try to save his future. It was the only way Hans-Der Lyro might be afraid enough to keep the House of Lyro from meddling with Shayne's life. Shayne didn't have the heart to admit to his friends that if Lord Riothin decided not to kill him, Shayne would still likely have to stay there for several years before he could slip away and return to the human world. That only then would things have passed over, and he might be free.

Years of casting fake smiles in an enemy House was better than a lifetime in a highest chair.

"What a fool." Cress fell into step beside Shayne and folded his arms. His scowl seemed fitting on the body he wore.

"You make a good Dranian," Shayne said. "Maybe you two should stay switched."

Cress's eyes rounded, and only when he spotted Shayne's smirk did he seem to realize it was a joke. "I'll not have you making such preposterous suggestions in my presence, Shayne," he stated. "We came all the way here for that body. Imagine how distressed I was to wake up from my nap and realize my eyes had changed colour, and my shapely hair was different, and my face—oh, my face! It's awful."

Mycra cast a mean look back at Cress. She took hold of Dranian's arm as if to assure him Cress was crazy, and Cress made a loud, repulsed noise.

"Don't you dare think about doing anything of the frisky sort in that form, Dranian! If you violate my precious body, if you even *think* about kissing that female with my mouth, I'll take your tongue and bury you in a cauldron of bloodsucking slugs!" Cress shouted in return.

Dranian tugged his arm away from Mycra, and they both stepped a few inches away from each other. But a minute later, Mycra leaned to whisper something to Dranian. Shayne watched how Dranian looked back at her with what might have been the grump's best version of a smile. How his eyes followed Mycra wherever she went. How he was always just an arm's reach away.

The fool was practically obsessed with her.

Shayne stopped fiddling with the button on his coat and chewed on his thumbnail instead. He'd considered more than once he might be best off to grab Mycra Sentorious and drag her back to the House of Lyro with him. She would be a good bargaining chip. She might be enough to give Shayne a way out in the end.

His gaze hit the ground.

Could he steal Dranian's happiness for his own? Even if Shayne miraculously found a way to use Mycra to set himself free, Jethwire and Massie would just make their returned dreamslipper haunt him like they had before. Eventually, Shayne would probably be driven mad. He might run himself off a cliff or face some other dramatic end of his own doing.

He didn't want to see Mycra as a prisoner again anyway. And he didn't want to leave Dranian alone. One of them had to take care of Dranian, and Shayne knew it wouldn't be him.

He never imagined when he first went to his childling home that he wouldn't be able to return to the human realm. That his blood brothers would know of his life there. That they would do this to him. He should have never left the café to begin with. He should have suffered through the nightmares for eternity.

Shayne's stare found Lily's back again. Truly, he'd thought he would eventually force Lily to marry him, and he could give her the happily ever after he knew she secretly wanted. He thought he might become a police officer too and terrorize the poorly behaved humans of the city at her side. He hadn't even found a way to steal a kiss from those tempting lips of hers yet.

"Did you know you were in love with a human?"

How many times had Massie's voice sang through Shayne's head with those wretched words? Shayne rubbed his forehead and pressed a hand over his heart as it flittered off for a beat. Massie was diabolical. He sputtered nonsense for fun. Just because Shayne had found comfort in his moments with Lily and had often thought of her over the long months of battling his nightmares, it did not mean he *loved* her.

It was just another trap.

Shayne chewed on the inside of his cheek as he watched the way Lily walked. The way her hair swished with her movements. The way she breathed. The way she—

He nearly fell when she looked back over her shoulder and almost caught him staring.

Shayne's hand found his chest again—right over his wildly thudding heart. He kept his eyes on the back of Dranian's head after that. Because...

Who was he kidding?

She was probably already his mate.

Lily didn't know what she did to him every time she spoke or breathed, or why she was such an attractive target to his hellish brothers. She had no idea why Shayne had tried to tether her to him with a vine after he saw her in his fairy realm. And he would never tell her.

She didn't like him back—Shayne knew that. It wouldn't have stopped him from chasing her day in and day out, but it was enough to make the impending separation easier for him.

Lily Baker, the proud human who thought she could do anything and solve anyone. She'd never solved him. His slow grin returned at the thought.

Perhaps in several years, when he finally caught up to the others in the human realm, Lily would be married to some human idiot half as handsome as Shayne. Maybe she would have childlings of her own. Maybe she would have found another happily ever after.

He frowned.

Nope. No, he did not like that one bit.

"We'll stop here," Mor decided, looking around. A crystal creek laid ahead with a shore covered in lush greenery. "There are rash weeds everywhere. Be careful where you step," he added.

Lily slumped to sit and catch her breath, and Mor sat down beside her. The two looked like they'd been attacked by an artist with all their tattoos peeking out everywhere. He didn't join them though. He waited.

Then, right on cue, the voice Shayne had been waiting for lifted from the back.

"I'll go fetch firewood," Luc said. It was stated in disgust as he looked around at all the rash weeds. The moment Luc headed into the trees, Shayne doubled back and went after him.

Luc must have heard Shayne coming, but he didn't react as he drifted down a slope and rounded a small cliff. It was clear though when Luc stopped walking and released a loud sigh.

He turned around.

Shayne punched him.

Luc's whole body spun; he caught himself on the cliffside before he could fall into a rash bush. He dragged his gaze back to Shayne and slowly wiped a fresh bead of blood off his bottom lip. "Fascinating," he said.

"How could you lead them here with breadcrumbs?" Shayne accused. "I'm going crazy every moment Cress and Mor aren't at home! You know what will happen to Kate and Violet in two days now that they're alone!"

Luc tilted his head curiously. He stood tall, folded his arms, and tapped a finger against his bicep. "Do I?" he asked.

The pretense only boiled Shayne's frustration more. He should have known not to trust a fox. What was Dranian thinking keeping company with an enemy?

Shayne pointed in Luc's face. "You might not care about humans like we do, Zelsor—"

"You're right. I don't." Luc angled his head again. "What are you saying, exactly?"

Shayne drew his fairsaber. Luc's silvery gaze flickered down to it. "I'm saying this goes beyond me being concerned for Dranian's feelings being hurt once you're dead."

A funny smile broke across Luc's face. "Oh dear." He pinched the bridge of his nose. "Do you mean to tell me that our dear Violet is in trouble—again? And it's not even because of me this time?"

Shayne's fist balled around his fairsaber handle. "You're out of your mind. Admit it." He pointed back to the others with his blade. "They have no idea how warped you really are inside."

"Ah." Luc nodded. "Probably not. But I suppose they don't know how messed up you truly are at this point either."

Shayne lowered his saber and worked his jaw. "I'm not messed up. I'm the *only* Lyro with a clear head. Even my family knows it, despite my best efforts to prove otherwise."

Luc licked the remaining blood from his lip and folded his hands behind his back. "Well, before you blame me for putting Violet Miller and whoever else in danger, perhaps you should consider what might put them back out of danger. No threat comes without a solution, North Fairy."

Shayne opened his mouth. Closed it. Opened it again and said, "I have a solution. Lord Riothin is the solution. And if that doesn't work... I'll do what I need to. I'm not afraid of that chair."

Luc's heart-shaped mouth pinched. He took too long to think. But finally, he said, "Excellent. At least we're clear on that." He stooped down and grabbed three thick, dry sticks, then stood and handed the wood to Shayne. "Don't stand around here with me then. I'm getting the feeling you're running out of time to save those humans."

"What do you mean, you're getting the *feeling*? You know I am." Shayne stuffed his fairsaber away and got a better hold on the sticks.

Luc smiled and said nothing else. He gathered four more sticks. Then he said, "Check your pockets, you fool," and he disappeared.

Shayne blinked at the empty space by the cliff. He looked down at his coat. He shimmied the wood to one arm so he could stuff his hand into his pocket, and he stilled when his fingers grazed a papery texture. His fingers folded around the shape as he drew it out and lifted it slowly. He stared in disbelief at the origami crane.

All the sticks fell from his arm and bounced over the ground. Shayne used both hands to open the note, and when he saw it, he stifled an airy sound of disbelief.

His own letter.

Luc had been bluffing. He'd burned his own note. The nine tailed fox had no idea why Mor and Cress shouldn't be in the Ever Corners, no idea

131

what would happen to the unprotected humans back home. He hadn't known anything—until Shayne had just told him. And now Luc had all the answers he wanted.

Shayne released an old fairy curse and trudged back to the creek by himself.

Shayne watched Luc guzzle fresh water from the creek. It didn't seem fair that one person could have the ability to do so many tricky things in one faeborn-cursed lifetime. Sure, Shayne was grateful Luc had saved his life. But he wanted to march up behind Luc, shove him face-first in the shallow river, and hold his head down for a while.

"What's going on with you?" Mor asked.

Shayne's gaze darted up. He hadn't even heard Mor come over.

Mor pulled off his jacket and sat down beside him. "And why in the name of the sky deities are you spitting daggers at Zelsor with your eyes?"

"I'm thinking about stuffing a handful of rash weeds down the back of his coat while he's sleeping," Shayne admitted, rolling a handful of berries between his fingers. He extended them toward Mor. He wasn't hungry.

Mor took the berries and flicked one into his mouth. "He'll only become a bigger pest if you let on that you're riled up, you know. You of all people should understand how that works."

Shayne tapped a finger against his knee. "Why haven't you demanded an answer?" he asked, changing the subject. "I lied and came here instead of going to fun-filled-Florida with Greyson. Cress hasn't even punched me for it yet."

Mor's brown-silver eyes turned sharp, and Shayne wondered if he shouldn't have brought it up. If maybe Mor was the one who'd be handing out the punches. If those punches were about to come this minute.

Shayne looked off toward the horizon sinking from pink to deep red and orange. The day was slipping away, and every minute passed too quickly. Soon it would be night. Soon it would be 'one day left'.

Mor huffed. "When I refused to take away your memories, Shayne, I didn't realize the alternative would be *this*." He nodded to the forest at their backs. "Now we're all here—some of us not by choice."

"I had my reasons for asking," Shayne said.

"It doesn't matter now. We'll go home in the morning." Mor tossed the rest of the berries into his mouth all at once.

Shayne closed his eyes and tugged on his hair. "Mor..." Mor was quiet as he waited. "Things are never simple here, are they?" When Shayne opened his eyes, Mor was frowning. "I think the first thing you should do when you get home is pay the Sisterhood of Assassins a visit. Bring them a cake or something. Try to get on Freida's good side for once."

Mor bristled. "Disgusting," he muttered. "And why are you speaking like you won't be there?"

Shayne angled toward where everyone was milling about, warming their hands at the fire, cooking roots, eating berries. He would miss Cress's temper tantrums. He would miss Dranian's moods. He would miss Mor's quiet insight. He would miss Kate's scolding, and Greyson's coolness, and Violet's observations. He would miss seeing Lily's pretty face. And her stink face. And her surprised face. And her annoyed face. And her *quit-getting-in-my-face* face.

Shayne shouted over the camp, "Just for curiosity's sake, if I tell you all to leave, as your rightful King, would you go home right now?" Then he added, "Without me?"

A series of expressions and grumbles lifted from all directions along the lines of:

"I would never leave my forever friend behind."

"That is preposterous!"

"Are you crazy, Shayne?"

"What an idiot."—That last one was Luc.

Shayne found a weak smile and looked at the ground. That was answer enough.

No, he couldn't tell any of them what was at stake. He was lucky Luc was keeping his mouth shut. It was clear Shayne's real brothers would try to stop him once they realized his predicament, and his one and only solution would be destroyed before he could even try.

He had one day left after today. One day to make sure his allies returned to the human realm and never came back. It wouldn't be easy, but there was a fairy here who might be obnoxiously clever enough to make it happen, and heartless enough to let Shayne walk into danger without putting up a fuss.

Because Shayne had to be long gone when they found out about everything.

Shayne shook the pretty human awake at midnight. His crossbow was heavy on his back as he brushed a strand of Lily's maize hair out of her eyes. The moonlight glowed over her cheeks as her lashes fluttered.

Mor, Cress, Dranian, and Mycra were all on the other side of the fire. Only Luc was nearby, and his snorty breathing was shallow enough to assure Shayne he was a light sleeper.

When Lily's gaze locked onto Shayne above her, she sat up quickly.

"What's wrong? What's going on?" She looked right and left, reaching for her atrocious gun, but Shayne grabbed her hand, and she stilled.

"Nothing." His tongue turned prickly. "Nothing at all, ugly Human."

She rubbed her eyes. "Then why'd you wake me up?" Her words were slurred with sleep. "What time is it? Is it time to go home?"

Shayne cracked a smile. "Soon." He pulled her to her feet with him and held her steady as she teetered. When she looked up at him in question with her half-open, sleepy eyes, he said, "Don't hate me. I need to do this just once."

Her lips parted, and her gaze flickered down to his mouth. He smiled—she got the idea.

"Shayne…"

"Shh."

He dragged her tight against him, and he kissed her.

The sky deities must have been jealous—he kissed her *well*. Lily's lips melted against his, her sharp, quiet inhale becoming music that rivalled the creek's trickling water. Shayne's thumb dragged along her cheek, pushing her hair back as he spilled every ounce of his enchanting persuasion into her soft mouth.

Magic rang in his ears when he pulled away. He'd expected to like the kiss, but queensbane, he hadn't quite expected his chest to erupt with flame. He brushed his fingers along Lily's flushed cheeks one last time as her wide blue gaze took him in. As the enchantment did its work and transformed him into the most gorgeous thing she'd ever laid eyes upon—though, that was nothing new for him. Just the same situation as always.

"Lily," he said. Truly, he liked using her real name when he could get away with it. "I want you to do something for me. Go right back to sleep after this, and in the morning, go home with everyone. Don't try to stay."

She said nothing as she absorbed his words.

"And miss me a lot," he added, just for the sake of it. "Don't go running off to find some ugly human male to fake date instead." Obviously, her enchantment would wear off long before that instruction was applicable. "Tell our friends at the station we broke up. They'll believe you this time when I don't come around."

He should have let her go then; time was getting away from him. He was lucky his real brothers hadn't woken up. "And last…" He bit his lips over a grin. "Tell me you've completely fallen head-over-heels in love with me. I want to hear you say it from those pretty lips before I go." He didn't care one bit that she had to utter it under an enchantment. That she might remember this later and wonder what in the world he'd made her do.

He'd revelled in fake dating her for ages. He could revel in a fake love confession, too.

Lily looked back and forth between his eyes. Her mouth twisted a little. Then, she did it: "I've fallen for you, Shayne," she said. She even held eye contact as she said it—it was the best.

Shayne smiled. "You'll never understand what you do to me, Lily Baker." He took her shoulders and guided her back to the ground to put her back to bed. Lily stared as he laid her back, as he dragged off his crossbow, pulled off his coat, and tossed it over her. "Ugly Human... you know I never thought you were ugly, right?" He pulled the coat right up to her neck and tucked it in around her shoulders. Then he flicked the end of her nose. "Sleep tight."

He waited until she closed her eyes before he refastened his crossbow, stood, and turned for Foxy Luc. But as soon as he turned, he found Luc standing there. Already wide awake. A peculiar look on his fair face.

It was a shame. Shayne would have liked to whack him out of his sleep.

Nevertheless, Shayne turned and headed for the creek. He waded through the shallow water in silence, careful not to flick a rock or hit a branch or do anything else that might stir his brothers awake. Luc was just as quiet as he followed.

They moved to the sound of squeaking moonbugs until they reached a nearby cave. And there, Shayne turned to Luc, grabbed his hand, and slapped his paper crane into Luc's palm.

"I don't trust you as far as I can throw you, Foxy. But I'm not a fool. I won't bring any of them with me to a House as dangerous as Riothin," he said. And then, "I'm going away for a bit."

Luc didn't object, but he raised a scarlet brow. "And how long will you be gone, exactly?"

"A while," Shayne admitted. He didn't want to think about whether or not *a while* would turn into *forever*. "Don't forget that you took Dranian's arm, and there's no fairy I care about more than that one. So make it right and die for him if you must." Shayne stepped in closer. "If I'm forced to become the next High Lord of the House of Lyro, and I find out you've let something happen to *my* best friend, I will hunt you down for as long as you live."

Luc smirked and twirled the paper crane in his fingers. "Try," he invited. "Please, North Fairy. I would really enjoy seeing how it would go for you, High Lord or not."

Shayne took in a deep breath and swallowed. "I don't trust you, but I'm counting on you because I must. Make sure they *all* go home. No exceptions. I want no one left here."

Luc grunted. "Yes, well, *my* bestie Dranian would hold it against me if something happened to the humans at home anyway now that I've summoned Trisencor and Cressica here. I'll get everyone home. You just keep your family issues away from my apartment and my dog."

Shayne folded his arms. "Tell me one last thing. Where do you keep disappearing off to?" he asked.

Luc smiled. He tucked the paper crane into his over-the-top black coat. "Just because I know your secrets doesn't mean I owe you mine." He paused. His nose wrinkled, and he sniffed.

"Well keep mine," Shayne snapped. "At least until morning when I'm long gone."

Luc pursed his lips and angled his head. "Oh dear. It might be difficult now, considering she already knows."

Shayne's brows tugged inward. "*She*? Who?"

Luc sighed dramatically. "How shameful, North Fairy. You've gotten so used to being unable to detect her feelings that you can't even tell when she's close enough to grab?" Luc airslipped to the cave entrance and reached around the corner.

He pulled Lily into the mouth of the cave, and Shayne's stomach dropped.

Oh.

'*She*'.

Curse the Ever Corner stars.

Lily's eyes were fierce and alert. Shayne studied the strangeness; how she seemed completely herself in that moment, in no rush to hold him, or climb all over him, or make the world a better place for him.

He wanted to ask what she was doing there, why she hadn't listened. But it was clear. It was so clear, it hurt—his heart and his pride.

It was the first time in his whole life he'd failed to enchant someone with a kiss.

"Let her go," Shayne whispered.

"Actually, I think she wants to be held right now," Luc said, tugging Lily a little closer.

"Let her go!" Shayne shouted it this time.

Luc's jaw slid to the side. But he slowly peeled his fingers off her. Then he said, "Say your goodbyes, dear Lily. When we get back to the others, we're going home."

Luc wasted no time backing up several steps and waiting at the entrance. He studied his coat, checked his pockets, but it was obvious he was still eavesdropping.

"Queensbane," Shayne said under his breath. "Ugly Human…"

"Don't call me that anymore," she rasped.

Shayne bit his lips. Then he said, "Lily—"

Lily stepped toward him and smacked his chest. He went still. He let her do it again a second later. She wasn't hitting him hard anyway. Not that he would have stopped her if she was.

"You're the worst," she croaked. It was a miracle of the sky deities she wasn't crying—thick tears rested in her eyes. They just couldn't seem to spill over.

The next time she tried to swat his chest, he grabbed her wrist. He slowly wrapped his arms around her, holding his hand tight against her back as her head came along his shoulder. She fought it with everything she had, but eventually, a cry slipped out, and Shayne's shoulder dampened.

It had taken her a million faeborn years to finally cry in front of him.

He hadn't wanted to leave like this. This was all wrong; she might not go home willingly this way. She might do something utterly foolish like try to stay. "Luc," Shayne called. "Can you take away her memory of this?"

Lily's gun was out so fast, aimed backward at Luc's heart—Luc went rigid in the cave's entrance.

"Don't you dare come near me," she said.

Luc eyed the weapon. "I think I'll stay out of this one." He bristled as his fingers dragged over the chain of his foxtail necklace. "But dawn is approaching—I shouldn't have to remind you of that."

Shayne pulled back and smeared away the last of Lily's tears with his thumb. "It might not be goodbye forever," he promised. "It might just be for a while."

Even he knew how ridiculous that sounded. Lily looked like she wanted to hit him again.

Shayne glanced out the mouth of the cave where the moon looked heavy in the sky and the stars threatened to disappear into a haze. "Luc," he begged. "Keep your word."

Luc put his hands on his hips and dropped his head forward. "Oh dear. She's going to dislike me even more after this," he muttered. In the same heartbeat, he airslipped to their side.

It was magnificent how Lily knew exactly where Luc would end up when she tried to punch him. Luc barely ducked before his foxy face would have been crushed, but he grabbed her—a pale hand around her tattooed arm— and Shayne felt Lily slide from his grip in an instant. They vanished.

The cave was empty.

It was quiet.

Shayne's hands slowly fell back to his sides.

He stared at the place Lily had been just a second ago. He adjusted the strap of his crossbow. He checked for his fairsaber. He rubbed his sore chest.

And he headed out.

It only occurred to Shayne once he was marching through the dark woods that Lily's love confession had come without being under the influence of an enchantment. His smile was weak and flat when he realized.

He was jealous humans could lie without feeling needles on their tongue.

"See you in another lifetime, pretty Human," he murmured into the wind.

CHAPTER

13

Lily Baker and the Homecoming Dance

This was worse than any joke Shayne had ever played. Lily sat by the fire, staring at the licking flames as everyone else woke up. Dew had formed along her bare arms in the early hours. Her skin was freezing; she'd been fighting shivers all night until the sun peeked over the distant mountains and warmed the forest. By then, she wasn't just devastated anymore.

She was angry. Angry at Shayne.

He'd promised her he was going home.

Shayne was a liar. How poetic, that he'd always accused Lily of being one.

The memory of the way he'd looked at her in the dark by the fire. Of his hand dragging along her cheek, finding its way into her hair as he'd pulled her into a kiss... Lily closed her eyes, angry all over again. She would never forgive him for doing that. For trying to trick her with heart flutters and honesty and telling her to do outrageous things like 'go home and live a happy life.'

"The vote is in," Luc announced as Dranian sat up, sneezed, and made Cress spring up with a startled gawk five feet away. "We're all going home."

Dranian blinked and looked around. He scanned the trees. Twisted to look back at the creek. "Wait..." He said it too quietly for anyone to notice.

"What in the name of the sky—why are Lily's ankles tied up?!" Mor roared. He strutted over to Lily and yanked the makeshift gag from her mouth first. Then he ripped the nest of branches from around her ankles, only to realize Lily's wrists were tied, too—with her own sweater. Mor's jaw tightened. He whirled. "Luc, what did you do?"

Luc sat upon a high rock, tearing petals off a flower one by one. "What makes you think I did all that?" he asked. When Mor's silence spoke volumes, Luc sighed. "I'm saving her life," he said nonchalantly. "She's just ungrateful."

"You're going to prison. You'll rot in jail forever for attacking a cop," Lily promised now that she could speak, pulling Luc's gaze off his flower. He scratched the side of his neck.

"Is there free food in human prison?" he asked.

Lily kicked a wad of dirt at him. It smacked against Luc's coat, and he snarled. Then he dragged himself off the rock, ignoring Mor shooting daggers at him with his eyes, and he crouched down before Lily.

"Dear Lily," Luc folded his hands, "I don't want to have to enslave you with your real name in front of all your puffed-up assassin guardians, but I will if I must. If I'm being honest, they don't frighten me as much as they think they do—"

Mor grabbed Luc's shoulder and ripped him back. "See what happens to your tongue if you try uttering her name," he invited. "You've gone too far, Zelsor!"

"Where's Shayne?" Dranian's murmur barely sailed into the conversation, but it made everyone look around. Lily watched them as they realized, way too late, that Shayne wasn't there. She saw Mycra turn and gaze toward the landscape. She was the only one who didn't look surprised.

Lily couldn't believe her eyes.

Mycra? The psycho stranger? *She* already knew?

Fresh frustration burned through her that Shayne didn't tell any of his assassin brothers what he was doing. That he snuck off in the night like a thief. That he didn't say goodbye to Mor, Cress, or even Dranian—he wouldn't have said goodbye to *her* if she hadn't caught him in that cave.

Mor dropped to a knee and untied the sweater from Lily's wrists.

"Careful," Luc warned. "She's a flight risk." He dug into his coat and pulled out a red paper bird. Lily watched him hand it to Mor. "But I have exactly what I need to ensure she comes home." Mor turned the bird over in his fingers. He exhaled a sigh of annoyance as he opened it.

"Mor knows we can't go home without Shayne," Lily objected, climbing to her feet. "No origami craft is going to change that. You're un-*real*, Luc!" she said. "For a minute, I actually thought maybe you were on our side. But it's pretty clear to me now that you're just crazy. Dranian is wrong about you!"

"Lily…" Mor's low-toned voice made Cress and Dranian look up across the firepit. He stared at the note in his fingers with an expression that turned something in Lily's stomach. Then he said, "We're going home."

Lily's mouth parted.

"What?" Cress demanded. "We are? We haven't even had breakfast yet."

"Yes." Mor handed the paper bird off to Cress, and Dranian huddled in to read it over his shoulder.

"Without Shayne?" Lily asked as Cress's face paled.

"Without Shayne," Mor agreed. He looked off, working his jaw, and folded his arms.

"It might not be goodbye forever," Shayne had promised. But nobody promised something like that unless there was a chance it *would* be forever. Lily had collected enough evidence over the last few days to determine that there was a good chance that kiss last night had been the last one he ever planned to give.

Lily released a sound of disbelief. "What is Kate going to say when we show up at home and Shayne isn't with us?" she said.

"Katherine is in trouble," Cress said through his teeth. He held up the note and waved it in front of Lily's face. "I'll not stay here another faeborn-cursed moment! Get your things, Human! We're leaving now!"

Lily's arms fell back to her sides. "What did you just say...?"

Kate?

Her gaze flickered across the camp to where Luc had found a comfortable spot leaning against a tree with his hands in his pockets. He hadn't said anything about Kate being in trouble.

Lily marched over to Cress and stole the paper crane. She read it.

"Give Cress his body back, Dranian," Mor instructed. "He's going to need it."

From the corner of her eye, Lily saw that Dranian's fists were balled. His borrowed turquoise gaze was aimed at the woods across the creek. He looked like he might run for it.

"Dranian," Mor warned.

Dranian turned his scowling face to Mor. Then to Cress. He reluctantly dropped his shoulders and nodded.

His hand came out slowly toward Cress.

"It's about time, you fool!" Cress snatched Dranian's hand out of the air, and they both shuddered. In the blink of an eye, they switched places.

Cress inhaled a deep breath and let it out slowly, patting himself on the chest. "How exhilarating to be back!" He even raised both arms and flexed his muscles. "Look, Mor. I'm gorgeous again." But his excitement vanished, his turquoise irises turning cold and sharp. "Now, let me go deal with whoever shows up at the café today." He swallowed.

Lily lowered the note. It slipped from her fingers in a gust of wind and sailed into the creek.

They were going... back?

Kate and Greyson were in trouble?

Fae scouts would go after them before the end of the day today?

Lily turned away from the others. She clutched her police hoodie in her grip, digging her fingers in.

Everything was happening too fast.

She let her eyes slide closed, and she swallowed. She'd never had a panic attack before. This couldn't possibly be what that was. But her hands shook, and an overwhelming wave of nausea washed through her abdomen. Was this what Dranian felt when he lost control?

Lily pictured Kate alone at the café. She'd probably been picking up double shifts to cover the counter after everyone left. She was vulnerable, like she'd been the last time a Shadow Fairy had appeared and kidnapped her, and had tied her to a chair, and had nearly...

Lily marched into the woods. The others continued their discussions, continued gathering their things behind her as she wove between trunks and stepped over fallen logs. Winged bugs spiralled past, and the same milkweed-like bulbs floated around, whisking away as she rushed by. She pushed strands of pink blossom-filled vines aside, carving a path through the flora.

She finally grabbed a tree, leaning against the trunk for support, her inhales tight and heavy. She clawed at the collar of her t-shirt, trying to remember breathing techniques through the haze of her mind. She squeezed her eyes shut.

This wasn't her. She didn't panic. She wasn't afraid of anything.

With the exception of one, single thing.

Lily had stayed by Kate's side, protecting her for all these years, only to leave her open to danger now. Everything Lily had done in the last year had been for Kate. Every design at Desmount Tech, every decision about the café, even allowing the fae assassins to stay around once she was finally convinced they were safe—that was all for *Kate*.

She only hoped that if Kate, her only sister, was in trouble, she would know to run. Because Lily had no other family left apart from Kate and Greyson. She hadn't been able to protect her first mother. She hadn't been able to protect her second mother or father, either.

"The girl who can survive anything... can she even save anyone?"

Lily's eyelids peeled open.

The music. High and fresh, curling over her skin like it was close enough to touch. She had the strangest urge to dance her way through the forest. To walk—no, *run*—to the source.

She realized her sweater was no longer in her hands. She turned to look the way she came, guessing where she'd dropped it, but instead of seeing the forest, an enormous teal sea spilled into her vision. She faltered before she took a step forward, looking down to find bubbly seafoam licking up the edge of a black rock beneath her feet. The sea went on for miles in every direction with no other shore or island in sight. The taste of salt moved along her tongue, and the wind turned warm and strange.

The Lady of the Lake. The one whose voice was trapped in a flute. Shayne had warned Lily not to listen.

She smacked her hands over her ears. She pressed so hard, she thought she'd crush her skull.

Like a painting being peeled away in strips, the vision of the sea disappeared, and she found herself back in the forest.

Bright emerald leaves fluttered overhead in a patch of breeze, distant birds chirped, and the creek waters echoed through the plants. Lily swallowed, realizing whatever tightness of breath and nausea she felt a moment ago was gone. She spotted the sleeve of her sweater on the ground a few feet away, mostly hidden by a blue quartz-like cliff. It wasn't where she guessed it would be. In fact, it looked like it was in the opposite direction of the way she came.

Lily marched over to it, flinging aside a string of pink flowers dangling from a crooked tree. She found herself on a cobbled path, and her feet came together. She'd never seen this path before.

A tune filled her ears, loud enough to tickle along her spine, poke at her insides, and wave her forward.

She spun, drawing her gun and aiming it at a being she knew was behind her.

The moment she saw two youthful fairies standing there with pure white hair, rich red coats inlaid with gold buttons, and glittering blue eyes, she knew she should have run instead.

One of them lowered a flute from his lips. His mouth curled into a twisted smile.

"Hello, Lily Baker," he said.

CHAPTER

14

Mycra Sentorious

What Followed: Part I

No one noticed when Lily Baker's rhythms tumbled into turmoil. Mycra watched the human's lashes flutter. Watched her spin around. Watched her leave the fire and sneak into the maze of trunks darkened by the morning's shadows.

And so, as the Brotherhood of Assassins devised a plan for which Shadow Fairy would transport which traveller, Mycra slipped away on silent toes to follow.

Lily must have been moving fast—Mycra couldn't find her right away. She smelled the changes in the air, followed the trail of warmth and worry. She hoped the human wasn't vomiting, but it seemed she may have been by the vibrations in the...

Mycra froze by a crystal rock face. She heard Lily's rhythms again, but something was wrong. The scents bled together with a familiar terror and, though something inside Mycra told her to flee, she leaped around the rock onto a stone path, reaching behind her for her spear.

There rested Lily Baker, collapsed. Her eyes were closed, her flesh was blueing, her breathing was shallow.

"Lily!" Mycra dropped beside the human and shook her shoulders. She turned to scream into the woods, to call for Lily's allies, but a net of sticky web came over Mycra, and a hand slapped over her mouth.

She thrashed as she was wrangled like an animal, the ropes tightening with every movement. Her spear was torn from her hands, and a dark, icy voice whispered into her ear; one she'd hoped she would never hear again.

"Welcome back, Dreamslipper. You've been busy."

"I'll destroy you," she said through his fingers, "if you take me back there."

A light chuckle followed. "Come Massie. Let's take our prizes back to Father."

15

Dranian Evelry
What Followed: Part II

Dranian instantly missed the energy and power that flowed through his veins when he'd been in control of Cress's gifts. But it was nice to be himself again. Shayne had once told him that all good things come to an end. That must have included unimaginable North power.

Though, he wondered if he might bother Luc for that walnut enchantment recipe. Just in case.

Dranian stared toward the East. He'd never been to the House of Riothin; he'd never imagined he would have a reason to go there, but somewhere beyond the sinking sands and the radish-growing villages, a great castle hosted a vile family who performed dirty practices and loved to murder their foes.

The humans were in trouble. How could Dranian possibly choose between Shayne and their humans? Dranian glanced over his shoulder at

Cress and Mor. The two were certainly strong enough to guard their humans on their own, weren't they? Would anyone really notice if Dranian went after Shayne?

But Shayne had snuck off. Like the first time when he'd not invited Dranian to return to the House of Lyro with him. Now Shayne was going somewhere else, pulling the same tricks for independence, and it put Dranian in a mood.

They'd always done everything together.

"No, Mor. *You're* taking me. I'll not go back with that fox," Cress announced.

"If Luc takes you, I can carry both females at once. And then one of us can come back for Dranian in a few hours," Mor returned.

Luc frowned. "You don't think I can carry two females at once, Trisencor? And why do you think it's alright to leave Dranian here alone? At least leave his fairy guard with him, and we'll both come back for them."

Dranian's brows furrowed when his observations quickly turned into the realization that the females had vanished. He turned all the way around. Luc spoke of the girl with no name, yet he didn't mention where she'd run off to. Dranian's gaze traced her footprints through a spot of mud, and a collection of broken branches at the trees' edge beyond that. He decided to leave travel arrangements to the loud fairies, and he scampered in the direction he imagined the girl with no name had gone.

His nose wrinkled as soon as he came into the woods. His sharp sense of smell seemed to be punishing him with all sorts of forest-y things. He thought he sniffed trouble in the air.

Three more steps in, he was sure of it. He picked up his pace, running, his faeborn chest lifting to a thudding ruckus as he came to a skidding halt on a tunnel-like path. He slapped a hand over his mouth when he beheld what was there.

A short spear lay upon the rocks. Beside it was a gun.

Dranian's hands balled into fists as they shook.

CHAPTER

16

Luc Zelsor
What Followed: Part III

All bickering nonsense between Mor and Cressica came to an end when a shout lifted from the trees just a fruit's toss away. Luc's hand slapped over his pocket where his fox bead was—he wasn't even sure why. It was the tone of the cry, he supposed.

Anguished. Fierce. Growling.

Dranian's.

Luc left.

The wind was thick as he leapt out, appearing at Dranian's side in the forest where the strange signs of a struggle littered the air, and… yes, just a wee, tiny spot of fairy blood was left on a flat stone.

Someone had been smacked.

Mor appeared beside Luc with Cress in his grip, but Luc hardly saw them as he stared at where Dranian was on his knees, clutching to himself a gun that had been pointed at Luc enough times for him to recognize, and a spear belonging to that sightly fairy who'd turned up out of nowhere several days ago.

Oh dear. This wasn't good.

Luc whirled to Mor. He grabbed him, and the two of them soared back into the woods, landing on their feet in the cover of a spindly tree trunk cove.

"Let me fix this," Luc said while Mor was still blinking back the shock, possibly still realizing what was happening. "You need me," Luc added. "Let me fix this, Trisencor," he said again.

Luc prided himself on his ability to jest and fool and meddle with others' emotions. But this wasn't that. He looked into Mor's brown-silver eyes as serious as ever—not because he wanted this horrid opportunity with bad odds, but because this was perhaps the one thing that would give him what he *really* wanted.

Mor's vision finally cleared. His gaze narrowed on Luc.

"Let me handle things here. Go home to dear Violet. I will fix this problem." Luc was sure he sounded like he was begging, and he bit down on his tongue after he said it.

"You don't fix problems, Luc. You make them. You're going to make everything worse—just stay out of this," Mor commanded.

Luc set his jaw and grabbed Mor's shoulder. At first, Mor blinked in surprise, until Luc flashed a broad smile. "Who's better at finding a solution than a fox?" he asked. "I'm the cleverest fairy you've ever met. Give me a chance to prove it."

A muscle shifted in Mor's jaw. "What's in it for you?" he asked.

"What's in it for..." Luc shut his mouth. He tried not to bite back with a sharp comment. Then, he dropped his hand from Mor and straightened out his coat. He couldn't *believe* it had come to this, but he said, "If I find a way to fix this, I want to be King of the High Court of the Coffee Bean."

"What?!" Mor growled. "Shayne's hardly gone and you're already trying to take his place?" He pushed Luc back a step. "You can't be a king just because you want to be, Luc! That's not how the world works."

Luc *almost* laughed in his face. "Trisencor, you have no idea how the world works. If you did, you'd have been able to keep your brothers and humans out of all this trouble."

He would have also realized that Luc didn't care one bit about being King of the stupid High Court of the Coffee Bean.

"Now," Luc brushed a few fluffs from Mor's chest and shoulders, "take Cressica and go home. We both know Dranian won't leave anymore, *so*, Dranian and I will stay and handle this."

A fire lived in Mor's expression; a series of pulling muscles and tipsy frowns. Just once, Luc would have liked to hear the turmoil that went on inside Mor's head.

Mor glanced with heavy eyes toward where they'd left Cress to deal with Dranian on the path. And by that one look, Luc knew he had him. "This isn't about you wanting to boast of your fox gifts, is it?" Mor asked, though it was more like a statement.

So, Mor did remember.

It was a relief. Luc was beginning to assume Mor was an idiot. An idiot who didn't recall that not long ago, Luc had promised that one day he would prove himself.

"If I don't bring Dranian and Lily Baker home, I'll leave the human realm like you want so badly, and I swear I'll never return," Luc swore. He reached out his hand, ready to bargain away his apartment, his dog, and his ice cream shop.

The moment the words left his lips, Luc's throat constricted. His other hand brushed over his chest where his last foxtail was hidden away. He decided not to mention that he had absolutely no idea how he was going to pull this off. He'd been waiting for a miracle from the sky deities for a week while living on the cusp of extinction himself. But as usual, the sky deities didn't care much for the fox. Not in his childling years, not now.

But Luc had always made his own luck.

Mor stared *way* too long.

"Why does it seem like there's a clock ticking over your head and soon you'll explode?" It was a very random, yet *very* accurate question.

"Oh dear." Luc considered his answer. "I just need some time to deal with a personal matter. And then I'll get right to fixing everything," he promised.

Mor's jaw hardened. "Lily won't have *time*."

"Trusting me is better than nothing. You need me," Luc stated. "Let me do this one thing, Trisencor. Either way, you'll get something you want in the end."

Mor looked like he was going to be sick for several moments. But when Luc extended his hand, to his surprise, Mor shook it.

CHAPTER

17

Cressica Alabastian
What Followed: Part IV

Dranian's mind was somewhere else. Cress talked at him, over and over, yet the fairy still wouldn't move from where he knelt on the ground, staring ahead at the empty path in the forest.

Finally, Cress shoved him off balance.

"Wake up, you fool," he said. "I need you to come to your senses! Where is Lily?!"

Dranian caught himself on his palm. He finally dragged his attention over to Cress.

Mor leapt out of the air, his feet landing on the cobblestones with a thud, and Cress slapped a hand over his heart. "You startled me," he scolded. "What is going on here, Mor? And where did you just go?"

"The Lyro House is on the move," Mor said. There was something in his gaze Cress didn't like when he added, "We have to split up." Mor dropped to a knee and put a hand on Dranian's shoulder. "We're leaving you here for now, Dranian. Keep your faeborn-cursed head on straight. And..." Mor's mouth seemed all twisty and pinched. "Stay with Luc," he finished.

"What?" Cress put his hands on his hips. "Don't be outrageous, Mor. We're not leaving Dranian here."

"You read the note. If Lyro decided to show up early, they might already have Violet and Kate," Mor said.

Cress closed his mouth. A gust of icy power slithered through his veins, making the blossoms around the forest curl inward in terror. A snap of lightning cracked over the sky, followed by a ground-rumbling roar of thunder. "Then they shall all die," he stated. He didn't have a chance to turn and scan the trees for Luc before Mor grabbed his arm.

"Agreed. Let's go."

Cress was tugged into an airstream, becoming a fairy in the wind. He held his breath, only sucking in when absolutely necessary. Though he hated airslipping, he could only think of one thing over the hours it took to reach the human realm gate and the following minutes they spent soaring across the city.

Cress was dumped on the sidewalk before Fae Café. Mor didn't wait around for him—the fairy vanished back into the air.

Sounds of car horns and chatty humans washed over the street, filling Cress with the same smells of the realm's nearby breakfast diner, the Sisterhood's repulsive yarn store, and the bread bakery down the road.

He listened first, tilting his head toward his café where he immediately sensed Kate was. He didn't hear a struggle. He didn't sniff fear or ill intent seeping from the cracks. In fact, a couple came out the door of the café, ringing the familiar bell as the door closed behind them. They were smiling. They were happy.

Even so.

Cress flung the door open and marched in. He looked around at the cozy atmosphere: the crackling fireplace in the corner, the coffee brewing behind the counter, all the bistro tables freshly washed, and a deli-cious-looking, steaming pie resting behind the glass display.

Kate turned when she noticed him. "You're back," she said with the brightest, most reassuring smile Cress had ever seen in his entire exist-ence.

He marched to the counter, rounded it, and he grabbed her. He pulled Kate in and held her tight, his faeborn heart mimicking a wild beast's as it slammed. He worried she'd feel it.

"Ugh," she said as her face smooshed against his broad chest. "Seri-ously, Cress? I just did my hair," she complained, trying to reach around his burly arms to smooth it down. "What's going on with you?"

"Not a thing, Katherine," he said. He set his jaw and glanced out the window at where clueless humans ventured down the street in small flocks. He dared the House of Lyro to try and come for Katherine Lewis.

His human.

The female who'd given him a simple life.

His simple human.

CHAPTER

18

Mor Trisencor
What Followed: Part V

The cathedral was far too quiet. Mor's chest thundered as he landed at the foot of the stairs. As he beheld the great towers of windows and steeples and boarded-up shutters. As he marched to the doors and flung them open and made his way inside.

"Violet!" he shouted.

He didn't have the patience to stop and listen, to try and pick up a tone, or...

"Hmm?" Violet peeked her head out of the kitchen. A large mixing spoon stuck out of her mouth. Her hair was pulled into a wild ponytail and the remains of some chocolate atrocity were speckled around her mouth.

She pulled out the giant spoon. "What's wrong?" She came all the way out of the kitchen in her slippers, and it took Mor several moments of staring at her in her stretched sweater and jeans with large holes in the knees, before it dawned on him that it was the weekend, and she was dressed that way on purpose and not because she'd been attacked or wrangled.

He swallowed. "You look…"

Violet glanced down at her outfit, then snorted. "I didn't want to get batter on my blouse," she said. "Come here and try these muffins."

Mor closed his eyes as his pulse settled. The rock-hard tension in his shoulders drained, and his hands unclasped from the fists he had them in.

Then he said, "I'd rather not."

THE
BACKSTORIES
THE
& FRONTSTORIES

19

Shayne Lyro and How it All Began in the House of Lyro

Shayne and Panola were enemies. In some ways, it was because they were natural opposites. Panola aimed to make the biggest ruckus of any Lyro whenever she could, always causing trouble, always laughing at inappropriate moments—including once during a political debate at the Silver Senate Tower. And Shayne was a more mischievous childling. He kept his ruckus quiet and secret. He never let on that he was the one behind the things he did. It was funnier that way, even if he did wish he could be loud sometimes like her.

At least, that was how it all was in the beginning.

Fairy nobles labelled Panola easily. "That female," they'd say, "is the Lyro troublemaker. What a commotion she makes everywhere she goes. If only someone taught her how to be quiet."

Little did they know that half the mischief Panola was accused of was really Shayne's doing as he giggled from the side and watched the drama unfold. Panola always took the blame. It seemed she didn't care. That defending herself was more work than her breath was worth. It wasn't a sport, exactly, but there was certainly competition involved when she would retaliate against Shayne later. And it wasn't that fun to compete, either—it was just something to do.

But on a crisp, sunny morning of their pre-teen years, Shayne came out of the maze in the House and overheard Panola arguing with Kahn-Der in the dining room, and everything that was once fun became infected by the same virus Kahn-Der infected everything with.

"You're an embarrassment, Panola. You must learn how to hold your tongue, or you'll lose it!" Kahn-Der scolded.

Shayne remained by the doors, watching through a slender crack as Panola threw her head back and laughed. "You think I'm an embarrassment? What about you, Brother? What about how Father has passed over you and means to hand the title of heir to one of us instead?"

The look that came over Kahn-Der's face was priceless. However, Shayne was too busy hosting his own startlement to revel in it. It was the first he'd heard anything about his father's selection. The first he had even an inkling that he or one of his siblings might be forced to step over Kahn-Der to take a High Lord's seat.

Shayne certainly wouldn't do it. Kahn-Der could have the title. Shayne would tell their father that if he was asked.

But Kahn-Der smiled at Panola crookedly. His icy eyes narrowed. "You don't really think he'd choose *you*, do you?" He stepped in a little.

Panola grunted. "Why would he choose me? I make noise, Brother. I throw fits and bring trouble wherever I go. I've worked very hard to ensure that I do not *ever* become the heir. But he won't choose you either. You're reckless and murderous, and I'm loud and embarrassing." She folded her thin arms. "And father would never hand over the chair to Jethwire who gambles away everything he owns, or Massie who's so terribly warped and cruel and tortures any living thing he comes across for fun." She laughed. "Don't you see, Brother? He'll choose Shayne. Shayne is the only Lyro with a sound mind. At least, that's what I've made sure Father thinks."

Shayne drifted back from the doors. He slowly lifted a hand and pressed it over his lips as those words sank in. This had to be a rumour; Hans-Der couldn't possibly pass over Kahn-Der and choose an alternative heir. Kahn-Der was the oldest. Kahn-Der was the most menacing. Kahn-Der always got what he wanted.

"You're lying," Kahn-Der said from the dining room. "Father is planning no such thing." But his voice wavered, a spool of anger unravelling as he seemed to think it through.

Panola smiled, her curling pink lips assuring Kahn-Der that she already knew this for certain, that she had perhaps come by the information to confirm it. "He will announce it tomorrow. And I will watch how you take the news from my seat." Her grin widened.

Kahn-Der bit his lower lip, his flesh tight over his body. Then he said, "I'll kill you for even suggesting such a thing if you're making this up."

Panola grunted. Then she turned, and to the whole House, she shouted, "Let's die together then! Tonight!" The invitation echoed down the hallways, making lesser fairies turn and bringing Massie out of his bedroom far down the hall. Shayne was sure there wasn't a single soul in the House who hadn't heard.

Panola leaned in toward Kahn-Der and added in a whisper, "If you really think I'm making this up."

The two stared at each other—crystal blue eyes and solemn faces. Until Panola smiled. And that gloating little reaction cost her.

Kahn-Der grabbed her by her Lyro coat.

Shayne burst into the room. "What are you doing?" he demanded as Kahn-Der dragged Panola across the dining room. Panola only laughed.

"Don't stop him, Brother!" she called to Shayne. "He doesn't have what it takes to be an heir, and he doesn't have what it takes to destroy me, either." She was yanked into the side entrance stairwell that led up to the pagoda roof.

Shayne decided to let them go. He shook his head as the sounds of her laughter echoed down the stairs. He turned to head back to his room, grabbing a handful of squish fruits on his way. He shoved them into his mouth and chewed them the whole walk back through the maze.

Panola was just trying to rile Kahn-Der up. Shayne had never been more sure of anything. He decided not to be worried about his sister's claims—about the idea that their father would hand the role of heir to Shayne.

That was, until the next morning when Shayne learned Panola was dead.

Word spread through the House, making the lesser fairy servants stir and putting the hunter fairies on edge. Hans-Der stormed through the spaces, a menacing sight for all to behold. Fairies were questioned; investigators searched rooms. Shayne stayed back and watched as his room was torn apart by hired officials in blue robes.

A trial was held. Hans-Der placed every suspect into a line before his High Lords' seat. Shayne was among them. So was Kahn-Der, Jethwire, and Massie.

Shayne peered over at Massie. The youngest Lyro appeared far too delighted at the sight of all the chaos. Jethwire, too, had reasons to hate Panola. She'd recently ousted him for betting with other young lords and collecting rare, magical items, some of which were banned in the North Corner of Ever.

But though Panola had shouted through the House, only Shayne had *seen* what had happened the day before. And as Kahn-Der leaned forward and glanced down the line, he locked gazes with Shayne. The oldest Lyro brother's icy eyes held a reminder. It was of Panola's voice, saying, *"Let's die together then. Tonight."*

Shayne had stayed quiet throughout the trial. He had not given his testimony. He did not point Kahn-Der's way. He wondered all the while if their father suspected Kahn-Der anyway.

Because the next day, Hans-Der sent an announcement through the House on crimson parchment. It arrived at Shayne's door in the hand of a lesser fairy. The scroll read:

THE HEIR HAS BEEN SELECTED.
SHAYNE LYRO SHALL INHERIT THE HIGHEST CHAIR IN THE
HOUSE.

That marked the day Shayne made a very important discovery.

Panola had never truly been naturally loud or crazy or insolent. She'd been brilliant.

Even as a childling she'd set herself up to avoid the one thing she didn't want. She made sure she'd be free of the chair and the chains that came with it. Panola Lyro would have gotten away with it, too, if she'd just kept her mouth shut one more week.

Shayne dropped his crimson notice in disbelief.

It wasn't too late. He was still young. Eight years was a long time, time enough to convince every watching eye that he was not the quiet, calculated being they knew him to be. It was more than enough time to walk the halls of the House without composure. To shout, and meddle, and attack, and toss tables. And laugh...

Oh, how Shayne wanted to laugh. To be free, like Panola. To be loud, just like her.

"Well done, Sister," he whispered into his dark, ripped-apart bedroom.

And he laughed.

He laughed until his stomach hurt. And then he laughed some more.

The sound of his laughter lifted across his room, through the hall of the maze, filled every nook of the ballroom and the dining room and the basement and the balconies, making heads turn and servants go still.

Perhaps it was because they thought they heard a ghost.

CHAPTER
20

Lily Baker and the Promise

Lily's braids were soaked with rain the day she ran into the hospital lobby. She nearly slipped over the floors from the water on her running shoes. She flew against the reception desk, and the lady there looked her over.

"I'm here for Katherine and Jessica Lewis," she stated. She yanked her hands back when she realized she'd flung droplets of water onto the desk. "They were in a car accident a few hours ago."

The receptionist made a face. "You look too young to be here by yourself. Did you come here with a parent?"

Lily tried to find a response but ended up just staring instead.

What could she say?

"Jessica Lewis is my parent." It wasn't true, even if Lily wished it was. Her fingers curled around the edge of the desk, and she said, "I'm old enough to be here. I'm in high school." Her gaze flickered up to the

receptionist to see if she'd believe it.

The receptionist sat back in her chair. "You can't just come in and visit people without their consent. You need to—"

"Lily!" Grandma Lewis came from a large set of doors. She cast the receptionist a ripe scowl and took Lily's arm. "Come with me. I'll show you where Jessica is. We don't have much time!"

"Much time for what?" Lily wanted to ask, but it seemed wrong to speak.

Grandma Lewis put a warm arm around Lily as they headed back through the doors. She kept it there as they ventured around a curved hallway and went into a room where the soft beeping of equipment filled the space. Lily's chest swelled. She was sure if she cried, Grandma Lewis would be able to tell, even though her cheeks were stained with rain.

Lily halted by the door. Jessica's eyes were closed, a breathing mask over her face. Her skin was covered in thick bruises and swollen to a point of her being nearly unrecognizable. Needles were taped to her arms with tubes that led to medical bags and machines. Only the thunderstorm outside hid Lily's inhale at the sight. Heat filled her eyes, but she blinked back any tears that tried to form.

Grandma Lewis was watching her. Lily didn't realize until she glanced over.

"Why don't you stay with her a minute, and I'll go check on Katherine?" Grandma Lewis patted Lily on the back as she said it. She turned to leave, but she paused at the door, and said, "Give Jessica my love if she wakes."

It was almost like the old woman knew something Lily didn't. But Lily didn't ask as she swept to the bed. As she looked at Jessica up close.

"I heard about..." Lily couldn't even say his name. The man who'd acted as Lily's father for the last year. The one who'd signed her homework book and called the school when she was sick so she could stay home and get better. The one who'd made her chicken soup on her birthday because it was her favourite.

The one who was already confirmed dead.

169

Arthur Lewis.

Lily sniffed back what she could, but the tears couldn't be stopped now. They rolled down her face as she sobbed, placing the back of her wrist tightly against her mouth so no one in the hall would hear.

"I'm so sorry," Lily said. "It's because of me—I think I'm cursed."

She placed both hands over her face and leaned forward on the bed, her cries shaking her body. She couldn't believe this was happening. It was too unreal.

A hand rested on her arm, and Lily lifted her head.

Jessica's eyes were open just a slit. She reached a shaky hand up and removed the breathing device.

"Kate?" she asked. She blinked rapidly and squinted her eyes.

Kate... Lily almost couldn't respond. Kate was somewhere else in the hospital.

Jessica reached out toward Lily, her eyes darting around in odd directions like she couldn't quite figure out where she was. "Kate?" she asked again. There were large red patches on her eyeballs, and one of her irises was extra pale.

"It's just me," Lily said—an apology.

Jessica cracked a weak smile. "Lily," she realized. Lily took her wandering hand and held tight. "Is Kate okay?"

"I think so," Lily said. "I haven't seen her yet. Grandma brought me here first."

Jessica's lips were dry, but she looked like she was trying to smile. "I don't feel well, Lily," she admitted.

"I know." Lily nodded and pursed her lips as her eyes grew warm again.

"I don't think I'll make it to Kate today," Jessica added. She tilted her head and pointed her wavering gaze in Lily's direction. "But I was told she's going to be alright." And then, "Can I ask something of you, Lily?"

"Of course," Lily promised.

It looked painful when Jessica tried to swallow. "It's going to be hard for Kate when she wakes up," she said. "I'm wondering if you can take care of her for a while. Until she's better and can take care of herself." Jessica cracked a smile again. "And keep an eye on Greyson—make sure he stays out of trouble. Stay by their side as long as you can in this life."

Jessica squeezed Lily's hand.

Lily couldn't smile through her puffy face.

Someone loved Kate this much. Lily couldn't remember how long it had been since someone talked about her this way. Jessica and Arthur had come pretty close a number of times. Lily cherished them for it with every piece of her heart.

But then Jessica spoke again, "Survive, Lily Baker. I know you can. Even when life gets hard, there's no one stronger than you. You're a good daughter. You're a good person."

Lily's breath caught.

"Please, Lily…" Jessica's lashes fluttered, her words falling away as her head rolled to the side. A few seconds went by where Lily was too stunned to speak or move. Something began happening to the machines around the room; noises sounded, and Jessica's grip loosened in Lily's hand. But Lily leaned in—Jessica hadn't finished what she was saying.

"J… Jessica?" she asked.

Jessica didn't respond this time.

Lily stared at the woman as nurses rushed in. Lily was shoved, her hand ripping from Jessica's as the nurses surrounded the rolling bed, all shouting in medical language. They pushed Jessica out the door and rushed down the hall.

All at once the hospital room was quiet. Only Lily stood there. Rain lapped against the window. The sky flashed yellow in the distance. The echo of thunder sent vibrations through the hollow space.

It took Lily several minutes to respond. But then she said, "I'll protect them, Jessica. I'll never leave their sides."

She got the news from Grandma Lewis an hour later that Jessica Lewis had died. Lily sat for hours in the hospital waiting room as it dawned on her that every family she'd found had left or sent her away, and the only parents who'd ever wanted to keep her had died.

She never told Kate about Jessica's final words. She worried Kate would be hurt if she found out Lily had been with her mother in her last moments and Kate had missed it all.

"Survive, Lily Baker... there's no one stronger than you. You're a good daughter. You're a good person."

Little did Jessica Lewis know that those words would become the spark in Lily's heart. That they'd be the fuel that would get Lily out of bed in the morning in the days and years that followed. That one phrase of truth by a loving mother would be the anthem she heard when she pulled on her police vest in the morning, the testimony she believed when trouble would come her way. The inspiration for the works of art on her flesh; the victory seals for every year she survived on her own after that. And she wore her paint like armour.

CH*A*PTER

21

Lily Baker and the Present Days that Followed

The soft smell of sweet metal filled Lily's nose as she was gently shaken awake. Her mouth was dry, her ears rang, and her head throbbed in pulses. She moaned as she opened her eyes, but the sound drifted away when she fixed her gaze on a set of blue eyes and a shock of white hair.

She thought it was Shayne. She almost said his name.

But her vision sharpened as the being's face spread into a twisted smile. And she realized this person leaning over her was the furthest thing from Shayne that existed.

"Hello, Human." The greeting had a musical pitch.

Lily inhaled shallow breaths as she looked around, finding herself in a room with dragons carved out of dark wood in the bedposts and dressers, and rich crimson curtains at the window. She couldn't remember how she got here.

Where were the baristas? Why wasn't she home with Kate?

A fuzzy memory flooded in of looking for her sweater in the forest. Of coming face-to-face with...

This fairy who sat at the foot of the bed.

"Where am I?" she demanded. Her voice cracked.

"Get up, Human, and I'll show you." The fairy's cold gaze narrowed. Then, when Lily didn't rise, he said, "Lily Baker, I said *get up*."

A gasp slipped out as Lily found herself sitting, tossing the covers off, and jumping out of the bed. She looked down at herself in horror, not sure how she even did it. It was like someone had tied puppet strings to her limbs and was jerking her around.

The fairy reached for the pillow she'd been lying on and carefully lifted a pinecone. He turned it over in his fingers. "You're quite a mess, Human. You brought half the forest in with you. We'll have to get you cleaned up." He tossed the pinecone back to the comforter. "I hope you enjoyed your beauty sleep in my brother's bed."

Brother.

Lily glanced back at the pillow. Was this Shayne's bed?

"There are just my brothers waiting for you at the other end of that song," Shayne had said.

The white hair, wide smiles, and deep blue eyes made it clear where she was.

"If you ever go see my brothers by choice, I won't go after you. I won't help you. I'll leave, and you'll never see me again." Shayne had also said that; like his brothers were so awful, he couldn't imagine facing them. Like he'd decided once and for all he would stay far away from them, regardless of what happened.

Lily's neck grew hot, her nerves standing on end. She hadn't come to see his brothers by choice—had she? She hadn't actually followed the music through the woods to them.

She studied the room, eyeing the window spoked with iron bars in particular. There wasn't much in the space, just a few books in a corner, an empty mannequin meant to hold a robe or coat, and...

A gilded crossbow hanging on the wall.

"Follow me," the fairy said as he headed for the door, and Lily's feet jolted after him. She tried to stop walking—she slapped her hands over her knees, but her legs kept moving forward. She tailed the fairy through a series of halls that all looked the same. She examined the walls, the floors, the mirrors, trying to mark her path so she could find her way back to escape, but after seven turns, she realized there was no way out of this labyrinth without a map.

Before she knew it, Lily stood in a wide room with bamboo-framed windows and a hot, steaming bath in the middle. Opposite the bath, a long red dress was fitted to a mannequin. Lily stared at the bath. The dress. Then she shook her head. "I'm not getting into that glorified water trough, and I'm definitely not wearing *that*," she stated, nodding to the dress.

"You'll do what I tell you," the fairy assured. "Now get clean and get dressed. And don't try to run. You have exactly ten minutes." He *winked*.

"Seriously?" Lily objected as she grabbed her own shirt. She whirled around to hide herself as she pulled it off, but when she glanced back at the door, she realized the fairy was already gone. She lifted her hands in front of her, cursing them for moving against her will. Then she proceeded to undress and sink into the bath. It was warm, and she should have been relieved after not being able to shower for days on end. But there was nothing natural about how she scrubbed herself clean and used the nearby soap on her hair, then dried with a towel and put on the dress.

What must have been exactly ten minutes later, the fairy returned. He found his twisted smile as he looked her over. Then he said, "Time for your commencement. Come, Human."

Commencement.

Lily hopped after him in bare feet since he hadn't provided shoes, and she followed him back through the network of halls to a great, wide room sprawling with crystal windows, enormous statues, and stunning murals across the walls. The carpet below her feet was rimmed with gold, and she stared at it all in amazement as she was led toward a platform where several throne-like chairs rested in a half circle. The one in the middle was the biggest.

A handsome, middle-aged fairy sat in it.

The man was the spitting image of Shayne, only older. He wore a wreath of twisted silver twigs with lively emerald leaves around his white-haired head.

All the fairies were here—the ones Lily had wanted to look in the eyes. Shayne's brothers, his childhood friends, his father. The despicable people who'd disowned him, then forced him back and tormented him. She found herself locking gazes with the man on the chair who had to be Shayne's father. Then she took in a younger white-haired fairy in another seat, and last, she eyed the fairy standing beside her. He held a flute in his left hand that Lily hadn't noticed until now.

"Shayne, what did these people do to you?" she wanted to ask. *"How can I make them pay for their crimes?"* She felt naked without her gun.

"She's perfect," the middle-aged fairy said from his seat. "I can almost taste her defiance. What an interesting flavour! The stubborn ones are the most fun to break, aren't they?" he asked the other fairies in the room. "She'll make a perfect peace offering once we're done with her."

Lily's arms went slack at her sides. She tried to gather information: a fruit bowl rested on an end table nearby, several fairies in rough-looking brown gowns were on a knee below the platform as if waiting for orders, and there was a leer on the face of the fairy with the flute at her side.

Still, Lily couldn't deduce what *"once we're done with her"* meant. There weren't enough clues.

The fairies in brown began moving. One brought the bowl of fruit and held it before Shayne's brother with the flute. The brother reached in and lifted a plump purple fruitlet. He turned toward Lily, but her hand flew up and she grasped his wrist before he could place it against her lips.

"Are you crazy?" she demanded. "You think I can eat right now?"

The fairy laughed, and it started a chain reaction that sent all the other fairies laughing through the room until the sound of it was deafening.

"We're all a little crazy here," he admitted. "And yes, I think you'll eat every one of these right now." His eyes glittered as he took the whole bowl into his hands instead and extended it to her. "Eat up, Human," he said, passing it over. He pressed the flute beneath her chin and tilted her face upward. Then he gazed into her eyes and said, "I want to see you dance."

Lily found her hand clasping around a fruit. She brought it to her lips while the fairy held eye contact, and she took a large bite, sweet and sour juices spearing into her mouth. She couldn't look away from his gaze, like a tether was holding her to him and her eyelids were stuck open.

"Didn't my brother ever teach you not to look a fairy in the eyes?" he asked with a chuckle.

Lily couldn't respond as she ate. As she ate and ate and continued to take new fruits from the bowl the moment she finished the one before. Warmth burned behind her eyes as they went dry from staring for so long. And then the threat of tears arose, but she swallowed her croak harder than she swallowed her food. She would *not* cry in front of these devils for anything.

However, she did beg. Not at first, but ten fruits in.

"Make it stop," she breathed. "Make me stop doing this, you psycho! ...*Please*."

The fairies laughed again in a chorus. And then, when the bowl was finally empty and Lily collapsed, holding tight to her stomach and fighting a rush of nausea, her toes began to curl and flex as she got the sudden urge to dance. It was the last clear thought that was still her own.

It went on for hours.

Then it went on for days.

She lost track of how long it all went on for; the eating, the dancing, the wavering songs, the teetering room, the voices, the laughs. But at some point amidst the blurs of music and feasting and twirling, she noticed the daily pattern of a golden sun rising, followed by a burning sunset casting light across the floor—her only indication of passing time.

But eventually, Lily was hardly able to see anything. The room spun even when she stood still. She teetered when she tried to stand straight and could never find her footing. She wanted to sleep more than anything. There were points where she was sure she was in and out of dreams, not fully awake but not actually sleeping either.

"Tie her with ribbons, put a wreath on her head, and sprinkle her with glitter!" The voice slipped through the haze and planted itself upon Lily's consciousness. "Let's prepare our peace offering."

Cold hands took Lily's arms and legs. There was a time when she might have kicked or screamed in a situation like this. But she hardly recalled her own name anymore, let alone how to fight. The only things that reminded her of who she was were the pictures depicted on her arms in ink. Sometimes she would look at those tattoos or read the names hidden within them, and she would manage to catch a thought through the haze, recalling a part of a story she was pretty sure was hers. But most days, she only knew food and dancing.

There was one exception. Somehow, she remembered Shayne's name. Every time she saw white hair and blue eyes in her blurry vision, she hoped it was him.

It was never him.

22

Shayne Lyro and the House of Riothin

He wasn't dead yet.

It was likely only a matter of time.

Shayne twirled a gold spoon in his glass of citrus, watching the fruity liquid move to the rhythm of the loud tune pulsing from the band working a variety of instruments Shayne wanted to smash. They weren't bad at playing their harps and lyres and beast skin drums, but the noise had a particular magical edge to it Shayne guessed was meant to pleasure Riothin's true allies and repulse his secret enemies throughout the room.

Shayne hadn't considered himself Lord Riothin's secret enemy at first. In fact, he'd come in sincerity to make an alliance. But he realized rather quickly that the House of Riothin was completely designed to weed out traitors or anyone with secrets or ulterior motives.

Shayne was probably all three of those things.

The scents of the House riled him. The water he used for bathing was ice cold to him. The music sounded sharp in his faeborn ears. And yet, he had to pretend through it all that he wasn't having problems with the smells, the water, or the music, lest he be figured out and dragged before the Lord in cold iron shackles.

It was a true Yule tidings miracle he hadn't been snapped in half the moment he reached the front gate seven days ago, smacked his fist against the great House doors to knock, and started loudly calling for the revered High Lord. If anyone apart from Meave Riothin had arrived at the gate and laid eyes upon him first, he'd certainly be a fairy corpse. But naturally, Meave liked what she saw when the gate was opened and Shayne was standing there, leaning against the stone frame like a god, sweeping a hand through his wool-white hair, and flashing the most delicious smile the female had likely ever seen with her wicked green eyes.

Meave Riothin; the second-eldest daughter of Lord Macewite Riothin. Next in line to be married after her older sister had been sold off in a bargain to form an alliance with one of the thirteen Low Princes of the South. In return, her father had been given a powerful army to wield in the South Corner, should he ever need it.

Meave was an easy target. The female was practically begging to be rebellious. Marrying the enemy was at the top of her 'to do' list in the foreseeable future.

That part had been easy. It was everything after that became difficult to bear. And it wasn't just the House repelling him with its natural safeguards and fairy charms, it was the people inside it, too.

Shayne stopped stirring his citrus and placed his spoon on the table. He leaned back in his chair and watched the dancing filling the room, right to the tall windows where fairies who passed by were meant to see the fun those in the House were having and grow envious.

A warm elftouch traced along the back of his shoulders. He pretended not to notice it.

Unfortunately, it happened again.

Shayne sighed. He turned in his seat and searched the sitting area for Meave. He found her watching him with a puffy-lipped smile. He gave her a cute little wave and winked. Then he begged the sky deities to keep her from coming over and asking him to dance. The dance floor was probably covered in tiles that would make the secret-keeping enemies of Riothin feel itchy and hot or some other atrocity.

He turned back to his citrus but found a noisy, nasty, black-haired menace instead.

Cosmo Flora sat across from him at the table. The fairy looked re-laxed with one arm slung over the backrest of the chair beside him, which was remarkable considering Shayne had only been turned around for a second and Cosmo looked like he'd been in that casual position for a hundred thousand years. The gold-braided wreath atop his head was crooked in an intentional, stylish way, and his picturesque, sultry smile made Shayne shiver in extra disgust.

Also, Cosmo was a heartless forest hog, and Shayne wished he could feed him bread in his sleep.

But Shayne smiled instead. Because only a perfect face with a perfect smile was weapon enough to stand up to the sultry smile of a heartless forest hog.

Cosmo reached for a cream-nut from a nearby dish. Not to eat it, of course, but to roll it around in his fingers like a godless fool.

"I don't trust you one bit," Cosmo said.

"Good. I don't trust you either." Shayne turned his smile extra flashy, even offering a cute nose scrunch with it. "But we don't have to trust each other. We only need to tolerate each other."

"Do we?" Cosmo laughed and chucked the cream-nut back into the dish. "What is it that you want with my cousin, Shayne *Lyro*? And how did you get Meave to notice you in the first place? She's quite cold and unwilling to give any male a chance these days. But she demanded my uncle not slay you. Yet."

"The attraction happened naturally," Shayne lied. "I have no idea what she saw in me."

Yes he did. He knew exactly what she saw, which was unrestrained gorgeousness, a smile to die for, and irresistible ex-assassin muscles.

Cosmo was just blind. And stupid.

Shayne chewed on his tongue as it tingled. Then he said, "And for your information, I came here for an authentic marriage bargain. I've betrayed my House. I have no reason to go back."

Cosmo angled his head. "I still think you're a Lyro spy."

Shayne grinned. "Your uncle thinks I'm an asset he can use against my House. And it really only matters what *he* thinks. Lucky me." He lifted his citrus to his lips, and he guzzled.

Cosmo rose from the seat. His finger glided over the table as he did, and when his hand reached a full goblet of citrus…

He nudged it over.

The entirety of its contents spilled across the table, rushing over the tablecloth and splattering all over Shayne's borrowed garments. A few fairies down the table giggled, but Cosmo roared in laughter that soared across the great hall and made heads turn.

Most fairies would have growled in outrage, but Shayne smiled. Chuckled. He flung off all the liquid he could, and he lifted from his seat. "Since it's clear you're trying to provoke me, I accept your challenge," he said to Cosmo. "Let's play."

Cosmo smothered a grin. "You'll never defeat me in this House." He waved a hand around at the décor and ambiance that all seemed to support him because of his heritage and alliance, and Shayne wondered if Cosmo had caught on to Shayne's secret difficulties with the smells and water and everything else. "But sure. I'd love to face off with a Lyro in a game of tricks. I'll defend the name of Riothin until my dying breath." He said it loud enough for those around to hear. "But let's make a bargain. If, after ten days, the House votes that I overcame you in easy tricks…" The way Cosmo smiled made it obvious he was fighting laughter as he let the words hang.

Shayne was a breath away from saying, *"No bargains,"* but he waited, worried he'd be scrutinized for refusing a Riothin relative before all these witnesses when the game had only begun.

"…You'll be the being we play around with for entertainment on the day of Yule."

Shayne grunted and sat back down in his seat. He brought his citrus to his lips. "What sort of beings do you usually play around with?" he asked around the glass before tipping the last of his citrus into his mouth.

"Humans," Cosmo said.

The citrus hit the back of Shayne's throat, and he spat it across the table. He dragged his wide eyes up to Cosmo as the drips rolled down his chin. He wiped them away with his sleeve.

It shouldn't have surprised him. It was what fairies did; ridicule and torment the 'lesser' species. There was a time when Shayne had hardly noticed what happened to humans who'd wandered too close to the fairy realm gates or, sky deities forbid, had been captured from their own world. Growing up in a rich household had given Shayne a front row seat on two or three occasions to such 'fun'. He hadn't cared for it as a childling.

He especially didn't care for it now.

"D…" Shayne bit his tongue, cursing it for how he stuttered. "Do you have one now?" he asked.

He shouldn't care. Whoever it was, this human wasn't one he knew or had agreed to protect.

Queensbane, what if Cosmo and the Riothin House had *many* humans?

Cosmo sniffed a laugh. "A what? A *human*?"

Shayne closed his mouth. He needed to stop asking questions if he didn't want to die today. "Never mind," he said. "I'll take your bargain. Let's have the House vote after ten days." He stood again, extending his hand across the table. "But if I win, I want *you* to become the Yule cele- bration's entertainment." How delightful it would be to see this fool humiliated before this entire House.

Cosmo nodded with a grin. "Maybe you're not so bad, Lyro. I think you might become fun for us." He shook Shayne's hand. The forest hog's fingers were too warm for comfort.

"I look forward to it," Shayne promised.

Also, 'fun' was Shayne's middle name.

"And no, we have no humans for the Yule day celebrations. Our scouts are on the hunt for some though, if you happen to know of any."

Shayne shook his head. "None at all."

A series of chimes clattered and the noise in the room hushed. Two large curtains were drawn to reveal the great Lord Riothin in a rich cobalt-blue coat. His black beard was braided at his front and his long hair was braided at his back, creating a remarkably symmetrical fae. People applauded politely as he entered the first Yule dance revelry, and Shayne followed suit even though he cringed at the sharp sounds of the chimes that rang in his ears long after they stopped making noise.

As soon as the High Lord was seated, Shayne swept far from Cosmo's presence and made his way around the tables. He paused when he was just an arm's length from Lord Riothin. It wasn't that he was intimidated, it was just that a hundred terrible rumours swirled in Shayne's head every time he got within reach of the male.

Rumours about Lord Macewite Riothin hunting the innocent on conquests that left entire villages in ashes and childlings without homes. About him dragging back some of those childlings to the House and turning them into lesser fairy servants. About how he often locked his servants away in dark rooms for making mistakes and sometimes he forgot about them for so long, they died.

Shayne took in a deep breath and let it out slowly. Truly, some High Lords deserved to be chucked off the nearest cliff to meet the sea dragons. Unfortunately, Shayne had heard so many terrible stories about this *particular* High Lord as a childling, he'd had recurring nightmares about being dragged off by him to the House of Riothin.

This House.

Shayne slid into the empty seat beside the High Lord. As soon as he did, Meave appeared on the opposite side of the table and took the seat across from him. Shayne flashed her a dashing smile. Her presence was probably for the best, since Lord Riothin almost always gave her whatever she wanted.

"I didn't see you there," Lord Riothin said to Shayne in his deep, dark voice. "What have you learned about my House so far, Shayne Lyro?"

Shayne *Lyro*.

Lyro, Lyro, *Lyro*.

They always called him *Lyro* around here.

"I'm not sure. I haven't really been taking notes." Shayne folded his hands and relaxed them atop the table. "You know I only came here to stick it to my own House. I imagined I'd just have fun and see what I could offer you while I'm at it."

Lord Riothin released a dry laugh. "So you say." He waved over one of the servants carrying a tray of spiked citrus. Shayne accidentally watched the servant a little too hard as she bowed before the High Lord and passed him a drink with shaking hands. Her feet were bare, probably cold in this weather. Normally Shayne would have been jealous of someone in bare feet, but not her.

He dragged his gaze back to Lord Riothin, and he leaned in. "I wonder if you've had time to send word to my House?" he asked. He pulled his hands beneath the table and clasped them.

"Not yet." Lord Riothin lifted his citrus and sipped. The way his eyes moved over the room made it clear he was aware of every single thing happening under his roof.

Shayne sat back. He bit down on his lips to keep himself from blurting something irrational. He settled on, "I wonder why you don't want to show off to my father that you've gained me as an ally? His own son? I'm sure you wish to see the House of Lyro humiliated as much as I do."

He began tapping his fingers against his knees. All at once, Shayne's mind went to Fae Café—a place he hadn't thought of in days, except for the moments when he dreaded that Hans-Der Lyro or his blood brothers had sent scouts into the human realm to seize his humans. His faeborn chest grew tight just imagining it. *All he had to do* was convince this man sitting before him to send a letter to the Lyro House informing them of Riothin's new alliance with Shayne, and they'd refrain from sending scouts or kidnappers into the human world. Every hour that went by made Shayne's skin crawl more at the thought that he might already be too late. It had already been a week.

"I'm in no rush," Lord Riothin stated.

Shayne nodded slowly. He turned to face Meave, swallowing his disappointment.

He would try again tomorrow.

"Would you like to dance, Shayne Lyro?" Meave asked from across the table.

"Of course he would," Lord Riothin stated. It sounded very much like a command, and Shayne flinched. It was like he was back to being a childling, stuck in a nightmare of this man's House. Only he was wide awake, living it.

This morning, Shayne had witnessed a youthful servant being dragged away at the High Lord's order and locked in the dusty East-wing attic. Shayne couldn't pass judgement though when his family had done many equal evils. But he still didn't like it. He didn't like overhearing the whispered rumours among the House staff of Riothin's cruelty. He didn't enjoy pretending to like a fairy who made his servants jump in terror and made young fairies tremble in his presence.

But Shayne ignored the rumours, ignored the sight of the fellow dragged to the East-wing attic, ignored the whispers. He wasn't here to do anything about it. He wasn't here to save the day.

He was here to survive.

And so, he rose from the table, he offered Meave his hand, and he danced until the moon came out.

The first order of business when the sun came up was to catch Cosmo off guard. One bonus about the fairies who ruled the House of Riothin was that they all slept in. Only Shayne was up before the sun, and he'd made good use of his time.

The morning feast was hot and delicious, and for the first time in days, Shayne ate well, slurping up cooked bird eggs in sugar cream, and gobbling down crisp beast meat in pepper sauce. The only thing the meal was missing was coffee.

He patted his stomach when he was finished and sat back in his chair to wait.

Sure enough, when the feasting table was nearly filled and only a few empty seats remained, Cosmo entered the banquet hall. His eyes were still half closed from sleep, his pristine coat was open, hanging off one shoulder and flapping slightly with his lazy strides, and, of course, an enormous mustache was scribbled over his top lip and a pair of human glasses were carefully drawn around his eyes with ink.

Shayne pressed a fist over his mouth so he wouldn't laugh out loud.

No, it wasn't exactly a trick. It was more of a lousy prank. But it was also a statement to remind Cosmo that Shayne could get to him while he helplessly slept, and therefore, it was worth every drop of ink Shayne had traded his last two arrows for.

Cosmo tugged a chair out and sat down. He looked around the table to see what the breakfast feast options were. Fairies around him began to place hands over their lips to hide giggles and release shallow gasps. It took Cosmo far too long to clue in, and even when he did, he was so confused by the attention that he simply sat there and blinked like a fool.

"Cosmo," Shayne drawled as he ran a finger over the rim of his goblet. "Do you not even look in the mirror in the mornings?"

That was it. At least a dozen fairies burst out laughing around the feasting table.

Cosmo rose from his chair and touched his face like he knew something was there but couldn't figure out what it was. He whirled and marched out of the banquet hall, his gaping coat fluttering at his back.

Shayne took a drink of his juice with a smile. It wouldn't be long now before he had the House wrapped around his little finger and giving him all their precious votes. He decided to help himself to another serving of beast meat. Every bite tasted like victory as the morning sun got higher in the sky, and Shayne eavesdropped on chatter about upcoming Yule festivities to take place in the House. He was particularly interested in the parade.

When he was finished, he dabbed his mouth with a silk cloth and considered what he might do for the rest of the morning now that his one, most-important task for the day was complete.

The banquet hall doors flew open. Someone was *thrown* into the hall.

A female hit the floor and rolled over twice before she caught herself. She whirled around on her knees and clasped her hands together. "Please!" she begged. "Please have mercy!"

Fairies around the table stirred and turned in their seats as Cosmo marched back into the hall. His face was clean, his coat was buttoned, and his expression was contorted with fury.

Shayne sprang from his seat. His hand still gripped the silk cloth, his knuckles turning white around it as Cosmo reached the young female, grabbed her by the hair and hoisted her to her feet as she wailed.

A few fairies of the House cringed, but most chuckled lightly and shifted themselves to watch the show. But that wasn't the disturbing part, nor was the aggression Cosmo displayed before the table.

It was that the female's hair was fashioned in a way to cover her ears. It was that her face was paler than a fairy's, her physique weaker than a fairy's, and her begging...

She was human.

Shayne threw the cloth to the tabletop. He fixed himself to march around the table and put an end to this horrid show. Everything in his faeborn chest twisted, his muscles flexed to move. But he froze there, his hands at his sides, his chest rising and falling with sharp inhales.

What was he to do? He was not this human's hero. He would die if he intervened.

When Cosmo hurled the human ten feet and she rolled across the floor, Shayne whirled around. He stared at the back wall as nausea built in his stomach. He could not endure this. But he *could not* intervene. He closed his eyes and grabbed a fistful of his hair.

The female shrieked and shouted and begged, filling his ears with pain.

"No," he muttered to himself. "Don't even think about it."

He bit his lips together, trying to think of something else. Why would Cosmo do this here? Was he so angry about Shayne's prank that he'd decided to take out his wrath upon a human prisoner? Was this all Shayne's fault?

Curse the faeborn sky deities.

Shayne turned back to the table. He grabbed a solid fruit. He hurled it across the banquet hall. It smacked square in Cosmo's left eye.

Forget the ink. Now the fool would have a bruise he couldn't wash away with soap and water.

A chorus of sounds erupted across the hall as the fruit fell to the ground and rolled across the tiles. As Cosmo's head snapped to the side, his hand flying up to cover his eye.

Shayne followed after his fruit in slow, easy steps, landing himself before where Cosmo was hunched. Conveniently standing right in the way of Cosmo's reach of the human still cowering on the floor. The smells in the air turned just a little more unbearable, the temperature growing uncomfortably hot. Even the sounds of distant music in the House turned screechy and sharp. Shayne pulled his face into a half-smile so no one would know.

"How cowardly of you," Shayne said. "If you're mad at me, take it out on *me*. Or are you too afraid of my abilities for that?"

Cosmo turned and stood slowly. He dropped his hand, revealing a patch of swelling flesh around his eye. His black hair was ruffled and out of place from Shayne's epic fruit throw.

When he stared at Shayne now, it seemed different.

"You said you didn't have a human," Shayne pointed out.

After a moment, Cosmo said, "I lied."

Shayne thought that was it. That they would all go their separate ways now that Cosmo's fit of anger had been handled. But then...

Cosmo's face spread into a smile.

And because of that, Shayne's smile faded.

"Everyone leave." Cosmo's command boomed over the banquet hall.

Immediately, every fairy in sight dropped their breakfast utensils and began rushing for the hall doors. They escaped two at a time, and soon the large hall was empty, save for Shayne, Cosmo, and the unfortunate human who'd found herself in the middle of a terrible fairy feud. The doors swished closed, and everything went quiet.

"If you care for that human so much, go tend to her wounds, Lyro," Cosmo invited. He nodded past Shayne with his chin toward the helpless thing still huddled on the floor. "Why don't you check if she's alright?"

"Ha! So you can stab me while my back is turned?" Shayne guessed, though he knew Cosmo wouldn't take that risk. "Absolutely not. I don't care for humans—I just wanted to see if you were afraid of me, and it seems you are. Admit it."

Cosmo shook his head in disbelief. "I can't believe it," he said, more to himself.

Shayne bit the inside of his cheek, wondering if he'd missed something. But his mind fled to the human on the floor behind him, possibly bleeding. Possibly terrified. If he could have kicked Cosmo out the banquet hall doors, he would have. All he wanted to do now was make sure the human wasn't broken, but he could *not* have a Riothin-blooded fairy see him tend to a human, and so, he folded his arms and waited.

"Well, then." Cosmo backed away, and to Shayne's relief, he turned for the doors. "I have other things to do today," he muttered as he marched.

Shayne waited. And waited. And waited. And *finally*, Cosmo left, the great doors banging closed after him and returning the banquet hall to silence.

It was the first second Shayne dropped the calm look from his face. He spun and fell to a knee, listening for the human's rhythms. He thought she'd passed out, until he saw her sitting there, alert.

"Are you alright, Human? Are you hurt?" he asked. Shayne lifted a hand toward her hunched shoulder, but he stopped short when she lifted her face to his.

Her once watery-eyed, startled face had changed. Shayne blinked in surprise, something dropping into the pit of his stomach at the sight of her wide, growing smile.

"No..." he rasped, tearing back.

The female threw her head back and roared in laughter, filling the hall with it. Her hair slid off her ears, showing their arched points, and Shayne realized just how much of a fool he was. Realized that Cosmo had tricked him into revealing something about himself none of his enemies should ever know. And that Cosmo was winning after all—not only in the game.

"Did you think I was really doing all that to a measly human?" Cosmo's voice came from behind him, and Shayne froze to the floor. Cosmo hadn't made a peep when he'd returned. "Those who know me know I can act viciously when I want to," he added. He crouched and leaned in to whisper in Shayne's ear, "And you should know; the things I do to real humans are much, much worse."

Shayne spun and punched. He knew better—*queensbane*, he knew better—but unfortunately his fist didn't.

Cosmo took the hit with a growl. His breathing was heavy when he spun back and sized Shayne up with glowing green eyes. He lightly touched his cheekbone where a new swell would soon match the patch from the fruit.

"What a poor sport you are. No fun," he said. "But I'm learning all sorts of things about you, Shayne *Lyro*. Including the best way to rile you up."

Shayne climbed to his feet and sped past Cosmo. He rushed for the doors, pushing out to brave the halls with a pounding heart. The scent in the hallway was metallic and icy, and Shayne coughed on the air entering his lungs. The agonies of this House created a vast sea where no direction seemed to take him to the surface.

He found himself in the backyard gardens minutes later. He wasn't even sure how he got outside. He looked back at the House of Riothin as his heartbeat settled. As he started to think rationally for the first time in several minutes.

"They know," he muttered. "Queensbane, they know." He dragged his fingers into his hair and began to pace along the stepping stones. Chilly wind whispered across his flesh and a sprinkle of snow fell over the garden, but he hardly noticed.

He cursed the sky deities and fell onto a stone bench, dropping his head into his hands.

"You fool," he snapped at himself. He'd come all the way here to ensure nothing fae, magical, or dangerous went near the human realm. He had one job to do; to ensure word reached the House of Lyro that Shayne was under the protection of Riothin. All he'd needed was for the High Lord to send that stupid letter, and the Lyro House would have forgotten about Shayne's humans, forgotten about forcing Shayne into the heir's seat, and might have eventually forgotten about Shayne altogether. Now, not only did his own family know about his affairs with humans, the House of Riothin had discovered it, too.

"It doesn't matter," he told himself. He dropped his hands and clasped them. "This doesn't change anything."

It wasn't like Cosmo's discovery would reveal anything about Shayne's connections in the human realm. In fact, Cosmo might not even tell anyone what Shayne had done in the banquet hall. It didn't matter one bit. Not at all.

Except that now Cosmo knew that he could control Shayne by torturing humans.

"Sky deities, why?!" Shayne growled. At least he hadn't been holding his crossbow during that catastrophe. He might have handled things even worse.

"If you're having a conversation with yourself, I can leave."

Shayne's head snapped up.

Meave stood by a willow bush, plucking the soft blossoms off as she watched him. A long, glamourous pink dress swept down her body, fluttering in the cold breeze. She was a being most fairies would find pretty,

Shayne supposed. But he wasn't really into 'dolled-up' or 'glamourous' or even 'pink'. He tried to picture Meave in jeans, or in a police vest, or even with messy hair all up in a ponytail.

He couldn't.

"How long have you been standing there?" he asked.

Meave's glossed lips shimmered in the sunlight when she smiled. "Long enough to determine that you're either crazy or brilliant with the way you ramble on when no one's around."

Shayne forced a smile. "Let's go with brilliant."

Meave laughed. Blossoms sprouted to full-faced flowers when her laughter sailed through the garden. Even the flowers of the House of Riothin responded well to their rulers. Shayne wondered if all his secret agendas would earn him some sort of plant rash if he stayed in this garden too long.

He stood from the bench and reached for Meave's hands. The female's fingers were pale and soft; too soft though—like she'd never thrown a punch or worked a long day in her life.

"I came to find you for a reason, Shayne," she told him.

Shayne's smile turned as relaxed as he could manage. Deep down, he truly hated that he needed her. She wasn't all bad, she just wasn't his type even if he was hers. She also threw ridiculous fits at least once a day that were eye-roll worthy, but not enough to deter him from following through on his plan.

But then she said, "My father has demanded you wed me." And curse him—Shayne's smile faltered.

"What?" He didn't mean to ask it with accusation, but he did.

"He will announce it as soon as I tell him to." Meave held tighter to his hands. "It's what you want, isn't it? And if you're having trouble with Cosmo, he'll yield to your authority the moment we exchange vows. You'll severely outrank him as the husband of the High Lord's favourite daughter."

For all his greatness, Shayne could only stare in this moment. Even though this was what he had come here hoping for. Even though the main part of his plan revolved around this very thing.

But perhaps he hadn't expected to be wedded right away. Perhaps he'd expected to have time to sort out his own feelings first and let a few things go from his heart.

"Don't you want this?" Meave's bright expression faded.

Shayne cleared his throat. "Of course." His tongue hurt. "Of course I do. I've wanted this since the moment I laid eyes on you at the gate— you know that."

"Then why wait?" Meave's face turned bright again. "I'm running out of time, you know. I don't want any of my father's warriors as a husband. I don't want my father to choose anything for me anymore."

Shayne released a quiet chuckle. Meave had made it so obvious that she wanted to marry a Lyro simply to stick it to her father that Shayne thought he'd struck gold.

And why wait? She was right. As soon as Shayne was the son-in-law of High Lord Riothin, as horrifying as the man was, Shayne would become untouchable. It would establish a stronger alliance with the House than him simply being present. It would undoubtedly force Lyro to withdraw any threats, and it would solve his immediate, pesky Cosmo problem. Cosmo would keep his mouth shut if Shayne demanded it.

He took in a deep breath and let it out slowly. "Can you give me three days to think before we announce anything?" he asked. "We haven't even known each other for two weeks. Three more days won't hurt us."

Meave's shiny lips spread into a bigger smile than ever. "Let me tell you a secret, Shayne," she said.

"Hmm?"

Meave's grip on his hands went so tight, it hurt. "Do you know why I want to marry *you* so desperately?" she asked. When he raised a brow, she said, "Because you're the enemy. And once I'm more powerful through the bond of marriage, I plan to throw a rebellion against my father. I plan to take everything he has for myself." Shayne blinked. He tried to pull his fingers away, but she didn't let go as she went on, glancing off at the garden like she was in another place. "He's a ferocious war fae and violent conqueror. But I shall be worse. I will take all the West villages. I will become the High Lady of Riothin whose name is spoken for generations to come."

A gust of wind rattled the bushes and the whole garden seemed to applaud. Shayne watched in amazement as a subtle shiver shook Meave's body. As she cringed like she'd smelled something foul in the flowers.

And it was then that it dawned on Shayne that even though Meave was the esteemed daughter of the House of Riothin, she was being repulsed by the House's magic, too. And she'd been hiding it much longer than Shayne had. Possibly taking cold showers and stifling gags at the scents, hearing dreadful music and dancing anyway.

Shayne finally managed to free himself from her grip.

This female was to be his wife? Someone who wanted to shed blood with her own fingernails?

A rebellion?

A takeover?

Everything she wanted would foil his plan. He'd hoped for subtlety and a quiet existence. He'd hoped to hide in the High Lord's shadow for at least the next several years. He'd expected an easy marriage, a lot of food, and the occasional fun-filled outing.

What a fool he was—for the second time today.

Shayne should have known that nothing was ever simple among fairies.

He should have known that a quiet, fun life in the Ever Corners didn't exist.

CHAPTER

23

Shayne Lyro and the Matches of Fairies

Even though Shayne hardly remembered his mother—a flighty female who'd taken off only weeks after giving birth to Massie—Shayne did recall his father speaking of her every now and then. Mostly bitter things, followed by curses and stories of her obnoxious, obsessive ways. But once, and *just* once that Shayne could remember, Hans-Der Lyro let slip a few words about the female, accompanied by a smile that did not appear cruel. Shayne had been just a childling at the time, five years old and sitting atop a thick book at his seat by the table so he could reach everything. His father had been standing by the window, gazing outside at the withering cherry blossoms shedding their petals to prepare for the short season of frost and ice winds that would cover the North Corner. The Lyro family and their loud friends had been making a ruckus as they passed around the heaping dinner platters, everyone talking even with full mouths. It was back during the time when Shayne had first learned to be quiet. Back when he didn't know he wanted to be the loudest of all.

Hans-Der, beneath the chatter, had said, "Jada always loved watching the trees lose their petals."

No one heard him, naturally, and perhaps that was why he dared to say it aloud. No one was even looking at him. No one, except for Shayne.

Though his hands were small, Shayne gripped a large spoon, holding it tight by his bowl of pudding. But instead of tasting the pasty chocolate, he watched his father's face create one of the only real smiles he'd ever offered in Shayne's five years of life. And it was at that young age Shayne realized that even though his father hated his mother's guts with the strength of a thousand blazing fires, he also maybe loved her.

Five years old was much too young to think about things such as *love*. But Shayne wondered about it anyway. He wondered for quite a while whether it would be worth it to ever love someone. Love was not a strong enough magic to keep his mother from leaving his father. It wasn't even strong enough to keep Hans-Der from being cruel to his offspring.

If love left people behind, perhaps Shayne didn't want it. Perhaps it just wasn't for him.

But as his years grew in number, Shayne found that what he did like was *flirting*. Not only because he was good at it, but because he could make others happy while also making himself happy, even if it was for just a short while. Offering a wink wasn't making a commitment. Blowing a kiss never forced him to swear himself to anyone. Even random acts of romantic chivalry could be used as a fun way to pass the time. But not once did he let himself fall in love with even the prettiest, most persuasive of fairies.

Not when love left people behind.

It was why Shayne had decided long ago he would never marry a fairy. Why he was so sure he wasn't 'marriage material' until he got to the human realm one year ago, and he wondered for the first time since he was a childling if perhaps love didn't have to end with one person leaving the other forever. If maybe love wasn't such a complicated, cruel thing. If maybe the reason he didn't want love was because he simply didn't want love with a *fairy*.

But of course, that was before. He was back in the Ever Corners now. And thus, he was grateful he hadn't fallen in love with anyone in his lifetime. What a disaster that would have been, since, as was the way of love, he would have been forced to leave her forever if he had.

Massie was wrong. Shayne couldn't possibly have been so foolish.

Shayne did not have a lover, and therefore would feel nothing about entering into a marriage with Meave.

The following two mornings in the House of Riothin arrived with the screeching of a woodwind instrument somewhere in the House and the fresh fragrance of someone's rotting, sweaty feet. And they absolutely weren't Shayne's. It got worse every hour now that he knew about Meave's secret plans. Now that he had two secrets to keep instead of one, and he was left with a splitting headache over it.

Cosmo hadn't hatched another trick yet, so Shayne figured it was his turn. He awoke to a dark dawn, wondering if the entire household was waiting to see what he'd do after his humiliating display several days ago. He meant to plan his retaliation, but as he sauntered out of his guestroom and made his way toward the conservatory to plan his heist, he heard a strange thing at the end of the hall.

"...Cosmo Flora's spy in the Lyro House..."

It was just a whisper, uttered by one lesser fairy to another. The young pair carried baskets around the bend as Shayne rubbed his tired eyes, but his hands went still when their words settled in.

At first, he thought it might be another trick. Why would two servants be foolish enough to whisper about the House of Lyro in front of a Lyro? It was almost funny, and Shayne might have laughed if a teensy little voice inside his head hadn't begged the question: What if it wasn't a trick?

What if the servants really hadn't realized Shayne was there? What if they thought no one was listening? No one in the Riothin House awoke before the sunrise, which was the ideal time for servants to share gossip and go about their duties in a relaxed state.

Shayne dropped his hand to his side and scurried down the hall with silent footsteps. He peeked around the bend and caught the fairies venturing down a narrow staircase in single file. He looked behind him to see if he was being followed. If this was orchestrated by Cosmo, the fairy would show up to watch.

The hall remained still and quiet apart from soft snores lifting from the nearest bedrooms. So, Shayne slipped down the hallway in the direction he'd seen the servants go. He tiptoed down the staircase and found himself in an unlit hall outside a rustic-looking kitchen. Three young fairy females were congregated in the tight space, speaking in hushed tones.

"Actually, Lord Cosmo sent word to his spy the moment the Lyro showed up. Apparently, the charming white-haired fairy is the rightful heir to the highest chair in the House of Lyro! It seems he didn't inform High Lord Riothin of that," one of the fairies whispered.

Shayne grunted. He would have admitted the responsibility he'd abandoned eventually. The bigger concern was that it was unclear how much Cosmo's spy might know about the Lyro family's discoveries regarding Shayne.

Shayne decided to walk into the kitchen. "Good morning!" he said, and three females jumped in surprise—one screamed.

Shayne grinned in his infectious way. "Don't worry, I'm not here to hurt you," he promised. "Unlike Cosmo Flora, I'm a *nice* fairy." He thought about that, then added, "With unmatchable killing technique and years of training that makes me nearly unstoppable." He wanted to be clear that he could kill every single one of them in the next three seconds if he wanted to. Not that he would, of course. He just wanted them to know.

Shayne took a step toward the servant who'd been dishing out the juicy gossip. "That's a lovely dress, pretty Fairy." He winced at himself as soon as he said it. Flirting wasn't going to get him anywhere with young servants, and her dress was practically made of boring old burlap and string.

Sure enough, the female glanced down at her outfit with an odd face.

Shayne cleared his throat. "Anyway, I must inquire what you were talking about. Tell me about Lord Cosmo's spy in the House of Lyro. I'll pay you."

The female's face paled. She, along with the other two, dropped to their knees and clasped their hands. "Please," the female begged. "Lord Cosmo will kill me if I tell you."

"I'll protect you from him," Shayne promised. "I need to know more about the spy."

The females all exchanged looks, and Shayne sighed.

"What do you want if not coin and protection?" he asked. "I can't marry any of you or anything. You're all too young for me, and I've already basically promised myself to Lady Meave." Then he mumbled, "And I'm out of time to avoid that promise."

The same female climbed to her feet. "I have something I want," she said. "I want you to deliver a letter to my mother." All at once, the other two females jumped to their feet as well.

"Me too! To my father!"

"Yes, a letter to my family!"

Shayne looked back and forth between them, his chest feeling a little squeezy all of a sudden. He rubbed it. "Frankly, I would if I could. But I don't think I'm leaving this House any time soon," he admitted. "Is there anything else I can trade for the information?"

The servants' shoulders dropped. It stirred so much disappointment into the air that Shayne moaned. "Oh, fine." He waved a hand around. "Why not? I'll deliver your letters if I can. Just tell me about the *spy*."

The gossipy female smiled for the first time. "The spy is a cook—an old friend of Lord Cosmo's that grew up here. Lord Cosmo writes back and forth with him. It's how the House of Riothin has been able to stay ahead of Lord Hans-Der all this time."

Shayne couldn't believe his ears. No wonder his father had never tried to attack the House of Riothin. He must have known that somehow Riothin would see it coming.

"Amazing." Shayne laughed to himself. "Tell me, what does this spy know about me, in particular?" he asked.

The fairy's face fell. "I'm not sure," she admitted. "The last letter didn't say anything else about you. I read it in secret when I fetched it from the delivery fairy at the front gate."

Shayne nodded. So neither Cosmo nor Lord Riothin knew anything about the human realm.

"This information has been very useful," he said. "Thank you." His mind worked as he turned for the dark hall, but he paused at the kitchen door. "Write your letters to your families and slide them beneath the pillow in my guestroom. I'll make sure they get delivered," he told the servants.

The fairies nodded, their smiles a tad bit infectious. One of them said, "You're so kind, Shayne Lyro! I wish you were the High Lord of the Riothin House!"

The words were like an icy wind wrapping around Shayne's throat. He swallowed. These fairies wouldn't say such things if they had his best interests in mind. Little did they know, Meave may soon try to make him that. And after all his efforts to avoid the highest chair at Lyro, he could find himself strapped to a chair at Riothin instead.

What a mess.

Shayne flashed them one last smile. It faded as soon as he turned and headed back through the dark hall and up the narrow staircase.

Cosmo was lounging on a fluffy sofa in a sunny room when Shayne found him. Birds with horns gathered on the windowsills, tweeting and eyeing the black-haired fairy inside. At first, Shayne thought Cosmo was napping. Ripe for another face-drawing. But as soon as Shayne drew near, the fairy opened his eyes.

"Ah. There you are." Though he said it, he sounded entirely uninterested. "I was wondering when you'd show up to retaliate. I'm ready," he promised.

Shayne plopped down in the nearest chair and filled the armrests with his muscular arms.

Not that he was comparing, but his arms were far more impressive than Cosmo's. He wondered if Cosmo had noticed. Shayne leaned, splaying his forearms and putting them in a direct beam of sunlight so they were easier to catch the eye—

"The servants are all whispering about you, you know," Cosmo said.

Shayne slowed his movements. After a few seconds, he drew his arms back and folded them tightly across his chest. "How odd."

"Not really. Though, some of the things they're saying are outright treacherous." Cosmo lifted to a sitting position and swung himself around to face Shayne. "I wonder if the gossip has reached the High Lord yet?"

Shayne became acutely aware of the dagger hiding in his boot. The birds outside seemed to refocus their attention and take him in. Even the early sun slid behind a cloud and cloaked the room in dimness, likely making his white hair stand out against the shadows.

"I came here to implore you to make our game fair," Shayne said in an effort to change the subject. "Isn't it cowardly to ask your spy about me when I have no spies to ask about you?"

Cosmo stared for a moment, his green eyes not moving a fraction. Then he smiled and huffed in disbelief. "Did you torture someone?" he guessed, tapping a finger against his chin. "A delivery fairy, maybe?"

"I came by the information on my own. Now all that matters is that I know you have an unfair advantage, and unless you want me to announce it to the whole House, I think we should make a new bargain." Shayne uncrossed his arms and presented them pristinely on the armrests again.

"All the nobles of the House already know about my spy. You were the only one out of the loop," Cosmo stated.

"Still. Humour me."

Cosmo's gaze flickered down to Shayne's arms, and Shayne's mouth tugged into a grin.

"What do you want exactly, Lyro?" Cosmo asked.

"Write a message to your spy-friend. Tell him to start a rumour in the Lyro House that I'm here. That I'm allied with the High Lord of Riothin. And that any actions they may wish to take against me will only stir up this House and threaten war."

Cosmo cast Shayne a doubtful look. "That's not true at all. I don't expect the High Lord to defend you if your family crosses you."

"Doesn't matter if it's true or not. Tell your spy to start the rumour immediately." Shayne cringed as he waited for Cosmo's answer. Some of the birds began to growl outside and try to beat their way in through the glass. One flashed its teeth.

Cosmo leaned back against the sofa, his lip curling into a snarl. "I suppose it would only benefit me," he thought aloud. "If you're telling the truth about why you've come, it would be nice to brag to your family that you're with us now. If you're lying about your reasons for being here, if you really are a spy for your House, then your father won't react with surprise to the news when he's informed of your whereabouts, and that would be grounds to have you executed here." Cosmo chewed on his lip. "But why would I help you? I don't care whose side you've flipped onto, you're a Lyro by blood, and I hate that you're still breathing."

Shayne brought his hands together and clasped them tightly. He ignored the menacing cries of the birds at the window, and he leaned forward to look Cosmo in the eyes so the fairy would know he wasn't lying. "If you do this, I will surrender this game to you. You will be the winner of the household, and I will be the next Yule fool to entertain the Riothin House. Just imagine how satisfying it will be for you to drag a Lyro around for your own entertainment."

Perhaps he could spare a human one evening of torment, too. It was worth it on both counts.

Cosmo didn't blink for some time. The questioning look in his eyes morphed into something else—hunger, maybe. Want. *Need.* Everything Shayne needed him to feel, even though the look made Shayne's skin crawl.

Shayne smiled and extended his hand. "I'll even make a bargain so I can't get out of it. If you stop hunting humans, I'll be their replacement here." He expected to have to use the other arguments he'd come up with, to spend the whole morning trying to convince Cosmo of this deal, but to his surprise, Cosmo's hand slapped against his, and Shayne found his fingers gripped tightly.

"There's no getting out of this one, Lyro," Cosmo warned. That strange look in his eyes darkened, and Shayne stifled a shiver, refusing to think about how far Cosmo might go. "You're mine when the eve of the Great Yule Morning comes."

Shayne shook Cosmo's hand, and the deal was sealed. "How long before your letter reaches your spy?" he asked.

Cosmo's eyes glittered as he replied, "Just half a day. I should have a response by tomorrow."

Tomorrow.

Shayne held his breath so he wouldn't let out his sigh of relief. Half a day, and the House of Lyro would know not to mess with Shayne anymore. They'd know better than to send someone against Fae Café, and Shayne could live the rest of his days here under Cosmo's cruelty until he married Meave and made Cosmo regret every decision he'd ever made.

It was difficult to avoid Meave, but Shayne managed.

Of course he was going to wed her. Of course he would tell her as much. Of course all was well.

But he perhaps wasn't quite ready to celebrate it yet. To sit through the engagement parties, be showered with presents, and have news of the betrothal travel to the surrounding Houses.

To have Meave lead an uprising with Shayne at her side and possibly ruin everything.

Shayne spent most of the day pacing. He wandered the gardens outside, stuck his feet in the stream around the manor, and avoided attending every meal of the day. At dusk, he ventured down to the kitchens to find himself something to eat, but he was surprised to find them empty. So, he gathered himself some figs and leftover rice, and he spent the afternoon in the drawing room painting for no reason. He wasn't even good at it. He tried to do a portrait and discovered his art skills were akin to that of a childling without hands.

Perhaps he would save the portrait and give it to his new wife once he was wedded. It was a lovely reflection of how he truly felt about her. The likeness was uncanny.

At midnight, he rolled up his horrendous artwork and tucked it beneath his arm, then headed down the hall to go store it in his guestroom. He shuddered thinking about having to share a room with Meave in the future, and he glanced down at his blue Riothin coat. Only today had he been presented with such a garment by the beautifiers claiming it was a gift from Lady Meave and that he belonged in this colour now. Never in his faeborn life had he dreamt he would wear the colours of a Riothin. What a strange turn of events he'd created for himself.

The lights flickered as Shayne reached the end of the hall and entered his room, sliding the portrait from his arm and setting it on his dresser.

He almost screamed when he turned around and saw someone standing there. The dagger was out of his boot and pressing into a fairy's throat in a heartbeat.

A young, female servant looked up at him with wide eyes. "Please don't hurt me!" she begged.

Shayne tore the blade back, almost stumbling out of the room when his back hit the doorframe. But he yanked the door closed behind him, and he blinked at the servant.

"Are you out of your mind?" he asked when he realized he knew her from the kitchen. "I told you to drop your letters beneath my pillow, not wait for me in person!"

She fell to her knees as if intending to beg for forgiveness, but Shayne strutted over, grasped her arm, and pulled her back up to her feet again. "Don't do that," he instructed. "Look me in the eyes and tell me why you're here."

The female shook a little. "I just wanted to tell you that I intercepted and read another letter from the spy."

Shayne's face changed. "When?"

"Just an hour ago. It arrived at the gate by messenger, and I went to fetch it," she admitted.

Shayne took hold of her shoulders. "Tell me everything. What did it say? Does my House know I'm here? Has the rumour been spread?"

She pulled her eyes up slowly. "It said nothing of that."

A squeak sounded in the room from the wind against the window outside as that settled in.

Shayne dragged a hand down his face in disbelief. Cosmo had fooled him again. Of course that fairy couldn't be trusted to keep his word. "What did it say then?" he asked.

The female didn't answer, and when Shayne glanced back at her, he realized she was pale and staring behind him in horror. "My Lord!" she shrieked.

This time, when she dropped to her knees, Shayne let her. His hand hung in the air where he'd been clutching her shoulder. He let it fall back to his side slowly. The wind continued to pound against the windows from outside, blending with the servant's desperate and terrified inhales, but apart from that, there was silence in Shayne's guestroom.

Shayne turned around.

Cosmo's hands rested in his coat pockets, his sleepy eyes settled on Shayne.

"You could have just asked me," Cosmo said. "No need to involve the slaves."

Shayne closed his eyes as his own words replayed through his head. *"Then I'll protect you from him."*

It had barely been a day, and he'd already failed to guard this servant from Cosmo. She didn't actually belong to Shayne. At present, Cosmo had more of a right to punish her, to do whatever he wanted with her, than Shayne did.

Cosmo reached into his coat and dragged out a letter. He unfolded it with care, and he scanned it for a moment before he said anything. "I'm not sure I want to tell you what it says," he admitted, "since you have your own ways of getting information." His gaze flickered over to the servant on the floor, and Shayne swallowed.

"This childling told me nothing. I found out another way," Shayne lied.

"She's hardly a childling. And I don't believe you," Cosmo returned. "But that's no matter. I don't deal with servants. That's the High Lord's job. I need only to report her to him, and she'll be dealt with by the merciless hand of the High Lord of Riothin."

The servant whimpered and slapped both hands over her mouth, making the muscles tighten in Shayne's chest. His instincts shouted at him to stand in between Cosmo and the servant on the floor as a barrier, but he knew it would do no good. She was doomed, and it was his fault.

"And as for your family, Lyro..." Cosmo carefully brushed a lock of black hair out of his eyes. "To my surprise, they say they're both *amused* and *comfortable* with you abandoning your House. Naturally I thought that was rather strange, since my spy never lies." He folded the letter to seal it up again, then slid it back into his coat. "Perhaps it's because they're confident they can still get to you, even if you're here."

"Get to me?" Shayne faked a chuckle, but he stole a look at the female on the floor as she trembled. He wondered how long it would be before Cosmo would leave. He wondered if he could rush the servant to the window and sneak her out through the garden. If it was even worth an attempt—

"Yes. Now that they have their dreamslipper back," Cosmo said.

The room froze in time.

Every thought Shayne had vanished, leaving only bits and pieces of confusing questions and nonsensical realities. He pulled his gaze back to Cosmo, but he didn't really see the fairy there; his green eyes, his black hair, his blue coat... It was all a blur as Shayne replayed that statement over in his mind.

No, Cosmo couldn't have just said... *dreamslipper.*

And he couldn't have been talking about Mycra Sentorious.

It didn't make sense because Mycra was in the human realm. Shayne had left the pretty fairy in the care of his real brothers. She was with Dranian. She was safe.

Everyone with her was safe, too.

It had to be a different dreamslipper.

Cosmo folded his arms and squinted at Shayne curiously. "You seem to know what I'm talking about, Lyro. It appears you're keeping secrets about your House. Why didn't you tell us your family has a dreamslipper at their disposal? Only an enemy would keep such valuable information from us."

Shayne still stared at the blurs of colour, at the air, at the fuzzy image of the dark-haired fairy standing before him he didn't really see.

No. Dreamslippers were so rare, his family wouldn't have been able to come by another one.

Why, in the name of the sky deities, wasn't Mycra Sentorious in the human realm?

Cosmo huffed in annoyance. "I could always torture the secrets out of you, Lyro. I think you and I are both aware at this point you're not really here for an alliance. Nor do you want Meave." He grunted in disgust. "You even acted like you *cared* for humans, but you hid that your own family has one. Who are you, really? You must be what I've suspected all along—a spy."

Cryptic words rang in Shayne's ears. Words that must have meant something else, because the facts couldn't possibly be true, and therefore, they didn't find a place in Shayne's sound mind to land. But even though it wasn't real, couldn't be real, Shayne's stomach dropped like a slow ball of flames lowering into his abdomen, crippling his nerves, hitching his breath. His blurry vision sharpened, and suddenly Cosmo became the clearest thing in the realm.

"You're lying," Shayne heard himself say. He shouldn't have said anything more to Cosmo, he shouldn't have revealed his tones, let his rhythms change. His hands should not have balled into fists, his flesh grown tight, his faeborn heart taken on a new, wild beat.

But it had to be true. Cosmo wouldn't have known about a dreamslipper or a human otherwise.

There'd been only one dreamslipper in Shayne's company before he left for the House of Riothin. There was only one human, too. And his blood brothers had been after her.

His blood brothers. *Her.*

For the next sixty seconds, Shayne only saw red.

At some point in those moments, he attacked Cosmo. He retrieved the letter.

He left Cosmo a mess of broken limbs on the floor.

He left.

CHAPTER

24

Luc Zelsor and the Freakshow

The Shadow Assembly's meeting place was possibly the most secret location in the Corners of Ever. Not even the Queene of the North herself had been able to discover the room hidden for centuries behind enchantments and layers of secrets and riddles. Its appointed chairs consisted of the highest-ranking members of the Shadow Court, a few powerful, greedy beings who just wanted to have a say in things, and only the richest and most influential nobles across the Dark Corner. It was not easy to gather them all in one place. It was not easy to stand in their presence, either.

Yet here Luc was. Standing.

The discussions had gone on for hours too long. Days, in fact. Luc had barely managed to slip away and return as much as required to convince everyone he'd been present the whole time. But it was a necessary, exhausting feat, considering he'd needed to be in two places at once. And he supposed he didn't mind that everyone wanted him. It was the curse of a fox—to be wanted all the time. To be so desperately needed by all who knew him. The High Court of the Coffee Bean needed him. The Shadow Assembly needed him. Mor needed him.

Unfortunately, Luc hadn't kept his word to Mor yet, despite his best efforts. It wasn't his fault though. As much as the High Court of the Coffee Bean needed Luc, the Shadow Assembly needed him just a little bit more at the moment.

It was, after all, his own trial. And Lily Baker, of all people, would understand the importance of a trial.

From where he stood on an onyx stage, Luc's nose scrunched at the thought of the mighty human trapped in an utterly horrifying situation. Would she be broken already? He bristled as he considered and calculated the days. As he wondered if she had far exceeded her expiration date for sanity and clear thinking. She was a strong-minded female, but no human could withstand fairy torment. Luc knew he should have done something about it, that time was of the essence, that Lily Baker might already be dead, and he would be in all sorts of trouble then, but...

Well, he did try to warn her not to come here. She should have stayed in the human realm. It wasn't Luc's fault she had a desperate need to prove herself all the time, though Dranian would be disappointed Luc had disappeared without warning immediately following Mor and Cressica's departure from the Ever Corners. Luc only hoped Dranian was still waiting where he'd told him to wait—though many days had passed since then, so it was doubtful.

Ah, it was all a bit of a mess.

The great Shadow Assembly's meeting room was in the heart of a black mountain, only reachable by airslipping. The magnificent candlelit space was filled with numbered velvet chairs, chatter, a dollop of shouting, and a fat portion of unnecessary judgement. People were far too critical of foxes. It hardly seemed fair.

"Are we ready to vote?" Luc interrupted the chatter to ask.

Approximately three hundred sets of silver and brown eyes turned in his direction. Most of them weren't that friendly.

"Vote? We've hardly discussed what's to be done to a traitor like you!" High Lord Bobin said whilst pointing. It seemed he might be trying to point at *Luc*, but his old finger was so crooked, it made a few heads turn toward the nothingness off to the side.

"Hardly discussed?" Luc scoffed. "You've all been discussing for over two weeks!"

Low Lord Ramoth leapt from his chair in the seventy-fifth position. "You *killed* the Dark Queene!" he shouted. Hundreds of outraged voices erupted through the meeting room, the noise so violent, Luc was sure the walls shuddered a little.

He thought about the accusation, tapping a finger against his chin. Then he said, "I don't think you can prove that was me."

The Army Commanders objected at once, shouting things like, "We all saw you do it!"

Luc's jaw slid to the side. They had a point.

He decided he would keep his mouth shut after that. There was no sense in trying to convince these fools of anything anyway—they were all cranky over the death of that heap of black-blooded hog meat they called a queene. People needed to get over things. He could have easily therapist-ed this group into recognizing that if they held grudges, they'd never be happy, but... well... Luc was a bit of a hypocrite in that regard, and he was afraid they'd all point it out.

So, instead, he sighed and looked out a window depicting a shimmering crystal mosaic of the great symbol of order the Dark Corner had abided by for centuries. The three standards of rule were written in the glass: Absolute Domination, Fearsome Power, Victory Over Enemies.

Yes, the Dark Queene had fulfilled those three obligations well. It was a shame she'd ticked Luc off so profoundly and it had all come to an end. Luc supposed his only option was to die now, should this Assembly require it, and if that were to be the final ruling, he'd already resolved he would vanish on site, head straight for the House of Lyro, break in with a clamour, snatch Lily Baker, drop her off in whatever crack of the forest Dranian had found himself in, then race the wind back into the Dark Corner where the Low Kings and Queenes would claim him as their prisoner the second he showed himself. At that point it wouldn't matter how enraged the House of Lyro was; one measly household wouldn't dare cross the boundary into the Dark Corner and risk a mighty face-off with the kings and queenes of the Shadows or the Shadow Army guarding its borders.

Luc tried not to think about the fact that humans rarely stayed in one place for too long once captured. They were worth too much for that, so they were given as gifts for parties, often traded or sold...

"Tell us, Prince, are you even the least bit remorseful for your actions?" The Great Judge brought the room to order with the question, and those in the numbered chairs hushed to listen. "It will help us decide whether to execute you publicly before the Corner," the Great Judge added with a fresh tone of resentment, making it clear which side of the debate he fell on.

It took Luc a moment to realize the Judge was speaking to him.

A 'prince'?

Luc nearly snorted a laugh as he dragged his gaze away from the windows' crystal mosaics and let it fall upon one Lord at a time. They looked back at him, waiting, perhaps hoping to see something in their fox 'prince' they had failed to see thus far. Perhaps hoping there was a shred of decency in him they might be able to rely on.

And so, Luc said, "No."

Roars of horror boomed through the room. The Assembly members who'd finally sat down leapt back to their feet. The Great Judge's eyes narrowed and he barred his shiny teeth.

Luc went on anyway, "I don't regret killing that disgraceful monarch you were all idiotic enough to recognize as your ruler, nor do I regret killing the High Prince who was the most disgraceful father in the Ever Corners. If you were looking for a nice answer, you shouldn't have asked such a stupid question."

Naturally, the meeting room boomed with a level of noise worse than before, a decibel strictly forbidden at Assembly meetings of the past. Luc's gaze drifted up the walls as the whole mountain rattled above, as though it too was angry at the fox who'd done a bad thing.

But 'bad' was subjective, and the mountain could kiss Luc's sorry—

A grape hit Luc's face. It was the first of a dozen mushy fruits and vegetables hurled in his direction, filling the onyx stage with the sour fragrance of a fruit salad gone bad.

It seemed the Assembly had made their choice. Luc might be stabbed with cold iron even before the vote took place. He glanced back at the window, sure he could slip through it in the blink of an eye and outrun these older, less fit fairies. He turned his body an inch, taking a small step forward to brace himself to fly...

An enchanted vine grappled his ankles and tore him off his feet. Luc fell forward, his face hitting the onyx, and he growled at whomever had provoked a powerful nine tailed fox. More vines slithered over him like serpents with minds of their own, constricting his wrists, squeezing his midsection, grasping at his throat, even. He tugged at the green stems, but it was no use. As soon as he'd touched the vines, airslipping was no longer an option, and he realized that whatever fate was decided for him in this shadowy Corner would be the one he'd face. As he sat up, bound in every way, he released a small huff-laugh of disbelief.

It was poetic, really.

He would finish his life a lonely fox, the same way he'd started it.

Admittedly, his last thought was of Lily Baker whom he realized he owed an apology to. Because despite his best efforts, or *partial* efforts, he wasn't going to make it to rescue her after all.

"I hope you're still alive, dear Lily," he murmured beneath the commotion around him as a dozen Army Commanders wrestled him to his feet. "I hope the sky deities care more about you than they do about me and you survive."

CHAPTER

25

The Human Who Forgot Her Name

She was sure she didn't forget her name entirely, but she couldn't recall it when asked. Nothing was clear anymore; not memories, not places, not faces. Everything had been swept away like the tide, sucked into an ocean too vast to explore, and cutting off her oxygen as she sank into darkness. Only on rare occasions did the human regard a name, though she was unsure if she owned it. Sometimes, when she managed to find brief moments of sleep, a voice shouted at her in the night, saying things like, *"Lily Baker, don't eat the food!"* and *"Lily Baker, if you give in, they'll break you and you'll never survive!"* But the voice always disappeared when the human was forced to wake up again.

And the day would start over.

But one day, when her feet were raw and her skin prickled from the effects of nearby music, she heard someone say, "She's broken now. Decorate her for the dress rehearsal tonight. In the morning, prepare her for transport. Our brother shall now learn the cost of his actions."

Several parts of the statement got caught in the human's ears as young women moved toward her with thin needles and began sewing flowers to her dress. They also combed her hair, braided it, painted her lips red, and placed an emerald-leafed wreath upon her temples as she tried to grasp onto certain words of the statement. The first was *"our brother"* because it told her answers to the mystery of who else was in the room. For the first time in days, the human lifted her eyes to look upon the people around her.

White hair abounded. Blue eyes. Lovely wide smiles.

Who were these people watching her being dressed up like a doll?

A memory tugged on her brain, one that felt like a case on the brink of being solved... Who else had white hair like this? Slanted blue eyes? A heart-fluttering wide grin? She knew someone, she was sure of it.

The second part of the statement that stood out to her was *"prepare her for transport"* because somehow, the human was positive that in a hostage situation, the likelihood of finding the victim decreased significantly if the kidnapper moved them to a new location.

Was that what she was? A victim? A hostage?

She looked around, finding it difficult to concentrate on the high walls with dragon paintings or the finely stitched tapestries or the family portraits or...

The human's gaze settled on the portrait in the exact middle of the line on the wall. She squeezed her eyes shut to try and clear them so she could see better, but the image of the person remained a blur when she opened them again. Still, the guy in the third portrait looked familiar with his shapely jaw and a certain curl to his smile. He reminded her of someone hiding a secret.

"Shayne." She whispered his name, not sure how she knew it.

She recalled his voice, too. She heard him say, *"If you ever go see my brothers by choice, I won't go after you. I won't help you. I'll leave, and you'll never see me again."*

Her gaze dragged back to the other young guys in the room, the ones who stood before her now. One of them had long white hair in a bun on top of his head. The other one, the slightly taller one, was the one who'd spoken before. His voice sounded eerily similar to Shayne's when he'd said, *"Our brother shall now learn the cost of his actions."*

Ah. The human nodded as she realized. They were all brothers, weren't they?

That was why the Shayne guy never came. Why she was here, and why he wasn't. It wasn't a lot of evidence, but it dropped an unusual ache into her chest. It made her realize that maybe she'd been waiting for him all this time. Maybe she'd hoped he would come for her anyway.

But no, of course he hadn't come. He'd been upfront that he wouldn't.

All these thoughts swirled as the women pinned gold trinkets into her braid and fastened glittering bracelets to her wrists. Someone tossed a pinch of sparkling dust over her that stuck to her skin.

The taller of the two guys stepped forward. He used a flute to push her chin up so he could look her in the eyes. His smile widened, and he said, "Perfect." Then he tilted his head and added, "You must be famished. Get the human something to eat!" The last part he said to those standing nearby.

A platter of berries appeared before her. She didn't have to be told what to do next, her hand moved like it was the only thing she knew. She took a small handful, and she pressed them into her mouth.

"Go get your beauty sleep," the guy commanded with a twinkle in his eye. He dropped her chin, and she obediently turned and headed for a hallway, dragging one foot in front of the other. The women who'd decorated her accompanied her. But as she walked, the sour taste of the berries grew sharp against her tongue, and a short memory of a warning trickled through her head.

"Lily Baker, don't eat the food!"

She stopped chewing, her mouth frozen around the berries. She had yet to swallow.

That voice had come to her several times in bouts of slumber, saying the same thing, but she hadn't regarded it as advice. It hadn't even crossed her mind that she should listen—she'd been sleeping, after all. It was only a dream.

An odd feeling came over the human as she reached her room. She brought her feet together and waited while the women tied a thick vine around her right ankle—one she overheard was there so she couldn't 'leap from the balcony'. The women set up her bed, tidied up her nightstand, closed the drapes of her balcony doors, and left.

Dizziness tried to sweep in as the berry juice leaked down the human's throat. But now that she'd started latching onto her judgements, she realized she *had* to get her thoughts back, that something incredibly important was on the line, and even though she couldn't remember quite what it was, she needed her head straight so she could think.

She channelled her willpower until the shuffling sounds of the women disappeared down the hall. Then she raced for the doors to the balcony, stumbling over the teetering floor, and she burst outside into the cold night air. She spat the berries over the rail.

The human inhaled deep breaths, clutching the railing with white knuckles as nausea washed through her stomach. She sank to a sitting position and hugged her middle, the vine pulling at her ankle telling her she couldn't take one more step or even attempt to climb down the side of this tall house and find a way out. Though, she couldn't imagine why she would run from these people. They fed her, clothed her, and gave her a bed to sleep upon.

So, what exactly was she trying to run from?

The human fell asleep on the balcony. The night came with the sounds of howling creatures, and when she awoke, shivering, she pulled herself to her feet and headed back inside, sealing the balcony doors closed behind her. She looked out the glass, realizing she could see many trees outside, their pink blossoms swaying in the wind. She realized she could see the room, too.

A shiver rolled up her body, and she rubbed her hands down her arms as she scurried over the floor to the bed. She curled up beneath the heavy duvet to get warm, but she couldn't sleep, and it wasn't because of the cold.

It was because she was thinking.

She had no idea how long it had been since her thoughts were clear. Since she remembered her name.

After hours of thinking, thinking, and thinking some more, the human whispered into the darkness, "Shayne, you'll come for me, right?" She had to believe it. Because if he didn't, she was sure she wasn't going to survive.

The sunrise came slowly, creeping over the floor inch by inch. Lily watched it all as it smothered the dim space. It nearly reached the bed when the bedroom doors swung open.

Fairies spilled into the room and took off her covers, lifted her off the bed, and dabbed her with wet cloths. They fixed up her hair so it was exactly how it had been the night before, and they tossed more glitter that stuck to her skin and made her glow in the morning sunlight. Lily observed them, took in their every movement, studied their patterns. But whenever one of them looked at her, she relaxed her face and stared off at nothing like she was in a daze.

As soon as they brought in a platter of food, Lily reached for it, pretending to be hungry. She shoved a handful of berries into her mouth and took a large bite of a crisp fruit on top of that. She chewed as the fairies straightened out her dress, but she shoved the wad of fruit beneath her tongue as they led her toward the door. The juices ran down her throat and she closed her eyes in concentration until the fairies turned her out of the labyrinth of hallways. She faked a few fumbles as they guided her through a lobby and out an enormous front door.

A large fountain took up the courtyard outside. The fairies led her to it and dropped her to sit on the fountain's ledge. The moment they headed back inside, Lily unearthed the wad of fruit and spat it into the fountain, brushing the juices from her lip in disgust. "Seriously…" she whispered as she watched the fruit get swallowed into the bubbling fountain waters. Her vision went in and out of focus, and she stifled a quiet moan as she teetered.

Even just a bit of the berry juice in her throat had been enough to leave her thinking she might tip right into the water.

A hand reached out and grabbed her shoulder, steadying her. Instead of looking back to see who it was, Lily glanced across the yard at a forest a short distance away, wondering if she'd make it if she tried to sprint.

The hand readjusted and took her arm. Lily was pulled to her feet and turned around. She found herself looking into the blue eyes of someone she knew by now was *Jethwire*. She tried to look dizzy, but the moment her gaze locked with his, a fire lit in her chest. She imagined throwing him to the ground and putting cuffs on him, and she forgot to drop her eyes.

The fairy's brows tugged in as he stared. He frowned. Then he said, "What is your name?"

Lily didn't answer. She forced her gaze from his and focused on something in the distance. She wavered on her feet, too, though she was sure it was too late; sure he'd realized she was no longer suffering from the effects of his magical berries and whatever else he'd been feeding her this whole time.

A series of other fairies appeared, including Lord Hans-Der—Shayne's father. New fairies were present too, ones Lily hadn't seen before. They rode atop giant beasts with fangs, and one of them carried a glistening blue banner with a symbol on it.

"Bring the peace offering," Lord Hans-Der said.

Jethwire pulled Lily over in obedience. His brows were still furrowed though, even as she almost lost her step.

Lily was shoved forward, and a new pair of large hands grasped her arms. A fairy in a strange outfit looked her over. "You're sure she's broken?" he asked.

"Yes," Lord Hans-Der said. But from the corner of her eye, Lily saw Jethwire hesitate. He leaned toward his father and whispered something in his ear. And Lily cracked a weak smile of disbelief as it became clear she would be discovered any moment.

"Let's check," the fairy holding onto her said. "What is your name, Human?"

Lily dragged her gaze up to meet the fairy's. She couldn't decide if she wanted to laugh or to cry. Yes, she'd finally gotten her thoughts back. No, she wouldn't get to keep them. But it had been nice while it lasted; she'd been able to remember everyone for a little while: Kate, Greyson, and Grandma Lewis. All her sword-wielding baristas. Violet, whom she'd developed an unexpected, common-ground friendship with. Even untrustworthy Luc—she would have liked to hold onto her memories of him over nothing. She wished she could say goodbye to them before they left her mind again.

"What is your name, Human? Do you recall it?" the fairy asked for the second time, tightening his grip on Lily's arms until it was painful.

Lily smiled—it was a pitiful smile, but the fairy was taken aback at the sight of it. She looked him dead in the eyes, and said, "My name is Lily Baker. And it'll take a lot more than that to break me."

The Lyro family's faces all changed at once. Some shouted and rushed forward while others passed blame. But Lily turned her head to make eye contact with *Jethwire.* She cast him a gloating smile; one last act of rebellion for the psycho who'd messed with her and Shayne. She did it knowing he'd speak her name, make her eat, and take away her sense of self again. She did it anyway, because just once, she wanted to be the human who outsmarted and embarrassed him after all the things he'd done.

Jethwire said nothing amidst the chaos; he only eyed her in return. So, Lily told him, "In my world, we call people like you *psychopaths,* and people like me would lock people like you and your whole family behind bars—"

The fairy who held Lily shoved her back against the side of a fanged beast, and it provided the perfect opportunity for her to kick the fairy in the shin. She hoofed him so hard, she was sure she broke her toes. The fairy shrieked and grabbed his calves, staggering backward, and it would have been satisfying, except that it took every ounce of energy Lily had left, and her own legs collapsed beneath her.

"You said she was broken! That she was a gift! What kind of gift is this?!" the fairy demanded while limping toward Lord Hans-Der.

Lily grunted a laugh as she fell over, rolling flat on her back in the dirt. The fairies continued to make noise and threats, but from her vantage point, she noticed Jethwire hadn't moved a muscle. He didn't seem angry as he studied her. In fact, a crooked smile curled up his lips. As the other fairies bickered, he sauntered over, dropped to a knee before Lily, and he tilted her face up with his wretched flute. "Well, Lily Baker. I'll admit, I wish I could keep you now." His grin widened. "But when a human is pretty *and* feisty, it's quite valuable to people like us. So why should we keep you when we can trade you for a high return?"

He pulled something out of his pocket, and Lily cringed at the sight of the berry.

"Eat this, Lily Baker," he commanded. "Eat and go with these fairies willingly. I don't care what you do when you get there, but you won't dishonour me again during this trade." He thrust the berry into her mouth.

Lily tried to shove it back out with her tongue, but as soon as she moved, she found herself chewing and swallowing it. Almost instantly, nausea trickled into her stomach, and she shuddered at the familiar, terrible feeling.

Jethwire smiled again. "I hope we meet again someday," he said. "Even though by then you probably won't remember me."

"For your sake," Lily said as she gritted her teeth, as the world around her began to blur, as her thoughts began to jumble, "you'd better hope I don't."

There was no way to tell if the day was long or short, starting or ending, or how much time had passed. Even warm and cold felt the same in the back of the caged wagon where the human found herself staring at the blurred tapestry of the sky. There were many, many turns and roads on her journey, through tall hills and mountains, around great cliffs and glassy green lakes. She couldn't make it out well enough to paint it or record it in her mind for later, but one thing she knew for sure was that wherever she was, it was very, very far away. Too far away to ever be found.

26

Shayne Lyro and His Nightmares Wide Awake

There sat his heartless father, his wicked brothers, and other young fair-ies who had once called themselves his friends. They all looked back at Shayne as he stood in the great hall. His own blood ran down his arm and over the handle of his fairsaber, dripping off the end and soaking into the red carpet. He'd fought a Lyro guard on his way into his childling home. And he had that rude guard to thank for leaving him with an open wound in his arm. But even amidst the fighting, the running, the pattering of his feet over the cold floors into the great hall, he hadn't uttered a word.

The twenty-four hours it took Shayne to get here were the longest of his life. And though he hadn't come on a straight path, and many things had happened in those twenty-four hours, he had felt a certain emptiness that was deeper than any he'd faced before. It had been twenty-four hours without smiling. Twenty-four hours of denial. Every step had been a

FAKE DATING A HUMAN 101

plea, an angry pursuit that had mimicked the pounding of his chest.

At the end of twenty-four hours, he looked into the faces of his past where his father and brothers sat in their chairs, unashamed of the works of their own hands. And Shayne said the first words he'd spoken since setting foot in this place.

"Give her back to me."

A few whispers flittered through the room. Massie tilted his head like a cat, and Hans-Der squinted as if trying to figure out what Shayne meant, even though it was obvious what Shayne faeborn meant.

Jethwire was a different story—he was the only one smiling. His icy eyes and twisted mouth made Shayne's insides curl with the story they told.

Lily was here in this room. At least, she had been recently. Shayne looked right and left, though he didn't see a pretty human with tattooed arms and long blonde hair. He didn't hear her rhythms, and though he could smell traces of her, she felt... He closed his eyes as he refused to acknowledge just how cold and far away she felt.

Queensbane, if she was dead...

Hans-Der leaned forward on his large chair and folded his hands before him. It was a posture he'd often used right before a righteous scolding. Shayne wasn't having it. He raised his fairsaber toward his father—a threat, and a statement: Speak or die.

Lesser fairies inhaled and scurried back as if afraid they might get caught in the crossfire of a terrible Lyro fight right in the middle of the great hall.

"Give *who* back to you? That human?" Hans-Der guessed, feigning innocence, and Shayne's jaw tightened.

"Yes," he said through his teeth. "That human. She's mine."

From his seat, Massie snorted a quiet laugh and placed a fist over his mouth.

Hans-Der's face spread into a smile, too. The look was infuriatingly charming and held a pinch of gloating. "I have no idea where she is," he said.

"Don't lie to me," Shayne demanded. He took a step forward, and Jethwire stood from his seat. It was a motion to assure Shayne that if he made another move toward their father, Jethwire would do something about it. Which was laughable. "What are you going to do, Jethwire? Throw your little flute at me?" Shayne guessed.

Jethwire couldn't find his stupid smile now.

Hans-Der chuckled as he relaxed against his chair. "My tongue would tingle if I was uttering falsehoods," he said. "It doesn't. I'm telling you the truth. I have no idea where that human is."

Shayne's fairsaber wavered. He stared at his father's face; one he'd been reading since he was just a boy. One that told him that perhaps this horrid man was telling the truth… until the corner of his father's mouth quirked.

"You're still lying, Father. And it's putting your throat dangerously close to being stabbed through with my fairsaber." Shayne took another step forward, and this time, Jethwire took two steps down the dais, his cold eyes whispering threats of their own.

Hans-Der, on the other hand, was smiling now, showing his teeth. Almost like he was *proud* Shayne could see through the falsehood, like he was realizing all over again Shayne was capable of figuring that much out.

"Very well. You're right, Shayne. I'm lying." He folded his hands and rested them on his lap. "Move, Jethwire. Sit down and let him be," he added.

Jethwire glanced back at Hans-Der with a look of question.

"Not only will Shayne refrain from killing us, he will also be taking his rightful place in the highest chair of this household tomorrow," Hans-Der assured as he stood. He descended the dais slowly, and he came to stand before Shayne, ignoring the fairsaber raised at his neck.

"Why would I ever do that?" Shayne asked. He inhaled; Lily's fragrance was everywhere—even in the carpet below his feet. He was sure if he just turned around, searched the House, he would find her.

Hans-Der reached up and pushed the fairsaber aside with the end of his finger. "Because once I tell you where that human is, I'm sure you won't want her anymore," he said, and Shayne's skin cooled. "This is the cost of your choice to disobey. I never fail to punish disobedience. You know this."

"Where is she?" Shayne thought to drop his fairsaber and grab his father's throat with his bare hand before all these witnesses.

"Swear yourself in as heir of this House. Submit to me and to this household, take your chair, and I will tell you where that human has gone." Hans-Der's voice was level, and Shayne's heart broke in his chest.

So, she was gone. Lost to the Ever Corners. Lily wasn't really here in this House, despite all the leftover traces.

The fairsaber nearly slipped from Shayne's fingers. Even if he set out immediately, he could spend years searching the Corners for a human, and he still might never find her. She could already be in the Silver Castle or in some other unreachable place, or she could be the property of the vilest fairies he'd only heard stories about. She could already have suffocated beneath the pressure of it all. She could already be dead.

No, he couldn't wait. And that was wildly unfortunate. Because Shayne knew not a soul in this House would tell him where Lily was unless he did the one thing they wanted.

His hand tightened around his fairsaber, but the rest of him dropped—his shoulders, his stance, his optimism. Could he really say goodbye to his true brothers forever? To the café? To the human realm? To Kate? To... to Lily? Could he say goodbye to Lily's police station, to secretly following her on her morning jogs, to her endearing scolds and the way he had her blushing schedule wrapped around his little finger? There was no going back to any of that if he did this, not even in a few years once things blew over. There was no sneaking away or maneuvering out of his position to live a happy life. In the whole North Corner of Ever, only Queene Levress had the power to stand against a household as influential as the Lyro's, and that was because she had all the armies of the North at her fingertips, and she was allied with Hans-Der.

No, there was no way out. And there was only one way to discover Lily's location.

Shayne released a growl and tugged at his hair. "I'll do it," he stated.

As the words left his lips, his cracked heart hardened to stone. He refused to feel anything more about this at all. It would destroy him if he did.

He sighed and dropped his hand from his hair. He knew this was coming anyway. He'd already decided on the way here what he would do. He'd already said his farewells to everything he would never see again.

Hans-Der's wide grin made the man look younger than he was. Shayne couldn't stand looking at it. Instead, he dropped to his knees and stared at the floor, letting his fairsaber fall away with a clamour. For all his years of running, all his time spent training with the Brotherhood to defeat people like this, for all his time spent among the humans... this is what it had led to: Shayne chained to a chair for eternity. To be quiet instead of loud. To never laugh again, because he wouldn't have anything to laugh about now.

"Bring the ring," Shayne said.

Hans-Der folded his arms and looked down the end of his nose where Shayne waited. "You know there's no way to trick the heir's ring. You can't get out of its bind. But just in case..." He nodded to someone Shayne couldn't see.

Sounds of struggling and a low, muttering voice filled the hall. Shayne turned on his knees to find two huntsmen dragging a scowling auburn-haired fairy over the carpet. They tossed him down at Shayne's side, and surprise filled Shayne's face.

Dranian lifted his head, growling about his 'one bad arm'. Shayne watched him take in the image of Hans-Der, the fairy who had purchased him all those years ago and had never once made things easy for him.

"I have no idea whether you were aware your old fairy guard followed you here or not, but now that I have him, I'm sure you'll follow through on your promise," Hans-Der said. "We shall have the swearing-in ceremony *tomorrow* night. And I'll keep your fairy guard contained until then to ensure you don't attempt any tricks." With that, Hans-Der crouched to a knee and looked Shayne in the eyes. "I have, after all, waited all these years to solidify an heir. I'd hate for you to get away again."

Shayne's mouth parted as Dranian was kicked by a hunter. Massie threw his head back and shrieked in high-pitched laughter that pulled Shayne's flesh into bumps. Dranian took in deep breaths, his lashes fluttered, but he focused long enough to tilt toward Shayne and mumble, "Don't worry. I understand why you had to come here and do this."

Warmth and dismay puddled in Shayne's chest. He struggled to spit out words, fighting the temptation to reach over and take Dranian's hand. His greatest, dearest friend, and the realest, truest, most loyal brother he'd ever had. "We'll always be the best of friends. You and me," he whispered back. "Regardless of where I am."

Jethwire carried over a bronze bowl. Everyone in the room leaned to try and see inside it.

Dranian was grabbed by the hunters again, and too quickly, his presence left Shayne's side. Shayne looked back over his shoulder; fear, worry, shock, and all sorts of other things pasted across his eyes. Dranian had the same sort of face, though he wasn't one for big expressions. Still, the two of them locked eyes that way, and as they did, Shayne gave his forever-friend a small nod. A nod of, *"Goodbye."* A nod of, *"Good luck."*

The truth was, he wasn't surprised to see Dranian at all.

But still… Shayne closed his eyes after Dranian was taken away. Knowing Dranian would come here didn't make what Shayne had to do any less real. He hated goodbyes.

"Let me swear in *now*, and then tell me where Lily Baker is," Shayne said to Hans-Der one more time. "I have no interest in waiting until tomorrow. I'll become the official heir right now."

Hans-Der reached over and lifted a gold ring from Jethwire's bowl. He studied the large Lyro crest stamped atop it. The gold band had a magical glow that radiated, casting flickers of light along his face. Shayne's stomach twisted into knots as he imagined wearing it. As he prepared himself for that ring to bind to his flesh where it would become impossible to remove. Where his role to govern the household would begin.

Hans-Der dropped the ring back into the bowl. "We'll get the preparations ready for tomorrow," he decided once and for all. Then, he turned, faced the room, and shouted, "Let's celebrate!"

Shayne watched as fairies leapt around the hall. Music began to play, but he closed his eyes. He couldn't bear to see them rejoice. Instead, he turned and headed for the maze, and he made his way around the curves to his room, expecting it to feel cold and abandoned like the inside of his chest.

The moment he entered, he gasped and slapped a hand over his mouth and nose.

Lily's scent was on *everything*.

It was like a caress of false hope, trapping him in a nightmare while he was still wide awake. She was everywhere, yet nowhere. Her fragrance was on his pillow, bound to his sheets, in footsteps on the floor, and resting in the air.

Shayne leaned on his bed, holding himself up by his fists. He whispered, "Where are you, pretty Human?" The room answered with silence. And so, he vowed, "I'm going to find you. Even if it takes me the rest of my life."

CHAPTER

27

Luc Zelsor and All His Hopes and Dreams

It was a bit unfair. One minute the Shadow nobles were calling him a *prince*, and the next, they were calling him a *traitor*. What a bunch of brainless fools who needed to make up their minds.

Luc had started pacing around his cold iron cell the moment he'd been shoved into it by a series of clammy Commander hands. After a few hours, he decided to sing. Normally songs were for fairies who were merry, and Luc didn't have many reasons to be happy, but despite the oncoming vote—which somehow *still* hadn't happened—he could think of one thing, one single thing, to be merry about. And for that, he sang, "There once lived a young fox who faced every obstacle with cunning and determination…" His lips curled into a cruel smile. "The fox grew to the capable age of twenty-five years and found he had reached the greatest measure of strength he would. And so, on a cold Wynter's day, he began a great trek up a mountain to face the greatest obstacle of all—

another fox!" He did a little skip and hop with that one. "One twice his age, and equal in power... And would you look at that? He won! The young, cunning fox beat the snot out of the old loser—"

"What are you rambling on about?" a prison guard hollered down the hall.

"None of your business, you eavesdropping slug!" Luc shouted back. Whelp. That did it.

A tetrad of fairies in dark green uniforms marched toward his cell. They walked tall like they carried authority, but with the way their scummy outfits gave off such bad style, Luc wasn't sure why they were so proud of themselves.

When they reached his temporary little home of cold iron bars, Luc flashed them a wicked smile and filled the prison with the scent of sweetness and delightful promises. He leaned toward the bars, and through them, he whispered, "How about you fetch me something delicious that tastes like human realm ice cream?"

The great and mighty guard with a gold medallion pinned to his chest stepped a bit ahead of the others. Yes, he loved himself very much for that gold medallion. It was obvious in the way he held his chin so high and said, "We have asked you several times to be quiet. Remember that we can make your last days in here quite miserable."

Luc slapped a hand over his eyes and laughed. "Oh dear," he said. "That's only if they vote to execute me. You've forgotten one very important thing." Luc dropped his hand and spun to face them, letting his metallic eyes sparkle. Sure enough, the guards' rigid stance shrank a little. "What if they vote *not* to kill me?" He returned to the bars, close enough that he might be able to reach through and snatch one of them without burning his flesh on the iron. "What do you think a scorned fox might do to his enemies if he gets to live? Before you refuse to wait upon me, remember that I might get out of this alive, and you'll wish you'd made the trek to the human realm to get me ice cream when I asked."

Another presence appeared at the end of the hall, too dark for Luc to see, but the slight sheen in his black pearl armour gave what he was away. Luc sighed and took a step back from the bars.

"Bring him," the Commander in black pearl said, and at the sound, Luc tilted his head in thought. The voice sounded a lot like his old Commander. The one he'd fought beneath for many years, the one he'd convinced to sign off on his first liaison spy mission into the human realm—after which he completely abandoned his post and never returned. Until now.

The lock on Luc's cell was wrangled a bit, but after a moment, it popped off and the guard with the medallion swung the door open. Luc waited for a moment until all the guards were wondering why he wasn't moving. And only after they became acutely aware of the wide-open space between the dangerous nine tailed fox and their fully exposed fairy flesh, only when their stances shrank and a spec of fear filled their eyes as they wondered what the fox might do, only *then* did Luc take his first step forward.

He glared at every single one of them as he passed.

At the end of the hall, the Commander didn't show a hint of recognition as Luc approached, even though the faded light revealed that Luc had been right—this old Commander was exactly the one who'd ruled Luc's Army division with an iron fist. One of the first fairies who'd come after Luc in the human realm when Luc had stopped checking in and sending news back to the Army.

The Commander stared at everything except Luc as he held out a fresh vine and waited. Luc released a sigh and obediently stuck out his wrists.

"You must have lost all your memories," Luc reasoned—it wasn't uncommon for Shadow Fairies. "Or, you're afraid of me."

The Commander's fingers stopped tying. He did look up at Luc then, with daggers for eyes. Luc smiled.

The guards ushered Luc out into a long, winding tunnel through the base of the mountain. "Are we going back to the Assembly?" Luc guessed as they walked.

No one answered. A loud crack of thunder boomed in the distance, echoing down the tunnel and making the only noise for several seconds apart from their marching footsteps.

"So, this is it, then." He nodded. The Shadow Assembly must have voted after all. It seemed his fate had been decided and he was walking out to—hopefully not too violently—meet it. "Did you know that foxes are known for defeating their enemies atop mountains?" he asked none of them in particular. "It seems we're also destined to die beneath them." He smirked at his own epiphany.

He was nudged to the right, and Luc braced himself to come face-to-face with whichever highest ranking Assembly members had been selected to bear witness to his demise. He considered himself brave, being a fox and all, but the truth was, if he saw an opportunity to escape, he'd probably take it.

Luc's old Commander opened a door with a loud screech, and the whole group of them came to a halt. Luc nearly bumped into the Commander's back, but it was the sounds of growls and flashes of lightning that made him lift his pretty eyes to the wide balcony beyond. He didn't realize they were up on a cliff, deep into the mountainside. A storm raged in the sky, and rain pounded upon slick stones where at least a dozen fairies in Shadow armour lay either unconscious or dead.

But what was utterly spectacular about the scene was the fool in the black, dandelion-speckled coat standing in the middle of the ring of bodies with a hood shadowing his face. A hood that carefully hid his curly hair, brown-silver eyes, and the fact that deep down he'd always been obsessed with Luc's well being—at least, Luc had speculated as much, but he'd never known for sure until this moment.

Luc bit down on his lips, but they still spread into a broad smile.

Mor Trisencor had been an unsolvable mystery for far too long. But now that Luc saw him standing there, drenched with rain and waiting like a beast of darkness who'd crawled from its cave to feed, Luc had his answer once and for all. And he snorted a laugh. Because he'd been right and Mor was wrong and everyone else in existence was wrong because the fact of the matter was that Mor cared.

The Commander drew his fairsaber and stepped out into the rain to go deal with the cloaked person he didn't realize was Mor Trisencor. And so, Luc wound up and kicked him in the behind as he left.

The Commander growled in surprise as he fell knees-first onto the wet stones. He sprang back to his feet in a heartbeat and lifted his fairsaber to Mor's throat. He heaved as he barked out his words like an animal, "Whoever you are, you will be punished by—"

"By whom?" Mor's distinct, low voice left his hood. "The Dark Queene?" he asked. Then he said, "I hear she's dead."

Luc bit his lips together so hard over his grin, he nearly chewed his own mouth off. "She is! She's dead!" he shouted into the rain. But then he glanced around at the guards who held him and added, "Not that I was there or am admitting to doing it."

No one saw Mor draw his fairsaber until it collided with the Commander's, and the guards around Luc drew their weapons. Luc kicked the nearest one back into the tunnel and ran out into the rain, leaping onto the Commander's back and swinging his tied arms over the Commander's head. He shoved the vines on his wrists into the Commander's gaping, growling mouth. "Bite down, you fool, or I'll rip out your teeth and use them to cut through these vines myself," Luc promised.

The Commander gawked when Luc pivoted to kick a guard in the stomach who got too close. The other three guards raised their blades and Mor swept past like a grim reaper. Very quickly, the last three guards stopped breathing.

"More Shadows will come," Luc warned Mor through thin lips as he tried to force his vines against the Commander's teeth. "There's supposed to be a grand spectacle of an execution today, and many will be arriving very soon to witness it."

"They haven't voted yet," Mor said back as he marched over, grabbed the top of the Commander's head and the bottom of his jaw, and slammed everything together. Luc felt the snap of the vines, and he slid off the Commander's back with his wrists raised as the vine tumbled to the ground.

"What do you mean, they haven't voted yet?" Luc asked as that settled in. Also, he wondered how in the world Mor knew that.

The Commander released a horrifying bark and spun with his blade out, but Mor and Luc were already gone.

The wind felt sweet, even though rain pelted Luc's face as he sped on the gusts after Mor. He hardly saw the Commander chasing them in the gales, until Mor's ankle was grabbed, and Luc watched him be lurched out of the current. Luc rolled out after him, landing on his feet at the foot of the mountain. Before Luc had a chance to breathe, a saber swung past his face. Mor smashed the blade back as he ripped his ankle free of the Commander's grip, and Luc took the opportunity to twist and steal a pair of fairsabers off the fairy who'd tried to run him through. It was the first chance he got to look up, and his rhythms faltered at the sight of all the fairies racing through the trees with their blades held high.

"What exactly did you do to make it to this mountain?" Luc asked Mor. "Not that I'm complaining you're here."

Mor collided with the fairies first—he ducked and slashed fae flesh, moving through the scattered warriors with decent technique, but certainly not the same sort of grace Luc moved with. Then he said, "I airslipped. All these fools chased me."

"Oh dear." Luc nodded with a wince. "I was hoping you came in secret or something." He spun into a series of stabs and kicks, dropping two fairies at once. "I should have mentioned I don't particularly want to cause any more trouble in this Corner, Trisencor."

"Why does that matter?" Mor asked. He took a punch to the mouth, but he still managed to shout, "You're already a breath away from dying if they vote to kill you!" Stab, stab, and another stab. Drops of purple blood competed with the rain, hitting trees, flailing in arches, splattering over Mor's scent-concealing coat.

"Hmm." Luc's mouth twisted. He paused his killing to contemplate. "I've just realized that you don't actually know what else they're voting on, do you?"

"Look out!" Mor shouted, pointing to a rushing Shadow Fairy.

But Luc had seen the fairy coming ages ago. He dropped to a knee and bent forward just as the fairy reached him, sending the fairy tripping over his back and flying into a tree. Luc stood and glanced after him. "What a loser," he muttered. Then he marched to where Mor was, stabbing and blocking as he did a quick count of the Shadows popping into view, calculating the energy he would spend trying to fight if the Army kept coming. And he decided he and Mor wouldn't make it.

"Let's run," he suggested. "And then you can tell me all about why in the name of the sky deities you came here." He smirked just a bit. "Though, I think I can already guess."

Mor scowled. "Don't flatter yourself," he warned as he cut a fairy thigh. He was sliced up the arm in return, and he gawked. Luc hurtled his left fairsaber through the Shadow Fairy's shoulder, and then he sighed because Mor was out of shape, and he wasn't sure if it would be polite to point it out.

"And they'll just follow us if we try to run," Mor added, clutched his bleeding arm. But he started backing away toward the mountain as he took in all the fresh Shadows flooding the trees.

"Then let's run to Cressica," Luc said. When Mor didn't reply, Luc's face fell. "You did bring the mighty North Prince, right? Please don't tell me you *actually* came here alone—"

Mor fled into the howling wind, grabbing Luc on his way. Naturally, at least a dozen war fae followed, eating up the gusts at their backs, swinging their weapons and coming dangerously close to cutting off Luc's limbs. Luc swatted one right out of the air as he rode the gales, staying on Mor's heels. They moved so fast that when they exited the airstream, they tumbled onto a patch of grass in a tangle of limbs, rolling over and sliding to a stop—Luc was flat on his stomach in the dirt.

"Where are we?" Luc asked with a wince. He'd lost his weapons somewhere in the wind.

"You're just over the border of the Dark Corner." A menacing, yet familiar voice filled the clearing. "And you're in my domain now."

Cress wore a hooded coat like Mor's, only his was short and looked to be made of leather for human motorcycle riders. Sunglasses covered his normally cold eyes.

"Oh, thank goodness." Luc let his face fall into the grass. He rested there as popping sounds filled the woods around them. "I was worried you hadn't brought him," he admitted to Mor who, coincidentally, was lying flat on his back in the grass at his side. When Mor turned his head, he glared at Luc, and Luc almost jumped in surprise at the expression. All Luc's merry thoughts about Mor coming to rescue him for 'caring reasons' went up in smoke.

So Luc grunted. "Figures," he muttered. Mor probably only came to force Luc to keep his promise about dear Lily and three-legged Dranian.

Luc looked around at the empty, damp forest, sniffing a few times.

Speaking of Dranian...

Cress suddenly pulled down his hood and tore off his sunglasses. Mor's wide-eyed reaction was enough for Luc to realize Cress revealing himself had *not* been part of their plan.

"Cress, wait!" Mor tried grabbing Cress's leg as the mighty North Prince stepped over him with his bright eyes taking in the Shadow Fairies.

"You've crossed into forbidden territory. I shall inform my Queene immediately of this treachery!" he shouted at them.

Half the Shadow Fairies looked startled at the sight of the North Queene's dreaded ward, alive and hungry for their blood. Most of them drew back, blinking wildly like they were sure they weren't seeing properly. It was only then Luc noticed his old Commander. The old brute had followed him all this way even though his teeth probably ached like crazy.

"Yes, I have returned to finish what I started with the Shadows," Cress went on. "That's the won-oh-won of being an assassin."

Mor closed his eyes and slapped a hand over his face. Luc, though, rolled up to a sitting position to watch. This was better than late night TV thrillers.

Cress drew his fairsaber handle from his pocket. The storm picked up, a bout of lightning burning across the North Corner skies, thunder crackling on cue, and the perfect amount of breeze fluttered Cress's hair as his fairsaber blade formed with a *buzz*. It was all terrifying, and totally magical. Luc smacked Mor's shoulder. "You're missing it, Trisencor. Wake up and watch," he urged.

Mor didn't. He remained lying there with his hands over his face.

"Who wishes to face me first?" Cress demanded.

There was utter silence from the Shadow Fairies, even though they stood there with their sabers drawn and their pearl armour glittering with rainwater.

And so, Cress shouted again, "Who will fight me?!"

Luc wondered why he was experiencing déjà vu. After a second, he snapped his fingers. "David and Goliath!" he realized. "Do you know that human realm story?" he asked Mor again. "That's what this reminds me of. Cressica is like a menacing giant, and everyone is too afraid to fight him."

Mor still ignored him.

So, Luc climbed to his feet and stood beside Cress. He cast his former Army companions a sweet, broad smile. "As you can see, I've aligned myself with the North Corner of Ever for the time being. Something even the Dark Queene herself was never able to do. So go back and tell that to the Assembly while they bicker like a bunch of childlings." He took a step forward, positioning himself directly before his former Commander, and to him, he said, "Do not bother me again until after they've voted, or you'll start a war that will end in the same terrible bloodshed that it did the last time we tried to stand up against the North."

The Commander's lip curled into a snarl, but he must have understood well enough. He turned on his heel and fled back into an airslip, the rest of the Shadows following close behind. They were all gone in exactly five seconds.

Luc exhaled slowly once the woods were clean, clear, and free of the Dark Corner presence. Even the charcoal clouds in the sky began to separate and disperse, leaving the wet forest gilded in bright light. He turned back to the two who had come to his rescue, but his smile fell when he saw Cress hunched forward and holding his stomach.

"What's wrong with him?" he asked Mor.

Mor finally lifted his hands off his face and rose to sit. He frowned at Cress. "He ate an entire box of doughnuts before we left the human realm."

An *entire*.... Luc placed a hand over his own stomach.

"Oh dear." He winced. Then he offered therapist-ing advice: "You should try ice cream. It's a much lighter option for someone with a binge eating disorder."

"I do *not* have a disorder," Cress snapped at him. "And this is all your fault, you fool!"

Luc pursed his lips and took a voluntary step back. "I don't really want to ask why you think so," he admitted, "but I will because I'm a strong and confident nine tailed fox." He bit his tongue, then he worked his jaw. Then he scratched the back of his head. "Alright, so why exactly is this my f—"

"You made me a promise," Mor stated. Luc hadn't even seen him climb to his feet, but Mor stood tall now, looking a tad bit more judge-mental than before when he was rescuing Luc and caring and everything.

"Ah, yes. And for your information, Trisencor, I was still planning to keep it," Luc returned. He slid a lock of his deep red hair out of his eyes, setting it nicely back in place. "You have no patience."

"No patience?!" Mor growled. "I trusted you, Luc! I trusted that you'd fix this like you said you would. I was crazy for believing you'd follow through and for leaving the people I care for in the hands of a conniving fox who's always been a risk!" Mor pointed in his face. "I knew you'd only make things worse!"

Luc's jaw slid to the side. Those nasty words didn't feel necessary, but he moved on. "I'm still fixing everything," he articulated. "I'm not finished yet, and you," he waved a finger up and down Mor's rigid stance, "are being rather ungrateful."

It was truly remarkable how Mor was so contained, yet sometimes he looked like he could burst at any moment and half the forest would explode.

"And, for the record, this does not count as the High Court of the Coffee Bean rescuing me. Even though things may have looked grave, I had everything under control," he promised.

Both Mor and Cress performed a rather excellently in-sync eye roll. They turned and headed into the woods, Cress returning his hood and his sunglasses even though he'd already been ousted to the whole Dark Corner and soon rumours would trickle to the North, South, and East that Queene Levress's deadly ward had made a return. The stress of that was written all over Mor's face.

"Where are we going? I can't go too far," Luc informed them. "I'm still in the middle of fixing everything, remember?"

Cress snorted at him. A moment later, he said, "We're fetching Dranian, and we're going home."

Luc stopped walking. His feet forgot how to move while he stared at Cressica Alabastian's broad-shouldered back. Not because returning to the human realm wasn't an option for him, though he had yet to tell Cress and Mor about that, but because Cress had used that word: "*Home.*"

Luc lifted a hand to his chest and rubbed over his heart where things got a little warm.

Cressica had used that word in reference to Luc. Like Luc was part of that home. Like he perhaps belonged there with them—like it was home to *all three* of them.

It was only when Cress and Mor nearly got lost in the forest ahead that Luc realized he was smiling. He dropped the expression from his face and airslipped forward to save himself the scramble.

"Oh dear. Going back to the human realm isn't possible for me," Luc said when he fell into step behind them.

Mor glanced back over his shoulder. "Don't lie," he warned.

Luc sighed loudly; it echoed through the trees. "You're exhausting sometimes, Trisencor," he admitted. "I'm not lying. You should find it within yourself to have a little patience sometimes."

"I ran out of patience in my childling years," Cress announced. "That's an absurd request for someone like me."

"Of course," Luc agreed. "But humour me and explain why you two came back to the Ever Corners and aren't in the human realm guarding our dear Violet and Kate Kole. And while you're at it," Luc looked around again, but he didn't see or sense another fairy anywhere, "tell me what happened to my bestie Dranian and why he's not here with you."

Neither Mor nor Cress seemed to care enough to respond, so Luc looked between the two and decided which one would be the easier target. After three more strides of silent walking, Luc came up beside Cress. He reached out, and he grabbed the Prince of the North's forehead to steal the memory for himself.

He didn't get it, and the cost of his attempt was a punch across the jaw with a fist of faestone. Luc collapsed into a dizzy heap at the foot of a tree, descending into a blackout slumber.

As Luc slept, he thought he heard someone knocking against the edges of his dream.

"Let me in," she said.

CHAPTER

28

Dranian Evelry and the Thing that Happened
Twenty-Four Hours Ago
(Before Mor and Cress Showed Up for Luc,
and Before Shayne Returned to the House of Lyro)

Snow.

Dranian scowled at the cold white stuff falling upon Toronto and hugged his arms to himself, his one good arm carrying the weight of the other. The streets rang with Yule carols and all the nearby humans looked cute with their pom-pom hats and their scarves jammed into the neck crevices of their coats. But even with the holiday tunes and the human-y cuteness in every direction, Dranian found he was temperamental, and not due to natural moodiness, no, but because he'd just *walked himself* across the entire North Corner of Ever to get back to the human realm and his feet and legs were bundles of soreness and silent complaints.

Naturally, as he was grouching about it to himself, muttering on about his circumstances—how the girl with no name had been stolen from him, how Lily had been human-napped and had vanished without a trace, how Mor and Cress had left him alone with Luc, and how Luc had disappeared for *days*—he stepped in a slushy bit.

"Faeborn-cursed-human-realm-slushy-bits!" he cussed as he shook off his shoe.

A mother cast him a scowl and dragged her childling to the other side of the road. Dranian looked up at her in surprise, realizing he'd startled the small human family. So, he attempted a smile, which must have been rather terrifying since the mother's face grew more horrified and her steps of escape became quicker.

Dranian snarled and turned back to his walking. His running shoes were every bit as damp, squishy, and repulsive to hike in as sticking his bare toes in swamp mud. But he finished the trek to Fae Café and paused outside when he noticed the new holiday drink menu in the window and the strings of lights flashing around the door. Something big and heavy sank through his chest. Half of him was so profoundly relieved to be back, to see this with his own two eyes. How he had missed this burgundy awning, the scent of fresh drinks, and the promise of warmth.

His eyes grew misty when he thought about Shayne never seeing it again. Never having this feeling of desperation and relief from standing before the café door. Then, he sniffed—loud and hard—to make sure none of his watery emotions showed. He even wiped his nose on his sleeve, then he grabbed the door a new man.

When he came inside Fae Café, he instantly craved cranberry desserts and caffeine. Even though he hadn't been gone from this place for long, he didn't realize just how much the separation had affected him. How much his fairy blood and empty stomach demanded to be filled with sweets and hot beast milk with whipped cream and tiny little crunchy bits sprinkled on top.

But then there was Cress. And Kate. And... queensbane, Mor and Violet were there too... and Greyson—oh no.

Dranian fell into a chair, threw his head back, and wailed a cry of self loathing.

Customers quieted their conversations, a few glancing over at him with strange faces. A female across the café even held a sizable piece of cake on her fork an inch from her mouth, frozen there at the noise.

Cress's wild turquoise eyes darted up, spotting Dranian. Then they moved around, taking in all the cringing humans, and his expression grew horrified as Dranian ruined his well-maintained level of customer satisfaction. To Mor and Greyson, he whispered, "Get him."

Greyson was smack dab in the middle of consuming a tart. He looked up as if to see if Cress was serious, and seeming to note the fairy's deadly glower, Greyson dropped the tart to his plate and rushed through the café after Mor. Mor didn't really need his help though—that was clear when Mor reached Dranian, grabbed a handful of Dranian's shirt at his shoulder, and tugged him up from the chair in one great heave.

"Come with me," Mor said in a voice far more soothing than Cress's had been.

Dranian shook his head. "You don't understand—"

"Apologies!" Cress shouted at the humans in the room even though they hadn't asked for an explanation. "This fool was raised by raging forest beasts riddled with itchy fur-lice. He *often* forgets how to act normal like the rest of us."

"Cress!" Kate scolded with a whisper as she flicked him. "That's a terrible thing to say!"

Cress leaned down to Kate's height, put on his *'I'm about to educate you'* face that Dranian had come to know all too well, and he whispered back, "It's essential to stay *ahead* of the problem. That's public relations won-oh-won."

Dranian was nudged through the kitchen doors, and the doors swung shut behind them.

Mor folded his arms as soon as they reached the back freezers. "Speak." He waited.

Dranian sorted through a variety of things he might say aloud. Nothing quite fit, but he decided he might go with—

"There can only be one reason you're here, Dranian. So, tell it to me,"

Mor said for him. "Where is Luc? What happened? Please tell me…" He paused and swallowed with difficulty. "Please tell me Lily is alright, and the two of you have found a way to rescue her."

Dranian grimaced and looked off to think.

A muscle feathered in Mor's jaw. "Where. Is. *Luc?*" he asked again. Even though Mor was normally the most understanding of Dranian's brothers, he had a particular way of sharpening his silvery eyes that could turn a fairy's blood cold. Thankfully, Mor only brought it out for special occasions.

It seemed this moment was one of those occasions.

"Dranian," Mor warned again, and so, Dranian cleared his throat.

"Luc… has vanished." He bit down on his mouth after he said it, every inch of him feeling like a disloyal, loose-lipped traitor.

Frankly, on his walk back here, Dranian had resolved he wouldn't tell a soul about Luc abandoning him immediately after Mor and Cress left. About how Dranian had thought about going after Lily and the girl with no name all by himself, and that he'd been so distraught by the idea that he had truly considered researching Luc's magic walnut enchantment and switching bodies with Cress again. In fact, he'd resolved that his primary reason for returning here was to get Cress's body back so he could return to the Ever Corners and save the day.

But alas, Mor had looked Dranian right in the eyes and asked *that* question specifically, and so, Dranian had revealed everything. He would apologize to Luc later—if Luc ever showed up again.

For now, Dranian's one plan was soiled. But perhaps it had been de-railed the moment Dranian had arrived and seen that everyone was present instead of *only* Cress. *Only* Cress would have been easier to trick into eating another walnut than everybody plus Cress. Dranian was no math wizard, but even he could tell that equation wouldn't add up to success.

It occurred to Dranian that Mor had not blinked in a very long time. He had not spoken, either.

Finally, Dranian murmured, "Aren't your eyes drying out—?"

"Do you know where Luc is?" Mor asked. "If you have an inkling, Dranian, tell me now."

Even if Dranian did know, he was sure admitting Luc's location to Mor when Mor's eyes were doing their sharp silvery thing would be a betrayal to Luc. Perhaps Luc had betrayed their High Court first, but Dranian had always been loyal to a fault—except when asked direct questions with eye contact.

None of that needed to be said aloud though. So instead, he went with, "I haven't a clue."

Mor closed his eyes and let out a growling sigh of disbelief. "I'll go get her then," he said.

Dranian's eyes widened. "Who?" he asked with dread.

"Lily, obviously!" Mor snapped back. He glared at Dranian for a moment, but then his shoulders relaxed. "I shouldn't have left you alone with that fox. This is my fault, not yours. Thank you for coming to tell us about Luc," he said.

Dranian opened his mouth to confess that he hadn't actually come here to tell Mor about Luc, but then he thought better of it. In fact, he went with it.

"Of course," he mumbled with a nod. "But Mor... how do you plan to get Lily back?" What he didn't add was, *"And will you be getting back the girl with no name, too?"*

Mor shook a hand through his hair, dislodging a wild curl from its bun. "I suppose I'll offer to purchase her, which will bind us to payments for the next twenty faeborn years at least. And if that doesn't work..." Mor's throat bobbed again, and Dranian wondered if he was thinking about instigating a death match—a one on one fairy battle that would result in the winner taking a very large prize—like a human. But Mor finished with, "I'm not sure what I'll do."

"That is outrageous, Mor!" Cress said from outside the kitchen doors. The doors swung open, revealing Cress, Kate, Violet, and Greyson who'd all been listening on the other side. "You'll not be going to the House of Lyro. Not today, not ever."

247

"What happened to Lily?!" Kate's voice rang over everything—and Dranian's heart stopped as he took in the humans and realized what they must have learned in this moment.

"Cress, are you out of your mind?!" Mor asked, nodding toward the humans. "Do you want Kate to have a heart attack? I thought we were going to tell her everything once we got Lily back!"

"Seriously, what happened to Lily?" Kate shouted as she took a step into the kitchen.

Cress jutted this thumb backward toward the café exit. "This is for Shayne to deal with. That was the responsibility placed upon him when he made the choice to fool us and run off in the night!" Cress tried to stand with his own words, but a slow, tight-lipped snarl formed across his mouth a second later. "Oh sky deities, have mercy. Fine, inform the Sisterhood they must be on guard," he stated. Then he turned to Kate. "Put on your sweater."

"What are you doing?" Mor asked him, and Cress lifted his eyes that were a fraction icier than they'd been a second ago.

"We're going to find Shayne and Lily ourselves like we should have from the start," Cress declared.

Mor put his hands on his hips, shook his head, and rubbed his temples. "You really trust the *Sisterhood of the Travelling Knit-Pants* to protect our humans if we leave?" he asked.

"No," Cress stated. "They're severely out of practice, and if I'm being honest, they're wildly unhealthy. They ride around on those mopeds all day like they've forgotten how to faeborn walk! But we'll strike fear into them with our dominance, and they will obey us."

Mor cast a look to Dranian indicating he didn't believe for one second the Sisterhood of Assassins would abide by Cress's fearsome demands.

Dranian noticed Cress's gaze dart to Kate while her back was turned. The sorrow that spilled into his turquoise eyes made Dranian shift his footing. Cress's tones gave off a story of worry that if he returned to the Ever Corners and his identity was revealed, he might be trapped there forever. It was as though Cress feared he might never hold onto Kate again, and that sent prickly guilt crawling all over Dranian's flesh.

This was the exact sort of situation he'd wanted to avoid when he had decided not to involve Cress and Mor and their humans in Ever Corner business in the first place. If something happened to Cress, Kate would lose her forever mate. She wouldn't understand why she felt her human heart torn from her chest without notice, why she would wait by a window for the rest of her life, or why she would never be able to forget about him or let him go and why time would not heal all things as the humans claim. She wouldn't understand because she was from a realm where the relevance and power of bonding to a mate were entirely unexplained. The same thing would happen to Violet if something happened to Mor.

Dranian glanced through the kitchen doors, out at the café, at the street beyond the windows, and he wondered just how different the human realm might become if the fairies in his company did not return home.

Thirty minutes later, three fairy assassins stepped out of Fae Café.

Cress pulled a pair of sunglasses out of his fashionable snow coat. He put them on as a warm gust of wind fluttered his silken hair, and a beam of sunlight pierced through the clouds overhead, turning him gold for a split second. Time seemed to slow as he flexed his jaw, his coat flapping while he took his first step across the sidewalk. Dranian's eyes got stuck; he couldn't look away from Cress's greatness. In fact, Dranian could have sworn he heard some sort of sweet-toned, stringed music rise from the ground that aligned perfectly with Cress's movements.

"Stop doing that," Mor muttered at Cress.

The slow-motion, the magical wisp of breeze, and the music all disappeared in an instant, and Cress's hair fell flat. Cress grunted and adjusted his coat which seemed far less flashy all of a sudden. "If I *can* do it, I *should*," he said back. "It's a great act of theft to all those watching if I don't."

Mor rolled his eyes and buttoned up his own coat; the long black one he usually kept in the closet at his cathedral. In comparison to theirs, Dranian's coat was pretty boring.

The sound of revving, chunky bicycle engines lifted from behind the buildings, sending ear-piercing echoes in all directions, and Dranian winced.

"Ah. Right on time," Cress said, looking at his wrist even though he didn't have a watch there.

The assassins turned toward the end of the street where two dozen mopeds inched their way around the bend, ridden by females wearing tight knit scarves, unsightly yarn vests, helmets, and bug-eyed goggles. The machines took up the whole road, and Mor shook his head.

The Sisterhood rolled up to Fae Café and stopped before the Brotherhood when they saw them standing there. Freida slid the goggles off her eyes and hung them around her neck as she looked Cress over first, then Mor. She hardly spared a glance at Dranian. "Well, something's not right," she said. "Where is Kate Kole?"

"She's *fine*." Cress made a tsking sound. "I take good care of her." He folded his arms and leveled his sunglasses-covered eyes with Freida's. "We're about to—"

"Go on a trip, I imagine. Isn't that right, Prince?" Freida interrupted. "Ah. I see you're all dressed up." She made a face at Cress's outfit in particular. "Not well, but dressed up, nevertheless."

The corners of Cress's frown tightened.

"We'll be back soon. *Please* keep an eye on our humans for us," Mor said, and Freida's gaze darted over to him. She had a cat-like way of looking people over, and even though Dranian wasn't the object of her attention, he fidgeted with his hands.

Freida folded her arms and tapped a finger against her ugly sweater. Then she said, "Fine. We'll watch over Kate Kole and the humans—"

"It's not an enormous request!" Cress howled out of nowhere. "Just say you'll do it! Or when I return, you will suffer my unrestrained wrath!"

Mor and Dranian leaned forward to look at Cress.

Freida unfolded her arms and barked at her fellow moped-riders, "Is he deaf, Hazel? I did say we'd do it, right?"

Hazel nodded but said nothing, and Cress's stance relaxed. "Oh," he said.

"We're a gang, Prince Cressica. *And* we're former assassins. We'll guard the humans well," Freida swore.

"A gang?" Dranian didn't mean to mutter it out loud or say it with doubt, but Freida's gaze—along with all the pointed gazes of the whole 'gang'—darted to him. At that moment, he felt a bit like he might melt into the sidewalk.

"Gangs ride around on bikes and are deadly to mess with," Freida challenged him. "Seems like we're a gang then." With that, she replaced her goggles, turning her back into a giant, fuzzy bug.

The Sisterhood filled the street with the scent of exhaust and screechy whining sounds as they flew three more doors down the road on their mopeds and stopped in front of the Yarn & Stitch.

And just then, Dranian was struck with the horror of what might happen if the girl with no name he'd spent so many years without decided to join that knit-wearing band of old women if he managed to get her to the human realm. The females were all on the same side after all. What if the girl was more loyal to the knitters than the café? What if Dranian was forced to whip pudding and cupcakes across the street at her? And— queensbane—what if she threw macarons *back* at him?

It was still on his mind as he and his brothers walked down the streets of Toronto. As they rounded the shops and made their way toward the gate that would take them back into the Ever Corners—hopefully for the last time.

When they approached the gate, that shimmering flicker of light and sweetness in the air that indicated something magical was on the other side, Mor said to Dranian, "So you really have no idea where Luc is?"

Dranian shook his head.

They hopped through the barrier one by one and found themselves in the lush, cold North Corner of Ever. No one was there guarding it, though that had been the case the last few times they'd crossed the gate. Levress must have been preoccupied with other troubles in the Silver Castle since she'd abandoned it.

"Let's find Shayne first. That's step one," Cress decided. "If we can infiltrate the House of Riothin, we may be able to drag him out, and then we'll remind him that this is *his* mess to clean up, and then we can beat him—royally—and after that—"

"There's no need for that."

Cress stopped talking. The voice that came from the trees' shadows was one Dranian knew well, one that reminded him of a fairy he wanted to both hug and kick just like Cress.

Shayne stepped out of the woods like he'd been waiting. Purple blood coated his hands, a piece of parchment was clenched in his fist, dark crescents shaded his usually bright eyes, and his hair was a mess—nothing like the slick style he always kept it in to catch the eye of human females. And his scowl...

Queensbane, his scowl...

It was so much bigger and greater than any scowl Dranian had mustered in all his years of scowling. Shayne was the new King of scowls. King of the High Court of the Coffee Bean *and* the King of Scowls.

Shayne lifted the letter toward them. Cress carefully took the bloody letter with the tips of his fingers and unwrinkled it to read.

"You're right," Shayne stated. "This is my mess. Lyro is my House, and Lily is my human." He glanced at the gate behind them, and a faint, sad smile shifted his mouth. "I've missed this place," he confessed. "But I can't go back in there without Lily."

"How did you get here so fast?" Dranian asked Shayne, but it mustn't have been loud enough because Cress spoke again, and everyone gave him their attention.

"Well, at least we know where Lily is now." He folded the letter and

FAKE DATING A HUMAN 101

handed it back. "And that she's alive."

"I'm going to get her. But I just wanted..." Shayne chewed on his bottom lip, his brows tugging together. "I guess I just wanted to say goodbye. Properly this time." He glanced at Dranian. "And to give you an opportunity to rescue Mycra, if you want it."

"Nonsense." Cress waved a hand through the air. "Bringing Dranian is a great risk—"

"I'll come." Dranian's statement was loud enough to shake the fruit in the nearby trees, and Cress slammed his mouth shut as he looked at Dranian in surprise. But even though Dranian had failed to steal Cress's body, he needed this one last chance to be epic. He needed to show up for the girl with no name, to pull her from the cage she found herself in, to make up for all the years she had waited before and he had not shown up.

Shayne nodded, and his modest smile looked real this time. "Let's go then. One last mission together, Dranian. Just the two of us, like old times."

"What in the name of the sky deities are you talking about?!" Cress demanded. "Are you planning to take that chair, Shayne? You know I was only joking when I said all those things a moment ago about this being your mess and all that."

"I knew it was my mess before you said it. And you know why you and Mor can't come with me. Dranian knows his way around my House, and if we're careful I can make sure he gets back out. But I can't say either of you would—especially you, Cress. You'd be sold off to the Silver Castle in seconds if you showed up there." Shayne sauntered over with his bloody hands in his pockets and stopped before Dranian. He pulled out an old key and held it up between them. His blood was smothered over it. "Come on," he said. "Our females might not have much time left."

Mor grabbed Shayne's shoulder. "Let us help you, at least. Maybe there's a way out for you."

Shayne's chest rose and fell. "Absolutely not. I've thought of everything," he assured. "There's only one way to save Lily, and I'm going to take it." He turned and looked at Mor. "Let me go, Mor." The words came out soft. It was a plea that was meant for far more than just this moment. It was, *"Let me go forever. This is goodbye."*

A silent inhale swept across the Ever Corners as Mor's hand slid off Shayne's shoulder. Cress looked like he might protest, but for the first time in his life, he didn't seem to have an argument. Bugs and birds chirped in the forest, making conversation when the fairies couldn't.

One second passed. Dranian still didn't know what to say. No one else seemed to either.

How was Dranian to let his forever friend go? Shayne was his charge, his fairy to guard. How was he expected to watch Shayne's final moments of freedom with his own two eyes? If he did not have a girl with no name to save, Dranian was sure he would not have been able to go to the House with Shayne for this.

Dranian looked down the line of them, wishing he could imprint this moment onto his brain. The image of four brothers standing side-by-side. Likely, for the last time.

CHAPTER

29

Dranian Evelry Being Epic Again

The basement of the House of Lyro was a bitter, cold place. Dranian breathed on his hands to try and warm them as he studied the bars of his cage and the deep darkness that laid beyond. His mind was muddled with the sharp memory of his 'bestie for the restie' kneeling before Hans-Der Lyro in the great hall, surrendering himself, his faeborn smile, his joy, his future.

Dranian would never unsee Shayne on his knees before the House of Lyro like that. Not once in their childling years had Shayne knelt before his father or his House. Not once had he surrendered in anything, until now. The sight had almost been enough to make Dranian scream as he was being dragged away.

It was the moment Dranian had officially failed as a fairy guard. And now his chest was utterly cold, his heart still barely beating where it was deserted on the red carpet upstairs, leaving a hollow, hungry space in his body that ate up the rest of him.

As soon as the guards left the basement, Dranian leaned against the bars and whispered the girl's temporary name into the dim space, "Mycra!"

He wasn't great at yelling, but when the girl with no name didn't reply, he cleared his throat and tried again. *"Mycra!"* he shouted.

The sound boomed through the basement, making a nearby bug spring off a ledge.

Still, nothing responded. And so, he waited through the night until the toe-curling sounds of celebration and partying died down upstairs. He passed the time by counting the stones in the walls and eyeing a few weapons on hangers as his eyes adjusted. Doing pretty much anything to keep himself from thinking about the white-haired fairy upstairs.

Only when peace fell upon the House did he draw the key from his pocket, slick with Shayne's blood. It must have been the early morning hours, though in the depths of the House, it was hard to tell. But if his history in the House of Lyro told him anything, it was that the fairies here rarely went to bed at a reasonable hour.

Dranian reached through the bars of his cage and shoved the key into the mouth of the bloodlock. It clicked, and his door swung open. He pushed out and looked around once more before marching through the basement, whispering for the girl, searching high and low through empty cages, closets, and rooms full of weaponry—where he took a few handy things for himself.

It wasn't easy to stay out of sight of the lesser fairies as they milled about and carried things from one place to another, but Dranian kept tight around corners when he ascended from the basement and braved the maze. He slipped right and left, checking bedrooms silently as Lyro allies slept, snoring and talking in their sleep. All the while, Dranian wondered what dreams the girl with no name was being forced to infiltrate, and what sorts of other things the Lyro household had been making her do since she was captured.

It took him until mid-morning before he finally found her, and the sight made his breath catch in his throat.

The ballroom. Of all places. The wide open, gaping ballroom.

The girl with no name rested in a golden cage, high in the air above the largest room in the whole House. She slept soundly in a white night-dress atop a glorious red velvet bed, a grand exhibition for all who visited the House of Lyro to marvel at. It was enraging and intimidating all at once. There was no easy way to fetch a fairy in the sky, not unless he could fly like Cress or airslip like Mor. And he realized just how foolish he was to come here on his own with only one good arm and no way to climb. It was the first moment he was tempted to turn back, to send some-one else in his stead. He turned away to leave when he spotted a thick rope tied to a curtain rod over a tall window. He followed the rope with his eyes and, realizing the rope was what held the girl's cage in the air, he filled his chest with air and courage. He might have only seconds be-fore the nobles heard his ruckus and awoke. Seconds to set her free once he started.

Dranian raced for a plush couch in the corner. He used the brute strength of his good arm to shove it from the wall and push it into the centre of the room. The screeching noise sang like a dying bird, echoing in every direction and flooding the House with clamour, but as soon as the couch was below the girl's cage, he turned, drew a dagger, and hurled it—aiming for the rope.

He missed. Terribly.

He tried again with a second dagger, and he missed that time, too. So, he drew out the handle of his spear, fired it to life, and he threw it toward the ceiling. The blade cut clean through the rope—he almost didn't spring out of the way in time as the entire cage came crashing down onto the sofa. Dranian scrambled to the cage door as the girl startled awake, looking around in a panic. He drew out the key, swiped a thumb-full of Shayne's blood off it, and jammed his thumb against the bloodlock. An alarm sang through the House as the cage door swung open.

The girl was already scrambling from the bed and out the door, pull-ing Dranian along with her before he could speak to announce what his plan was.

"Hurry," she said, reaching for him—at least, he thought she was until she grabbed his last dagger from his belt. "Huntsmen will be here in seconds… too late. They're here."

Dranian spun to find a dozen fairies in red Lyro lamellar armour rushing into the ballroom. His stomach dropped just as a loud smash tore his attention to the shattered window. The girl no longer had the dagger in her hands when she grabbed Dranian's good arm and jerked him toward the windy opening. As soon as they reached the window, the girl wound her arms around Dranian's middle, and she *leapt*.

Dranian released a shriek as his body was torn from the House, out into the open air with nothing below to catch him. The girl reached upward toward the sky, her white dress rippling around his body, her hair fluttering over her face. He didn't know what she was reaching for until a pale hand stretched out and clasped around hers.

Dranian was sucked sideways into an air current in the girl's embrace. He held on tight, his hands clasping around her back, his shrieking stifled behind his teeth. His surroundings appeared as he hit the ground, rolling through a bright wheat field, and he landed on his shoulder. He winced as pain seared down his arm, and he lifted his head to see the girl who'd landed a foot away.

Her chest rose and fell, wheat sticking out from a variety of places in her black hair. She opened her bright eyes and looked over at him.

"What just happened?" Dranian asked her.

"I was infiltrating someone's dream when you woke me," she said through heavy breaths.

"Who's dream?" Dranian sat up and looked around, but the voice came from behind him.

"Mine."

Luc walked into view, swatting at wheat bits and shaking out his scarlet hair. An enormous, swelling purple ring surrounded his left eye. He stopped his fussing and scowled at the girl. "If you ever invade my slumber again, I will torture you far worse in your waking hours than you can with me in my sleeping ones!" he promised. "Dreamslippers have no business being in my powerful mind."

Mycra lifted herself on shaking arms. She stood to her full height when she faced Luc. "Shadow Fairies are the most useful," she said to him even though he hadn't asked for an explanation.

Luc finished swatting wheat off his coat. "Will one of you tell me what in the name of the sky deities happened to you all after I left?" he demanded, looking at Dranian in particular. "It's driving me crazy not knowing!" Before Dranian could answer, he added, "And where's dear Lily? I have a lot on the line to lose if she's really vanished into the Ever Corners."

Dranian looked back in the direction of the House of Lyro. He couldn't see the House; the great field and at least one forest separated them from its tiered pagodas and tall dragon statues. But one last time, he thought about the forever friend he'd left there. The one he already missed with every fairy fiber of his being even though he'd seen him the night before.

"It seems only Shayne can find her now," he said in a quiet voice.

CHAPTER

30

Lily Baker Spinning Around and Around and Around...

There was a garden in the new place. The realization didn't land right away, but after the fragrance had washed over Lily enough times, she was sure there had to be flowers somewhere nearby. She didn't recall seeing bright blossoms or bushes on her way in, although, she didn't remember much of the walk at all. What she did remember, however, was the danger of the food.

It took her only a day or two of refusing to swallow what she ate and spitting it out when no one was looking to clear her head. It was a miracle Jethwire hadn't told her new captors that she'd learned about the food, or that she might try to keep from eating it. But when she was led through the halls, she continued to stumble around and stare off in a daze so they wouldn't realize she was coherent.

The music was odd. It reminded her of a stringed melody in an orchestra except that it moved around in a different way, like a tangible current rolling over her skin and shivering down her toes, making her want to dance. She fought the urge day and night, clasping her hands together in front of her and counting to one hundred over and over so she wouldn't be tempted to start twirling through the room they locked her in.

After two days, her stomach ached with hunger, and her arms trembled in weakness. She wasn't sure she could resist anymore. The scent of food washed through the room three times a day, but by some miracle, whenever a fairy arrived with a tray for her, she still kept herself from eating.

Lily curled into a ball and hugged her knees to fight the cold in the evenings. She rocked back and forth and sang in a raspy voice to distract herself from the things pressing in, threatening to drive her crazy. It was Kate's favourite song—a catchy one about a breakup. A large tear slid down her cheek when she realized.

"I can't do this, Kate," she said in apology. "I'm not going to make it back to you."

It had taken Lily too long to come to grips with it. But now she knew.

She'd lied to Jessica Lewis. She wouldn't be there to protect Kate and Greyson because she wasn't going to survive this. She was already crumbling, teetering on the cusp of losing her mind, and the pressure was only growing heavier by the minute.

At least her siblings had the baristas to look out for them now. Maybe they didn't really need Lily anymore anyway. Maybe she'd been fooling herself this whole time thinking that she could do a better job of keeping Kate and Greyson safe than the fae. Maybe Lily had been stupid to try and come up with all those gadgets and weapons at Desmount Tech. All that research and technical design seemed like a far-off dream now, something of the past. Just another thing she'd distracted herself with instead of spending time with the people she loved.

Now she was trapped in a haunted house like something from a terrible movie she and Kate would have clutched each other through as they watched. Only this horror movie was filled with pretty creatures who ate and drank and danced and sang and mocked her.

She lifted her hands to study the rough cuts along her knuckles, her chipped fingernails, and the dirt caked into every crevice. She didn't even have clear memories of what the mess was from. Then she hugged her knees again, laid her head down upon them, and resumed humming Kate's favourite song.

"What song is that?"

Lily sprang from the bed and landed on her feet.

A black-haired fairy stood at the door. She might have met him before, but she didn't remember her first day of existing in this place, and therefore she had no idea who this was. Bruises and lacerations covered his face and neck, and it looked like several of his fingers had been broken and put back together like he was some kind of Frankenstein doll.

The fairy's eyes roamed up and down her body, taking in her red dress, all the strands that had come loose from her braided hair, and her feet glued to the floor. "You were humming just now, weren't you?" He drew into the room, and Lily took a step back toward the bed. "And since you're not dancing," his gaze flickered up to hers, "I'll assume you're unaffected by the enchantments of the food and music of this place, which is interesting to say the least." He grabbed her hand when he was close enough. He lifted her arm and studied her tattoos, tracing a finger over the ones at her shoulder.

Lily tore herself away. "You're right," she said, then swallowed. "Your food doesn't affect me, so you can stop trying to feed it to me." Her empty stomach hated her for the comment. "I won't be any fun to you or the rest of the fairies here. I was a waste of your money, so you should just chuck me outside and get rid of me."

Her argument was so unconvincing, she was almost embarrassed she'd said it aloud.

The fairy laughed. "No human is immune to fairy food," he remarked. "If Shayne Lyro really cared about humans so much, he should have told you that while you were in the care of his household."

Lily's stomach turned.

Shayne Lyro? The fairy had said it clear as a bell.

Shayne... *knew* this fairy?

Lily looked him over, but she didn't recall hearing anything about a fairy with jet-black hair and a reason to be all banged up. There weren't many clues to work off either. Apart from his dark blue coat and the yellowing marks on his jaw and fingers, he seemed like every other fairy she'd crossed—calculated, manipulative, and greedy.

"How do you know Shayne Lyro?" she asked. "Are you friends?" A bit of hope slipped out with the question.

The fairy laughed again, throwing his head back and barking at the ceiling. "Friends?" he asked when he was finished. He shook his head. "We're something of the opposite, I'd say. More like enemies." He scratched his head.

Lily's heart sank. "Ah." She glanced around the room, but there wasn't much in it useful for self defense. Not even a pen or a rock. "So, you couldn't deliver a message to him for me?"

"A message? Certainly not. But you could have delivered it to him yourself if you'd asked sooner," he said, and Lily looked up at him in surprise. "He just left."

She had to blink a few times before that settled in. "He just... left? Here?"

No, that couldn't have been right. She glanced in the direction of the hallways, thinking about the various rooms she'd been in. If Shayne was in this place, he would have come to find her. He would have at least shown himself. He would have tried to help her.

The fairy clasped his hands behind his back and sauntered around the room. "Yes, Lily Baker. He just left *here*. It seems to be terrible timing for you, too, since he enjoys meddling when I'm trying to mess around with humans," he said. "But he is engaged to my beautiful cousin, so maybe if you ask her to deliver a message, it might reach him. I should warn you though—she's the jealous sort, and you're quite pretty. She might poison you instead."

Lily stared. She watched the fairy move about, studying the room.

Shayne was engaged? Already? He gave himself to someone that fast? Someone *here*?

She studied the fairy's mouth, eyeing his tongue. He didn't chew on it or make faces like it was prickling or numb.

Her eyes dragged back toward the hall. So this was the place Shayne had run off to when he left her in the forest. He'd been prancing around here, meeting a beautiful fairy, getting engaged, not worried about Lily or the people he left behind. It seemed like things were going well for him here.

"Did... Did he know I was here when he left?" Lily asked, because she had to. Because she needed to know, even though half of her regretted asking the question the moment it came out.

When the black-haired fairy didn't answer right away, fear sailed in. Lily knew Shayne—she knew he cared about her—he'd admitted it by the fire the night he snuck away. But what if he'd changed his mind? What if he left this place on purpose after she arrived because she'd done the exact thing he'd warned her not to do? He'd had a plan, he set out to do it, and she'd gotten captured. Maybe he couldn't veer from his plan regardless of what had happened to her. Maybe he was upset.

The black-haired fairy turned and settled his gaze on her. He squinted his eyes and tapped his chin for a moment. Then he said, "Yes, he knew you were here. And he ran away anyway." He tilted his head. "It looked like he was trying to avoid you, Lily Baker."

Lily's hope dissolved like steam. She felt like a flower drying out, its life breaking off in brittle pieces. She sank to the floor, her knees coming against the cold tiles.

He. Knew. You. Were. Here. And...

"...he ran away."

So that was why Shayne never came. All that time she'd spent in his childhood home, he never showed up to try and get her out. He'd chosen to keep his course and had forgotten about all the times they'd spent together in the human realm, about every moment he'd interjected himself into Lily's life, about every locked gaze or heart flutter or whisper he'd given her when no one else was looking. Frankly, she thought he cared about her more than he'd even let on by the fire that night when he'd kissed her. But he was a fairy, and now that Lily had experienced the Ever Corners firsthand, she realized that fairies were never what they seemed. Shayne must have been prancing around the human realm all that time just for fun. He'd only kissed her to enchant her, and now he couldn't stand to be around her. Maybe from guilt that she was stuck here, and he didn't plan to help her at all.

Still though. Still, she asked in a small voice, "Why would he leave if he knew I was here?"

The fairy shrugged. "I'm not sure," he admitted. "Maybe he didn't want to see you dance for us." The fairy took in a deep breath and let it out slowly. "But enough chatter. I'm here to ensure you're ready for our first great Yule Celebration on tomorrow's eve. You and I will dance the night away, I think. Until I get bored and decide to make you entertain the House." He put a finger in the air, then added, "And I should introduce myself since I already know your name. I'm Cosmo Flora, nephew of the High Lord of the House of Riothin." He reached into his coat and drew out a handful of what looked like peanuts, but Lily knew they weren't ordinary food. A thick tear trailed down her cheek.

"Please don't make me eat those," she begged. It would break her— she'd be done. She couldn't suffer through forgetting who she was again, skipping from place to place until her feet were sore and she wanted to collapse. Waiting around for a fairy she now knew wasn't coming.

No, Lily wasn't a survivor. She'd been denying the truth for too long.

She knew it for sure when the fairy walked over, slid a hand into the hair behind her head to hold her still, pushed the peanuts toward her mouth, and said, "Lily Baker, eat."

The sea was spinning. The human was sinking in it.

Breakfast was berries and meat.

Lunch was apples and blossoms sprinkled with sugar.

Dinner was… well, by that point, she could no longer tell what she was eating.

A large mirror was placed before her—or maybe she was placed before it—and she saw the fuzzy silhouette of a dazzling young woman with tattoos on her arms she didn't recognize. There was a window at her back, and she briefly thought she spotted twinkling stars and a heavy white moon through it in the reflection.

Garland was wrapped around her head in a wreath, and bright red lipstick was carefully dragged over her mouth. She was tossed with gold sparkles and silver tinsel and fashioned with a set of small antlers. Her feet were strapped into golden heels with ivy laces that wound up her calves, and bells were attached to her ankles, making noise wherever she went.

In the blink of an eye, she found herself in a bright room with abundant noise. People swooshed by her in blurs, the colours all melting together while the floor felt like the ceiling and the ceiling felt like it might have become the floor.

Someone strapped a basket of fruit to her head between the antlers. She was pushed to a wall, and she stared into the haze at figures who appeared to be lifting bows and shooting arrows at the fruit. It fell around her whenever someone hit one. Voices burst into cheers when a large, bearded man shot the whole basket right off her head.

"Lily Baker!" a guy with black hair called to her every now and again. His hands found her arms, her hips, her waist as he pulled her around and around, pausing every now and then to tell her to do things.

"The High Lord wants a show," he whispered in her ear after a while. He shoved a slice of carrot into her mouth, then he pushed her away.

The human tripped and found herself in the middle of an empty floor. All the people that had been moving only a second ago were at the edges of the room now. Many eyes were upon her. The carrot—at least that's what she thought it was—rolled around on her tongue. It was sweet like candy, and she wanted to swallow it.

She couldn't climb to her feet; she tried and fell over again. The people standing around laughed, and when the black-haired guy returned to help her up, he called to a heavy-set man with a beard sitting on a throne at the far end of the room—the same one who'd shot the basket off her head. "I think I fed her a little too much," he admitted. "Shall I make her vomit?" He spun the human around and pressed her back tightly against him like he was about to thrust his palm hard against her stomach.

But the strangest thing happened. Without thinking, the human grabbed his forearm, and she flipped him over her shoulder, dropping him to the floor where he landed flat on his back. Gasps and chuckles erupted around the room as the human blinked down at the guy.

Self defense. That's what she'd just done. Though, she wasn't sure how she knew how to do it. And it didn't quite feel like *enough* for some reason.

She spat the carrot on him. He shrieked and rolled away as it hit his face.

Laughter rose again, including from the bearded man in the throne-like chair.

"Psycho," the human said, though the word came out muffled. She wasn't sure if she was talking to the guy on the floor or the man up on the chair watching it all and doing nothing to stop it.

Her name. It came back like a wave on the tide, sweeping in then threatening to drift away again, not tangible enough for her to grab onto and keep.

Lily Baker.

That was it.

Her hair was grabbed.

She shrieked as her head was tipped upwards. The black-haired guy gazed down at her with darkened eyes. "Tonight is going to be fun," he said with a growl, *"Lily Baker."*

Lily Baker. Lily Baker. Lily Baker. She couldn't forget. No matter what, she couldn't forget that name—

A loud boom shook the room from two large doors smashing open, and the black haired-guy's grip fell from her hair. Every soul in the space went quiet as the noise reverberated and women's skirts fluttered in a cold wind. Someone marched in.

Lily's eyes fell on the newcomer, but she couldn't quite make him out. She thought he had white hair and blue eyes, but she knew better than to believe it—she'd seen that enough in the last place; she'd fallen for that trick over and over. It wasn't him.

Chatter erupted and nearby people gasped and yelped as he pulled a crossbow around from behind his back. Muffled whispers of, "Isn't that the Lyro?" and "Isn't he now the Lyro House heir?" reached her ears.

"Lily Baker," the guy shouted over the space.

Lily Baker... that was her. Lily's muscles flexed, and her body jolted like it was standing at attention. Then he shouted, "Punch him. And make it good."

Punch *him*? Who?

As if her body knew even when her mind didn't, Lily turned toward the black-haired guy. Her big eyes settled upon him, and his face blanched.

She clocked him.

The guy took it right in the teeth, sprawling backward and ending up on the floor again.

"Ha! That was perfect," the newcomer said. His grin was wide and hazardously handsome, and Lily stared at it as something doubled over in her chest.

It was a delusion. He wasn't real. She'd thought she'd seen him so many times already, she refused to believe that this thing standing before her was anything but a hollow figment of her imagination. She even whacked him to prove it, but her hand collided with a strong chest.

She stared at her hand, at his chest.

His hand lifted and wrapped around hers. A gold ring she hadn't seen before circled his forefinger.

"You can't have her," he shouted up at the bearded man in the chair. "She's mine."

"Shayne..." Lily tried to whisper the word to ask, but her mouth made no sound; just rasp came out. She cleared her throat to try again.

"It's me."

Lily's question dissolved in her mouth. She stared at where a warm hand held hers against his chest.

He tugged her to him, wrapped an arm around her shoulders, and began leading her in the direction of the large doors he'd come through. Murmurs rang through the space, filling Lily's ears.

"Heir of the Lyro House," the bearded man's voice boomed. "You can't take a human from a banquet unless you wish to die—"

Shayne turned around, lifted his crossbow, and he fired.

People screamed as the arrow split through the air and pierced the bearded man's chest. The room erupted in noise and running and shouting. Burgundy blood blossomed around the arrow as the man's eyes went wide in shock. He crumpled off his decorated seat.

"You're all correct!" Shayne shouted at the people. "I *am* the future High Lord of the House of Lyro! And my House wishes for war!"

Fresh panic made the noise in the room unbearable. People grabbed each other—one fainted. Some of the men pulled out weapons as whispers of war between Riothin and Lyro flitted through the space.

Shayne didn't stop moving. He pulled Lily through the doors as he slid his crossbow onto his back, and the second they were in the hall, he scooped her off her feet and began running with her in his arms. Wailing alarms filled the building, and one or two men rushed out the large doors after them, but they were far behind. Lily looked around as her thoughts crystalized, as it dawned on her that none of this was imaginary, and that Shayne...

He was really here. He held her tightly, his fingers curling around her side and locking her legs against him as he turned down a hall and followed a path of bodies littering the floor. Dark liquid covered his hands, leaving fingerprints on her dress, and Lily wondered how many men he'd killed on his way in.

No, not men. Fairies.

She looked up at him in surprise. The sudden movement made him tilt his face toward her, bringing it close enough that his features were clear, cancelling out any doubt she might have had left about who this was.

"Shayne." She said it with volume this time.

"Lily," he said back as he turned and slipped them sideways through a doorway. "I'm in a bit of a rush right now. Can we talk later?" he asked.

"I…" Her mouth and tongue were thick. "I thought you weren't coming for me," she admitted. Warmth pushed behind her eyes as her own statement rang in her ears.

"As if." He shook his head. "You're crazy, ugly Human. How could you think for one second I wouldn't come?" He spun and pushed a door open with his back.

Cold air brushed over Lily's skin as Shayne sprinted through a garden. Flowers and leaves slapped against them until they reached a metal gate, and Shayne kicked it open. Lily almost screamed at the sight of a giant beast with fangs waiting on the other side. Shayne pushed her up onto its back, then leapt behind and reached around her to yank on a set of reins. The beast turned and galloped through a courtyard where more bodies made a path to a large gate hanging open before them.

"Is… is this real?" Lily had to check one last time. What if this was a dream? What if she woke up in a minute and all of this was taken away, and she was forced to eat and dance again?

"Absolutely," Shayne promised into her ear beneath the roaring of the wind and the grunting of the beast. "I'll prove it to you. Just wait."

It was real.

Her body relaxed; she leaned back against him.

As they flew threw the opening, broke through the treeline beyond, and were consumed by a dark forest of trees, Lily felt Shayne hug her a little tighter to himself, and he whispered, "I'm sorry I was late."

CHAPTER

31

Shayne Lyro, Heir to the House of Lyro

Warmth trickled along Shayne's stomach and down his side, pooling at his hip and soaking his shirt beneath his coat. He didn't notice it until the thundering of his chest subsided, and at that point, he felt the sting of the cold iron cut along his forearm, the gash in his left shoulder, and the ache of the needly slices up his legs, too. But especially, he felt the stab he'd taken in his side from the first guard at the Riothin gate. The stab that threatened to steal his alertness now and put him into a passed-out state that wouldn't be good for him or Lily.

Ah, Lily. He'd stolen her back.

He smiled, hardly able to believe he'd found her at all, but revelling in the fact that she was actually where Hans-Der said she was, and Shayne hadn't been forced to hunt the Ever Corners for the rest of his faeborn life.

The crossbeast grew tired from the sprint, so Shayne slowed the creature to a walk once he was sure they were far enough away from the House of Riothin. They wouldn't have loads of time, but a few moments to rest would be enough for now. He slid off the creature's back, then he turned and held his hands up for…

Lily was looking at him, but it sort of seemed like she wasn't really *looking* at him.

Shayne's mouth twisted to the side as he contemplated. He knew she'd snap out of it eventually, but it wasn't exactly easy to see her this way. Even in her weakest moments in the human realm, she'd always seen him and known him, and probably wanted him a little. Not that he cared about any of that now.

He reached into his pocket and drew out a small bottle. "Drink this," he instructed. "It'll help you shake off—"

Instantly, Lily slid off the beast, grabbed the vial, uncorked it, and began to chug.

Shayne held his breath as he watched. He'd forgotten for a moment that he'd enslaved her. Shame on him. Shame, shame, shame.

"Lily," he said, but she didn't stop drinking until the vial was empty, even as a cold wind swept in and she shivered. She handed the vial back and wiped her mouth, and Shayne bit his lips. "In any other situation, I would have so much fun with this," he admitted, more to himself. He sighed and took the vial, then he pulled off his crossbow, shrugged away his coat and threw it around her shoulders. "Give it a minute. Any second, you'll be back to feeling yourself again, and I'm sure you'll have plenty of things to say—"

"What happened to you?" she asked in a stern tone.

Shayne took a step back and looked her up and down. Was she back to her senses already? He'd never heard of fairy medicine working that fast. He followed her gaze down to his tunic and realized it was soaked with blood. "Ah, yes. This." He pointed to his side where he'd been brutally stabbed. "It's just a little scratch. I'll be fine."

Her eyes darted up to where he chewed on his tongue.

"Don't lie to me," she said. "Seriously, Shayne, you look like you're going to pass out."

"Huh," Shayne glanced down at himself again. "That's strange. I feel fine."

His faeborn-cursed tongue fattened and itched. He was quite focused on it, trying not to bite on it right in front of her, until he noticed the glisten of moisture in the corners of her eyes, and suddenly his measly tongue felt like the least important thing in the entire forest.

He sighed and ran a hand through his hair. "Lily…"

She folded her arms and waited, and for all her attempts to appear strong, he only saw how her ankles wobbled in her heels, how her fingers dug into the flesh at her biceps, how the tears threatened to escape the corners of her eyes. It was all rather baffling, and so like her. How could she still be pretending after all this time?

He exhaled a heavy breath, and he said, "No human would be okay after all that." He nodded back toward the way they came. "Even fairies break under those circumstances."

Her face contorted, just a smidgen. One of those glittering tears escaped, but she smacked it away in an instant. And even though his chest got all twisty watching her try to fight it, he smiled. How he'd missed her; every little quirk of her face, how she scrunched her nose, how she glared, how she folded her arms to show off her scrawny little human muscles, how she tried to stand tall when she was never going to be as tall as him, and how it all made her such a perfect person for him to obsess over.

But, alas, his lashes fluttered, and his arm flew out to catch the tree beside him. "Queensbane," he muttered. He tried blinking the dizzy spell away, cursing that pesky little stab wound in his side.

"Shayne," Lily warned. "I swear, if you die, I'll kill you."

He burst out laughing, and, oops, it made him lose his balance. He slid down the side of the tree and rested in the grass, taking note of the crossbeast out of the corner of his eye in case the creature quickly decided he was food in this state.

273

Lily dropped into the grass beside him, grabbed a hold of his shirt, and tore it open.

"Pfft. Don't be so obvious," Shayne said as he leaned his head back against the tree. "If you want to see my abs so badly, just ask, ugly Human."

Lily ignored him as she studied the wound. She swore under her breath and tore the rest of his shirt to pieces, then reached around him to tie one of the strips around his middle. "This is really bad! Why didn't you tell me before if you were in this condition?" It sounded suspiciously like scolding when she said it. "I'm not joking—I'm seriously going to kill you if you bleed out. Shayne, this isn't funny!"

He was still grinning anyway. He reached up to touch her jaw, and she slowed her 'undressing him' attack, bringing her gaze up to his. Her eyelids were coated in gold dust, making her blue eyes sharp even in the darkness. He studied the silver decorations in her hair, the garland crown she wore, the stunning red dress, and the heels...

It was despicable. Unfit for her.

He reached up and removed the antlers from her hair along with the garland. The motions put his fairy brain into a spin, and he was sure he would pass out after all if he wasn't careful. If he couldn't keep himself together, he might not get her away in time, and that was the most important thing.

"What are you doing?" she asked—her voice was nice and raspy. "You need to hold still."

"I don't like these things," he admitted, tossing the garland aside. "I want to see you in a bulletproof vest. And a cozy knit sweater. And in that adorable little Fae Café apron I designed that fits you so well."

She hesitated. Then she asked, "All at once?"

He laughed. "Sure."

Even though she was being all serious, the corner of her mouth tugged up just slightly. Then she shook her head. "Unreal," she muttered. "You're such a child."

"I want to go home, Lily," he admitted. Something about the way he said it made her stop her fussing with his injury again. "With you," he clarified. He was sure he'd regret this conversation later, and that he wasn't at all in the right state of mind to say such things. But maybe confessions were easier when it was dark, and one was bleeding out against a tree. "You know I've loved you since the beginning, right, ugly Human?"

Her throat bobbed. Lily kept her eyes down on his wound. "I told you to stop calling me that," she whispered.

"Since the moment I made you laugh at your department fundraiser, I realized I liked being your fake boyfriend," he added. "I know we were only pretending to date all this time, but it was never really fake for me."

"Stop talking, Shayne," she said. "I don't think you're with it enough to tell me these things."

He thought about that. "Probably not. Don't hate me for it later." He knew she didn't like him back, not the way he liked her, which was astounding considering every other female in the human realm adored him. What a rebel.

Lily finally lifted her eyes to his. "Why even bring up the topic of going home then? Why wouldn't you go home?"

Shayne lifted his hand and splayed his fingers. She looked at his hand oddly, clearly not seeing the evidence, even though it was right there, clinging to his forefinger in a gilded statement that spoke volumes and felt as heavy as a brick.

She pushed his hand back down, because she didn't get it.

Ah well. He'd tell her later.

"Apply pressure here," she said, apparently forgetting about the whole conversation. She took his hand and pressed it against his side. He winced as pain seared through his middle.

"Absolutely not. That's the worst." He shook his head and yanked his hand away.

Lily huffed a sound of disbelief and stood, but her ankle gave out and she almost fell in her heels.

"Don't you want to take off your shoes?" Shayne asked. "You'll appreciate the feeling of the grass on your bare feet, trust me."

A rattling sounded in the distance, followed by heavy breathing and the stomping of hooves. Shayne turned his ear in that direction, hoping, praying to the sky deities, pleading...

He closed his eyes and his hands slowly pulled into fists. He'd hoped the House of Riothin would have been more preoccupied with trying to save the life of their High Lord than coming after him, but he supposed that was just wishful thinking.

Lily had no idea how close they were because her human ears failed her. "You need rest," she said. She looked around in the forest. "I think I see some kind of house up ahead. Let's go there."

"No, Lily." Shayne grabbed the tree at his back. He winced as he pulled himself to his feet, clinging to the bark with a shaking hand. "We need to keep running. They've found us." He padded his waist for his fairsabers, but he found something else instead. "Speaking of which..." He drew out a human gun—one meant for killing fairies. He held it out to her. "I brought your favourite thing in the universe."

Lily blinked a few times like she was second guessing what she was seeing. But her thoughts were taking too long, so Shayne grabbed her hand and shoved the gun into it. "If I pass out," he said, and her eyes darted up to his with ample wildness, "shoot everything in sight and run." He pulled a few cartridges of ammo out of his pockets, too.

"Shayne..." she whispered.

He already knew. Even before she'd said his name with such fear and begging, he knew this was not a fight she could handle. That everything she just went through was racing through her mind, about to drive her into madness. That she was *very* close to breaking; a strong creature in a fragile state. That she had perhaps learned the hard way that in the Ever Corners there were things far worse than death. And all at once, he decided he could not ask her to fight them, even if she did wish to be considered an always-strong-and-never-weak sort of human.

And so, he picked up his crossbow. He put a hand on her cheek as his eyes darted up to the fairies racing through the trees toward them, sliding off their deer and drawing their fairsabers. There were at least a dozen. He kept his gaze on them as he leaned against her ear and whispered. "Lily Baker," he said. "Close your eyes and count to ten."

Her eyes slid shut. Shayne stepped around her and raised his crossbow. He fired at the nearest fairy, and then he drew his fairsaber to take care of the rest.

"One," Lily obediently said behind him.

He dug his fairsaber deep into all the fairy flesh he could reach.

"Two."

Someone got a hit in against his wrist and he jerked back.

"Three."

He spun, cutting two at the same time, but he missed the third and got stabbed through his leg.

"Four."

He growled and threw his fairsaber at the fairy who'd stabbed him. By some miracle, it went clean through the fairy's body and the fairy toppled over. Shayne rolled out of the way before he could be crushed.

"Five."

He picked up a rock and hurled it at the others as he scooted backward over the grass, his leg leaking blood through his pants.

"Six."

A fairsaber appeared over him and he sprang to the left as it stabbed downward, missing him by an inch. He kicked the fairy in the stomach.

"Seven."

The fairy wobbled, so Shayne stole his fairsaber and sliced his legs.

"Eight."

The same fairy grabbed Shayne's hands and tried to wrestle his fairsaber out of them until Shayne grabbed a handful of dirt and whipped it into the fairy's mouth.

"Nine."

Shayne leapt to his feet, but his leg gave out instantly. He tumbled to a knee as three fairies surrounded him, their blades raised toward his chest and head. He went still.

"*Ten.*"

Blasts erupted through the woods as three bullets were fired. Fairies fell to the ground, and Shayne jumped to his feet, putting the weight on his good leg as he swung at the last fairy. The fairy moved too fast, smacking Shayne's fairsaber out of his hand and brushing *past* him. Shayne tried to grab him as he rushed at Lily who was reloading. The fairy swatted the gun from her fingers, and she scrambled backward against a tree.

In a heartbeat, Shayne picked up the gun, shoved the cartridge in, and aimed it at the back of the fairy's head.

A rather satisfying blast filled the woods.

And there was Lily, gripping the tree at her back, her chest rising and falling. Not broken. Not at all.

Shayne smiled. He whispered to her, "Survivor."

He fainted.

CHAPTER
32

Lily Baker and the Fox's Big Juicy Secret

The woods went quiet. There'd been so much shouting and so many growls only a second ago. Lily felt stuck against the tree, her hands shaking as she held tight to the juts in the bark. Her mind was a mix of blanking and flashing, and she was sure she could hear the sirens for an emergency situation going off in her head.

Shayne was passed out. Reason told her to start performing first aid. But she stared at the three fairies on the ground; the ones she'd taken out with her own bullets. Up until the moment she'd raised her gun, she wasn't sure she could still protect herself anymore, or protect Shayne. It had been instinct, and it had kicked in just like it was supposed to. She thought she would cower, or scream, or run. But she didn't.

She'd fired.

She'd fought back, and she'd endured.

Her attention dropped to where Shayne lay, his face relaxed and his body sprawled. It hit her all at once that Shayne was bleeding out on the grass, that the creepy fairies of the Riothin House would probably send more people to try and find her, and that—

She shrieked as the huge beast they'd ridden here on wandered past her and began helping itself to the fairy bodies on the ground. She slapped a hand over her mouth, and she rushed to Shayne's side, afraid the grotesque creature might consider Shayne to be free meat along with the others.

"Shayne!" She grabbed his shoulders and shook him. "Shayne, wake up!"

His body lurched along with her movements, but he didn't open his eyes. There was so much blood everywhere; his clothes were mostly dark purple.

"Shayne," she begged. "I can't protect you if you don't wake up!" She looked around at the dark forest, not seeing a path or a clear direction to head in. She wasn't sure she could even carry someone of Shayne's size. She definitely couldn't outrun more fairies if they came.

Lily grabbed the sides of her head. Even though she'd started to think straight after whatever potion Shayne made her drink, she knew she was deprived of nutrition and likely on the verge of passing out herself. She gasped as the beastly creature turned and began heading in Shayne's direction.

"Seriously, what do I do?!" she whispered to herself. She used to be good at problem solving, but she wasn't sure of anything anymore, except that she needed someone stronger, someone who wasn't a malnourished human on the verge of losing her mind.

It was crazy, but it was her last shot. She started screaming.

"Mor!" She shouted it into the darkness, her dry voice cracking over his name. She knew Mor couldn't hear her. She knew she was grasping at straws. But she begged him to come anyway. "Mor!" It echoed through the trees, and critters she couldn't see stirred in the branches overhead. "M—"

Someone appeared in front of her, and she gasped. The hem of his long black Dracula coat fluttered in the wind. Luc folded his arms as he looked her over. His silver gaze lifted to the hungry beast heading in her direction, then dropped to where Shayne lay in the grass.

"You called?" he asked, doing nothing about any of it.

Lily blinked. She really hadn't expected someone to hear her screams. "I wasn't calling you," she said from a strained voice—though, she wasn't sure why she said it.

Luc nodded. "Ah. Then I'll leave." He turned and Lily grabbed the hem of his coat.

"Wait!" she begged. "Luc…"

When Luc twisted back, he was clearly trying to hide a smile. He stared down at her, and Lily wondered if this was the first time she'd ever been alone with Luc. She swallowed and glanced over at the beast.

Luc sighed and tugged his coat out of her grip. When he turned himself toward the beast, something came over his eyes; a darkness that sent a shiver through the woods. The leaves rustled overhead. Lily smelled smoke.

The beast stopped in its tracks. It stared at Luc. Then it shrank and released a quiet whimper before backing up a step.

"That's right. Shoo, cow." Luc flung his hand at it.

The beast snarled as it turned and headed into the woods. Lily watched it until it disappeared into the shadows of the trees. She realized she was gripping tight to the grass.

Luc crouched, levelling himself with her. "I need you to stay alive because of a promise I made, dear Lily, not because I've started to like you or anything," he stated. Then, he added, "Just so there are no misunderstandings about why I'm here." He stood and extended a hand.

Lily eyed him. No one would come rushing like that just because of a promise.

"What about Shayne?" she asked. She unclasped her fingers from the grass and reached up to take his hand. He took a step forward so she didn't have to reach so far.

"He's not really a part of my promise," Luc admitted.

Lily stopped. She jerked her hand back. "What?!"

"I'm just being honest." Luc shrugged. "I said I'd bring you and Dranian back to the human realm. I said nothing about him." He nodded toward Shayne. "Besides, with that ring on his finger now, it's not like he can come back anyway."

Lily's gaze snapped to Shayne lying peacefully in his purpled clothes. A large gold ring hugged his forefinger. She'd been dizzy back in the Riothin ballroom, but she did recall the whispering fairies talking about Shayne like something had happened to him. They'd called him '*Heir*'.

"I can't go without him," she said, not sure if she was speaking to herself or Luc.

What did it mean that Shayne was 'Heir'? Why did a ring have the power to keep him from staying with her?

Luc released an exasperated sigh. "Ughhhh, you humans. Fine." He folded his arms. "I'll fix his problem too, since I'm fixing everyone else's at the moment. You're all so needy, do you know that?"

Lily was still thinking about the gossip from the ballroom when a fairy materialized beside Luc, making her jump. The fairy wore a similar black coat. He tore down his hood, and Lily's chest swelled at the sight of Mor. "Lily," he breathed in his low voice. Mor's hands were balled to fists at his sides, his face contorted with worry.

Lily wanted to cry, but she sucked back her tears as she tried climbing to her feet. Her legs shook, and Mor stepped forward, lifting her until she was balanced.

"Ah, there you are. I was wondering how long it would take you to catch up," Luc said to him.

"Lily..." Mor said again. "I would have come—" Out of nowhere, Luc pushed him out of the way and took Lily's hands.

"I was here first," he said. "At least let me carry the pretty one."

Mor frowned. "Not a chance." He shoved Luc back and yanked Lily to himself. In an instant, she felt the world around her slip away. Mor cradled her head against his warm chest.

It felt like only seconds before everything stopped moving, and Lily's feet were set on solid ground. Cold grass curled over her heels, and wind filtered through nearby trees. Mor kept a firm hold on her arm, keeping her balanced. When Lily turned around...

She saw Cress.

And Dranian.

She even saw psycho Mycra. There was something familiar about the woman, and Lily settled her gaze on her for a moment, wondering if they'd spoken recently. Wondering why she remembered Mycra's voice in her head.

Luc arrived with Shayne a second later and practically dumped him on Dranian's lap.

Lily wasn't sure what to say to everyone, but at the sight of them in arm's reach, and with Mor a shield at her side, every one of her tense muscles unspooled. She collapsed into the deep, peaceful sleep she'd been craving for weeks.

Luc's voice sounded like a sweet song, even when he was complaining.

"So, let me get this straight. Now we're being chased by the House of Lyro *and* the House of Riothin, and on top of that Cressica has revealed his identity to the whole Ever Corners and will certainly stir the North High Queene to chase after him, and on top of *that*, it's too dangerous for any of us to return to the human realm, even though at any moment the Lyro House could send spies to burn Fae Café to the ground, and the only ones watching over your humans there are the yarn-covered females whom I nearly destroyed all on my own this summer?"

Luc chuckled after his long list of grievances. It stirred Lily awake. She didn't know how long she'd been sleeping, but it had to be almost a full day because the air was cool again. She saw treetops fluttering over-head in a soft breeze, and the blue sky was starting to turn grey.

Luc clapped slowly. "Well done, everyone. How embarrassing."

"Am I the only one who wants to punch him?" Mor murmured to Cress.

Lily sat up, and just then, Shayne's guttural scream filled the woods.

Her body went cold. She whirled to see Dranian *snap* Shayne's leg back into place. She blinked. Then a gag hit the back of her throat, and she smacked a fist over her mouth to hold everything in.

"There. Now it can meld," Dranian mumbled. "Try not to walk on it for at least..." His voice trailed off as Shayne climbed to his feet.

Shayne's chest was slick with sweat, his body was covered in dry blood, and his eyes were red with bloodshot. Lily's mouth parted at the purpling bruises and the gash in his side and leg. He needed to be in a hospital, not walking around in the woods. He didn't seem to know it though as he stretched like he'd just woken up from a nice nap.

Lily rose to her feet too, and the movement caught Shayne's eye. He wandered over and took hold of the flaps of his coat she only now real-ized she was wearing. He had a devilish smile when he tugged her to him. Then he stuck his hand into his coat pocket and pulled out a handful of folded papers.

"I have some letters to deliver before it's too late," he said to every-one, even though his gaze stayed on Lily. "And while I'm at it—I shoved a young fairy through the gate into the human realm earlier. If you could find her and give her a job at the café, I'd appreciate it. She was a servant, so she'll be a hard worker." He glanced back at Cress now. "Should work out for the best since Cress is always complaining about how under-staffed Fae Café is."

Cress grunted. "I do *not* always complain about that."

"Why are you asking us to find her? Why can't you do it yourself?" Lily asked him. Shayne's attention drew back, his smirk not as wide an-ymore. He twisted his lips to the side like he was contemplating what to say, but he didn't end up saying a thing.

A small, pathetic smile found Lily's own face, and she looked at the ground. "I'm not stupid. I know you think I'm the only one here who hasn't clued in yet that you're staying in the Ever Corners," she said.

At that, Shayne's smile vanished altogether.

Luc's grew though. "Oh dear," he murmured, seemingly to himself. He pinched the bridge of his nose as his grin broadened, but he didn't explain what he found so funny. Lily thought about throwing a rock at him.

Shayne swallowed and straightened up her coat, brushed dirt off the shoulders, folded down the collar. Then he dropped his hands. "You'll be promoted to a detective in no time, ugly Human," he said to her. "It pays better anyway." He bit his lip for a moment, then he added, "Don't worry about me. You've spent all this time immune to my witty words and dazzling looks. There's no reason to start caring too much."

Lily's mouth parted. She really couldn't tell if he was putting on an act, or if he was really that oblivious.

Immune to his 'witty words' and 'good looks'? Not *once* had she been immune to him. She'd spent the last year losing her mind over him. He'd always made sure his presence was everywhere, even if he wasn't physically with her. There wasn't a single workday in the last six months where she hadn't stolen glances at the front door of the station to see if he would visit, or a single shift at the café she wasn't aware of exactly where in the room he was standing.

Lily's jaw remained dropped as Shayne reached forward and ruffled her hair in a *'see you later, buddy'* sort of way. Like they were just friends, and all was well. Like it shouldn't bother her that he wasn't coming home.

She stared at him, even when he couldn't meet her eyes. He took in a deep breath and plastered a smile back onto his face as he huffed it out. "We should get moving," he called to everyone.

"Agreed. We need to get Lily back to the human realm before Levress and the Brotherhood of Assassins find our trail," Cress said. A large crease hung between Cress's eyebrows when Lily's wide gaze fired over to him next, and even though Lily had made a few conclusions by now, that one, she hadn't seen coming.

"Wait... you're staying here, too? I thought Luc was just rambling about all that," Lily said. When Cress didn't deny anything, Lily took a step toward him. Pain burned up her legs from her long hours of being strapped into fairy heels. "What about Kate?" It came out high-pitched.

Had all these fae lost their minds? Was this a joke?

From the other side of the clearing, Luc squeaked another laugh.

Cress clasped his hands together. "This is for Kate," he said as his mouth tipped down at the corners. He wasn't chewing on his tongue. "And I haven't yet decided what to do. We likely only have hours before everything chasing us closes in." His turquoise eyes settled on the fire in the middle of the group. "We'll take you back home immediately. Then we'll stand in front of the human gate and guard it for as long as possible. If we succeed in holding them off, you'll be safe. If they kill us, the forces of the Ever Corners won't have a reason to go into the human realm anymore anyway—"

Laughter rang through the trees. Luc slapped a hand over his mouth and slid behind a tree trunk, but it was no use. It echoed deep into the woods.

"What in the name of the sky deities is so funny, Luc?!" Mor growled and folded his arms.

"Oh dear. I think I've given myself away." Luc peeked out around the tree and bit his bottom lip over a grin.

Lily stared at him in disbelief. "Did he hit his head on a rock while I was gone or something?" she asked the group.

Mycra sighed across the clearing and poked at the fire with a stick, making Dranian's head snap toward her. "Wait... do you know what he's laughing about?" he grumbled.

She shrugged. "I saw his dreams. But it's not my place to voice what I see inside people's heads." She tossed something into the fire. A second later, she smirked too. "It is pretty funny though," she admitted.

"Why don't we place bets to see who will find us first?" Luc suggested. "I think it'll be the House of Lyro."

"Why would we place bets on that? That is outrageous," Cress barked. "And why Lyro?"

"Because they're already marching up the hills past this forest?" Luc guessed, but by the look on his face, it didn't seem like a guess at all. It dawned on Lily that he was telling them all to move.

"He's joking, right?" Lily asked Shayne as she yanked his coat off and handed it to him. "They're not actually coming…" Images of Jethwire's twisted smile filled her head. She turned and looked into the trees.

A small red object soared through the air above. It spiralled down, and Lily flinched as it sped past her face and landed by Shayne's feet. Shayne looked like he'd been slapped when he stared at it.

"Is that what I think it is?" Cress asked from across the clearing.

No one answered. There was no denying the bright red paper bird resting upon a bed of moss.

It took Lily a second to realize her hands were shaking. She balled them into fists.

"They're already here for me?" Shayne's question was quiet, like he was asking himself. "I thought I'd have more time."

Mycra jumped to her feet. Whatever humour was on her face before had fled. She whirled toward Luc. "I think it's time to go now," she urged.

Luc sighed. "Not yet, Dreamslipper. Have some patience."

"We can't face off with the House of Lyro!" she argued. "This isn't funny anymore!"

"What are you two talking about?!" Cress marched between them and looked from one to the other.

"Actually, it's hilarious," Luc corrected. "But not to worry…" He sniffed and turned around a few times like he was looking for something in the woods. When he couldn't seem to find it, he scratched his head.

Just then, a robust fairy with a menacing face and black armour materialized in the clearing.

Cress and Dranian jumped, Mor's sword buzzed to life, and Lily gasped as Shayne pulled her behind him. Mor took one step toward the fairy with his sword raised before Luc lifted a hand to stop him.

"It took you long enough!" Luc snapped at the Shadow Fairy. Mor slowed his steps while Luc laid his hand flat before the newcomer. "Give me the documents," he demanded.

The Shadow Fairy looked around at the group, taking in faces. After a moment, he reached into his armour and unearthed a thin scroll. "The vote was close," he said in a dark voice as Luc unrolled the scroll. "You foxes and your nine lives," he added with a mutter. The Shadow Fairy took a step back like he was about to do something, like drop to the ground, but Luc suddenly kicked him in the knee.

"Not in front of the others, you fool. You're ruining the surprise." Then, to everyone else, Luc shouted, "I would like the record to show that I, singlehandedly, fixed *everything*. That none of you fools were clever enough when it was needed, and that every time one of you was in trouble, it was me who showed up. And if you ever forget it, I'll ruin you." He rolled the scroll and stuffed it into his pocket.

Shayne put on his coat and pulled out his fairsaber handle. The blade formed with an electric popping sound. "You're crazy, Foxy," he said. Then to Lily, he instructed, "Go with my brothers. I'll hold off my family while you get home."

Luc's jaw nearly hit the forest floor. "Did you not hear everything I just said, North Fairy?!" he shouted at Shayne's back. With a tight-lipped scowl, Luc marched across the clearing and *grabbed* Lily by the arm. "Try to keep up unless you really want to lose her!" he snapped at the others. "We're going somewhere dark!"

The last thing Lily saw in the clearing was Shayne spinning and his eyes going wide as he lashed out to try and grab her back. Everyone leapt into motion, but no one reached her.

Lily was sucked into a speeding tunnel of air. Luc's arm secured her as they flew, veering around shapes Lily didn't have time to focus on.

At least thirty seconds passed before they slowed. The world spun around her even after they stopped and Luc let her go. Lily grabbed the side of her head and fell into the grass. She held her breath against a wave of nausea before she could look up and take in her surroundings.

This place was dimmer than the forest. A big, turbulent cloud swirled overhead, and cold air swept over her flesh. A long, narrow clearing surrounded them, where a dark line of ash or some other black substance stretched across the space in both directions as far as Lily could see.

"Where are we?" she asked.

"We're in the Dark Corner of Ever, dear Lily," Luc told her.

"What?! Why did you bring me *here*?" she said back. "And why in the world did you just steal me from the others?"

Luc spun around, knelt, and poked his finger beneath her chin to tilt her face up. His eyes were a little wilder and brighter than normal. The gesture reminded her of a certain white-haired fairy with a flute, and she smacked his hand away, making Luc's heart-shaped mouth twist. "You make yourself a target for fairies, you know. Being feisty like that makes you more valuable. Even I'm tempted to sell you at this point." He snarled a little as he stood and turned away from her. "I'm here now," he shouted at the trees where shapes and shadows shifted.

Lily fell back on her hands when Shadow Fairies emerged from the forest. "Luc…" she said in warning. Or maybe it was a plea, or an accusation; she wasn't sure. "What's happening?"

Mor burst out of the air. His fist was up and swinging at Luc as he landed, and Luc hardly dodged it in time. Luc whirled and kicked Mor off his feet. "Get a grip, Trisencor. In a second, you're going to be very sorry you attacked me here."

When Luc strode over to join the Shadow Fairies, Lily crawled over to where Mor balanced on one elbow. Mor's hair had come loose, and a grass stain covered his arm where he fell.

"Just stay behind me," he warned Lily when she reached him. She realized Mor was trembling as he dragged his feet beneath him and crouched like he was bracing himself. She watched his brown-silver eyes dart between the Shadow Fairies emerging from the forest and drawing their weapons. They slinked forward in silence, making an odd formation that gave Lily the feeling they were being surrounded.

Luc grunted a laugh. "Don't worry, you two. The rest of your High Court will be coming soon. We weren't that far from the border—I imagine the sprint will only take them a few minutes," he said. Then he turned to the rest of the fairies, and he said, "Prepare yourselves."

"Mor…" Lily whispered. "What's happening? Were we just betrayed by Luc?"

Mor's throat bobbed. "I'm not sure," he admitted. "I don't think so, but truthfully, I'm finding it hard to tell." He climbed to his feet and pulled Lily up with him. Lily watched his fingers slide into his back pocket and pull out his fairsaber handle.

Someone broke through the trees. Cress's pinched face was focused as he raced over the black line in strong, even strides. He skidded to a stop and tipped forward with his hands on his knees a foot away from Mor and Lily. "Ah, yes." He nodded, though his face was red like he was going to faint. "I knew I was the fastest," he said.

Mycra and Dranian came next, half carrying Shayne as he limped. "Just trust me!" Mycra shouted at the other two as if they were in the middle of an argument. "Hurry!"

The three of them stumbled across the black line, and to Lily's amazement, none of the Shadow Fairies rushed in to capture them. Lily jogged forward in her wobbling heels to help Mycra and Dranian, but Shayne pushed their hands off.

"I'm fine!" he stated. He marched away from them and met Lily halfway. "Did he do anything vile to you?" he asked her with a scowl before scouring the clearing. "Where is he? I'll kill him."

"I do hope you're not talking about me," Luc warned. He shook the dirt off his Dracula coat and wiped off his sleeves. "It would be rather tragic if you're really threatening me in front of all these witnesses."

Shayne's jaw tightened. He took a step toward Luc just as hundreds of hunters in red flooded through the trees. They scattered down the line, their bows drawn, their blades forming, and Shayne grabbed Lily instead.

Lily's heart squeezed in her chest as she recognized faces. She spotted Jethwire with his flute in his hand, resting high upon a reindeer. He made eye contact with her, his gaze icy, and Lily found herself gripping the back of Shayne's coat. Fuzzy memories spilled in; Jethwire nudging her face around, his commands for her to eat, the fairies with him laughing. The dizziness, the sore feet, the dancing in circles... all before Shayne's father; Hans-Der.

The middle-aged man sat upon a reindeer, too. He stared at Shayne darkly. Lily had never seen him furious.

She realized just how vast and strong the Lyro army was as it took several moments for them to assemble their lines. Lily's shoulders dropped as the warriors seemed to keep coming forever. There would be no fighting her way out this time. They would take Shayne. They might take her, too. She bit down hard on her lips at that thought.

Hans-Der slid off his reindeer. He kept his attention solely on Shayne as he stepped forward. He came to the black line of ash and moved to step over it...

"Uh oh," Luc said.

Four Shadow Fairies appeared around Hans-Der with their blades out. The Lyro army raised their bows in reaction, but Hans-Der hesitated. After a moment, he lowered his foot back on his side of the line. He raised a hand, and the bow-wielders of his army lowered their weapons.

Luc sauntered forward with his hands clasped behind his back. He sighed and shook his head. "I thought the House of Lyro wanted to *avoid* a war, not start one," he said. As he moved, a dozen Shadow Fairies in black armour inched along with him.

"Who are you?" Hans-Der asked, his lip curling in revulsion as he took Luc in. "Aren't you the fool who killed my oldest son?"

Luc put a hand against his chest, feigning shock. "Oh dear," he said. "I think I'm offended. First—your oldest son had it coming. Second—I don't think that's any way to address the King of the Dark Corner of Ever."

Lily felt Shayne flinch past the fabric of his coat. His hand tightened on her arm as his brows furrowed. He tilted his head as if taking in Luc for the first time.

"Speaking of which…" Luc looked around. "Someone should really get me a crown."

Hans-Der's face changed from disgust to surprise, to curiosity, then to doubt. "Nonsense…" he uttered.

The Shadow Army all raised their weapons at once, aiming for each and every fairy in red across the line of ash. One of them parted from the hoard and lifted his sword at Hans-Der. He said, "How dare you address His Royal Majesty with disrespect. Surrender to be tortured for it, and we shall let your army live."

This time, Hans-Der spoke through his teeth. "What?!"

"Hand over our prisoners," Jethwire interrupted. His gaze cut back to Shayne. "And our heir. Then we shall leave peacefully."

Luc tapped a finger against his chin. He took a while to deliberate, glancing over at Cress first like he was considering it, then at Shayne, then at Lily. Finally, at Mor—who's face was heavy with different emotions. One of them was definitely accusation.

Luc scrunched his face at Mor's expression, and he turned back to Hans-Der. "Nah," he finally said. "Mostly because I don't want to, and therefore, I don't have to." He marched forward and stood before the High Lord of the Lyro House. "You see, the thing is, I've been black marked by the House of Lyro. I was threatened by *your* own paper crane. And what a wicked and foolish thing it is to black mark a High King with an Army the size of mine." Luc's silver eyes blazed. Hans-Der shifted his weight as murmurs trickled down the line of Lyro allies, and for a moment, Lily thought Hans-Der might actually apologize.

But Luc wasn't finished. "I demand justice. Either we go to war, and you can fight the entire Shadow Army right now with your measly handful of hunters, or you sacrifice the heir of your household to me. Only the age-old custom will suffice. I demand blood for blood—as you have vowed to take mine. Black mark for black mark. Your highest seat for the throne you threatened." His words were cutting and dark, making the leaves throughout the forest shiver and tree trunks groan and snap. Some of the Lyro army drew several steps back from the line of ash.

Hans-Der opened his mouth, but he closed it again. He glanced over at Shayne, only this time, it wasn't with a glower. In fact, a strange smirk crossed his mouth. "You wish for my son's blood?" he asked.

Luc's smile broadened into something truly evil. "Desperately."

"And this will erase any transgressions from my household toward the Dark Corner throne?" Hans-Der took a slow step back from the ash, like his army.

"You'll avoid war. For now," Luc agreed.

Hans-Der nodded. Then he grinned, a look of malice spreading over his blue eyes. "Done. Kill him."

Luc drew his blade, and Lily didn't have time to process what was happening before he strode over, tore Shayne from her grip, and plunged his fairsaber through Shayne's stomach.

Lily heard herself scream.

Everything around her froze in place, except for the blade being torn back out of Shayne. And Shayne's body falling…

Falling…

She was still screaming as he collapsed in the dirt, as his blood leaked onto the soil. She buckled beside him and yanked his coat open. She slammed her palms against the stab wound, applying pressure. Sobs escaped her as she tried to hold him together, as she fought to keep him from losing the last of his blood and dying beneath her hands. Shayne's mouth parted as he stared up at the sky, his eyes losing focus, his limbs going slack.

"You're…" Lily croaked. She didn't even know what she was yelling. She thought she would die right there beside Shayne. "You're a *monster*, Luc!" she shouted through her tears.

Luc stared down the end of his nose, watching her. He didn't look like he regretted anything. In fact, he seemed to stifle an eye roll as he bristled, and he turned his back to her.

Lily knew Luc didn't like Shayne. Luc had threatened Shayne many times, but she didn't really think he'd... he'd...

Dranian stood nearby, his expression slack, his face white. Mor and Cress were as still as statues. Until...

Mor reached out and grabbed Cress's arm to hold him still. To keep him from helping, maybe. The act was so strange that Lily looked back to Luc again.

"Your household's debt is paid, High Lord," Luc said to Hans-Der. "But be assured that if you ever threaten the Dark throne again, or even bother me in the slightest, the House of Lyro will be burned to the ground with fairy fire so searing that even your *name* will be wiped from existence." He raised his hand and flung it at the whole Lyro line. "Now get out of my sight, peasants," he said.

Hans-Der took one last look at Shayne's body on the ground, bleeding beneath Lily's fingers. He snarled as he turned and walked back to his reindeer. With a shallow bow toward Luc, he mounted his deer, turned it around, and fled into the woods. The army in red followed him, groups breaking off from their lines and stampeding through the trees.

Jethwire was one of the last to leave. His mouth was pinched to the side, and his eyes were narrowed like he was waiting for something as he watched Lily hold Shayne's wound. But finally, he turned his reindeer and followed his family.

The second he disappeared, Luc whirled. "Hurry!" he shouted at the Shadow Fairies standing around. "Hurry, hurry, hurry!" He pointed down at Shayne. "Save him or you're all dead!"

Lily's hands were pulled off Shayne as Shadow Fairies swooped in and began performing strange practices: digging for nearby roots, pulling his coat off, splashing water over his face. "Wait..." she said to one when he shoved a handful of something into Shayne's mouth and held his lips shut around it. "You'll suffocate him..." But she didn't fight them. She scooted out of the way, watching as they jolted him around.

After a moment of it, Shayne's chest began to rise and fall. Mor appeared beside Lily and helped her to her feet, but she kept her stare glued to the parts of Shayne she could see between the Shadow Fairies surrounding him.

"Bring him to the Shadow Palace healing rooms," Luc instructed. Two Shadow Fairies lifted Shayne and vanished with him. Then Luc said, "And didn't I tell someone to bring me a crown?"

33

Shayne Lyro and That Time He Almost Died

Everything smelled like darkness. Shayne found himself wincing as he stirred awake, as he inhaled the fragrances of death and destruction around him. He smelled smoke, too, but not the nice kind; not the sort from campfires or the warm fireplace at Fae Café. This was something stranger and laced with far more shadows.

When he opened his eyes, he thought he was alone in a long room with bottles lining shelves and various forest herbs tied in bundles by the windows. But when he sat up, his leg bumped an arm covered in tattoos, and he took in the human leaning against the foot of his bed, fast asleep. She wore black clothes now, almost as unfitting for her as the red fairy dress and gold heels had been. The black dress hugging her body was definitely something of Dark Corner fashion, and it had Luc Zelsor written all over it.

Shayne's first priority became finding Lily something else to wear.

He leaned forward to brush a strand of her hair out of her face, but agony speared through him and he inhaled, grabbing his midsection and realizing that reaching and stretching and all manner of other big movements wouldn't go well for him for the next little while. So, he studied her instead.

He could still hear her screams. She'd practically turned into a human explosion when Luc had stabbed him.

Speaking of the fox devil, Shayne glanced around the large room to look for him. Even though Shayne had caught on to Luc's plan the moment Luc had turned his fairsaber on him, he didn't exactly care for the way Luc had gone about doing it.

Shayne lightly touched his tender stomach, thinking about Lily's reaction all over again.

He bit his lips together as a smile formed. She would kill him if she awoke and saw him smiling like this, but truly, that had been a lot of screaming for someone who didn't have feelings for him. Maybe she wasn't there yet, but Lily Baker was certainly on her way to falling deeply, madly, head-over-heels in love with him. It was only a matter of time now.

But his face changed when he thought back to the moment after he'd rescued her where he'd been bleeding out against that tree and had babbled all that nonsense about "loving her since the beginning" and whatever else he'd said under the influence of potential oncoming death. He stifled a moan. Why did he do foolish things like that? Why did he run his mouth? He sighed, only finding consolation in the fact that she'd tried to shut him up at the time, which meant she'd used her powers of case solving to deduce that Shayne was *not* in his right mind. Had he been, he would have confessed far more stylishly.

Or, he likely wouldn't have confessed at all.

He took in the great stone walls around him and the misty forests beyond the windows. He'd certainly never been here before, but after what happened at the border…

This *had* to be the Shadow Palace. Of all places. Somewhere he never in his wildest dreams thought he'd set foot even once in his faeborn lifetime.

Shayne's mind raced as he went back to his last memory before he'd been nearly gutted before the House of Lyro and left in the grass to die. He had thought he was dead, truly. He thought he might make it to human heaven after all. But he was alive, and he was here—with Lily.

Queensbane, after all the months of Shayne's wrestling through plans and tossing them to the wind, Luc-Foxy-Zelsor was the one who'd found a way to free him. Shayne brought a hand to his forehead as he considered what it meant now that his blood family thought he was dead. He dropped his hand to stare at that ring—the one he'd bound to himself, the one that would never come off. The one Hans-Der hadn't even asked to get back after Luc's stunt. The one he'd felt sick to slide onto his finger in the first place; a thick chunk of gold that was now powerless. He tugged at it, even though he already knew it wouldn't budge. And then he laughed because, even though he was free, he would forever have a reminder of his heritage, of the last name he wished to scrub from his life, of his memories of the Ever Corners he'd tried so hard to convince Mor to take away.

"Stupid ring," he remarked, dropping his hand to his lap.

The doors at the end of the room squeaked open, and in walked Luc wearing an extravagant black coat that was almost as ugly as his other coat had been, and a spindly black wreath-crown with jagged spokes, black opals, and silver moonstones. Luc even carried a large scepter he used as a walking stick that made Shayne laugh. "You look like a clown," he promised when Luc was close enough, even though Luc was the Dark King and the Shadows who tailed him wouldn't like the insult one bit.

"I look menacing," Luc corrected. "Which is fitting since I *am* menacing. I'm also the one who saved you, in case you haven't figured that out yet, North Fairy."

All his loud self-glorifying made Lily stir. She batted her eyelashes as she woke and lifted from the bed. She inhaled slowly, then reached her arms high in the air and stretched.

Shayne clasped his hands together and squeezed them, his faeborn heart nearly bursting as he watched her be that cute. "Stop it," he warned her, and she looked over at him in question. "You're supposed to be tough and angry like always."

She raised an eyebrow, but didn't ask what he was talking about. Instead, she lifted from her seat and came closer. "Are you alright?" she asked, and he revelled in every bit of concern in her tone. He was obsessing over it too hard to notice that Cress, Mor, and Dranian had followed Luc into the room.

"One of your minions just told me you sent a letter to Queene Levress," Cress said, taking over the conversation about two seconds after he arrived. He rushed over and put a hand on Luc's shoulder that caused the trio of Shadow Fairies around him to glare. "What did you say to Levress?" Cress demanded.

Luc carefully peeled Cress's fingers off his shoulder. "I threatened war," he told him. "I told her the great Cressica Alabastian was in fact alive, as the rumours claim, and that he was allied with *me*, the Dark King, and if she ever tried to find you or send one of her assassin guard dogs after you, or if she ever dared to send one of her loser North Fairies into the human realm to spy on you, I'd send the greatest army in the Ever Corners—"

"Second greatest," Cress mumbled in objection.

"—to the Silver Castle, and she would regret the day she broke the delicate peace between the Dark and North Corners." Luc shrugged. "Simple." Then he looked around from fairy to fairy—to human—and back to fairy as a slow, broad smile split his mouth. "Don't you all want to know how I became King?" he asked.

"Not really," Cress grumbled. He folded his arms with a slight pout. Mor pressed a fist over his mouth like he was trying not to laugh at him.

"Let's get one thing straight, Foxy," Shayne said as he pulled the covers off himself. He turned with a grimace, pain shooting through his whole faeborn body, and he put his legs over the side of the bed. Then he glared at Luc. "You practically *killed* me."

"Yes, well, you killed me first," Luc reminded him. "And I did say I'd get my revenge. We're even now, North Fairy. And just in case you're all dying to know, I became King because I slaughtered the Queene of—"

"Eiw." Lily covered her ears.

"—the Dark Corner on her throne, and then I gave the Shadow Court two options. I told them to gather and vote on whether they'd execute me for treason or to *fully* King me. It seems I was right about what they'd decide, since I pointed out I was the last living member of the royal family, and my bloodline has remained in power for seventeen generations." He snapped and pointed. "I'm also not the first one in my family to assassinate a King or Queene to steal the throne. So, I had that going for me."

"Congratulations," Mor mumbled in a low voice. It was hard to tell if he was being sarcastic or not.

Luc did a spin so that everyone could see his coat from all sides or something. "You can all thank me now. I fixed everything, like I said I would." He pointed his scepter at Cress. "I even fixed your thing, when I didn't have to." Then he jabbed it toward Shayne. "And yours, North Fairy."

Dranian clapped, and Shayne shot him a look that made him clap slower and then eventually stop.

The candlelit dinner in the Shadow Palace was every bit as horrifying as Shayne could have imagined. He'd never spent much time thinking about the Dark Corner or its practices, or its decorations, or the things the Shadows considered to be valuable. But it was clear now as he looked down the black tablecloth at the gloomy curtains mostly covering the dim, filtered light slipping through the twisting cloud in the sky outside.

Tall silver candlesticks speared the air like broken fingers, holding candles that dripped wax all over the tablecloth. But the cherry on top was the fox sitting at the head of the table in his heavy black crown, now fashioning a *new* coat with slick black feathers around the collar that seemed to be swallowing him whole. Luc picked at a plate of meat he seemed too revulsed at the sight of to actually eat. If Shayne didn't know any better, he'd think Luc was secretly plotting to escape this dungeon of darkness, even if it did seem to suit his evil personality.

The rest of Shayne's brothers, Lily, and Mycra sat around the table, nudging their plates every now and then so wax wouldn't drip on their food.

Cress leaned over to Mor and didn't whisper quietly enough, "This is worse than your cathedral, Mor. It's like we're trapped in the underworld."

Mor bit down on his lips, but a smirk still formed. "I think we'll go home after this," he said back to Cress. "I'm a Shadow Fairy and even I'm going to have nightmares from looking around this place too long."

Naturally, Lily was every bit as oblivious as usual about how mighty she seemed as she braved the meat first. She took a bite, and Shayne watched her chew and swallow it. He sat back in his chair and folded his arms, waiting for the sassy remark he knew would be coming next.

Dranian leaned and mumbled something to Mycra.

Cress nudged Mor, then pointed down at something on his plate in disgust.

And *then*, there it was: Lily lifted her head, glanced down the table at Luc, and said, "If this food makes me feel dizzy, or dance, or do literally anything but be normal, I'm going to shoot your head off."

Shayne had to plug his nose so he wouldn't snort a laugh all the way down the table.

But if that wasn't enough, Lily turned to the others and added, "And seriously, does this taste like garbage to anyone else?"

Luc's rosy lips spread into a tantalizing smirk. "You'd make a great fairy queene, dear Lily. Only the fearsome ones throw fits over their food."

Shayne's smile fell. "Easy, Foxy," he warned as he reached for his water goblet. "We might mistake that for a proposal."

Luc shoved his plate away, then lifted his pale hands and folded them on the table. "It can be one if she wants it to be one," he said. When he smiled, a sweet fragrance rippled down the table, and the candle flames flickered. Everything grew a little warmer, and Lily's gaze was sucked in Luc's direction like he held the end of a magnet. Shayne's fingers tightened around his goblet. It was already horrid enough that Lily was dressed in a sleek black dress from Luc's palace and had her hair brushed by his servants, but now she was breathing in his furry fox fragrance?

Shayne slammed his water against the tabletop and stood from his seat. "I have something to go do," he claimed. He turned and marched for the hallway, only realizing once he was there that he'd been gripping his water goblet so hard he forgot to let it go.

As soon as he was in the hall, he peeked around for doorways, certain he could find a room *somewhere* with *something* better inside it for Lily to wear. Even if it was burlap.

But he hadn't taken three steps around the bend when he heard Lily's hushed voice sail through the dining room and ask, "Does Shayne have feelings for me? Like, for real?"

Shayne's feet came together on the cold floor. He realized he was stuck there, blending into the rows of ancient fairy statues lining the walls.

Had she actually forgotten how fairy ears worked—again? Did she really not realize Shayne could hear the question loud and clear even down the hall?

It was Mor who replied with certainty. "Sky deities, *no*," he said.

Shayne breathed a sigh of relief. At least Mor had his back. He was lucky Lily hadn't asked Cress or Dranian. Neither of them would have kept their cool.

"Then why can't you look me in the eyes?" Lily asked Mor, and Shayne grabbed his hair in his fist.

It wasn't like she didn't know. He'd already told her; he'd already yacked his faeborn face off and spewed everything into the air. It shouldn't have stressed him out to have her flat out ask about his crush after all he'd said already. But still…

Shayne whirled around and tiptoed back toward the dining room. He leaned in, spying around the doorframe just in time to see Mor shove an enormous clump of meat into his mouth which Shayne knew full well was so that he wouldn't have to answer Lily's question.

The scheming little detective went on, "When Cress liked Kate, you could all sniff his fairy crush. Shayne can't possibly like me without you knowing, right?" She didn't admit to them all the nonsense Shayne had said to her in the woods.

Dranian spoke up out of nowhere, "That's because Cress had no experience with romance and females and bumbled around like a fool. The inexperienced ones can't hide it. But Shayne has plenty of experience with females and romance and hiding things and—"

"Never mind!" Lily waved a hand to shoo him off, her face all twisted and bothered now. "I wish I never asked," she mumbled as she pushed her plate away.

Shayne relaxed against the wall. He wanted to give Dranian a high-five for being the winner of the conversation and for bringing it to an end. It was all good now. It was all safe—

"You're an open book though, dear Lily." The sound of Luc's voice was like a dull knife scratching against a sleek rock. Shayne's head whipped back to see Luc level his silvery, creepy, unblinking gaze on Lily until she shifted in her seat.

Mor cast Luc a doubtful look. "What are you talking about? I've tried reading this human a hundred times. She's not an open book."

"You forget that I steal secrets, Trisencor. And I stole all of Lily's secrets a long time ago," Luc stated.

"What?!" Lily dropped her cutlery. "When did you steal my secrets?! That is such a violation of human rights!" She pointed at him with her knife. "That's why no one will forgive you for what you did to Violet, you moron! Un-*real*!"

Luc sipped his water and leaned back against his glitzy seat. "Then I should add that I didn't *need* to steal your secrets, dear Lily. I figured out everything about you long before I stole anything," he said. "And also—I'm not a human, so your 'human rights' rule doesn't apply to me." Then he raised his glass toward Mor and Cress. "If you all practiced studying people a little more instead of relying on your fairy senses to tell you things, you might have picked up on her feelings a long time ago."

"What feelings?" Cress demanded. He leaned forward to see around Mor, and he looked Lily over. "She doesn't have any feelings. She's like a lump of rock. She feels nothing."

"She does, actually," Luc corrected. "She's just one of those rare humans who fairies can't discern, you fools."

Cress grunted and folded his arms like he didn't believe it for one second. Mor cast Luc a look of warning, but it did nothing as Luc tapped the table with his forefinger like he was leading some absurd group therapy session no one wanted to be a part of.

Shayne almost barged in and put an end to it. He had the thought to go flip over Luc's chair with him still in it. He swished out from behind the wall and marched into the room, but he froze in place when Luc said, "Dear Lily, you are so madly in love with that barefoot North Fairy that it's hard to notice anything else about you."

The smashing sound of a goblet hitting the floor rang through the room. Shayne didn't realize it was his goblet. That *he'd* dropped it. That all the noise was coming from him, and now his feet were wet and his pantlegs were damp with cold water.

He only realized it when Lily's face turned toward him and her mouth parted, her eyes wide. Her cheeks became pink like all the flowers in the universe blossomed inside them. "I... That's..." She shook her head. Then she stood like she had something important to say—to him, to everyone. But she said nothing.

Nothing.

Nothing, nothing, and *still* nothing.

So, Mor spoke up. "That's ridiculous," he said in what sounded like a feeble attempt to come to her defense, but he waited with strange, worried eyes like he was also wondering why she didn't deny it.

"Want to help me out, Dreamslipper?" Luc said to Mycra. "You saw inside her head."

Mycra instantly raised her hands. "I'm staying out of this."

And that was it. That was proof enough.

Shayne gasped. Loudly. He slapped both his hands over his mouth, and he pointed right in Lily's human face.

"You're in love with me!" He bellowed it for the whole Dark Corner to hear, accidentally producing the biggest smile he'd ever formed.

He found himself moving across the room, pushing aside a chair, kicking over candlesticks and stepping in Dranian's food as he scurried *over* the table to close the gap between them—even though she backed away and continued to shake her head like the little liar she was trying to be.

"It's alright, Trisencor." Luc was still talking for some reason. "You wouldn't have been able to sense it. *He* should have figured it out though." He might have nodded toward Shayne's back because he added, "And you call yourself a romantic. Idiot." He sighed. "That's why she'd be better off with me."

"You like me. Admit it!" Shayne demanded of Lily. "Tell me the truth, ugly Human!"

Instantly, Lily stood at attention and blurted, "I do like you. I would take a bullet for you if I had to." But her jaw dropped, and her mouth hung open. Her hand came over it, and a strange sort of deadly accusation moved across her eyes, telling Shayne he'd done something wrong even though he had no idea what. That was, until he realized...

"Oh..."

Shame. Shame on him for forgetting—*again*. Queensbane, he was really in for it now.

He grinned anyway. A love confession under the force of enslavement was still a love confession.

"How do you feel about marriage?" he asked her. "Do you want to get married before Cress and Kate and rub it in their faces?"

Lily and Cress growled at the same time, "What?!"

Shayne grabbed Lily's hands so she couldn't flee, or hit him, because she was giving off slight '*I want to punch you*' vibes.

"No, Shayne!" she said. "I don't need a guy to take care of me, which is why I've always said I'm not getting married—"

"Yes, you are," he corrected with a chuckle. "And when you do, I'll take your last name. Mine sucks. Everything *Lyro* sucks."

Somewhere behind them, Mor was trying so hard not to laugh, he squeaked. Then, in his low voice, he said, "I apologize, Cress. But this is quite possibly the funniest thing I have ever witnessed in my entire faeborn life."

"I'll wear hoodies all the time and push up my sleeves to my elbows," Shayne promised. "You'll love it." He clasped Lily's hand and tugged her back to the table, then he nudged Dranian out of his seat so he could sit beside her—*Lily*—the human who loved him so much she could die. Who probably was having a hard time keeping her hands off him now that they were engaged.

Females.

"This is outrageous!" Cress stated. "That does *not* count as a proposal! I'm getting married first! I call the human right of dibs!"

"We'll see," Shayne said.

Luc rubbed his temples at the end of the table. "Oh dear. You're all exhausting sometimes," he muttered. "I was planning to return to the human realm, but in this moment, I'm considering just being King and ruling over my subjects with an iron fist. It would be less annoying than dealing with all of you."

"You're returning to the human realm?" Mor asked in surprise. "Will the Shadow Court allow that?"

Luc sighed. "I'm King, Trisencor. I can do what I want. Besides, I have a job now in the human realm to go back to."

"What job? I didn't hear of any job." Cress looked around the table like he was trying to figure out if anyone else knew about it.

"I already told you; I rescue puppies from trees and save babies." Luc lifted his goblet and took a long drink. "Oh—" he lifted a finger "— didn't I also say I volunteer in an old-people's-home or something?" He tapped that same finger against his chin. "I don't remember."

Mor rolled his eyes and folded his arms. "You and your lies," he said. "Just once, I wish you'd tell us the truth straight up."

Luc smiled devilishly. "One day, Trisencor, you will see just how many times you thought I was lying when I wasn't."

"Will you still be living in our apartment with me and Dog-Shayne?" Dranian murmured.

Shayne's head snapped toward him. "Who is Dog-Shayne?" he asked. "And what do you mean '*living in our apartment*'?"

"Of course," Luc replied to Dranian. "I just spent the last weeks pretending to be in two places at once, and I've discovered I'm good at it. My fellow Shadow Fairies never even realized I was gone. It won't be that difficult to check in every now and then and do some King-ish things. Throw a few royal fits. Maybe snap a few necks while I'm at it."

Shayne watched Lily wince and shake her head.

"Let's go home, then," Cress decided. "Immediately. I'll lose my faeborn-cursed mind if I stay here any longer." He glanced up at the vaulted, web-covered ceiling heights of the Shadow Palace.

At the mention of home, warmth spilled into Shayne's chest. "Home," he whispered to himself. It drew Lily to glance over at him. He smiled as it settled in that he was going there, back to the human realm, back to Fae Café, back to the box of space he'd promised to share with Dranian, back to wearing his burgundy apron, and enchanting coffee drinks. Back to peace and simplicity. Back to everything he loved. And especially, back to where he belonged.

A hand slid into his beneath the table. His gaze darted over to Lily, and he realized he'd maybe reached human heaven for a split second when he caught her smiling. "You're such a child," she whispered, filled with all the endearing, '*I'm-completely-obsessed-with-you*' feelings she would totally deny later.

"And you're not as ugly as you think, ugly Human," he told her.

Her face changed like she couldn't decide if that was a compliment or not. "I told you not to call me that."

"Ah, you're right." Shayne nodded. "I think I agreed to call you *Messy-Haired Scarecrow* from now on, didn't I?"

She pulled her hand out of his. "Shayne," she said flatly.

"Scarecrow?" he asked in all innocence.

Lily rolled her eyes, but there was a teensy smirk on the corners of her mouth. Shayne stared at that mouth of hers, with its little quirking movements and its bad habits of lying and being sassy. He'd never wanted to kiss anything so bad. She'd probably shove him off if he tried it in front of everyone though since she wasn't one for public displays of affection—something he would have to make her change her mind about since he was excellent at public displays of affection.

Yes, he'd kiss that mouth *very* soon.

CHAPTER

34

Luc Zelsor and Home

There was a particular smell in the old-people's-home that most of the human realm workers claimed to not like. Luc was probably the only being in existence who found comfort in it. It was filled with old stories, peaceful tones, and untapped wisdom. Humans didn't realize all the available knowledge hiding away in their elders. If only humankind would take a glance at their history every now and then, they might find solutions to their problems instead of repeating the same mistakes over and over.

Luc opened the front doors and headed inside as he adjusted his backpack, then he nodded to the young receptionist at the desk who cast him a shy wave and pushed her hair behind her ear. A variety of paper trees had been hung up along the walls—likely the patients' most recent craft.

He made his way around the bend to his locker, shrugged off his coat, and dragged out his scrubs, slipping them on over his jogging clothes.

He was still fastening his shiny name tag to his chest when the head caregiver, *Mary*, came around carrying a clipboard and a rather heavy-looking teetering tray of rolled towels. Luc almost didn't make it to her in time before she would have dropped everything. He lifted the tray while the middle-aged female caught her balance and wiped a bead of sweat from her brow. She flashed him a smile.

"Thanks, Luc. I was on my way to distribute those to the rooms on the second floor, but... well, I got a little dizzy," she said. "They're a lot heavier than they used to be."

"I'll do it," Luc said. He cast her a smile in return that might have actually been authentic and cruelty-free. "How is patient 112? Any new trauma symptoms?" he asked as he moved the tray to one hand and used the other to replace his backpack. They headed back by reception toward the stairs, and Mary laughed.

"They're people, Luc, not patients. This isn't a hospital. And you should learn their names!" she reminded him. "I think it's so funny you always call them by their room numbers. How do you remember everyone's numbers like that anyway?"

"Not everyone's," he admitted. "Just the ones I like, I suppose."

Ten minutes later, Luc set the empty tray on the cart at the end of the second floor hall and ventured down to room 112 with the last towel. He knocked lightly, and when there was no answer, he cracked the door open.

"Ms. Hunter?" he called gently. "I've brought towels."

"Come in," a voice called back, and so, Luc slipped into the room.

A female sat in a wheeled-chair by the window, making a study of everyone outside. Wreaths of woven flower stems and long grass hung in various places around the room.

"How are you today?" he asked her, and the female turned in her seat. She smiled when she saw him—she had a lovely smile. Heart-shaped and kind.

"Luc, was it?" she asked. "Sorry to ask—my memory isn't great. I'm not sure I can trust my own mind anymore even though you come in almost every day."

"Your mind is just fine," he told her as he sat on the bed and pulled his backpack around. "So are your legs," he added, eyeing the wheeled-chair. "You don't actually need that thing. Why bother with it?" He un-zipped the backpack and reached inside.

"Of course I don't need it. I'm younger than all the people here," she said, waving toward the other rooms. "But if I tell the staff how good my legs are, I'll have to start walking everywhere."

Luc chuckled. "Fair." He pulled something out of the backpack and held it up so she could see. "I brought you a present," he told her.

Ms. Hunter turned in her chair to see it closer, eyeing the tight wreath of the crown, the glittering black opals, and the expensive moonstones that had been sacred to the Dark Corner for generations.

"What is it?" she asked.

Luc reached forward and placed it on her head. "It's something that will ensure you're never ruled over again," he told her.

She released a laugh as she balanced it atop her head. It compli-mented her smooth, pale skin, her silvery eyes, and her pointed ears. "How do I look?" she asked.

"Like someone who belonged at the Queene's table all along," Luc said. He tossed his backpack aside and stood, then he reached to adjust the crown, but he paused when her hand came up and rested along his. He found her studying him the way she studied all people.

She cracked a modest smile. "Oh dear. You know, the strange thing about having Alzheimer's disease is feeling like you know someone but not remembering why," she said, and Luc frowned. He lowered his hands as she took him in. A second later, she laughed at herself and shook her head. "Maybe I should be worried I'm forgetting something important."

Luc's shoulders relaxed. He found his own smile and he stood again, walked around her wheeled-chair, and took the handles. "That would only apply if you actually had Alzheimer's disease, which you don't," he informed her. "You have a simple case of amnesia. And you have nothing to worry about in here. As long as you remember that I'm your favourite caregiver in this place, and they continue to feed you three times a day, and they let you play board games with your friends, and they take you out for long, lovely walks in the park, I imagine it's much better than whatever life you had that you can't remember."

He turned her chair toward the door as she nodded.

"Maybe you're right," she said with a sigh, and she laughed again. "You seem clever."

Luc's grin widened.

"Now, since you're so determined to take advantage of these chairs on wheels and get pushed around instead of walking on your perfectly good feet, why don't we head out for a walk? There's an ice cream place not far from here that I've recently discovered is open year-round."

Ms. Hunter's room filled with the sounds of her clapping. "Yes! I *love* ice cream."

CHAPTER

35

Lily Baker and Fae Café

The street smelled of freshly ground coffee beans, car exhaust, and new possibilities. The whole city blinked with red and green Christmas lights, and slush coated the sidewalks, bringing in a sweep of fresh winter weather. All the good things about Fae Café seeped out from the door whenever it was opened; the chatter, the smell, the warmth.

Lily stood on the opposite side of the street gripping a burgundy mug and watching customers filter in and out of the café she'd created with Kate; a business built on the desperation to pay bills, dreams of making it in the future, and the promise to look out for each other forever. A place that had become so much bigger and more meaningful than she'd expected the day she and Kate had sat cross-legged in her apartment and had decided to "do their future" together by starting a business.

She shivered as icy air trickled in through the cracks of the slouchy, cream-coloured sweater the Sisterhood of Assassins finally made for her after Shayne had harassed them about it for the last five days. Freida only agreed to give Lily a fairy-yarn sweater if Mycra knitted it, which was a task Mycra took pretty seriously since it was her first mission with the Sisterhood. Mycra's handiwork was actually impressive though; the sleeves of the sweater were a little too long and hung over Lily's knuckles, but otherwise, the oversized garment was exactly how Lily would have made it herself.

She wrapped her hands around her warm mug, letting the coffee's heat sooth the biting chill of winter. If she knew Dranian was going to take this long to hang the Christmas lights, she would have worn her coat.

"How's that?" Dranian's mutter was way too quiet from where he was perched atop a ladder all the way on the other side of the street. If his mouth hadn't moved, Lily wouldn't have even known he'd spoken.

"What? I can't hear you!" she called back.

She smirked when Dranian wrenched himself around to scowl at her. "I said…" She watched him take in a large chest-full of air. "HOW'S THAT?!"

The earth shook below Lily's feet; a few people jumped out of their skin as the roar echoed across Toronto. Lily took a sip of coffee to hide her giggle. She raised her other hand toward Dranian with a thumbs up.

The door to Fae Café swung open and a handsome fairy with styled white hair and a fitted burgundy apron poked his head out. "Come inside before you get sick!" he shouted at her. Then he added, "Scarecrow!"

Lily's body jerked into motion. She bit back a grimace as her legs brought her across the road, over the sidewalk, and right back into Fae Café. Instantly, the warmth of the space enveloped her, and although Shayne deserved a good swat upside the head for bossing her around like that with his 'master' powers, she was relieved to not be freezing out in the snow anymore.

Speaking of Shayne…

She looked around, but she didn't see where he'd hidden after he'd hung out the door and yelled at her. Cress was charming some poor, innocent girl by the counter, trying to convince her to add six slices of pie

FAKE DATING A HUMAN 101

to her coffee order. She could see Mor through the cracked-open kitchen door, whipping up a batch of gingerbread cookies like it was nobody's business.

"Shayne?" she called. She turned all the way around once before she was grabbed and dragged into the narrow hallway by the door.

Shayne was biting his bottom lip over a smile as he nudged her against the wall and slinked his fingers into her hair without warning. "I have an idea!" he said in a loud whisper. He began twirling her hair around his fingers.

"Great." Lily sighed. She took another sip of her coffee to hear him out, even though she knew in about two seconds she was probably going to have to try to talk him out of whatever his new idea was.

"Let's host a pie eating contest at Cress's wedding!" he said with so much excitement it *almost* rubbed off on her.

"That's a terrible idea. He'll kill you in front of everyone. Literally," she said.

Shayne shook his head. "You're wrong. I'm doing it."

She wasn't ready when he swooped in and pecked her on the mouth with a kiss. She stood there, frozen for a minute as he scurried off. Her hand rose and pressed against her thudding chest. Then she brushed her fingers along her lips where leftover traces of him warmed her skin. She snapped out of it a second later and wandered after him.

"Shayne! Let's talk about the pie thing…" she called, but when she came out of the hall, she found him sitting at one of the bistro tables with Luc, Dranian, and Greyson.

"He'll be in the kitchen for a while. Let's hurry," Mor said as he scooted into the chair beside Dranian. Cardstock paper covered the tabletop along with a handful of pens that looked like they either came from Mor's cathedral or Shayne's pockets.

"What are you doing?" Lily asked.

"We're writing 'best wishes' letters to Cress for his wedding day," Mor told her. "We read about it in one of the bridal magazines Cress has upstairs."

"I don't know what to write," Greyson said. He tapped his pen on the table and turned to Luc who was already scribbling across his piece of paper. "What are you writing?"

"An ancient proverb," Luc replied without missing a beat.

"Nice," Greyson said with an odd face. "I don't know any of those. Which one did you choose?"

Luc finished, picked up his tiny espresso mug and sipped it with his pinky in the air, then lifted his letter and read, "Cressica, you're quite fast."

Greyson waited, and when Luc didn't explain, he nodded. "Cool—"

"Because intelligent thoughts have always chased you," Luc went on. "But you were always faster." Luc lowered his letter and sipped his drink again. His gaze shot right to Lily like he expected her to comment.

And she did. "Seriously?"

Luc set his espresso carefully on the table and said, "I'm not changing it."

"Yes, you are. Write something else, Luc," Mor said as he focused on his own letter.

Luc grumbled as Lily abandoned her coffee on the nearest table and folded her arms to watched them. She had to admit, it was pretty thoughtful that they came up with this on their own.

"What are you writing, Mor?" Greyson asked.

"It's a secret. It's only for Cress to know," Mor returned. "It's between brothers."

Greyson tilted his head. "I'll *actually be* Cress's brother after the wedding," he pointed out.

Luc yanked a newly scribbled letter into the air and began reading: "Cressica, it's better to stay silent and have people wonder if you're a fool than to open your mouth and have everyone know for sure."

"Luc," Mor warned dully. "That's not true. Cress isn't a fool when he speaks."

"I'd agree with you, Trisencor, but then we'd both be wrong." Luc folded his letter, stuck it in an envelope, and then sat back to sip on his coffee while the rest of them finished.

Shayne lifted his letter and read aloud, "To the Mighty Prince of the North: You are wise in everything regarding fairies. But when it comes to human-y things, unfortunately, it's people like you that are the reason cleaning products have warning labels."

Mor bit down on a smile.

"Are you saying that because he used bleach to clean Kate's sofa that one time and left it all patchy?" Dranian asked in a monotone voice. Lily burst out laughing.

"Yes." Shayne folded his letter.

"You can't say that!" Mor wiped the smile from his face to scold Shayne, pointing his pen at him. "Say something nice!"

"Fine. If I have to be nice, I'll write my letter to Kate instead." Shayne grabbed his pen and spoke aloud as he scribbled, "Dear Kate. If you change your mind about Cress, come find me. I'll be an excellent husband. I'm totally husband material. Feel free to tell Lily that."

Lily shook her head as she brought her mug over to the sink to wash it. "Don't be mad because I refused to get married before Kate. There are some friendship rules that shouldn't be broken, you know."

Shayne cast her a doubtful look.

Suddenly, Cress banged out of the kitchen doors, and very quickly, all the fairies and Greyson scrambled to hide their terrible letters of well wishes.

SPRING
IN THE HUMAN REALM

**There are three important rules to follow
if you want to get married to a fae:**

1. If possible, don't ever tell him your real name, but if it's too
    late, make sure you at least know how to enchant him with a
    kiss to even things out.
2. If you're an author, try not to let him anywhere near the novels
    you're writing, or he'll offer unsolicited advice until your ears
    fall off.
3. Just let him take over the wedding plans. Seriously, trying to
    get involved isn't worth it. He's just going to go with the accent
    colours he wants regardless of what you say.

36

Kate Kole and the Wedding Day

The thing about Kate Kole was that there was a time she felt like she didn't exist. She'd been a student who sat at the back of the class under a fake name, a struggling entrepreneur with debts to pay, and a mostly noiseless presence apart from those rare occasions when she saw something unfair happening and felt the need to intervene instead of minding her own business. The days before fairies had been slower, quieter, and frankly, easier in some respects. But she wouldn't go back to that life if given the choice. She wouldn't choose to return to the mundane feeling of nonexistence. Not after she'd learned what it felt like to be the centre of someone's entire universe.

Well… sometimes, anyway. Cress was the centre of his own universe on a normal day, but there were moments where Kate knew he would have abandoned everything in a heartbeat if it would bring a smile to her face. The fae Prince who'd barged into her life ready to kill her in a revenge hunt had come a long way since the day he'd shown up in a stolen police uniform and pinned her back against the café wall with death in his trained assassin eyes.

The mirror in the back room of the church was so big it made Kate look like a giant. Her hair fell in soft, burgundy waves around her shoulders, making her feel like a full-fledged fairy queen. She and Cress had been at odds for the last three months about what colour her hair should be for the wedding. He'd finally won, claiming he would "tangle it into elf-locks the night before the wedding" if she didn't comply with the 'burgundy theme' of his *once-in-a-lifetime* wedding. He hadn't looked like he'd been joking either.

Frankly, Kate didn't really care what colour her hair was. It had just been funny to see him argue about it so hard, and sometimes she was just curious about how far she could push him before he would snap out some ridiculous claim that actually had nothing to do with her or the wedding and she'd get to watch him binge-eat cookies for three days straight.

"You look awesome. Seriously, Cress will faint," Lily said as she entered the back room with a grin. Her long burgundy bridesmaids' dress fit her so well, Kate was sure she'd turn heads. Kate had chosen the sleeveless style for Lily to wear on purpose so everyone could see her tattoos.

"I hope not. He'll be so mad if he misses his own wedding after all this planning." Kate set her bouquet on an end table and swished her dress back and forth in front of the mirror. "This is pretty poofy. Should I change dresses at the last minute and give Cress a heart attack after he shopped for the perfect dress for like four months?"

Lily laughed. "Spare us all the next ten years we'll have to listen to him complain about it," she said. A moment later, she leaned and peeked out the door. "They're ready for us. Greyson is waving us over."

Kate took in a deep breath. She wasn't nervous, really, it was more like excitement jitters. Even though her boyfriend was unconventional, Kate had always imagined she would get married one day, unlike Lily, who'd spent her young adult years claiming she'd stay independent—though Lily's mind seemed to have been changing lately. Kate caught her staring at Shayne's back all the time when he was turned around. The two were practically magnets that couldn't stop being pulled together.

"Mom and Dad would have loved Cress, right?" Kate asked as Lily swung the door wide open so she could fit through. "I mean, Grandma Lewis did. Greyson does."

"Totally," Lily said. "He's pretty solid in the 'capable of protecting his wife' department. And he works hard, he's good at selling coffee, and he wants to be a dad. That's a lot of wins."

Kate chuckled as she slid out of the room, filling most of the hallway with her dress. "Yeah, we let him get away with too much though. Grandma Lewis would've let Cress have it for enslaving me, even though he saved my life. She would have kept Shayne in check now that he's enslaved you, too."

"Well, now we have Mor for that." Lily reached over to adjust Kate's skirt and hair as they reached the entrance to the sanctuary. Greyson jogged over in a dashing suit.

"You ready?" he asked Kate with an enormous smile.

"Cress wouldn't let me leave even if I wasn't," Kate joked. "You two are going to have my back when I tell him I only want four kids maximum, right?"

"Sure," Greyson said with a shrug. "I can't wait to be an uncle." He stuck out his arm, and Kate took it. "Oh… and before we go in, I should probably warn you…"

Kate found Greyson wincing when she glanced over. "What?" Her smile fizzled away. "What happened?"

"Well, Cress is just…" Greyson shook his head. "Never mind. Go on ahead, Lily. They're playing the song."

Lily flashed Kate one last smile before heading through the entrance and making her way down the long aisle scattered with burgundy rose petals. It was the first chance Kate got to peek into the sanctuary. She saw hundreds of people she knew filling the pews and the fae baristas standing in a row at the front. Shayne bit his lips over a closed-mouth smile when he saw Lily. Then he mouthed the word, "*Hot*" at her.

Lily blushed and shook her head as she headed to the opposite side of the stage. She stood alone over there as Kate's sole bridesmaid, so it was pretty obvious who Shayne was ogling at when he leaned forward to see past Mor.

The Sisterhood of Assassins took up the front rows of the church, fashioning full-on knit dresses—all but Mycra who wore a bright green summer dress that matched her eyes. Behind them was Violet with her interns—Remi and Jase—and behind them were a few acquaintances Kate knew from high school and college. Luc sat at the end of a pew, holding tight to Dog-Shayne's leash. Some of Grandma Lewis's old friends had even made the trip, and a few of the neighbours of Fae Café had come, too. Greyson waved at Lincoln and Tegan in the back row.

The song increased in volume, and it was exactly the second Greyson tugged her through the entrance on his arm, the same second she felt the stares of all those hundreds of people upon her, that she noticed Cress.

Cress was bawling too hard to keep his eyes open. It was so dramatic, Kate almost stopped walking.

"Keep moving," Greyson said through his teeth behind a plastered smile.

Cress sniffed, took in a deep breath and composed himself for about a second. Then he opened his eyes, saw Kate, and released a loud wail before starting to cry all over again. This time, Greyson pressed a fist over his mouth and snorted a quiet laugh.

From the pews, Kate heard Luc mumble, "What a loser."

"Sorry," Greyson whispered to Kate. "I can't stop laughing. It's like he's doing this to himself."

"Has he been like this all day?" Kate asked quietly.

Greyson scratched the back of his head. "You don't wanna know."

Kate watched her strong, handsome fae Prince make a complete fool of himself in front of everyone, and a slow grin spread across her face. If she was being honest, Kate would have preferred to ditch the wedding, grab Cress, and run away with him for a while. If nothing else, his antics would keep her amused for the rest of her life.

Greyson let her go when they reached the front of the sanctuary, and Kate almost didn't have time to pass her bouquet to Lily before Cress leapt forward and clutched Kate's hands tightly in his.

"This is the best day of my faeborn life!" he announced. "You're everything I ever wanted, Katherine." He loudly sniffed—for a long time, too. Mor was fighting to stay straight-faced behind him. The pastor opened his mouth to begin the ceremony, but Cress cut him off and went on, "Katherine Lewis, you're so simple."

Kate's face changed. "What?"

"Everything about you is simple! And *so* plain," Cress loudly declared. "You don't have it in you to form cunning, manipulative, tricky thoughts. Even your thoughts are simple." He put a finger against his pursed lips and shook his head.

Kate released a strange laugh and pushed her hair behind her ear as she murmured, "Uh... I don't think you realize what it means to call someone *simple* in this realm, Cress—"

"You're just so ordinary and simple!" He practically shouted it. "It's perfect for me. I'm like a glowing star. There can't be two glowing stars in a relationship—it would never work!"

Shayne leaned back and whispered to Dranian, "I should have brought popcorn."

Somewhere past that handsome face of his, Kate was sure Cress actually thought he was flattering her. And with the way he held both of her hands, facing her before the church... Kate's eyes widened.

"Are these your vows?" she asked in horror. She glanced over at the pastor who didn't seem to know what to do at this point.

"Absolutely not!" Cress stated. "My vows are exceptional. Just wait until you hear them." He dropped one of her hands to reach into his suit pocket, and he drew out a paper. He took one look at it, then burst out crying again. He shoved the paper behind him and mumbled something along the lines of, "I can't. I can't do it, Mor. You must read it for me as the Best of the Men."

Mor sighed and took the paper, and everyone in the sanctuary relaxed a little. Dranian didn't have much of an expression, but Shayne was grinning ear-to-ear.

Mor raised the paper to read Cress's vows before the whole church. He cleared his throat, and read, "Kate, you're so simple..." He paused. Mor's eyes scanned the rest of the vows on the page, and after a moment, he seemed to think better about reading them. He folded the paper and tucked it into his own suit jacket pocket. Then he looked up at Kate and said, "He loves you, Kate. That's all."

"I love you, Katherine!" Cress growled it for the entire human realm to hear, and people shrieked and threw their hands over their ears as the pews rattled and a large crack formed across one of the stained-glass windows.

Kate's jaw dropped, and her hand flew to her forehead as she took in the ruined glass. "*Unreal*, Cress!" she said, but her mouth tugged at the corners. Then, against her better judgement, she burst out laughing, because she only had herself to blame for thinking this day might actually happen normally. She grabbed her stomach and lost her balance as her laughs filled the stage, and Cress almost didn't catch her before she would have hit the floor.

"What's wrong with her?" Cress demanded. He set Kate down on the dais stair, stood, turned, and *glared* at everyone in the pews with menacing, cold eyes. Clouds formed in the sky outside, blotting out the sun and blanketing the church in darkness. "Who fed her enchanted laughing weeds?" he growled. Then, he pointed through the crowd, right at Luc. "Was it you, Fox?" he asked. "You look awfully suspicious!"

Luc lazily raised both hands. "Wasn't me," he promised in a bored voice.

"Cress..." Mor warned. "You're turning your wedding into a trial."

"Great! Is the wedding over then? Is it time for presents yet?" Shayne asked. He reached past Mor and poked Cress in the back of his shoulder. "I brought *lots* of pie as your gift. You're going to love what I have planned," he said.

Kate sighed as Cress reached down and lifted her, draping her over his arms without difficulty, even with the extra weight of her dress, like he planned to march her right out of the church. His jaw was set when he looked into her eyes, but even though he was scowling, Kate smiled and planted a deep kiss on his mouth in front of all their friends. A few whistles and cheers lifted from the nervous guests.

The hardness melted from Cress's face. After a second, he dropped her legs and pulled her tight against him, molding into the kiss like it was suddenly the only thing that mattered in the universe.

When he drew away, he gazed at Kate. She flashed him one more smile for good measure, and she said, "I love you too, Cress. Happy wedding day."

Cress burst out crying.

"This is the greatest day, ever!" he shouted. "Let's go eat Shayne's pie!"

The Happy Faeborn End of Everything

Thank you for reading *Fake Dating a Human 101*
If you liked this book, please leave a review!

Join Jennifer Kropf's newsletter at www.JenniferKropf.com to
be alerted to all new book releases!

Christmas fantasy books by Jennifer Kropf:
(for ages 10+)

A SOUL AS COLD AS FROST

A HEART AS RED AS PAINT

A CROWN AS SHARP AS PINES

A BEAST AS DARK AS NIGHT

CAROLS AND SPIES

ACKNOWLEDGEMENTS

To God: Thanks for creating me the way you did. Little did I know that all those years I spent struggling to focus and pass in school because I was daydreaming about fantasy worlds would be the thing that made my career when I was older. You always have a plan.

To Phil, Chase, Ellie, and Austin: You guys are everything.

To Mom, Dad, Steph, Melis, and Jesse: Thanks for the years of laughter and humour that made me weird enough to write funny and bizarre characters.

To my beta readers, Anne Lawson, Vickie Grider, Chandelle Huerta, Audrey Moore, and Kailey Marie: You guys are the best crew and I'm so lucky to have you in my life. Thank you for all the feedback and encouragement!

To my core Patreons: Lyndsey Hall (who's been such a great friend all these years we've both been writing books!), Redlac (best brother ever), and to Danielle, Sarah Breed, Amanda Ross, Lydia Woodward, Mimi Anderson, Vickie Grider, Stephanie York, Eden Mayers, Anne Lawson, Betsy Squires, austengirl_710, Audrey Moore, Sarah, Chandelle Huerta, and Kailey Marie. You guys keep me going. Thank you for all your input about covers, character art, story concepts, beta reading, and literally everything else related to this job. It's been amazing to get to know many of you personally over the years!

To my favourite editor of all time, Melissa Cole: I was very tempted to put a bunch of misspelled mumbo jumbo in this paragraph just to see if you'd catch it. Also - sometimes I wish the rest of the world knew how funny we are whenever we're in the same room. You're outrageous, and you make cool potato stamp paintings.

To my agent, Brent Taylor: You're killin' it. I've lost track of how many book deals you've gotten me. How many languages is this series being translated into now? A thousand? (Thanks to everyone else at Triada US Literary Agency too for all you're doing!)

And last but not least: Thank you to all my family and friends who've been offering in-person support all these years that I've been writing books. You're a big part of the reason any of my books ever got published in the first place.

www.ingramcontent.com/pod-product-compliance
Lightning Source LLC
Chambersburg PA
CBHW031153050726
47495CB00019B/1657